THE RENEGADE

Silent Phoenix MC Series: Book Three

SHANNON MYERS

SHANNON
MYERS

stories that stick with you

Cover Model: Sonny Henty

Photographer: Wander Aguiar

First Printing: 2017

Paperback ISBN- 978-0-9994716-1-6

❀ Created with Vellum

ALSO BY SHANNON MYERS

From This Day Forward Duet
(David & Elizabeth's Story)

From This Day Forward

Forsaking All Others

Standalone Novels
(Travis & Katya's Story)

You Save Me

Operation Series
(Dakota & Zane's Story)

Operation Fit-ish

(Kate and Nate's Story)

Operation Annulment

Silent Phoenix MC Series
(Grey & Celia's Story)

The Deserter (Book One)

The Protector (Book Two)

The Renegade (Book Three)

The Traitor (Book Four)

The Savior (Book Five)

The Mercenary (Book Six) *Coming 2022*

Fairest Series
(Charm & Neve's Story)

Through The Woods

To the Mikes and Laurens of the world—the ones who were dealt a bad hand, but proved their worth regardless.

TERMINOLOGY

1%er (One-Percenter)- *If 99% of motorcycle riders are law-abiding members of society, the rest is the 1%. Advertised through a patch or tattoo, usually on a diamond shaped back field.*

13 - *Patch worn by a biker, usually a 1%er. May stand for the letter "M" (13th letter of alphabet), and indicate the wearer smokes pot, or uses "crank" (methamphetamine). Can also mean "The Mother Club", or original chapter of a motorcycle club.*

1916- *The nineteenth letter of the alphabet (S) and the sixteenth (P). Stands for Silent Phoenix.*

3-Piece Patch- *Configuration of back patches, consisting of: a top rocker (club's name), a center patch (club's emblem), and a bottom rocker (geographical territory).*

69 - *Patch indicating someone who has performed cunnilingus with witnesses present.*

Air Condition- *Riddle with bullets*

ATF- *Bureau of Alcohol, Tobacco, Firearms and Explosives.*

Broad- *A female whose sole purpose is being used as a sexual object; similar to a one-night stand.*

Cage- *Non-biker's car/truck.*

Church- *Club meeting.*

Club Whore- *Also known as a Mama. Sexual equivalent of a public well. Anyone can dip into her, at any time, as often as he wants. These are woman who belong to the club at large. They belong to every member and are expected to consent to the sexual desires of anyone at anytime. They perform menial tasks around the clubhouse, however do not attend club meetings.*

Colors- *Patches, logo, or uniform associated with a motorcycle club.*

Fly Colors - *To ride on a motorcycle wearing club's kutte.*

Gathering: *A scheduled social event or meeting. This is not Church.*

Grocery-getter- *A biker's car/truck.*

Hang Around- *a person that hangs around a motorcycle club and may be interested in joining.*

Jacket- *Arrest record*

Kill-Light- *A flashlight used as a weapon.*

Kutte- *A jacket which has had the sleeves cut off. All club patches are sown onto kuttes, which are worn as the outer-most layer of clothing. Most, if not all, outlaw clubs have kuttes as their basic uniform.*

Mother- *Founding/original chapter of the club.*

Nomad- *1) "Nomad" on a bottom rocker patch means that motorcycle club member travels between geographical chapters. Kind of like working in a secretarial pool, a Nomad goes where he's needed. 2) "Nomad" on a top rocker patch or car plaque means "Nomad" is the name of that club.*

Ol' Lady- *Wife or long-time girlfriend of club member. She is considered property of the member and is off-limits to other club members.*

Property Of- *displayed on a shirt, patch or tattoo to show who the woman "belongs to." Example: Monica wore a "Property of Torch" vest in Renegade. That meant that she associated herself with Torch and would do anything he needed/wanted.*

STRUCTURE WITHIN CLUB

National President- *Many times the founder of the club. He will usually be located at or near the national headquarters. He will be surrounded by bodyguards and organizational enforcers.*

Territorial or Regional Representatives- *In some cases called the National Vice President in charge of a specific region or state.*

National Secretary / Treasurer- *He is responsible for the club's money and collecting dues from local chapters. He also records any by-law changes and records any minutes.*

National Enforcer- *This person answers directly to the National President. He acts as a body guard and gives out punishment for club violations. He has also been known to locate former members and retrieve colors or remove the club's tattoo from them.*

Chapter President- *This person has either claimed the position or has been voted in. He has final authority over all chapter business and members.*

Chapter Vice President- *This person is second in command. He presides over club affairs in the absence of the president. Normally, he is hand picked by the Chapter President.*

Chapter Secretary / Treasurer- *This is usually the member with the best writing skills and probably the most education. He will maintain the chapter roster and maintain a crude accounting system. He is also responsible for collecting dues, keeping minutes and paying for any bills the chapter accumulates.*

Chapter Sergeant (SGT) at Arms- *This person is in charge of maintaining order at club meetings. Because of the violent nature of outlaw gangs this person is normally the strongest member physically and is loyal to the Chapter President. He may administer beatings to fellow members for violations of club rules. He is the club enforcer.*

Road Captain- *This person fulfills the role of a logistician and security chief for club sponsored runs or outings. The Road Captain maps out routes to be taken during runs, arranges the refueling, food and maintenance stops. He will carry the club's money and use it for bail if necessary.*

Members- *The rank and file, fully accepted and dues paying members of the gang. They are the individuals who carry out the President's orders and have sworn to live by the club's by-laws.*

Prospect- *These are the club's hopefuls who spend from one month to one year in a probationary status. They must prove during that time if they are worthy of becoming members. Some clubs have the prospect commit a felony with fellow members observing in an effort to weed out the weak and stop infiltration by law enforcement. Must be nominated by a regular member and receive a unanimous vote for acceptance. They are known to carry weapons for other club members and stand guard at club functions. The prospect wears no colors and has no voting rights.*

Associates or Honorary Members- *An individual who has proven his* *value or usefulness to the gang. These individuals may be professional people who have in some manner helped the club. Some of the more noted are attorneys, bail bondsmen, and auto wrecking yard owners. These people are allowed to party with the gang, either in town or on their runs; however, they do not have a voting status or wear colors.*

AUTHOR'S NOTE

Please be aware that The Renegade is not recommended for readers under the age of eighteen, as it contains strong language, sexual situations, drug use, and graphic violence.

If you, or someone you care about has been a victim of sexual assault, RAINN is available to provide confidential support.

RAINN Hotline: 1 (800) 656-4673

RENEGADE

/ˈrenəˌɡād/

noun
   noun: **renegade**

   1. a person who deserts and betrays an organization, country, or set of principles.
   2. An individual who rejects lawful or conventional behavior.

adjective
   adjective: **renegade**

   1. having treacherously changed allegiance.

PROLOGUE

Lauren: April 2004 (Age: 17)

Denver, Colorado

"So, here we are yet again, Ms. McGuire. As much as I enjoy our weekly chats, I'm sure your teachers would prefer to see you in class every once in a while." Mr. Santiago sat back in his desk chair, resting his arms behind his head. With his dark, slicked back hair, he might have passed for attractive were it not for his obvious affinity for Budweiser.

I rolled my eyes. Mr. Santiago was the guidance counselor for Thomas Jefferson HS and probably the least intimidating person I'd ever met. If the school was hoping to scare me straight, they really should have reconsidered sending me here.

"Always a pleasure, Joshua," I offered, staring past him at the motivational posters adorning the cinderblock wall behind him. It was like being inside a prison.

He shook his head in frustration. "It's Mr. Santiago to you, Ms. McGuire. Are you just going to sit there and completely ignore the fact that you got caught slamming another student's head into a gym locker?"

I pursed my lips as if I were debating it, earning me yet another glare from across the desk. "That doesn't ring a bell. Get it? Ring a bell?"

He inhaled a sharp breath. "Lauren, I can't protect you from the consequences of your actions any longer. The girl's parents are considering pressing charges—at the very least, you're going to be expelled. Can you give me anything, any reason, that might convince the school to let you stay? You're an excellent student, but your behavior makes you a liability."

What could I say—that Becca Graves had discovered I showered every morning in the girl's locker room, so she and her posse of bitches confronted me over it?

Nope.

It would probably just make things worse for me. So, I turned my lips up into a smirk and replied icily, "I heard that she's been talking about getting a nose job, so I saved her parents some money and took care of it myself."

If I left now, I could be gone before they pressed charges.

The chair groaned loudly as he stood up. His belly bumped up against the side of the desk, sending papers flying, and I wondered how many times a day he knocked things over like this.

He finally made it around the desk and placed a light hand on my shoulder. "We tried calling your mother, but the number was disconnected. When we called the work number listed in our records, they said she hadn't worked there in months. Can you tell me where we can find her?"

In a bar?

On a corner?

Take your pick, Joshua.

Instead, I repeated the lie I'd used countless times before. "My mother is out-of-state visiting her sister. No, I don't know when she'll be home. I don't have a good phone number for her, as she's staying with different relatives."

While Mr. Santiago looked skeptical, he didn't press for more details and released me to go back to class until the school could decide what to do with me.

I wasn't waiting around for that and skipped out before the dust settled.

———

I made it back to the rundown duplex I called a home just as the sun drifted behind some clouds. It was probably going to rain. I looked forward to it. I could pop open the window and let the cooler temperatures act as free air conditioning.

It was only April, and already it was unseasonably warm. I'd been prepared for a spring blizzard, not blistering heat. The girls at school had taken the weather as an opportunity to show off as much skin as possible, while still following dress code.

Then there was me, dressed in winter gear, regardless of the season. I'd tried cutting the sleeves off of a pale lavender sweater, but the whole thing unraveled. From then on, I'd stuck with rolling the sleeves up and dealing with it.

There was a note taped to the door, the edges flapping wildly in the breeze. I pulled it free and despite the heat, my blood turned to ice in my veins.

EVICTION NOTICE

———

Ms. Monica McGuire,

You are hereby notified to vacate the premises named above due to non-payment. You are required to vacate on or before May 1st, 2004, being ten days from the issuance of this notice. Failure to vacate will result in civil proceedings against you for unlawful detainer.

Thank you for your prompt attention to this urgent matter,

Oaklawn Duplex Management

———

Ten days.

I had ten days until I was homeless.

I had no job. No license. No birth certificate. Monica wasn't really the type of mother to cut the crusts off your sandwiches after staying up late to scrapbook your latest achievements. When I was fifteen, I'd wanted to take Driver's Ed and had approached her for my birth certificate and social security card. She'd looked at me as if I'd grown two heads before going back to staring blankly at the television screen.

That was two years ago, and I was still no closer to finding my birth documents. Other kids my age were applying to colleges and preparing to take the SAT, while I was going nowhere. It didn't help that this was the longest Monica had been gone, either. She'd taken off in February, promising that she had a job lined up that would get us back on our feet. I'd given her my last twenty dollars so she could take a cab.

Stupidly, I'd believed her... for a week or two. By then, I knew she'd fallen back into one of her three vices: men, booze, or meth. Once the realization hit, I'd resorted to stealing again just to stay alive.

I never took more than I needed—a couple of dollars from several unlocked gym lockers would hold me over for a couple of days. It was also unlikely that someone would miss it enough to search for a thief.

I'd learned early on how to stretch my money and make it last. Dollar stores carried everything from body wash to canned soup. I even saved enough to buy a couple of plates and cups, just in case I ever had company. I never did, but it was nice to know I was prepared if the opportunity ever presented itself.

Now, it might've all been for nothing. I'd been able to survive with no water or electricity, but out on the streets, I'd never make it.

At least the management office would find that, while I couldn't pay the rent, I'd at least kept the place nice and tidy.

I couldn't worry about that now. I'd worry about it later.

I tugged my arms out of the sleeves of my sweater and chucked it across the back of the metal springs posing as a couch before sitting down to do my homework by flashlight. I just needed another month; another month to graduate and then figure out what the hell to do next.

I had almost all of it completed by the time the sky began to rumble and fat drops of rain fell angrily against the window. I stood up and stretched my back before opening a can of chicken noodle soup. It wouldn't fill me up, but it would get rid of the hunger pangs that caused my stomach to cramp up.

I sipped the cold soup slowly, trying to trick my brain into thinking I was eating a much larger meal. I'd done it as long as I could remember. CPS had placed me in foster care twice when I was younger, and I remembered both families being astonished by how much I could eat.

Inevitably, Monica would get her shit together just long enough to be granted custody again and I would miss the way my stomach had felt so full I thought it might burst.

I finished my soup and slipped out of my jeans before lying down on the couch, trying to align my body on the parts of the couch that still held cushion. The lack of food and fight from this morning had left me exhausted.

I closed my eyes, still hearing Becca's taunts.

"What's the matter, White Trash? Don't they have showers in the trailer park?"

She'd yanked my damp hair and continued when I'd remained silent, *"I'd just bet that with hair that red, your mom fucked a leprechaun. That true, White Trash? You got a pot of gold we should know about?"*

I didn't know what was different about today, but for whatever reason, I just didn't feel like taking the abuse anymore. I waited for her to pause long enough to take a breath and then I grabbed her by the throat and walked her backward toward the lockers, nothing but adrenaline coursing through my body. Her posse's laughter ended, but not one of them made a move to help their leader.

No, they'd all run screaming from the locker room as Becca's head connected against the metal with a dull thud. I could still hear the sound in my head.

The storm died down outside and I realized I could still hear the low thud. A floorboard creaked in the back bedroom and I knew I hadn't imagined it. Someone was in the duplex with me.

My eyes flew open, but I remained frozen on the couch. If they were looking for anything valuable, they'd realize soon enough that they'd picked the wrong unit.

The footsteps grew louder, as if the intruder was making no attempt to hide his or her presence. I briefly tried to remember if I'd left the bedroom window open, for all the good it did. I quietly slipped my sweater back on and tried to make myself disappear into the couch.

Maybe they'd find whatever it was they were looking for and leave. There was movement in the small den and I realized belatedly there was more than one person inside with me.

I willed my body to remain still, hoping that they might not see me in the dark.

"See, what'd I tell ya? Home alone." I recognized the man's voice as the neighbor two doors down. The smell of cigarette smoke only confirmed his identity.

Just as I realized their true intentions and decided to run, hands were on me, pinning me back down to the couch.

"She's feisty, I'll give her that. Shhhh... calm down, girly. We just wanna have some fun with ya," the other man muttered in my ear, as if there was nothing out of the ordinary going on.

I raked my fingernails down the side of his face in response and began kicking wildly. My neighbor's hand came down across my cheekbone, stunning me.

That was when I began screaming.

The second man's hand covered my mouth and my neighbor rocked back on his heels, laughing. "Scream all you want. No one's gonna come running in here to save you."

I bit down on his accomplice's hand and tried to run for the door, but my neighbor caught me, pushing me face first into the dirty carpet. He held something sharp against my throat briefly before using it to cut through my sweater and bra.

He flipped me over onto my back and I saw the lust in both of their eyes. I knew what they were planning to do to me—and they weren't the type to let me go after.

I raced through my available options. Even if I made it outside, my chances weren't much better. I didn't exactly live on Sesame Street.

There was a loud knock at the door and the second man crept over to look through the peephole while my neighbor held the knife against my throat again.

"Don't even think about screaming," he hissed.

That was it. I knew I could either die after being raped and tortured or I could get it over with immediately. I inhaled and screamed as loud as I could. My neighbor must have been expecting me to remain quiet, because in his shock, he dropped the knife and I rolled away from him.

It all happened in a matter of seconds. The door imploded, and I dove behind the sofa for cover as shards of wood flew in every direction. I didn't know if the person at the door was my savior or just another junkie with a penchant for teenage girls.

"Lauren!" the voice called out, and I froze. It was Mr. Santiago.

Why the hell was he here?

I slowly poked my head over the sofa, using the worn fabric to cover my exposed parts. His shoulders relaxed once he saw me. The room was empty with the storm raging outside and lightning illuminated our faces every few seconds. My attackers must've booked it once he kicked in the door. "Hey there, Mr. Santiago. Didn't know you made house calls."

He surveyed the small room before his eyes came back to mine. "Jesus, *mija*. You've been living here?"

I nodded, and he gestured toward me. "Why are you behind the sofa? Come out."

I nodded again, this time a little more shakily, as I realized what I'd just escaped. "Um, I don't have anything..." I trailed off, hoping he'd catch my meaning.

His eyes widened, and then immediately narrowed in anger. "Did they rape you?"

I shook my head and responded, "No, you uh—you got here just in time, Mr. Santiago."

He found a blanket lying near the couch and tossed it over to me. "Joshua, Lauren. Call me Joshua. We're beyond formalities at this point."

I wrapped the blanket around myself and headed toward the small bedroom near the back of the duplex to find something to wear. Joshua stood silently outside the door, waiting for me to change, before instructing me to grab anything I needed.

The night air was warm and slightly sticky from the recent storm, yet I shivered uncontrollably in the passenger seat of his Ford Taurus.

I pulled the blanket from the floorboard and wrapped it around my shoulders as we pulled into a fast food parking lot. The smell of greasy, fried food wafted in through the vents, and my stomach grumbled painfully.

Joshua didn't ask questions; he just pulled through the drive-through and ordered three separate meals and watched me devour two of them like an animal.

I ate until my stomach felt as if it would explode before making eye contact with him again. He pursed his lips as if trying to solve a puzzle. "How long has it been like this, Lauren?"

I swallowed a sip of Dr. Pepper before answering, "It's always been like this. Monica's a little neglectful, I guess."

His eyes almost bugged out of his head. "A little neglectful? Mija, you were living in *miseria absoluta* and you call that a little neglectful? Jesus—what if I hadn't shown up, huh? Those men—they would've raped you... or worse. *Ay Dios mío!*"

He was so worked up that he kept switching between the two languages while I struggled to follow along. I closed my eyes and leaned against the window as he continued his tirade. Apparently, he'd shown up to visit with my mom about my behavior. He hadn't been able to reach her by phone and didn't trust me to give her the letter the school sent home.

I cracked one eye open and looked over when he paused to take a breath. "Can you take me back home now?"

He put the car in reverse. "No, I'm not taking you back to that hellhole. You've been going without electricity or running water—that's unacceptable. No, you're coming home with me until we figure out something else. I'll keep you safe, *Mija*—you have my word."

I settled for a small nod, too exhausted to argue, and went back to staring out the passenger window. It wouldn't last. Monica would get her shit together long enough to get me back and I'd be right back where I started.

It didn't mean I couldn't enjoy it while it lasted, though.

CHAPTER ONE

Mike: March 2014 (Age: 31)

When I told David I sold my soul to the devil, I'd only been half-joking. Keeping the club—and, ultimately, Grey—happy was single-handedly the hardest job I'd ever had.

I'd become his bitch, for lack of a better term.

I parked my truck in the spillover lot at *Nick's*, scanning the rows of parked vehicles for David's truck. Seemed the old place had gotten pretty popular since I gave up drinking for Grey not fucking me over in Galveston.

A year in, I made the mistake of researching the statute of limitations on voluntary manslaughter in the state of Texas. Within two minutes, my phone was ringing.

"Gettin' cold feet on me again?" Grey laughed, but my skin had broken out in a fine sheen of sweat as I shut down the browser.

I doubt I took a shit that he didn't know about within minutes.

SPMC had no statute of limitations when it came to me. My life belonged to the club, and they had done a hell of a job keeping my hands nice and dirty in the years since.

Just last night Grey had called, wanting me to do something else for his club. "Got a new club whore here. She's an addict, drivin' a really nice Toyota. Somethin' about this ain't settlin' well with me, kid."

He gave me the plate number, and I ran it through the database. Unsurprisingly, it came back stolen. When I broke the news, he'd sighed, "Yep, that's about what I thought. I'm gonna take it to Comedian's shop and have him buff out all the dings and replace the upholstery. Looks like a fuckin' bullet hole in the back window—gonna need to replace that, too. Give me forty-eight hours and then close the case. I want nothing on that vehicle tracin' back to me—we clear?"

After promising to handle it, I went back to work. I didn't know what his plans were for the car—didn't really give a shit, honestly. The less I knew, the better off I was.

I shouldered my way through the crowded bar before spotting David out on the patio. Since the wedding, life had taken us in different directions. By the time he and Elizabeth got back from their honeymoon, I'd already moved out of our old college house and bought a place outside the city limits. Grey had eyes everywhere, but I liked the illusion of privacy country living provided.

Then John died, and David shut himself off from everyone, refusing to answer my calls and texts. I tried not to take it personally, but John had been like a father to me, too. I'd long seen David as a brother and thought we'd get through his death together. Instead, my closest friend in the entire world built a wall and kept me out.

"Hey man, good to see ya." I shook his hand, and he pulled me into a rough hug, almost as if in apology. Maybe tonight was his way of coming back around.

David ran a hand through his unkempt hair and leaned in, close enough I noticed his bloodshot eyes. "So, I cheated on Beth. Do you want a beer?"

I frowned, waiting for the punchline. "You're shitting me, right? Is this a joke?" This time, I looked around, certain a camera crew was about to pop up out of nowhere.

His head dropped onto his chest. "No, I fucked up. It's just been so hard since my dad—we were fighting all the time. I didn't mean for it to happen, but Jess was there—"

I held my hand up and stopped him. "Wait, just so I get this straight. You're telling me you couldn't deal with John's death, so you went out and fucked your wife's best friend?"

I'd witnessed enough shit early on that I never put stock into the whole marriage business. Men weren't made to be monogamous—how many times had my old man used that line on me?

But David didn't live in the world that I did.

He was supposed to break through all of that and live happily ever after or some bullshit. It seemed he'd chosen to play both hero and villain in his fairytale, which only reinforced my thoughts on marriage.

What pissed me off was that he'd done it to Elizabeth, one of the sweetest people I'd ever met. Hell, anyone else would have run the other way had they been unfortunate enough to walk in on me in the middle of a three-way.

Not her.

The thing was, she could've been a complete bitch to me and I would've admitted that I deserved it, but Elizabeth was always quick to greet me when she came by the house, pretending as if the entire thing had never happened. She took the time to get to know me—well, the parts of myself I could share with the world.

I may not have had any faith in the institution of marriage, but there was one cause I was fiercely loyal to—my friends.

And I considered her one.

David shook his head, keeping his focus on the deck. "I don't know what I was thinking. I was drunk and when I came to, she was there— said we'd hooked up. Jesus, you gotta help me."

I stared at him with raised brows. "And how would you propose I go about doing that, David? Want me to write a letter to the past you to say that fucking your wife's best friend is a bad idea? Maybe I could send myself back to knee you in the balls before you unzipped your pants? What in the ever-living fuck can I do to fix your mess? Bring John back? Jesus Christ, David, I'd do it in a heartbeat if I could. Your old man was one of the good ones."

David kept his head down and pinched the bridge of his nose, nodding along with me. "I don't know, Mike. I don't even know where we went wrong. My dad wanted me to make her a priority, and I failed at that. I thought by taking on more jobs, that it'd bring us closer."

As I sat there and listened to him try to justify his promiscuity, I couldn't help but feel a little grateful that my work with Grey had kept me from having much of a social life at all.

I couldn't even remember the last time someone had punched me in the face.

CHAPTER TWO

Lauren: March 2014 (Age: 27)

The first seventeen years of my life read like the instruction manual on a Little Miss Meth Head starter kit.

Addict mother.

CPS visits.

Foster care.

Class 3 misdemeanor charges resulting in juvenile probation.

Check. Check. Check. And check.

My school guidance counselor had risked not only his career but his reputation by taking me in, something my mother wouldn't have bothered to do. With a full belly and access to running water, I'd been able to finish my senior year without a single visit to his office.

Given the drama that seemed to follow wherever I went, Joshua Santiago would have been well within his rights to end our little arrangement the moment I turned eighteen.

Only, he hadn't.

Not even when Addict Monica turned up one month after he took me in, only to skip town hours later with most of his things and the graduation dress he'd just bought. Also missing was the first piece of jewelry I'd ever owned, a sterling silver necklace with my initial and small butterfly charm.

The shame and embarrassment were too much, and I tried to bail. Joshua stopped me, insisting my mother's actions didn't reflect on me. A sane person would have kicked me to the curb and been done with it, but he said something that night that had stuck with me ever since.

"You might walk out that door and make it on your own, but you shouldn't have to. Let's face it, mija. You need me, maybe just as much as I need you."

My tough as nails persona was no match against Joshua and his big dumb heart. As if on cue, his name flashed across my cell phone screen.

"*Bueno, mija*, missed your call this morning," he said in greeting.

"Josué, you will be the death of me," I responded with a grin, unable to resist using one of his mother's—my *abuelita's*—favorite phrases. "I was running late and meant to text, but I'm fine. Alive and well. Shouldn't you be at work?"

"I'm in the parking lot. I just needed to hear your voice and know you're okay. You know I worry with everything that's happened. Have you heard anything on the car?"

"I'm sorry I made you worry." I carefully avoided his second question and straightened the pens and pencils on my desk, all while choking on the guilt of disappointing the only person on the planet I wanted to make proud.

"Mija, did you call Toyota yet? Listen, if the dealership is still giving you the runaround, you need to go directly to the source. You shouldn't be saddled with a damn lemon, and if you need me to make the call, I'll do it."

"Left a message, just waiting to hear from someone," I lied, hating myself a little more. "I know I've had the BMW much longer than I said I needed it for. I can get by without it if you need—"

"¡Basta!" He growled. "It's not that. I'm just ready for you to have a reliable form of transportation and—"

I heard her throat clear milliseconds before Dr. Mulloy poked her head into my office. Perhaps office wasn't the right word as it was the size of a closet, with just enough room for a desk, filing cabinet, and chair. I damn near had to turn my body sideways just to reach my desk.

Her gaze narrowed on the cell phone pressed to my ear. "Ms. Santiago, might I have a word with you?"

"I've gotta go, *Josué*. I'll call you when I'm headed home tonight."

"Sounds good, and *mija*? *No hay mal que por bien no venga*."

Something good always comes from the bad.

The advice was only slightly reassuring as I slipped my phone into a desk drawer and turned to face the firing squad.

"Sorry, Doc, my dad was worried when he didn't hear from me this morning."

Sandra met my overly bright smile with a frown. "Honey, we've been over this—during working hours, I'd prefer it if you referred to me as Dr. Mulloy. It sets a nice precedent for the rest of the staff—are you okay?"

I blinked against the sting of tears and nodded toward the open spreadsheet on my computer, shoving my volatile emotions down deep. "Yeah, just finished reconciling the credit card statement from last month."

"Lauren," she sighed, letting her forehead rest against the door frame as if it pained her to look at me. "You know I need you on top of things. If you're already a month behind, then you'll have to stay late to catch up. I can't have anything slipping through the cracks because you'd rather spend working hours making personal calls."

I resisted the urge to scream.

The clock read eight sixteen—a record for her. "Well, I can only reconcile the previous month right now. So, I guess you could say we're all caught up."

She gave me a patronizing smile. "I hired you as my office manager because you seemed like someone who would keep my practice running smoothly. If that's not the case anymore, then you need to make me aware of that. Okay?"

You need this job.

You need this job.

You need this job.

It had been like this for the past seven years. I could tell her that the sky was blue, and she'd sniff in a deprecating way before informing me I'd need to stay late to fix it.

I pasted a smile on my face. "It's taken care of. You have nothing to worry about."

She gave me an absent smile in response before being called into an exam room for her next patient. I got the distinct impression she'd only popped in for a visit, hoping to bust me doing something wrong.

Never mind that there was more than enough work to keep me busy for the next ten years—both real and imaginary.

If I died tomorrow, Sandra Mulloy certainly would not mourn. No, she would be the one to show up to my funeral, complaining to anyone who would listen about how typical it was of me to create more work for her by dying before finding a replacement.

The revelation had come to me four years ago while driving home from Elizabeth's wedding in Galveston, or as I would always fondly remember it—*The Road Trip from Hell*. Sandra had spent most of the nine-hour car ride glued to her phone, only looking up every so often to critique my driving skills.

By some miracle, I'd graduated in the top tier of my high school class and had been awarded a scholarship by Texas Tech. The subsequent business degree had paved the way for a comfortable career and stable life.

But I wasn't naïve enough to think the world would come to a grinding halt if I was gone.

Sure, I no longer worried about the electricity or water being shut off anymore, but I didn't have a spouse to come home to. Someone who would notice if I didn't show up.

My rent being paid on time was probably the biggest impact I'd made in my twenty-seven years of life, which wasn't much of a legacy. There were no children to keep my memory alive.

I didn't even own a dog. One who would wait by the front door for me, night after night.

Except for Josué, who was busy living happily ever after six hours away in Austin, my inner circle was non-existent. There was a strong possibility my body wouldn't be discovered until the neighbors complained about the smell.

Even if I hadn't played it safe with dating, my work schedule all but guaranteed my only relationship would be with the phallic sculptures tucked away in my dresser and the handful of fantasies involving a certain blond-haired surfer with a sexy as hell southern accent.

What did it say about me that my last kiss was with a man who hadn't even given me his real name?

A fantastic kiss I hadn't quite managed to recover from almost four years later.

I often cursed the fact that I'd spent the first half of David and Elizabeth's wedding reception alternatively monitoring Sandra's alcohol intake and hiding out in the bathroom just to buy a moment's peace. I'd missed most of the toasts and speeches given by the wedding party, and Jack's in particular.

When Elizabeth returned to work after her honeymoon, I briefly considered asking for a rundown on the groomsmen until reality and all its baggage paid a visit in the form of Mom of the Year Monica. After finding me on social media, she'd shown up outside the office with the stolen necklace in hand, claiming she'd found God.

By the time I realized the woman whose first love had been cocaine —with meth coming in a close second—hadn't suddenly turned over a new leaf, it was too late.

After reconciling the credit card statement, I checked to ensure Sandra wasn't lurking nearby before retrieving the mail from my purse.

Just like ripping off a bandage.

There were more than usual this month, and I winced before opening the first one. Initially, I refused to pay the fines until they informed me they would issue a warrant for my arrest, as the car had been registered in my name.

By the time I finished going through the stack, parking and toll tag violations littered my desk, and my bank account was leaner.

On paper, I was a goddamn catch. One of those independent women Destiny's Child had been singing about in the nineties. I had found success, despite my circumstances—circumstances Monica had caused.

But underneath the shiny exterior, my life was messy. It seemed everywhere I looked there was something else waiting to be cleaned up.

CHAPTER THREE

Lauren: March 2014 (Age: 27)

By the time I made it home, I was bleary-eyed and ready to devour my takeout before falling into bed.

Until I saw it, parked under the awning near my apartment building.

A 2007 dark blue Toyota Camry.

"How? Is this some kind of joke?" I dropped the bag of food, babbling as I made a slow circle around the vehicle.

It was no joke. The license plate confirmed it.

My car, last seen merging onto I-27 with Monica in the driver's seat, had miraculously been returned to me in better condition than before.

I'd reported it stolen immediately, for all the good it did. Once the officer assigned to my case discovered the carjacker was my mother, he'd treated me like a suspect, not a victim.

And there was no way in hell I could tell Josué what happened—not after he had given me strict instructions to take her to a shelter when she'd shown up in the freezing cold with no place to go.

Directly to the shelter.

Do not pass go... do not collect two-hundred dollars.

What was I supposed to do? Call him up and say, *Hey, remember when you told me under no circumstances should I let Monica get in my head? Well, somewhere out of nowhere, I took her to a diner where she waited for me to go to the bathroom before ditching me and stealing my car. Hilarious, right?*

No, the truth would have destroyed any faith he had in me being better than her. As absurd as it was, it had been better for him to believe my car was in the shop every week rather than know what an idiot his adopted daughter was.

"You Lauren?" a gruff voice asked.

I yanked my hand off the hood and gripped my keys in the other like a weapon before turning around to face the giant leaning against a car two spaces over. He looked like a goddamn viking with his blond hair and piercing blue eyes.

Eyes that reminded me of the ocean.

And Jack.

Jesus, read the room, heart.

Not the time.

"D-Do I know you?" I stammered, mentally calculating the distance between him and my apartment door.

The giant shook his head and clicked his tongue against his teeth. "You don't, but that's your car, right?"

Fuck.

What had Monica gotten herself into this time? Better yet, what had Monica gotten *me* into?

Had she used my car as collateral?

I nodded dumbly, and he smiled. "Name's Jamie. I'm a—uh—friend of your mom's. She's detoxin' and after checking into it, saw the car was registered to you."

I swallowed past the lump in my throat. Maybe he thought there'd be reward money involved, but any spare change had gone paying off toll violations. "I don't have any money, if that's why you're here—"

Jamie shook his head. "It's not. Just wanted to return the car to you. It's got a full tank of gas and just had an oil change. Don't owe me a thing."

He held out the keys, and I reluctantly took them from his hand and tucked them into my purse. He seemed like a nice enough person. It felt wrong to let him go without a warning. "You—um, you might think you know Monica, but just be careful. She'll feed you any sob story to get what she wants—which inevitably ends up being more drugs."

Jamie nodded, as if he was actually taking my words to heart. "Yeah, I think that's how she used to be. Maybe once she's clean, you could get to know her again."

I shook my head and bent to retrieve my bag of food from the pavement. "No, thank you. Been there, done that more times than I care to admit to a perfect stranger."

Or the only father I'd ever known.

"Monica's addiction cost me a lot of material things, not to mention any respect I might have had for the woman. You're welcome to her—just keep her the hell away from me."

He agreed. "Absolutely. Take care of yourself, kid."

As he walked off, I called out to him, "Thank you... for bringing my car back."

He waved and then disappeared into the dark parking lot.

I couldn't believe what had just transpired. Addicts stole, but rarely bothered replacing. Monica had somehow held onto my necklace and my car, ensuring I'd gotten both back.

Well, she'd let her scary boyfriend handle the car. Still, none of it made a damn bit of sense. I walked up the stairs in a daze, still trying to piece together a rational explanation for why my car was back in my possession.

Maybe Murder Viking was telling the truth and Monica was working to get clean.

Or maybe the universe had finally decided to stop taking a shit on me.

If that was the case, then I had another request. "Uh, Universe? Think you could send me a man while you're at it?"

Hey, it never hurt to try.

CHAPTER FOUR

Mike: May 2014 (Age: 31)

"Hey, man. Glad you made it."

I surveyed the empty living room before turning to David. "Hey—Where's the talent for tonight? I didn't sign up for a sausage fest—"

His smile faded, and he rounded on me. "Look, tonight's not a date."

I pinched my gray button up between my fingers. "Then why the fuck am I dressed up? I'm not putting out for you now, asshole."

David sighed. "It's just, Lauren is Beth's friend—and her boss. She's off-limits for obvious reasons."

I nodded. "And... what about her other friends? You said, and I quote, 'Mike, come out for a surprise anniversary blah blah with Beth and our friends, blah blah.' Friends implies more than one. So, where are the other ladies? You know, ones who aren't off limits to me."

"It's just the four of us, man," he responded easily. "There isn't anyone else coming."

"See, to me, that sounds like a date. And last I checked, Elizabeth had another friend. Hmm..." I tapped my index finger against my lips with a smirk, enjoying the way the color drained from his face. "Now, who could I be thinking of?"

He glanced down the hallway before lowering his voice. "You know why Jess isn't here. Don't fucking bring it up again."

"Then don't fucking tell me who I can and can't hit on," I snarled in response.

God forbid I actually get to make any decisions regarding my own life.

He turned away from me and yelled down the hall, "Beth, c'mon! We have to leave no later than seven. You have five minutes."

"So, does this Lauren chick know we're not on a date? Because I would sure hate for any of us here to be under the illusion we're gonna have fun tonight."

David spoke through clenched teeth. "Doesn't matter. She's off-limits. End of story. And I will sure as hell knock that shit-eating grin off your face if you—"

The click of heels against the wood floor stopped him mid-tirade and saved me from embarrassing him on his special night, which was sounding like something I was going to bail out of the first chance I got. I turned, and for a split second, couldn't seem to find my breath.

It was her.

Charlotte.

Charlotte was Lauren, Elizabeth's boss. I didn't know whether to be relieved that she wasn't one of David's relatives after all, or furious that the asshole had put a woman with a body like hers on the no-touching list.

She was even wearing the same dress she had at the wedding, although it looked better than I remembered. And the red hair I'd wanted wrapped around my fists had grown longer in the last four years.

I watched with a smug sense of satisfaction when she stopped mid-stride, green eyes widening as they moved over my face in recognition.

David and Elizabeth were talking, but I couldn't hear a damn thing. Couldn't focus on anything but her.

Her pink lips curved into a soft smile as she extended her hand toward mine. "Hello. Lauren Santiago. Nice to meet you."

I gripped it tightly in mine, before croaking, "Mike—Mike Sullivan."

So, one of us had recovered from their shock more gracefully than the other.

David ushered the two of us out front while he and Elizabeth locked up the house. One of his 'big surprises' sat waiting at the curb, a stretch limo that felt like overkill, even to me.

Infidelity... limousines. Seriously, where did it end with this guy?

"So, how's that surfing career panning out?" Lauren asked, biting down on her lower lip, instantly taking me back to the moment I met her.

My heart pounded with lust, but I forced a grin, as if seeing her again was no big deal. "I gotta say, surfing's not so good here in the desert. You know you still owe me that drink."

A part of me wanted to ask why she'd never shown up to meet me, but Comedian hadn't raised a pussy.

Her smile faltered slightly, but she recovered enough to say, "I do still owe you a drink. Let me buy you a round tonight?"

I shook my head like a defiant toddler and muttered, "It doesn't count."

The garage door went up, revealing David and Elizabeth. Her eyes went round at the sight of the limo and she turned to David in shock.

"Happy Anniversary, baby," he said, grinning from ear to ear.

Lauren bounced up and down in excitement. "We pulled it off!"

Any irritation I may have felt vanished as the momentum made her tits jiggle beneath the dress, and I wondered how she'd react if I threw her over one shoulder and hauled ass back to my truck.

I let out a low growl at the thought of taking off with her like some deranged kidnapper, earning more than one confused glance from the others.

"You planned all this?" Elizabeth asked, bringing a hand to rest against her chest. "How in the heck did you keep it a secret?"

David slipped an arm around her waist and steered her over to where the driver stood waiting beside an open door. "I've got a few tricks up my sleeve. I can still keep some things from you."

His words triggered another surge of anger. Sure, it was all well and good for him to fuck his wife's best friend, but god forbid his single and ready to mingle buddy be given the same opportunity.

I grabbed the brown paper bags from the backseat of my truck and looked up just in time to see Lauren bend over to retrieve something from the backseat of her own car. The green dress rode up over her hips just enough for me to catch a peek of lace from the black boy shorts she was wearing.

"Knew it," I whispered to myself, while simultaneously wondering how in the hell I was going to keep my dick locked away for the evening.

Lauren reappeared with a large paper bag in hand and slammed the car door shut with her hip. I followed her into the limo like a stray dog, wracking my brain for something to say—preferably something that wouldn't end with me getting laid out by my best friend.

Between the two of us, it seemed we'd purchased enough alcohol for a frat party. The minute my ass hit the seat, I began doling out beers, needing a second to get my thoughts and emotions under control.

I planned on only having a couple—nothing that would put me on Grey's radar. As he'd specifically mentioned hard liquor, I figured a beer or two wasn't likely to earn me an ass beating from a club prospect.

I'd keep a clear head and honor David's request like the goddamn gentleman I was.

That plan went sailing out the window when Lauren wrapped her pretty pink lips around the bottle and tipped it back to take a swig.

I ran a hand over my face and took a long drink from my beer, not even tasting it. No, I was fighting a raging hard-on, imagining Lauren's lips around my cock—picturing the sounds she would make as she took me deep.

She laughed at something Elizabeth said. Like, really laughed, with her head back and eyes closed. Christ, the woman was even more beautiful than I remembered her being four years ago.

David caught my eye and ran the flat of his hand over his throat—a warning to keep my hands to myself.

Unfortunately, my brain hadn't quite latched onto the concept and was spinning fantasies that were wild, even by my standards.

I was well and truly fucked.

CHAPTER FIVE

Mike: May 2014 (Age: 31)

"Found any up-and-coming artists I need to know about?" I asked, alone with Lauren for the first time all night.

After buying a couple of rounds for everyone, she'd disappeared, leaving me to act as third wheel for two people who were missing a prime opportunity to make use of the bench seat inside the limo.

I finally extricated myself and found Lauren leaning against the patio railing, staring off into space.

She turned toward me with a distracted smile. "You know the art world, always changing..." Her voice trailed off, and she looked down to pick at her nail polish.

The playful banter we had in Galveston was noticeably absent here. Maybe I'd been ditched at a hotel bar because she'd known even then what I was just figuring out.

It had all just been a game of pretend.

I skimmed Lauren's bare arm with my fingertips, desperate to know if the jolt I felt the first time we touched was still there.

Instead of leaning into me, she pulled away as if my touch burned her skin.

"Hey," I said, keeping my voice low. "Did I say something to piss you off?"

Lauren lifted her head to face me, eyes overly bright, as if she was on the verge of tears.

Fuck.

I didn't know what to do with a crying chick. My hand itched to reach out and touch her again, but I wasn't sure my ego could handle being rejected a second time.

Her lower lip quivered. "I'm sorry. I've built up this image of you in my head, and it's still surreal to think that you're here right now. You've been here the whole time—I'm just trying to reconcile you with Jack."

Jack?

Right. The fake name I gave her that night.

I rested my forearms against the railing and looked straight ahead, trying to keep the edge out of my voice. "Do I... do I not measure up to who you imagined me to be?"

I held my breath as she struggled to find the right words. Maybe the girl four years ago had considered a romp on the beach with a stranger, but I worried the woman in front of me wanted much more than I would ever be capable of giving.

She started and stopped four different sentences before she got out what she needed to say. "It's not that simple. At David and Elizabeth's wedding, I wanted to meet you for that drink—I did. But I was worried about what you'd think about me after. The woman who came with me, Sandra, said I shouldn't do it. Said I'd hate myself in the morning."

Ah, fuck.

That explained a lot of things. Her 'friend' might have hit the nail on the head with her assessment of me and my motivations, but she'd only done it to help herself out.

Lauren pressed her lips together before admitting, "You know, I've often wondered what would've happened had I gone back to your room with you."

This time, when I reached out to touch her, she didn't pull away. She moved closer, bringing her palm up to rest against my chest. It was a cause for celebration and more drinks, but instead of letting her go, I kept my arm wrapped around her shoulder as I guided us back inside.

Shit-eating grin firmly restored, I decided to go for broke. "Let's grab another round and you tell me more about these thoughts you've had. And be honest, am I wearing clothes in them?"

Lauren patted my chest and shook her head. "Leave it to a man to turn it around and make it about sex."

"Darlin', looking at you, it's hard to imagine much else."

She tilted her chin up at me defiantly. "Is that right?"

Oh, I was so getting laid tonight.

I nodded dumbly and lowered my head. Lauren's eyes fluttered to a close, but just as our lips were about to touch, all hell broke loose in the bar.

"You wanna get your fucking hands off my wife, or do you need some help?"

Given my track record, I immediately assumed he was talking to me and all but shoved Lauren away.

Fortunately—or unfortunately, depending on how one viewed these types of situations—David was the one preparing to brawl. Then I saw the grin on his face and knew shit was about to head south.

Frowning David? Completely normal.

Smiling David? People were going home in body bags.

A man I'd never seen before in my life released Elizabeth and held his hands up in surrender. "Sorry, man. Been drinking and she looked like someone I know."

David didn't waste a second pulling her against him while I waited, trying to decide whether to intervene. I finally settled on standing at his side, hoping the drunk guy would take a hint and walk away.

Before going, he turned back to Elizabeth with an affable grin. "Again, I'm sorry. I meant no disrespect."

Lauren made a sound of surprise and I glanced back to find her face had gone pale. She stared at the man as if she knew who he was before turning her glare on Elizabeth. It was over in a matter of seconds, but had lasted just long enough to pique my curiosity.

"I—I can't breathe," Elizabeth gasped raggedly and Lauren stepped in, leading her back to the patio and leaving the two of us in the narrow hallway by the bathrooms.

"C'mon, man. He's not worth it. Don't let this drunk idiot ruin the evening," I said, injecting as much calmness in my voice as I could muster.

Most people didn't enjoy getting angry. David wasn't most people though—the guy was completely content to take up permanent residency in the great state of rage.

Growing up, I was the scrappy one. The surliness had appeared not long after the whole Patrick thing.

Maybe I'd created a monster.

Something flickered in his gaze, and he exhaled slowly.

I slapped a hand lightly on his back. "You alright? You wanna step outside for a minute?"

David shook his head. "No. I wanna stay and dance with my wife."

I waved away the concerned staff and turned back to him. "I think that's a good plan, but first, take a walk with me outside. Let's clear your head before you Hulk out on us. Then we'll grab another round and you can get that dance."

In another life where things weren't completely fucked up, I probably would have made a kick-ass parent. Pulling David out of a rage couldn't have differed from calming a toddler after a tantrum.

Shit, it was probably easier to deal with the toddler.

CHAPTER SIX

Lauren: May 2014 (Age:27)

After ensuring nobody was about to throw down, I rejoined Elizabeth on the patio. She was standing in the exact spot I'd been in just minutes before, staring vacantly toward a nearby playa lake.

"He's gone now. Nobody had to throw any punches either. Looks like Mike's trying to calm David down."

Elizabeth's behavior over the last few months had been strange. At work, she'd become distant, often completing tasks with little to no emotion. But when David reached out to ask me to help plan a surprise anniversary, I'd agreed immediately.

We might not have been close friends, but theirs was a modern-day fairy tale—proof that my soulmate was out there waiting for me. Marriage hadn't changed things. If anything, it had only strengthened their bond.

David sent flowers to the office—and not just for special occasions. What I found odd was that she'd read the card with a secret smile before running it through the shredder.

Personally, if I had a husband and he was giving me sexy love notes, I'd keep those bad boys in a box to read on the days when I wasn't feeling it.

Which brought me to my next question. "Wanna tell me why the guy who delivers flowers to the office was holding you like that back there?"

Elizabeth closed her eyes. "I cheated on David."

"No," I said automatically. "You two are so happy, and the flowers —" The flowers. *The goddamn flowers.* "Aren't from him, are they?"

She shook her head and cleared her throat before whispering, "That was Landon. The flowers were from him. David's dad died, and he'd been taking all these out-of-town jobs."

If they couldn't make it work, then who could?

I stumbled over my words. "Did you try talking to him about it?"

"I did, Lauren. When he was home, I tried to support him. I let him know I was available if he ever wanted to talk about how he was feeling. But he didn't want to talk. He shut down and shut me out. I just felt like nothing I did mattered." She wiped away the tears on her face before adding, "It's over now. Between Landon and me, I mean."

"Is it?" I hissed, my pulse speeding up. "It didn't look very over from where I was standing. And I didn't even know it had begun!"

Elizabeth rubbed her temples with a sigh. "I don't know why he was here, but I didn't start things up again, if that's what you're getting at." She lowered her voice on the last part, as if David might pop up out of the playa lake at any moment. I pictured him spitting out a snorkel and screaming, "I knew it!"

I pursed my lips together, struggling to keep a straight face as I reached for her hand. "I believe you. It just doesn't make sense that he would approach you like that, especially if he saw you were with your husband, does it?"

David and Mike chose that moment to reappear, saving Elizabeth from having to answer my question and pulling my brain in a vastly different direction.

The man I'd spent the past four years fantasizing about was right in front of me. And he had apparently spent a good chunk of his time in a gym, because his body was rock solid muscle.

The sight of his biceps straining against his dress shirt dredged up every single lustful thought I'd had. It had taken everything in me not to jump into his arms.

And that beard... *purr.*

Unfortunately, Elizabeth's revelation wasn't going quietly into the night. No, it kept poking its head back in, leaving me feeling conflicted.

David approached and wrapped his arms around her waist. "You okay, Beth? God, you just looked so scared. Amazing how some guys have absolutely no respect."

I turned away, afraid the truth was written all over my face.

"Something you wanna share with the class, darlin'?" Mike whispered in my ear.

And suddenly, I was back in Galveston—weighing the pros and cons of sleeping with him.

Sure, I'd tempted fate a bit while getting the alcohol out of my car back at the house, knowing his eyes were glued to my ass. But that confidence had faltered by the time we reached the bar.

Casual sex while on my quest to find Mr. Right was one thing. But Jack—*Mike*—had always been The One. Now that he was here, I didn't know what the hell I was supposed to do.

Everything had changed suddenly and without warning.

Elizabeth had once let it slip that she hadn't slept with David until she had a ring on her finger. Sandra swore soulmates were something only found in movies, saying, "You've got to just get it, get it, get it until you can't get it anymore."

Seriously. Those were her exact words.

Sandra was also the one who'd convinced me that Mike was a man with one thing on his mind. And with Elizabeth smack dab in the middle of her own crisis, I couldn't exactly verify whether it was true.

"I don't know what you're talking about," I said, turning to face him. It seemed my entire exercise had been futile, because the minute those piercing blue eyes met mine, the cons disappeared. "W-wasn't there something you maybe wanted to share—before all the drama?"

Or finish—like that almost kiss?

His mouth curved up into a playful grin. "Now, I'm confused. You'll have to enlighten me, darlin'."

Bastard.

Deciding two could play that game, I ran my fingers over the lapels on his shirt and moved in for the kill. Placing my lips just inches from his, I whispered, "I thought there was something you were trying to tell me earlier. Guess I was wrong."

He exhaled a low growl before catching my wrists in his hands. "Are you coming on to me, Lauren? I'm not that kind of guy. And in the interest of honesty, I'm actually seeing someone already."

The balloon in my chest burst, and I pulled back, wondering how I'd completely misread the situation between us.

He had a girlfriend?

I stared down at my peep-toe heels as if they held the answer, cheeks growing warmer by the second. With my fair skin, I probably resembled a tomato.

Mike nudged my upper arm. "Red, I'm screwing with you."

"You are?" I squeaked out, feeling relief seep into my every pore.

Unable to hold it in any longer, he burst out laughing. "Of course I am. Christ, you should see your face!"

I finally recovered enough to ask, "So, if I said I was coming on to you—"

"I'd fuck you in the bathroom right now if you let me. Get it out of our systems."

"Get it out of our systems," I repeated slowly, waiting for the punchline. But when I looked into his eyes, I realized he was serious.

I knew next to nothing about Mike—at least nothing that was true. What I did know was I would be nothing more than a notch on the man's bedpost.

And just like that, my four-year fantasy came to an abrupt end on a bar patio.

Maybe instead of viewing David and Elizabeth as some great love story, I should have seen them as a cautionary tale. It didn't matter if life served up a happily ever after on a silver platter. Eventually, someone was going to screw it all up.

Even if I had met Mike for that drink in Galveston, it wouldn't have mattered.

He wanted a one-night stand, and I was worth so much more than that.

I'd just been holding out for something that didn't even exist.

CHAPTER SEVEN

Lauren: May 2014 (Age: 27)

"Thanks for inviting me. I had a blast." I almost tripped over my heels in my haste to get out of the limo and away from him.

While David and Elizabeth danced like they didn't have a care in the world, I'd spent the rest of the evening picking apart a napkin while Mike pretended I no longer existed, even though I was literally sitting across the table from him.

"Red! C'mon, Red. Wait up." Mike jogged after me.

I was still fumbling around in my purse for the car keys when he caught up to me.

"Talk to me, Red."

My eyes stung, and I had to bite down on the inside of my cheek to keep it together before looking up. "My name is Lauren."

Mike ran both hands through his hair with a muttered curse. "Let me walk you to your car—it's the least I can do."

I pointed at the window. "We're at my car. Now, if you'll excuse me, I just want to go home. It's late."

He sighed. "Right. How about we go back to your place and talk?"

The request sent a jolt of longing through me, and I knew if he came back to my apartment, I would forget why sleeping with him was a bad idea.

Clearly, my lady-bits were morons.

"Yeah, think I'm gonna pass on all that," I said, waving a hand in his direction. "Thanks for the offer though, and good luck with... whatever the hell it is you do for a living."

Keys in hand, I got the door unlocked and open, only for Mike to slam it shut again.

"Just hear me out, Lauren. I don't know what you're expecting, but—"

"You're not it," I finished helpfully, before reopening the door and climbing in.

It wasn't the truth.

The truth was, I wanted him just as badly as he wanted me. But being vulnerable would only cause more hurt in the end.

Why couldn't he have seen me as more than just his next conquest?

Didn't what we shared in Galveston mean anything to him?

I made it to the end of the block before the sob broke free from my chest.

He probably used the same spiel on every girl he met. The thought left me pounding my fist against the steering wheel and rage screaming before dissolving into full-blown weeping.

By the time I reached my apartment, I'd come to two conclusions. One, I would never be one-night stand material. And two, wanting someone to stick around was apparently too much of an ask—something I should have recognized by now, considering my upbringing.

I'd also decided I'd been born in the wrong time period. I wanted a love like Darcy and Elizabeth's in *Pride & Prejudice*. While their relationship was certainly rocky, I couldn't imagine Mr. Darcy asking Lizzie to 'fuck in the bathroom.'

Maybe I'd wasted the last few years holding out for a love that wasn't attainable in the age of online dating.

I parked and rubbed the remaining tears from my eyes. It seemed I was going to have to make my peace with dying a lonely, cat-collecting spinster.

First things first, I needed to go out and buy some cats.

What I would not do was waste one more tear on a man who wouldn't know a great love if it jumped up and slapped him in the face.

"Hey, Lauren."

My chin dropped to my chest, and I contemplated climbing back into my car and speeding off again.

Instead, I released a long sigh and turned around. "Monica. I'm starting to think you must have a radar that goes off just when things in my life are looking up. Ding! Time to fuck up Lauren's world! Sorry to disappoint, but someone already beat you to it tonight."

She cautiously took a couple of steps toward me and I realized it was the healthiest I'd ever seen her. She'd put on some weight, but it looked good on her. Her hair had been washed and straightened, and while her makeup had gone out of style when the eighties ended, she was at least wearing some. She was also wearing a leather vest, for some inexplicable reason.

"I didn't mean to startle you. I just wanted to see you," Monica ventured, taking another step toward me. "Have you been crying?"

I gave a half-hearted shrug. "Does it matter? Cut the crap. What are you here for—the car? My wallet? The apartment? I'd rather skip the holier-than-thou lecture this time and just get right to the point. What are you here to steal?"

Mike had officially used up the last of my fucks.

She shook her head. "I'm not here for anything like that. I've actually got my own thing going on now."

"Doing what?" I asked with a bitter laugh. "Running a motorcycle gang?"

She bit her lip. "Something like that. I'm an Ol' Lady. It's real classy. See?" She twirled around and there it was in bold letters on the back of the leather vest.

Property of Torch.

I bobbed my head up and down slowly. "I see. So, what does an 'old lady' do?"

I didn't care and couldn't fathom why I was humoring her. I wanted to get upstairs to my apartment, kick off my heels, and forget this night ever happened.

She swallowed before admitting, "I just do whatever needs to be done for my man—I started out as a club whore, which just meant that anyone could use me for sex or—"

I held a hand up, stopping her. "Okay, I've heard enough. I'm just going to head upstairs and get some sleep. If you're planning on stealing anything, just let me know and I'll make sure I just leave it out for you."

She reached out and grabbed my arm, and I wrenched it back, knocking her to the ground. "Do not touch me! Don't you ever touch me!"

"Lauren, I didn't mean to scare you. I'm sorry. I'm not here for anything, I swear. Been sober for sixty-three days, and I wanted you to know." She reached into her pocket and pulled out a wad of cash. "I also brought you some money to pay you back for the car and for other stuff I took from you."

There she was, sitting in the parking lot ,offering me the money she'd earned by performing sexual favors for bikers.

It was a pathetic sight.

I tightened my grip on my purse strap. "I don't want your money. Just leave me alone."

She moved onto all fours and got herself upright again. "I under-stand you might need some time to think it over, but you can accept this—free and clear."

My jaw ached from clenching my teeth and I barked out, "I don't need some time, Monica. I don't want anything you're offering. Not now... not ever. I just want you to leave me the hell alone. Can you do that? Can you just disappear?"

She wiped at her eyes, and I realized she was crying. "I'm sorry, Lauren. I'm so sorry for not being the mom you deserved—"

Unable to stand a moment more in her presence, I turned and jogged up the stairs to my apartment—heels be damned. It had been an evening of unfulfilled wishes and dreams that had suddenly morphed into nightmares.

I couldn't bear listening to her sudden regrets over the shitty hand she'd dealt.

CHAPTER EIGHT

Mike: June 2014 (Age: 31)

I wanted to say life returned to normal after the platonic date from hell. That I moved on from a certain redhead, free to get back to the things I loved, like casual hookups with no strings attached and more casual hookups with no strings attached.

Instead, I'd handled the rejection about as well as an alcoholic would an open bar. Lauren waltzed in with her curve-hugging green dress and promptly fucked up my entire world.

If we'd had our one-night stand as planned, I could have gotten her out of my system and been on to the next one. But my sex life for the past month had been nothing more than me fucking my fist after drowning myself in tequila.

Grey was going to nail my ass any day now over the drinking. Maybe I'd just send him Lauren's way, as the thing was entirely her fault. Making my dick want what he couldn't have.

My phone vibrated against the nightstand, David's smug ass grin lighting up the screen.

This was partly his fault, too. Instead of taking responsibility when I confronted him over it, the shithead had laughed in my face, telling me I was just pissed that Lauren had seen through my act. His parting shot was some bullshit about love and... *insanity?* Honestly, I tuned most of it out and hadn't talked to him since.

Maybe he was finally seeing the error of his ways. If so, I would graciously accept his apology and let him make it up to me in liquor.

"Hey, cocksucker. Missed me?"

The other end of the line remained eerily silent. I pulled the phone away from my ear and glanced at the screen to see if the call had been dropped when I heard the choking sound.

"We were in an accident—the car was in an accident. Beth—she didn't wake up, and they took her—"

Suddenly sober and with my heart feeling as if it was seconds from exploding, I forced out, "I'm on my way. Where did they take her?"

He told me and, despite the boatload of Cuervo and adrenaline running through my veins, I somehow made it to the hospital in one piece.

The automatic doors of the emergency room parted, but instead of David, I found Lauren. She perched rigidly on the edge of a gray plastic chair in the corner, completely pale and bouncing her legs like an addict in need of a fix.

"Is Elizabeth—" My voice cracked. "Did she?"

I couldn't finish the question—didn't want to hear the answer. What had seemed so important to me hours ago no longer mattered. This changed everything.

She pushed a trembling hand through her red hair, eyes brimming with unshed tears as she stared through me. "I—I don't know. They just told me to wait here."

I dropped into the empty chair beside her with a nod. "I'll wait with you."

Lauren stopped bouncing her legs long enough to look at me. Really looked at me. Her green eyes were a stark contrast against her pale cheeks and in this moment, I hated that her fair skin gave her away. Hated that I could see the fear projected across her face.

She forced a watery smile. "That's really not necessary, you see—"

I reached over and cupped her knee, her jerky movements vibrating through my palm. "Stop," I said with an authority I typically saved for work. "Neither one of us should be alone right now."

"She's not, actually."

I glanced up at the douchebag in the suit and rolled my eyes. "And you are?"

He handed Lauren a coffee, not bothering to look at me as he said, "Her date, Brant. Who are you?"

Who was I?

Fuck, who was I?

The tool who'd tried to get in Lauren's pants first?

"He's David's best friend, Brant," she answered wearily, before choking up again.

And there it was.

She had relegated me to the inferior role of acquaintance, just one step above complete stranger. All because she was looking for monogamy, while I was more of a ménage kinda guy.

Now that someone else had moved in, I was reconsidering things.

Before I could plan something resembling a response, David approached, looking like he'd been through the ringer.

"Hey," he managed, before his jaw tightened. "Thanks for uh— thanks for coming."

I stood and pulled him into a hug. "Hey, what are they saying?"

He held a fist up to his mouth and exhaled slowly. "Beth was on the side that got t-boned. She hit her head and lost consciousness. They're running tests and scans—I don't know."

Lauren broke and pressed her hands to her eyes, her shoulders shaking with silent sobs. Before I could swoop in and save the day, Brant slid into my empty seat, pulling her to his chest.

Asshole.

David left soon after to speak to a nurse. I took a seat across from the woman who had me questioning why I hadn't offered dinner instead of a bathroom quickie.

I was busy staring at the yellowed linoleum floor, lost in my head, when someone tapped me on the shoulder.

Torch, decked head to toe in SPMC gear, had his arm slung around a blonde I'd never seen before. I avoided the clubhouse, if I could help it and wouldn't know a club whore from an Ol' Lady.

"What the fuck are you doing here?" I hissed, cutting my eyes over to where Lauren was inexplicably trying to fold herself in the small chair.

Her awkward movements didn't escape anyone's notice, least of all the woman's. "Lauren?" she asked, waving her hand. "Hey, what are you doing here?"

Lauren gave a weak wave in return. "Monica—hi. Just waiting for a friend."

Torch jerked his chin toward the exit. I sighed before following him outside.

"Grey said you were here. We got a problem. Eli's on a run with some guys, and Cage has appendicitis or some shit. We need you to get us in and out of here, no questions asked."

I pinched the bridge of my nose. "You're fucking kidding me, right? My best friend and his wife were in a car accident and Grey thinks now's a good time for me to do club shit?"

My voice got louder and louder until I was shouting directly into the biker's face. He didn't seem fazed by it—just whipped out his cell phone. "No problemo. I'll just let Grey know you refused."

Fuck.

I shook my head. "Fine. Get him here, and I'll see what I can do."

Torch nodded. and we reentered to find the blonde Monica occupying the seat I'd vacated. Given the pinched expression on Lauren's face, the two seemed to be having quite the conversation.

Once Torch and the mystery woman left, Brant stood with a stretch. "Listen, I've got to go into the office tomorrow, so I'm going to have to call it a night. You ready, Lauren?"

She glanced toward the double doors that led back to the exam rooms, fidgeting again. "But, but we don't know if she's going to be okay or not."

He sighed heavily. "I can't hang around all night. Can you get a ride home?"

Lauren's eyes immediately went to me, and I nodded, earning a shaky smile in return. "Yeah, I can manage. Thanks for dinner and the wine. It was really nice."

"Mm-hmm," he mumbled, looking down at his phone. "I'll call you."

Twenty bucks said he wasn't going home. The bastard was going to get laid. The disinterested look in his eyes when she talked told me everything I needed to know about him. He probably thought he'd take her to dinner and then get in her pants. I imagined the whole best friend being in a car wreck thing had really thrown a wrench into his plans.

This guy was a Grade-A Prick.

"You alright, Red?" I asked as soon as the douche nozzle left, sitting down across from her again. I considered taking said douche nozzle's former seat, but didn't want to press my luck.

Lauren took a slow breath and let it out. "I'm fine. So, how do you know Monica's biker?"

"Torch? Mainly from work," I admitted, making a mental note to remind Grey the next time I saw him that having his guys show up in public was drawing a lot of unnecessary attention.

"Your work," she repeated. "And what exactly is it you do for a living, when you're not desert surfing?"

The question annoyed me. Yet another reminder that my M.O.— my lies—hadn't charmed this woman into bed. If the snark in her tone was any indicator, it had only pissed her off.

"I'm a cop."

Lauren's laugh sounded anything but amused. "Why does that not surprise me? You act just like one."

Instead of diving into what the fuck that little dig had meant and giving her the pleasure of knowing she'd gotten under my skin, I forced a grin and asked, "Enough about me. How do you know the biker's girlfriend?"

She squirmed in her seat, suddenly finding the floor the most interesting thing in the room.

"Red?"

Lauren blew out a frustrated breath, which lifted her hair up off of her forehead just enough for me to see her eyes. "Monica? She's just someone I used to know."

I was wise enough to know when to quit and let it drop in favor of a topic I cared a hell of a lot more about. "So, Billy Bob seemed nice."

She lifted her head, shooting me a look that would have turned lesser men to stone. "His name's Brant, and don't patronize me."

"Wouldn't dream of it, darlin'," I said with a grin, wanting to patronize the shit out of her. "I think we both know a guy like that is no good for a girl like you, though."

If that guy was a stick of dynamite, then I was a block of C-4, but we'd cross that bridge when we came to it.

"And what about you?" Lauren asked, cocking her head to the side as if genuinely interested in my response.

I settled back against the plastic chair, putting my arms behind my head. "Darlin', I'm starting to think I just might be your soulmate. It's gotta be fate, us running into each other again, don't you think?"

I was serving up some high-quality chick flick shit, expecting her to eat it right up.

Instead, she frowned. "Fate? Try again. Your best friend is married to my best friend. That's not fate—it's logistics."

Time to bust out the big guns.

"What if?" I leaned forward and ran the toe of my boot over a scuff mark on the floor before meeting her now curious stare. "What if I wanted more than one night? Would it change things? Because I haven't been able to get you out of my head since the night we went out."

Lauren's mouth opened and closed like a fish's, and I held my breath, knowing it could go either way. When a flash of red moved from her chest up into her cheeks, I knew it was going to swing in my favor.

"But..." she began.

I held a finger up, silencing her again. "I'm not asking you to decide anything right now, Red. Just think about it."

She gave me a shaky nod in return and slumped down in the chair, her legs parting slightly. From where I sat, I had a clear view of her black panties. A gentleman would have let her know, but no one had ever accused me of being that.

Maybe she knew just what she was doing.

Regardless of what she was planning to say, it sure as hell seemed like her body was already giving me a yes.

CHAPTER NINE

Mike: June 2014 (Age: 31)

"Take a right on Utica and the complex will be on your left." Lauren pointed ahead. I slowed my truck to take the turn, fighting exhaustion.

We'd stayed until a little after two in the morning, when David insisted we go home and try to get some sleep, promising to call if Elizabeth's condition changed.

While Lauren dozed in a chair, I'd distracted myself by getting Cage fixed up for Grey, amazed as always at what flashing a badge and smile could accomplish. I'd woken her when it was time to go, and she'd unfolded herself from what had to be the most uncomfortable position known to man. The sleepy smile she gave as I helped her up left me wondering what she looked liked after sex. Because her face looked anything like it did now, I'd be keeping her ass in bed for days.

"What are you doing?" Lauren asked, when I parked the truck and got out.

I nodded toward her apartment. "Walking you up." When she frowned, I added, "Red, it's just me walking you up to your apartment —not a marriage proposal."

She pressed her lips together and jerked her chin in a stiff nod. "Okay, but I'm not sleeping with you."

"I wasn't offering to put out," I said, dragging my gaze away from her ass to refocus. "Still waiting on that drink. Remember?"

While small, her apartment looked like something out of one of those home design magazines, arranged in a way that made the rooms seem more spacious. No empty cereal bowls piled up on the coffee table or lacy underwear poking out from under the couch cushion.

Not one thing looked to be out of place.

She had to be one of those neat freaks—the ones who make you use a coaster and take your shoes off at the door. This was new for me. The girls I usually spent time with had half a dozen roommates and their homes looked as if a tornado had recently blown through.

Interesting.

"What happened to '*I'm just walking you up?*'"

I had to move a couple of throw pillows before sitting down on the couch. "I would love a cup of coffee. Thank you."

Lauren's eyes went wide. "Oh, no you don't. I'm not falling for that. It's late and you need to go."

"Exactly. It's late and I'm dead on my feet. Doubt you'd wanna be the one responsible for sending me home in this condition. What if I fell asleep behind the wheel?"

She held her index finger up and then dropped it with a sigh. "Okay, one cup and you're gone. Deal?"

I nodded and settled my feet on the small coffee table in front of the couch.

"Also, no shoes on the furniture," she called from the kitchen. "In fact, just leave them by the door. There's no telling what we picked up at the hospital."

Neat freak with a dash of germaphobe. It was a weird turn-on.

I unlaced my boots and placed them near the door with a chuckle before settling back in on the couch, socked feet on the carpet.

Lauren reentered the living room moments later, carrying two mugs. "I didn't know how you take it, but I'm out of milk. I might have some sugar in the pantry, though."

I took the mug from her hand. "Black is perfect, thank you."

She set her mug down on a coaster—*called it*—and moved to the opposite side of the couch, facing me as though I was about to try something.

While I couldn't say the thought hadn't crossed my mind, I wasn't a predator.

"So, you doing okay?" I started off. She still owed me an answer, and I wasn't leaving until I got one.

"I'm fine." Lauren took a small sip before her eyes welled up again. She used her free hand to brush away the tears. "I'm sorry. I just keep picturing David's face and can't imagine the person I love being in a coma—not knowing if they were going to be okay."

I hadn't really considered it until she said something. I pictured her lying in a hospital bed with tubes running out of her body, and it was as if the world slowed down. The thought left me with an ache in my chest.

"I—I can't imagine what he's going through," I admitted quietly, still seeing Lauren's bruised and broken body in my mind.

I'd seen a lot of shit, both in the club and as a cop, but imagining her like that was by far the most painful thing.

I knew what my problem was. I'd gotten hung up on women in the past. Once we fucked, things went back to normal. I was going to have to put forth a little more effort if I wanted this to work. Once I got inside of her, then I could think straight again.

"You look like you're lost in thought over there. What are you thinking about?" I blinked and there she was in front of me again, healthy and watching me with a curious expression.

And three, two, one...

I cleared my throat. "I was just imagining how I would react if it were me and I got a call that you were hurt."

Her green eyes narrowed, waiting for me to turn it into a joke, but I kept my face blank. When she realized I wasn't laughing, her lips parted on a soft exhale. "Oh." Then she glanced down at her watch. "It's getting late..."

I set the coffee mug aside and scooted closer to her. "Did you think about what I said?"

Looking into her eyes, I tried to calculate how many dates it would take me to seal the deal.

She looked like a five-dater. Usually, when I spotted a five-dater at the bar, I'd run the opposite way. My life was too fast-paced to commit to anything for more than a night.

The five-dater expected flowers—roses to be specific. She wanted to be wined and dined at the nicest restaurants in the city. She'd wear something with a plunging neckline, but kiss you goodbye at the door. In her mind, she was banking on the guy getting attached before she gave it up.

I was a good detective in a lot of areas.

"There's just so much going on, and I—"

I leaned in just close enough that I could feel her breathing in and out. Her eyes widened, but she pushed her lips into a pucker. When our lips were just about to touch, I whispered, "Please give me a chance."

She nodded, clearly rattled to have me so close. "O-okay, but this is exclusive, right?"

I nodded, "Of course."

Wait, what did she mean by exclusive?

Ah, fuck.

What had I just agreed to?

CHAPTER TEN

Lauren: June 2014 (Age: 27)

Just as my love life was taking off, David and Elizabeth's relationship was falling apart in spectacular fashion. The car wreck and Elizabeth's short-term amnesia were nothing compared to the discovery of dual infidelity and a pregnant mistress.

"Can you believe it? He found out she was pregnant and just drove through a red light! Then, he tried to act like it hadn't been his fault."

Dr. Mulloy nodded sagely. "Well, honey, he was probably trying to get you out of the picture so he could marry her free and clear."

Elizabeth looked stricken by the thought and then began sobbing. *Again.*

And this would be the last time I offered to host a girl's happy hour at my apartment. I'd thought it would be a good way to blow off some steam from work, but once Dr. Mulloy found out, she'd insisted on joining us.

"Lauren, do you have more cheese? We're running low in here." She waved the near empty platter at me as though I were a waitress in a restaurant.

I wrestled it from her hands and went into the kitchen to add more. I'd really wanted to announce that I was going on a date with

Mike, but the conversation kept reverting to Elizabeth and her failed marriage.

As much as I loved her, I also kind of hated her right now.

She had become a close friend over the past month and while I couldn't imagine losing my memory in a car wreck and being forced to rely upon other people to remember the past, she'd brought this on herself—whether she remembered it or not.

My phone chimed from the countertop.

Mike: Hey, Red. How's ladies' night going?

I smiled and peeked over the half wall into the living room. Another coworker was arguing with Elizabeth over the logistics of whose cheating was worse—hers or David's.

Me: Just reliving the demise of the Greene marriage over here.

His reply was almost instant.

Mike: You in need of rescuing?

And there it was. Tummy flutters and a racing heart. It had been happening a lot over the last two weeks. We'd made plans to go out the weekend after he drove me home from the hospital, but had been called in to provide relief for David and Elizabeth instead.

Since then, we'd been trying to find space in our busy schedules to reconnect, often settling for text messages and a few late-night phone calls.

As much as I wanted to believe the man I met on a beach in Galveston was real, another part of me felt it was too good to be true. Plus, with Monica lurking around every corner and my friend's marriage ending, the timing was all wrong for a relationship.

It didn't mean I couldn't enjoy the distraction, though.

I surveyed the chaos in my living room and debated, knowing if I sat back down, I'd be forced to offer my opinion on the entire ordeal. If I let Mike rescue me, then I'd be walking a tightrope of emotion.

As much as I wanted to sleep with him, I needed more time and could only hope he would be patient enough to wait it out. Modern romance had become a race to the finish line, but what happened to taking things slow?

Brant had been my first foray into online dating. When he brought up sex before the appetizer even arrived, I knew it would be my last. I'd just taken a bite of a bread stick when he asked about my birth control methods and ended up choking on it. I had spent the next five minutes downing water and avoiding his gaze.

"We'll come back to that one after dessert," he'd ominously suggested.

David's phone call had saved me from having to undergo any further interrogation in my sex life, or lack thereof. By the time Mike arrived at the emergency room, I couldn't even determine if I was crying over Elizabeth or my horrible experience with dating anymore.

"No, it's definitely worse because she was my best friend! Landon was just a nobody," Elizabeth proclaimed loudly from the sofa.

I rolled my eyes from the kitchen and briefly considered slamming my head into the cabinets until I had amnesia and could forget tonight ever happened.

Dr. Mulloy raised her voice. "Lauren! Honey, where's the cheese? I need to soak up all this wine."

Decision made, I picked up my phone.

Me: I direly need of rescuing. Know anyone who could help me out?

Mike: Be there in five, darlin'.

I couldn't wipe the stupid grin off my face. I quickly emptied the tray of cheese into a plastic bag and hid it behind a carton of milk before rejoining the girls in the living room. "Hey guys, we're out of food and I need to go. I just remembered I made plans."

Sandra eyed me skeptically, while Elizabeth nodded sadly. "I'm so sorry, Lauren. You brought us here to have a good time, and I just brought down the mood."

Yeah, you sure did.

I shook my head. "You're fine." I gave her a quick hug and ushered her over to the front door. "I'll call and check on you tomorrow."

The others followed Elizabeth out, and I began speed-cleaning the apartment—straightening throw pillows and dumping empty wine glasses into the sink.

Once I was certain that the living room was pristine again, I bolted into my closet and searched for something sexy, yet casual. I chose a basic black sundress and stripped off my t-shirt and athletic shorts.

It was right about then that the front door opened and Mike walked in. As if he had a sixth sense about this sort of thing, he immediately looked down the hallway and paused when he realized I was standing in nothing but my bra and panties.

I immediately tried and failed to cover myself with my arms.

He fought a grin and held up a small bouquet of red roses. "I—I—uh, here are some flowers for you. I knocked, but you didn't answer. Do you always leave your door unlocked? That's really not safe."

I held up my index finger. "Can you?" I squeaked, "Can you just give me a minute?"

He nodded as his gaze moved up and down my mostly naked body. "Sure. You need any help?"

I slammed the bedroom door and called out, "No. No, thank you. I'll be just fine."

I rested my forehead against the door. *Okay, so we'd established that physically he was into me.* I just wish there was a way to ensure he'd stick around until morning.

I looked at the sundress, now mocking me from its hanger, before retrieving my discarded clothes off the carpet.

Baby steps, Lauren. Baby steps.

Mike had made himself at home on the couch by the time I finished changing and was flipping through the channels aimlessly.

He took in my baggy t-shirt and shorts with a mock frown. "I gotta say, I liked your first outfit better. I got you these."

I swatted him playfully on the arm and took the roses from his hand. Most people would have been over the moon to have gotten flowers, but I was missing the elegant bouquet gene. I just didn't see the point to them.

"Uh, do I put this little packet thing in the water now?" I called from the kitchen, struggling to read the tiny print on the package.

Mike spun around on the couch to face me, one eyebrow arched. "What do you mean? You've gotten flowers before, right?"

"No," I admitted. "I'm not really a flower girl. Wine and chocolate girl? Absolutely. But flowers have never really been my thing."

His face fell, so I quickly added, "But I love these! These may turn me into a flower girl, just as soon as I can figure out what to do with the plant food."

Mike hopped off the couch and joined me in the kitchen. "You're such a bullshitter, Red. Let me see the little packet. Surely, between the two of us, we can figure it out."

Less than a minute later, he gave up trying to decipher the faded print on the packet of plant food and resorted to Google. I found and washed a glass pitcher while he trimmed the ends of the stems over the trash can.

"Do you have baking soda?" he asked, reading the screen. "Says here that a little mixed in with the plant food and water will make the roses last longer."

I found it on a shelf in the refrigerator and triumphantly raised the box before handing it over. We worked side by side in my small kitchen—close enough I could feel the heat of his skin but not close enough to touch.

If someone had told me before tonight that a man arranging flowers was a turn on, I would have politely assumed they were crazy. But there was something decidedly erotic about watching Mike carefully place each stem in the pitcher. He rolled the cuffs of his shirt up to his elbows, displaying a kaleidoscope of tattoos spanning both arms.

"When you go to bed, put them in the fridge and then just take them out every morning."

I nodded along, not hearing a damn word he said. If floral arranging had this effect on me, I could only speculate what would happen should the man decide to pick up a toilet brush next. Or a vacuum.

"Red? You with me?" Mike waved a hand in front of my face, pulling me from a fantasy montage no sane person should be having.

"Sounds good," I squeaked, nodding like a bobblehead doll. My blood pulsed with the need to shed the buttons on his shirt and pay homage to his muscles.

He leaned in and, for a moment, I thought he was going for a kiss. Something I was completely on board with. Instead, he pressed the backs of his fingers to my forehead. "Are you feeling okay? Your face got really red there for a second."

I wasn't okay, and his proximity wasn't helping matters. It was causing my brain to short-circuit and had left me with a strong aware-ness of my heartbeat.

"Fine—I'm fine. Everything's fine. Flowers are weird. Like how did something that dies within a week come to symbolize love and romance? Not that you got them because you love me, per se—" I was rambling and didn't know how to stop. "That's silly. We just met. Do you want a glass of alcohol? I might have a beer or two in the fridge. Yes? No? I think I'll have wine. I think the situation calls for wine."

Mike gave me a bemused smirk and dropped his hand on my shoul-der. "I can't, I'm on call. But if you show me where you keep your cups, I'd be happy to pour you a glass of wine. It's clear you need one."

CHAPTER ELEVEN

Lauren: June 2014 (Age: 27)

While Mike filled a wineglass to the brim with pinot noir, snagging a bottled water for himself, I placed the pitcher of roses on the small ledge separating the kitchen from the living room and talked my libido down.

We settled on the couch, much the same way we had a couple of weeks ago, with me occupying one end and him the other. Clearly not a man of patience, Mike allowed me to take one sip of my wine before plucking the glass from my fingers and setting it on the coffee table. On a coaster, no less.

"Come here," he commanded, patting the cushion next to his thigh.

"Why?" I asked, feigning disinterest, despite the heat wave currently making its way through my body. "You miss me already?"

His tongue darted out to press against the corner of his lips. "Darlin', if I'd known you walked around in your underwear, I would have been over here every goddamn night, wine and chocolate in hand."

Ridiculously pleased by the comment, I began inching my way over, but not fast enough to suit him. Mike latched onto my arm and tugged me the remaining distance before nestling me under his arm.

What the hell was he doing to me?

Hours later, I woke to him kneeling beside the couch, his fingers lightly tracing the curve of my jaw.

"I got called in," he whispered in apology, before leaning in to press a kiss to my cheek.

The television was still on, running a World War Something documentary from the History channel I'd said I enjoyed watching.

Lies.

But in my defense, the man was rubbing small circles against my shoulder with his thumb when he asked, and I couldn't think clearly.

"What time is it?" I asked with a yawn, resisting the urge to pet his beard. *Barely.*

His eyes dropped to his watch before coming back to mine. "Just a little after three. I didn't want to wake you, but figured you'd probably didn't wanna sleep on the couch."

This sweet, caring side of Mike was unexpected, but not unwelcome in the slightest. Maybe it was nothing more than a ruse to get me into bed, but it had left me second-guessing the decision to take things slow.

I looped an arm around the back of his neck and brought his face down to meet mine. "Stay," I begged against his lips. "Please."

Mike used the back of the couch to brace himself as I pulled him closer, almost as if he was resisting. I was past the point of reason and rules as I lightly nipped his lower lip with my teeth.

Any restraint on his end snapped, and then he was kissing me. His tongue thrust against the seam of my lips and I moaned, allowing him to take everything from me.

My legs moved around his waist, trying to pull him down to me. He obliged, running his erection over the seam of my shorts until I was arching up to meet him. Everything in me ached for more.

With a growl, Mike broke away and brought his forehead to rest against mine before panting, "Fuck, I want to. I do, but I can't stay."

"Can you be late?" I moaned, reaching between us to grasp the hem of my t-shirt, slowly peeling it up to reveal my stomach.

"Don't fucking do that," Mike warned, his hand locking around my wrist.

"We could be quick—"

He squeezed his eyes shut, holding my wrist even tighter in his grip. "Not gonna happen, Red," he finally managed through clenched teeth.

"Okay," I said as I pushed myself into a sitting position, wondering what had come over me.

Mike pressed a quick kiss to my lips before standing. "How would you feel about coming over tonight and letting me make you dinner?"

I forced my eyes up to meet his. He was still visibly hard. Like dick print against slacks hard. I wanted to continue admiring it, but the man was waiting for an answer. "O-kay."

"Seven?" he asked.

"Yep." I was back to staring at the outline of his dick again. His *dickline*. It was impressive.

"I'll text you the address."

"Yep," I repeated, deciding that the weapon he was packing would put my phallic sculptures to shame.

"Lauren?"

"Yep," I murmured, still completely transfixed.

"You wanna walk me to the door so you can lock up behind me or just sit and stare at my cock some more?" he asked with a wicked grin.

I got to my feet, catching my shin on the edge of the coffee table after sneaking another glance. Mike's arms shot out to steady me and I let him lead me over to the front door.

"I'd tuck you in," he whispered, tucking several strands of hair behind my ear before leaning down to nuzzle against my neck. "But I think we both know how that would end."

In orgasms?

Tears of happiness?

"And that's bad?" I croaked, sounding as if I'd just run a marathon.

Mike smiled down at me like he found the question amusing.

"Darlin', when I get you into bed, it won't be for a quick fuck. I plan on taking my time getting well acquainted with every square inch of your body. Could take days—maybe even weeks."

Yes, please.

My vision blurred, and I took a shaky breath, fighting to stay on my feet when my mind took the declaration and ran with it.

To my utter disappointment, instead of another toe-curling kiss, Mike pressed his lips to my forehead and promised to text me his address.

The bastard even had the audacity to wink on his way out the door, taking great pleasure in leaving me and my lady bits to suffer. I flipped the lock and slid down to the entryway tile, needing one or a hundred cold showers to come back down to earth.

CHAPTER TWELVE

Mike: June 2014 (Age: 31)

I was developing carpal tunnel in my right wrist. Since my blindingly stupid decision to reject Lauren's offer for a quickie early this morning, I'd *badgered the witness* more times than I could count. My hand hadn't seen action like this since I was a teenager.

Every time I talked my dick down, I'd hear her voice in my head, begging me to stay. The feel of her legs wrapped around my waist. Then I'd find myself in the private bathroom connected to my office, jerking off to visions of her on top of me, under me, upside down, right side up, backwards, forwards, spinning in fucking circles.

Despite what she'd said while half asleep, Lauren was a five-dater, which meant I was realistically looking at another five to six weeks of this bullshit.

My brain was a sadist, offering helpful reminders throughout the day that said otherwise.

Can you be late?

We could be quick.

Those weren't in the book—not like there were any actual guidelines for me to follow. I was flying blind here.

Patience was the name of the game. Hell, if I could manage Silent Phoenix, surely I could handle a feisty redhead. A few more weeks in my prison of self-imposed celibacy, and then I'd fuck her brains out and move on with my life.

My jeans immediately grew tighter, and I cursed. I was going to have to think of something else or spend the evening in agony.

Fuck me.

I fired up the grill and then glanced down at my watch. We agreed on seven, which gave me all of five minutes to get my baser instincts under control.

Yep. That would work.

By the time I reached the upstairs bathroom, I already had my jeans unzipped and my cock out. I considered kicking the door shut behind me, but Fantasy Lauren was already beneath me, demanding my full attention.

I squeezed my dick, picturing her hand instead of my own. My vision blurred as I stroked myself harder. Faster. In ways that made my toes curl and the muscles at the base of my cock contract far quicker than I planned.

Didn't matter.

I wasn't going for longevity, but for sanity.

My breaths were ragged. Animalistic. I made the mistake of looking up and caught my reflection in the mirror. I clenched my jaw tight—my face contorted in a mask of agony.

This was what she'd turned me into. One taste and I was hooked. I pumped into my hand viciously, as if punishing myself for letting her get inside my head.

A car door slammed from somewhere outside.

Christ.

I was so close to coming, too far gone to stop now. My balls ached and my spine tingled with the need to blow my load.

"Lauren," I growled through gritted teeth, coming so hard I saw stars. But I couldn't stop myself. No. I continued jerking my cock, coating my knuckles, the counter, and even the mirror in the throes of what I could only describe as a full body convulsion.

Once my vision returned and I regained full use of my limbs, I snagged the cleaning supplies under the sink and got to work. By the time I headed downstairs, I was feeling much better. Calmer.

"Hey," Lauren called through the screen door on the front porch, giving me a little wave.

Less calm now.

I unlatched it and let her in. "Hey. How long have you been waiting?"

Translation: How much of that did you hear?

Her face was a mask of innocence as she said, "Just pulled up a second ago—I'd just knocked when I saw you coming downstairs. You're really out of breath. Were you working out?"

Nah, darlin'. Just playing a little game of pocket pinball.

I rubbed at the back of my neck and let out a small laugh. "No, just got the grill going and then ran upstairs to make sure I put away everything."

"This place is amazing. I don't know the last time I saw a house with a wraparound porch," she said, taking it all in. "Not having neighbors has gotta be the best part of country living. I hear my downstairs neighbors arguing almost every night."

I took her purse and hung it on the coat rack behind the door. The farmhouse had been a steal, mainly because it needed a shit ton of work that most investors didn't have the patience for. With the help of David and his construction company, we'd been able to restore the old place to its former glory.

Grey had even shown up on multiple occasions, putting his woodworking skills to use.

"You help me, I help you. What'd I say?"

It had felt like more than that, though. When he said it, it had come out like an apology, as if he'd regretted pulling me into the club's dealings.

"Is this the original flooring?" Lauren asked, pulling me from my thoughts and over to where she was kneeling in the entryway. Her fingers stroked the wood, much like I'd stroked my wood minutes earlier.

She looked a hell of a lot better doing it. Several strands of cinnamon-colored hair were fighting to escape the braid draped over her left shoulder as she caressed my floor in a way that might have left me jealous if I was a lesser man.

Meanwhile, I stood in silence, rendered completely stupid by what she'd chosen to wear.

A fucking sundress?

It was short and cut just low enough for me to glimpse a flash of shadow boob with the way she was bent over. She was trying to kill me.

I shook my head, muttering, "Five-dater."

"What's that?" Lauren looked up with a frown.

"I said it is the original flooring. Now, what do you say we get those steaks on the grill?"

She stood back up and smiled again. Her smile was like that of a child's—given completely and without provocation. As if everything amused her.

The evening sun highlighted the freckles scattered across the bridge of her nose and cheeks as we stepped out onto the back patio.

Goddamn. Could she be any more adorable?

Adorable?

What the fuck, Mike?

"What can I help with?" she offered, but I shook my head.

"Just sit there. Do you want a glass of wine? Beer?"

She sat down in the chair at the small patio table. "Just water for now. Thanks."

I snagged one from the fridge, along with the marinated steaks, and brought it to her on my way to the grill. After getting her preference—medium rare—I closed the lid and joined her at the table.

"So, Red. Tell me about yourself. Where'd you grow up?"

Lauren paused mid-drink, amused by the question. "Are we telling the truth this time?"

"Yep," I responded, annoyed, until I realized it was the same line I'd used in Galveston. "This time, we're doing it for real."

"Well, I grew up in Denver—"

"How'd a nice girl like you end up in Texas?"

She leaned against back of the chair with a relaxed smile. "Well, it's a funny story. Tech offered me a scholarship, and J—my dad pushed me to take it. But I could tell he was struggling with me being so far away, you know?"

I did. I had spent most of the last month struggling, and she was just inside the city limits.

"I just didn't want to leave without knowing he was going to be okay, so I created a dating profile for him on a site that probably isn't even around anymore. And that was how Isaac came into our lives."

"And your dad didn't care that you did this behind his back?" I couldn't resist asking. My old man would have loved me finding him a fuck buddy, but I imagined normal people probably didn't want their kid playing matchmaker.

Lauren bit her lip to keep from smiling and shook her head. "Not exactly. I mean, he tried giving me a lecture on boundaries before curiosity got the better of him. Once he saw who I'd picked out, he couldn't stay mad. Isaac lived in Texas, and after a year of long-distance dating, he proposed."

"You got a bonus dad."

She gave up fighting it, allowing her lips to curve up in a beaming grin. "I did. He's a pretty kick ass one too."

I picked at an invisible thread on the thigh of my jeans. "It's a little intimidating."

The smile faded almost instantly. "What do you mean?"

"Meeting one father is hard enough when dating a girl. Now, I've gotta meet two? I'll be lucky to leave with my balls intact."

That was the thing with five-daters. They loved talk of the future. And mention meeting their parents? Well, that was foreplay to them.

"You're skipping quite a few steps. Let's just see how tonight goes first." She tipped the water bottle to her lips, while I tried to come to terms with what had just occurred.

I'd expected a hopeful grin—maybe even a laugh. Instead, I'd been served a line I was used to delivering. And it tasted like shit.

"Mike?"

I looked up, expecting her to admit she was kidding before begging me to meet her dads.

Instead, she pointed over my shoulder and somberly announced, "I think the grill's on fire."

CHAPTER THIRTEEN

Mike: June 2014 (Age: 31)

One hour and several well-done steaks later, I was beginning to question the skills that had gotten me laid in the past. The roles I'd played to get what I wanted. It was like my head wasn't in the game anymore, and I was fucking things up at every turn.

I was also starting to suspect Lauren was a witch in disguise.

The woman asked me about my own parents, a topic I typically avoided at all costs, unbothered by the beef disguised as hockey pucks.

I hadn't spoken to my father since the morning after David's wedding. He'd called me a traitor and a traitor to Michael Sullivan, Sr. was as good as dead. Since then, Grey or another biker had handled anything related to me.

Last I checked, he was still making regular trips down to Beaumont to hook up with my mother, though. I think that was the most disappointing thing. She'd done well on her own, but then Patrick got killed and she'd taken him back almost immediately.

As if she hadn't been capable of living on her own.

Desperate, I'd informed her about the cheating, convinced she'd change her mind and kick him to the curb. But she knew. She'd known all along.

The two of them were no better than addicts—their drug of choice just happened to be the other person.

I had shared more with Lauren in the last sixty minutes than I had ninety-nine percent of the chicks I'd been with over the years. The one percent being a therapist I saw after a brutal case. I'd opened up to her about my feelings and after our last session, she'd opened her legs to me.

My reluctance to discuss my parents hadn't fazed Lauren. She studied my face in a way that suggested she was reading my thoughts before moving on to a more neutral topic.

"It's sad. I've lived here for almost a decade and don't know that I've ever sat and watched the sunset," Lauren admitted, almost wistfully.

We'd moved from the patio to the front porch swing, something I hadn't planned on installing. Grey and David had both insisted that every old farmhouse needed a good porch swing.

I extended my arm along the back, my fingertips brushing against her shoulder. "The only way to experience a real west Texas sunset is out in the country. This is actually one of my favorite spots at night. It's quiet and the perfect place to decompress from the day."

I had to be careful, or I was going to end up pouring my heart out to her like some fucking *Lifetime* movie. It really called my intentions into question, because I had never gone to this much trouble just to get laid.

She sighed happily and murmured, "I don't think I'd ever make it inside. I'd just kick my shoes off and spend the night out here."

I glanced down at her bare feet. "Well, you're halfway there already."

Lauren scooted closer and nestled her head against my shoulder, flooding my nostrils with lavender. I didn't know if it was her shampoo or a perfume, but the scent was quickly becoming one I associated with her.

"I didn't know you had all these tattoos until last night," she said, reaching for my left arm. "I guess I've only ever seen you in long-sleeved shirts." Her fingers traced the intricate designs lightly. And that, coupled with her smell, was sending my body into overdrive.

"I only planned on getting one, but couldn't seem to stop," I said with a soft laugh.

"What does this mean?" She pointed to the quote wrapped around my forearm and up onto my bicep.

"'He who knows when he can fight and when he cannot, will be victorious.' It's a quote from Sun Tzu." Seeing her blank expression, I added, "He wrote *The Art of War*."

Lauren nodded and lightly dragged her finger over to the one next to it. "And this one?"

It was single-handedly the most erotic thing I'd ever experienced while sitting on my front porch.

Jesus.

"'Perfer et obdura, dolor hic tibi proderit olim.' It's Latin—be patient and tough. Someday this pain will be useful to you."

It seemed nearly all of my tattoos were related to pain and war. Coincidentally, I'd started getting them right around the time I sold my soul to the club.

If a therapist ever got wind of it, I was certain they'd piss themselves with excitement.

The quote from Ovid had come courtesy of Celia after a surprise run-in at *Inked on Broadway*. Coincidentally, it was also when I learned the depths Grey's enemies would go to—the people they would hurt to send a message.

"They teach you these things in cop school?"

Cop school?

"No, darlin'," I said with a laugh. "Although, I think it's adorable that you think I went to 'cop school.'"

"I don't know what you call it."

I grinned. "Most people refer to it as the academy, but I'm mighty partial to Cop School now."

"Ha-ha," Lauren said in mock annoyance, all while continuing to stroke my arm. "It really is beautiful work, though. They should put your arms in an art gallery."

I tilted her chin up so I could see her face before remembering she hadn't had anything to drink other than water. She was completely sober.

"You wanna put my arms in an art gallery? Where's Charlotte when we need her? She'd know if these babies were the next van Gogh."

She bit down on her lip and smiled lazily. "I like you, Mike."

I felt like puffing my chest out. I'd done it. Four more dates and she'd be mine. "I like you too, Red."

The swing creaked as Lauren stood up suddenly.

I frowned. "You going somewhere?"

She swayed slightly before coming to stand in front of me with a smile I didn't trust. I didn't know if she was about to knee me in the balls or perform a strip-tease.

"Is this okay?"

"Is—" The word was barely out of my mouth when she placed a knee on either side of my legs, sinking down to straddle me.

Okay? It was fucking terrific. I never expected to get this far on my first night with a five-dater.

Fuck. Me.

It felt like a test.

"Hi," she whispered breathlessly, brushing her lips over mine. "Is this okay?"

I closed my eyes and nodded, trying to get my body under control. She pressed her lips to mine again, this time with more firmness, letting her hips rock over the front of my jeans.

"And this?" She whispered again.

I bobbed my head again, like a puppet on a string. Any sudden movements on my part had the potential to break the spell she was under.

The sun had set at some point, casting Lauren in shadows and making it harder to read her facial cues. The buzz of nearby cicadas mingled with the sounds of our heavy breathing, creating a soundtrack that I would forever associate with summer. And her.

Lauren caught my bottom lip between her teeth and I groaned, conflicted. Old me would have lifted that pretty dress and shoved her underwear to the side so she could sink down onto my painfully hard cock. New me was supposed to be respecting the fact that she was a five-dater and keeping my goddamn dick in my pants.

I was so screwed.

She sat back and rubbed at her swollen lips before deftly unfastening the red microscopic buttons on the front of her dress. Just as the top of her bra came into view, she asked, "Is this okay?"

My nod was shakier this time, and I watched with rapt attention as she slipped the strap down on one side and then the other until the dress fell around her waist. Sensing I wasn't about to make the first move, she reached for my hand and brought it up to rest against her tits.

"What about this?"

She was fucking with me—that had to be what this was. She wanted me to agree to all of it and then it'd somehow prove I wasn't long-term material.

Not that she would have been wrong.

I needed to stay focused on the task at hand. I was going to pass her little test until date five. By date five, you could bet your ass I was going to be motor-boating the hell out of her tits.

I jerked my hand back as though it had been burned, and Lauren's eyebrows bunched together.

"Why don't we find a movie to watch?" I suggested through clenched teeth, fighting to hold on to my last thread of sanity.

She moved closer, cupping the back of my neck in her palm. "Is that what you want?" Her hips rolled forward, until my cock was nestled up against her pussy. The friction was going to kill me. "To watch a movie?"

"No," I snapped. "It's taking everything in me not to tear your damn dress off and fuck you. But I can't."

I squeezed my eyes shut, hearing the desperation in my voice. She may as well have stripped me bare with as vulnerable as I was.

"Why can't you?" she asked, as if she didn't already know. "You want to touch me and you didn't mind me touching you. What's the problem?"

"The problem?" I growled. "The problem is that we're still taking our time getting to know each other. I wanna pursue you properly. You know, take you out for fancy dinners and stuff before... that."

The lie was bitter on my tongue, but with her mouth and tits pressed up against me, my brain had gone haywire. I didn't know if anything I'd just said made sense. I had zero experience with five-daters and this proved it.

"What in the 1950s are you talking about? Pursue me? I'm not prey, Mike. And I don't need fancy dinners and 'stuff' to want to be with you."

"What do you need, Red?" I whispered, suddenly wanting her more than anything in the entire world. More than tequila, which was really saying something.

"I need you to drop the act. I'm not looking for a ring. Just be with me tonight." Then she reached behind her back and unfastened her bra, letting it fall onto the porch before adding, "It's a damn good thing you don't have neighbors, Tex."

Lauren may have been a tiny little thing, but *goddamn*, did she make up for it with her breasts. My hand was halfway up before the bra hit the porch, ready to cop a feel. I was betting she was a C... maybe a D.

Pale pink nipples hardened due to the slight evening breeze, and my hands ached to cup them.

She hadn't called me Tex since Galveston, back when I'd just been Jack the surfer. Could things be as simple as they'd been that night? If so, I was going to get my life back sooner than planned.

"You want me." A statement. Something old me would have said within seconds of meeting a woman.

"I do, you idiot," she said with a giggle before leaning in to kiss me again. "Now, what are you gonna do about it?"

CHAPTER FOURTEEN

Mike: June 2014 (Age: 31)

W hat I didn't do was wait for Lauren to grab her bra.
Not when the most fantastic tits I'd ever seen smashed against my chest, stimulating my primal brain and short-circuiting the more rational lobes. I carried her up the stairs with her pretty little sundress still bunched up around her waist, wholly focused on getting those babies in my mouth.

I laid her back on the king-sized bed, and she shimmied the rest of the way out of her dress before kicking it into the corner.

"You're not drunk, right?" I asked, hand hovering over the button on my jeans.

"Sober as a judge, officer," she giggled. "Neither one of us drank, remember?"

Right. I knew that.

Tonight was a first. Sex and alcohol had always gone hand in hand for me. I couldn't recall ever being stone-cold sober for the act, a fact which suddenly left me with a little performance anxiety.

While she trailed kisses along my jaw and down my neck, I raced to get my jeans off, thankful I'd shed my shoes after dinner. Deep down, a part of me was afraid she'd change her mind if I took too long.

Within seconds, my shirt joined her dress on the floor and I stood at the foot of the bed in nothing more than a tented pair of boxer briefs. I cocked an eyebrow and began lowering them, silently daring Lauren to lose the sexy little hipster panties next.

Her tongue swept over her bottom lip as she rocked back onto her heels and spread her legs, sending a painful throb through my dick. She was soaked, the silky material clinging to her skin and framing the lips of her perfect pussy.

"Is that for me?" I asked, shaking my head in disbelief.

Mine. All. Mine.

She nodded and used her thumbs to push them over her hips, wide eyes locked on my erection.

"He won't bite, darlin'."

"I know that," she mumbled, still staring. I let my teeth graze along her collarbone before pulling her mouth back to mine.

Four years later and she was still the only woman whose lips had me hooked.

One of her hands tightened against the back of my neck, while the other stroked along my jawline. She had me pinned in her grip, but the siren song of her perfect breasts was impossible to resist. I lowered my head, nipping her flesh with my teeth.

Lauren shivered and began roughly petting the side of my face. Her fingernails scraped against my skin with every pass, but I barely felt it. I was busy grinning like a madman because—thanks to proper hand and mouth placement—I now knew with certainty she was a D.

Thank you very much.

I alternated between breasts, savoring each little gasp of pleasure. Unfortunately, my dick wasn't enjoying the lick-suck rhythm I'd perfected as much as the rest of me. My spine tingled, warning me that taking my time would not be an option for much longer. Thanks to a certain redhead keeping me in a perpetual state of arousal, I was on a strict three-hour masturbatory schedule.

I needed to be inside her right the fuck now.

"Roll over," I commanded, after taking another pull from her nipple. I'd had enough sex at this point in my life to have a preferred method. I started with Basic Doggy, before easing into Hissing Cobra and Cat's Meow. If the mood was right, I'd work in a Swinging Reverse

Cowgirl and, for my grand finale, a little Crouching Lion, Hidden Cock.

Anything face to face was out—it was too personal.

Lauren moved onto all fours and rested her weight on her forearms, hips thrust back in offering. Well, well, well. Seemed we were changing things up and starting the evening's festivities with Cat's Meow.

I paused with the condom in my hand, mesmerized by the shape of her. On a scale of one to ten, she was a twenty. The most beautiful woman I had ever had the pleasure of seeing naked.

"Mike?" she questioned, watching me curiously over her shoulder.

"Just admiring the view, Red," I admitted softly, running my hand over her lower back. "Give me a minute here."

"It's just—"

"You ready for me?" I whispered, sliding the condom down my length.

Her eyes widened considerably, but she managed a jerky nod before lowering her face to the comforter.

"Is that a yes?" I asked, because there was no reason on earth this woman should have even been in my bed.

"Y-yes," she whispered, her voice muffled by the bedding.

I ran the head of my cock up and down her slit, coating myself in her arousal, and locked one hand around her hip. Instead of rocking back to meet me, Lauren broke away and skittered across the mattress, throwing her hand up in the universal sign for *wait*.

I also detected notes of *not fucking happening tonight, pal*.

"Lauren?"

"It's fine," she muttered to the comforter. "I can do this."

While I enjoyed a good self pep talk from time to time, something was clearly off here.

"You sure about that, darlin'?" I asked, trying to keep my tone light even though my dick was turning an angry shade of purple.

"Yep. Just do it."

Just do it?

Excuse the fuck out of me?

My cock had been reduced to an athletic slogan meant to sell overpriced footwear. Worse, she said it as if fucking me was a chore she'd been avoiding. Some annoyance she had to suffer through.

Her shitty mantra was fucking with my vibe. I had half a mind to tell her to leave. Unfortunately, the other half of my brain resided between my legs. And when she slid a finger into her body with a moan, I could barely remember my name, much less what I'd been about to say.

"Please," she begged, slowly drawing her finger in and out. Torturing me.

I bobbed my head in what I hoped was an affirmative direction before moving over again. This time, I took a cue from the Lauren playbook and replaced her finger with my own.

Testing the waters, so to speak.

Her body recognized the difference immediately, and like a bouncer, refused to let me past the velvet rope. I tried again, but she was on lockdown.

And I was *persona non grata*.

Lauren lifted her head and turned to face me. "This isn't working."

"Okay," I hedged, refusing to admit defeat, even as everything in me screamed that I'd lost my touch.

Before I could properly theorize what I was doing wrong, she was scrambling up and over, guiding me back onto the mattress.

"Stay like this," she commanded.

I considered telling her I wasn't into missionary, but her eyes had a manic look about them. An unhinged expression that encouraged me to keep silent if I enjoyed my balls being attached to my body.

Why were the crazy ones always the best in bed?

Lauren snagged her lower lip between her teeth and settled over me, planting both palms on my chest. Her face was a mask of concentration—which, to be honest, wasn't boosting my confidence any.

"If you're not feeling it, we can do something else," I suggested, fighting to keep the disappointment out of my voice.

Thanks to the moonlight streaming in through the window, I witnessed the flush of red work its way up her throat and into her cheeks.

"It's not that—"

Realization washed over me, and I froze. "You've done this before, right?"

She reluctantly met my gaze and admitted, "I have—just not with another person."

Jesus. There was a fine line between crazy and criminal, and the woman on top of me was straddling it.

"Explain."

She swallowed. "My partners have been more of the phallic sculpture variety."

"You're a virgin?" My relief was short-lived. I'd done a lot of things. A virgin was not one of them. I was suddenly having second thoughts about the entire thing.

I tried shifting her weight onto the mattress, but she stopped me.

"Please. I want this—with you." Flustered, Lauren shook her head and tried again. "I mean, I want my first time to be with you. I'm not expecting a relationship or any commitment beyond tonight. We can even do it the way you want."

Her blush seemed to deepen, which only highlighted her inexperience. What I didn't understand was how.

How was she a virgin?

It didn't make a goddamned bit of sense.

She turned back around and placed her face against the comforter, completely submissive. It felt wrong. She deserved for her first time to be special—I wasn't a complete animal.

Without saying a word, I gently rolled her onto her back and knelt down between her legs, sliding a finger through her wetness. The answering gasp let me know I was off to a good start.

God, I couldn't remember the last time I'd gone down on someone—I was practically popping my cherry again. Using a figure-eight pattern, I stroked her body, praying I was hitting the right spots. Instead, Lauren's noises of pleasure tapered off into soft breathing.

Okay, on to Plan B.

I brought my face down and licked along her slit like an inexperienced teen. She moaned, hugging my head with trembling thighs. Bolstered by the response, I began lapping at her clit like a kid would a water hose on a hot summer day, quickly realizing why I never performed cunnilingus.

My fucking tongue was cramping up. Hell, I was probably developing TMJ. But goddamn, her taste made it worth it.

Lauren's pants grew louder, so I went for broke. While maintaining rhythm with my tongue, I tried introducing my middle finger again. And this time, her body let me past the door.

Within seconds, she was writhing against my face. I wanted nothing more than to feel her wrapped around me and, brushing her arousal from my beard, moved into a pushup position over her.

"Darlin', are you sure?" I asked, pressing a kiss to her mouth. Then her neck. She had to be a witch. It would explain why I couldn't seem to get enough of her.

"Please," she whispered, her green eyes looking up at me in trust.

I aligned my cock and pushed in a couple of inches, trying to let her body adjust before going deeper. "You ready for me?"

She nodded, fear quickly replacing trust in her wide eyes. Her body disagreed and inched up the bed in retreat, leaving me feeling like a prick.

Her first time should've been with someone special.

Someone who wasn't me.

I pressed another gentle kiss to her lips. "It may hurt, but I'll go slowly."

The statement earned me another nervous nod. Moving at a snail's pace only seemed to increase her anxiety, causing her body to tighten further.

I pulled back until I was almost out and lowered my head to whisper, "You are absolutely perfect."

Lauren gave me a small smile in return. I waited until I felt the tension leave her body before thrusting all the way in.

I'd done it. I'd just deflowered a virgin.

God, I bet my mom would be so proud.

She cried out and dug her nails into my shoulders. I kissed her over and over again, murmuring what I hoped were words of praise—telling her how strong she was.

I'd imagined her countless times, spread out before me just like this, but my fantasies were nothing compared to the real thing. My hands roamed freely down her arms, drawn to her tits like a moth to a flame.

"You feel so fucking amazing," I whispered, and those green eyes tilted up to meet mine again.

She did too. Her pussy gripped my dick, pulling me in deeper. Once she adjusted to my size, her hips rocked forward. An involuntary rhythm I knew all too well.

Knowing how awkward my first time had been, I felt like I had this standard to meet with her. It had suddenly become my job to ensure that Lauren had an orgasm. I picked her up and her legs instinctively wrapped around my waist as I backed her against the wall.

The position gave me better control. At this angle, my dick was thrusting right up against her front wall, and I knew within a couple of seconds that I was hitting her G-spot. Her body went stiff and her mouth fell open, but no sound came out.

Gripping her ass tightly in my hands, I forced myself deeper. Lauren grew louder again, so I moved faster, trying to keep up. The heels of her feet stroked my lower back and my balls tightened, encouraging me to join her.

My thrusts became quicker and shallower as she raked her nails down my back and cried out something unintelligible, milking my cock for all it was worth. I thrust once more and then joined her in a freefall with a roar.

My face was completely numb.

It should have been impossible, but I'd just had the best sex of my life with a virgin.

I stumbled back over to the bed and settled her against the pillows before heading for the bathroom to dispose of the condom.

When I returned, I did something else unexpected. I climbed into bed and pulled her back to my chest before whispering, "Stay the night?"

Lauren nodded sleepily and nestled in closer as I pulled the comforter over our bodies.

It was still dark outside when I woke, rock hard and ready for her again. I shifted down a bit and lifted her leg, surprised to find her pussy still wet. She awoke with a loud moan when my dick brushed against her clit and I paused. She was probably sore as hell and not in the mood for more sex.

"Please," she begged, reaching back to guide me.

What was it about this woman that made her feel like home to me?

When did I start thinking like a greeting card?

Would the wanting her go away?

I was so beyond fucked I needed a new word to describe it. One night would not be enough. And now that I knew no one else had ever been inside of her, I wasn't sure I was going to be able to share.

Now, who was the clingy one?

CHAPTER FIFTEEN

Lauren: June 2014 (Age: 27)

The pillow beneath my head was lumpy. I blinked to clear the sleep from my eyes and surveyed the unfamiliar room before remembering I was in Mike's bedroom.

I'd done it.

I'd lost my virginity.

I probably should've done something about it when I was a teen, but given Monica's benders, my concerns had been limited to frivolous things like food and shelter. By the time I got to college, I was so hell-bent on proving to Josué and Isaac I wasn't going to turn out like Monica that I'd all but chained myself to the desk in my dorm room.

After college, I focused on finding a career. And by then, it was too late. My virginity felt like some shameful secret—a topic that had ended more than one first date before we'd even gotten to dessert. To them, sex with me was a life sentence. As if wanting to get to know them better was some sort of trick to trap them into marrying me.

A month ago, marriage was the goal. But with Monica turning up at the most inopportune times, things were complicated. I couldn't imagine trying to juggle a relationship, too.

Which suddenly made Mike Sullivan the perfect choice. He was at least upfront and honest about who he was and what he wanted.

I stretched and was rewarded by a foreign twinge of pain from my pelvic region. Mike shifted in his sleep and mumbled something before his breathing evened out again.

Why was I still here?

Sleeping with him had been the equivalent of diving into the shallow end of the pool. I saw the signs warning against it, but still jumped.

I rolled onto my elbow and glanced at the alarm clock on the night-stand. Just after six. If I left now, I could avoid any awkward conversation and subsequent rejection.

No. There would be no walk of shame with me. I was an independent woman who could handle myself with dignity and grace.

I slid out of bed and down onto my hands and knees to search for my clothes, holding my breath as if it would somehow make me quieter. I was exhausted and longing for sleep. It seemed just as I would get comfortable enough to doze off, Mike's erection would nudge me awake again.

Not that I was complaining.

I'd lost count of how many times we'd done it, but the evidence was currently running down my leg. Had he used a condom every time?

Okay, not a problem.

I was a responsible, independent woman and would head over to the pharmacy once it opened for some Plan B, as my birth control plan until tonight had been what's the point? I found my underwear near the foot of the bed just as Mike bolted up.

"He shot them. Grey, he just shot them." His eyes were open, but it was clear he was still asleep. He muttered something unintelligible before falling back against his pillow.

Meanwhile, I lay clutching my chest in fright. When my heart returned to a normal rhythm, I army-crawled along the hardwood floor before spotting my dress on his side of the bed.

As much as I wanted to sit and watch him sleep, it wasn't worth it. A guy like Mike wouldn't offer more than one night, a truth I was painfully aware of.

Four weeks ago, I thought I could convince him to love me. Me.

With my emotional baggage? If it didn't cut me to my core, I might have found the thought laughable.

I paused at the top of the stairs and pulled my underwear and dress back on. My bra was still out on the porch somewhere. Without reason, though, my feet led me back to his bedroom.

He was still lying in the same position on his back, one arm resting behind his head. The sun peeked through the blinds just enough for me to see him without squinting. A flash of color caught my eye. I turned toward it, feeling a pressure in my throat and the sting of humiliation in my eyes.

My blood. On his white sheets.

Well, there was no way in hell I could ever face him again.

I couldn't look away from it as I backed out of the room, knowing there wasn't a snowball's chance in hell I could ever face Mike Sullivan again. Not with the evidence of my inexperience on his bedsheets.

With that, I made it downstairs and found my purse and sandals before recovering my bra from the porch.

And then I ran.

CHAPTER SIXTEEN

Lauren: June 2014 (Age: 27)

"What?" I grumbled into the phone. Its incessant vibrations had woken me from a dead sleep. One of those where I didn't know if it was morning or afternoon. Was I late for school or was it the weekend?

"LoLo, it's after nine. Why are you still in bed? Are you sick?" Josué peppered me with questions, bursting my drowsy bubble and making me remember I was an adult who hadn't had to worry about missing a school bus in almost a decade.

I rubbed the sleep from my eyes, along with last night's mascara, before responding, "No, I just stayed up late watching a movie. What are you up to?"

"Well, I'm staring at an envelope full of cash and a note from your mother."

I bolted upright, suddenly wide awake. "What? How did she get your address? Is she there now?"

He sighed, "She's not here—it came in the mail. LoLo, it's a lot of money."

I rubbed my temple with my free hand. "How much money, Josué? And, what—what does the note say?"

He cleared his throat. "It's uh—it's about seven... grand." I gasped, but he continued, "The note just says that it's payment for what she stole and for taking care of you. She also talks about her rehab—apparently, she's been sober since March. Oh, and she said to tell you to stop being stubborn and take the money from her."

My palms went sweaty. When I saw her at the hospital, she'd been adamant that I take the cash—said it would help clear her conscience.

The second time around, I'd seriously considered taking the offer. She looked so good—her eyes were clear, and someone had obviously spent the money to get her hair highlighted and trimmed. Minus her teeth, there was no evidence of her ever being a drug user.

"Oh." I didn't know what else to say.

He cleared his throat again, obviously uncomfortable with the topic. Early on, Josué admitted he was afraid Monica would turn up one day, demanding to have me back. Her sudden reappearance had to be dredging up those old feelings.

"She left a phone number and said I could give it to you."

I didn't want her number, but wrote it down, anyway. Monica had made her bed years ago, long before I arrived. Spending the rest of her life knowing her only child wanted nothing to do with her was a fitting punishment.

Josué didn't ask how she got the money—which was good, because I wasn't sure I had the heart to tell him. If he knew she was in deep with a biker gang, he and Isaac would be on the first flight to Lubbock.

I was twenty-seven. I needed to handle Monica like an adult. An adult who'd learned the hard way how life worked with an addict, but an adult nonetheless.

Before we hung up, he made me swear to keep my valuables at home if I contacted her. I plugged my phone into the charging cable and laid back down, conflicted by the conversation.

Reconciling the beautiful woman who approached me at the hospital with the addict who had made my childhood a living hell felt impossible, but eventually, I was going to have to do just that.

I'd just reconnected with the sweet spot on my pillow and was hovering in an almost asleep state when someone began pounding on my front door.

Someone who was about to regret the life decision that had led them to my apartment.

I stumbled out of bed, stubbing my toe on the nightstand and letting out a very unladylike "fuck."

"M-Mike?" I stammered as I threw open the door, ready to attack the idiot on the other side. "What are you doing here?"

The plan was supposed to be simple. Dinner, sex, leave, sleep, pharmacy, and then trying to forget last night ever happened. At no point was he supposed to show up at my house.

He held out a coffee. "Brought you this. Why'd you leave?"

I took the cardboard cup from his hands with a forced smile. "You didn't have to come all this way to deliver me coffee."

He took a step forward, leaning against the door frame like it was made for him. "You didn't answer my question. Why'd you leave?"

I sighed. "I thought that's what you'd want and was trying to make it easier."

He jerked his chin in an abrupt nod. "So, that's it? You just use me for sex and then leave without so much as a goddamned goodbye. You could have at least had the decency to explain how you remained a virgin for twenty-seven years."

I grabbed the front of his shirt and quickly pulled him into my apartment, slamming the door shut behind him. "Thanks for announcing that to the entire complex."

Mike gave me a lopsided grin that made my insides turn to mush. He enjoyed tormenting me. "Darlin', we could've had this discussion out in private if only you'd stayed."

I gestured to the couch, and he sat down with a stupid grin. "Do you want coffee? I think you're gonna need coffee. God knows I need coffee." His grin only seemed to widen, causing me to snap, "What? Why do you keep looking at me like that?"

"Because you're gorgeous when you're mad. As for coffee, I'd love some. Thanks." He turned away from me and began taking off his boots, but the grin remained firmly affixed to his face.

After presenting him with a large mug of black coffee, we moved to our respective corners of the couch and sipped our caffeine in silence.

"You've got some pretty serious charges stacked against you, Ms.
—"

"Santiago," I supplied helpfully. I'd slept with a man who didn't
even know my last name. I didn't know whether to laugh or cry.

Mike leveled his icy blue gaze at me. "Right. Well, the evidence
doesn't look good. I want to help you, but you're going to have to be
honest with me."

Oh, he was good.

I shifted against the cushion, unsure of how much to reveal to him.
He was supposed to be a one-night stand. If anything, he was the one
who needed to come clean. "I don't know why we're having this
conversation. What we had last night was good, but—"

Mike frowned. "Good?"

"Fine, it was spectacular. Happy now? Not that it really matters,
though, because we both know you're not looking for more."

"Don't do that. Don't pin this on me. Sure, maybe I didn't know
what I wanted, but I'm not the one who left this morning."

He had me there, but I wasn't ready to throw in the towel and
admit defeat just yet.

I picked at a strand of hair on the back of the couch, avoiding his
glare. "You're right. I left because I thought it's what you wanted, and
leaving hurt a lot less than being rejected."

Sure, he was here now. But for how long?

"I don't know how this works," I admitted with a sigh. "The whole
relationship thing is out of scope of expertise, mainly because I've
never been in one. God, that makes me sound like a loser."

Mike set his coffee down on the side table and pulled my hand
away from my face. "No, I'm the same. If we're being honest—fine—
I've never been in an 'exclusive relationship.' Hell, most of my dates
haven't lasted past the morning. What happened between us was
something I've never experienced before—"

I cut him off with a bitter laugh. "What? Never had sex with a
virgin before?"

He shook his head. "Not even once. That's not what I mean,
though. For me, it's always just been sex. Last night was something else

—it meant something. But I still have questions, like why did you tell me Galveston that you weren't a virgin?"

I pulled my hand free from his and wrapped my arms around myself. "You said I couldn't tell the truth... so I didn't."

Mike smirked and scratched along his jawline. "You're fucking with me, right?"

I shook my head. "Not even a little. And I was going to lose my virginity sooner, but my life was... complicated."

He nodded and took another sip of coffee, clearly waiting for me to go on.

I had an ache in the back of my throat and a strong desire to confess everything. He was a cop, though. What cop wanted to hear their new—what was I to him?—person was the daughter of a drug addict?

If I wanted a relationship built on honesty, I was already off to a shitty start with the whole virginity thing.

"Okay, here it is," I said, choosing my words carefully. "I didn't have the easiest childhood, and with everything going on, my virginity was the least of my concerns. Then I got older and wanted it to be special."

It sounded stupid.

And more than a little desperate.

I should have just told him about Monica.

His fingers stroked the back of my hand, and I stared down at them, somewhat in shock that he was still here. "Mike, what are we doing?"

He exhaled softly. "I don't know, Red. All I know is that I want to keep seeing you."

So, it wasn't some great admission of love.

But it was a start, right?

CHAPTER SEVENTEEN

Mike: June 2014 (Age: 31)

While Lauren waited in line at the pharmacy, I moseyed over to the family planning aisle to stock up on condoms.

Condoms.

Those were pretty fucking important.

She casually asked if I'd used a condom every time, dropping a bomb in my lap. I couldn't remember. I'd just woken up and let my baser instincts take over.

There was no freak out or emotional breakdown. She just said she'd run to the pharmacy for some emergency contraceptive. The woman, who until twelve hours ago had been a virgin, was going to casually pick up some Plan B on her own.

That was the thing. Lauren threw everything I thought I knew about women right out the window. I was fluent in getting the job done and getting the hell out, but I'd never been on the receiving end until I woke up to an empty bed this morning.

Turned out, I didn't like it much.

Look everyone, Mike's the girl now.

The redhead had turned me into a stage five clinger.

Me.

The guy who avoided commitment like the plague suddenly

couldn't stand the thought of Lauren with anyone else. Getting her out of my system? Never gonna fucking happen.

What the fuck was I doing?

Had I agreed to monogamy?

I began gathering condom boxes by the armload, earning me a judgmental look from a woman buying tampons.

"Safety first," I joked.

She shook her head in disgust and walked away.

I was working on formulating a response when there was a gentle tap on my left shoulder. "Hey, I got it. We can go."

I turned and Lauren held up a small white paper bag with a smile that seemed to wobble as she took in my haul.

"Do you really need all those?" she whispered.

I nodded solemnly. "This should get us through the next week, and then I'll see if I can order them in bulk online."

Her eyes widened, but she held on to her poker face. "Whatever you say, Tex."

As we checked out, I couldn't help but recall David's words to me on his wedding day. I'd given him a hard time about forfeiting bachelorhood to sleep with one woman the rest of his life, something he had found hilarious.

"Mike, there's going to be a day when a woman comes along and throws your entire fucking life upside down and you won't want it to go back to the way it was before. And when that time comes, I will laugh my ass off and tell you I told you so."

It felt like a curse. Hell, even now I had the urge to pay him a visit. Just so I could punch him in his smug face.

His words meant nothing.

We were just seeing where things went. No crazy long-term commitments.

―――――

"Hey, do you have plans for the fourth?"

Lauren froze, hamburger halfway to her mouth. "No—why?"

Her t-shirt had slipped down her arm again, and I couldn't help leaning over to press a kiss to her shoulder. "Because I wanna do something with you."

We'd spent most of the afternoon watching movies on the couch and despite how much I wanted to be inside her again, I was following her lead. Taking it slow. A phrase that was right up there with *I love you* on a list of things Mike Sullivan Jr. would never say.

She took a bite and chewed slowly, watching me through a narrowed gaze. "You sure you won't be tired of me by then?"

See? Completely unassuming.

"Well, it's just next weekend," I said with a shrug. "I probably won't try to get rid of you for at least another couple of weeks."

She slugged me playfully in the arm. "You're such an ass."

"Your ass. Remember that. Come over... I'll cook for you again. We can sit on the porch and watch the fireworks."

Jesus. What was she doing to me?

I couldn't even sit next to her for a movie without being hyper-aware of her scent and the feel of her hand in mine. My head was a goddamn wreck.

Lauren shook her head. "No."

It felt like my stomach had just dropped through the carpet and into the apartment below. Seeing my expression, she clarified, "I'll come, but I want to cook for you."

"Deal. Come here." I pulled her into my lap and twisted a strand of red hair around my finger. She shifted forward and then her eyes widened when she felt my hard-on. I shook my head. "We can wait. It's okay."

She regarded me thoughtfully. "Am I supposed to wait? We have protection."

And with that, all rational thought left the building. I pulled her oversized t-shirt off with a growl as her hands pawed at my belt, trying to get it undone.

I unhooked her bra with one hand, while the other untied her sweat pants. As much as I wanted to sink into her, I took the time to grab a condom before sitting back down on the couch. Lauren climbed back into my lap and I almost came just from watching her mouth as I slowly sank into her. It opened wider and wider until it looked like she was screaming soundlessly.

It was right about then that my cell phone started ringing. I ignored it and thrust up into her, eliciting a soft moan from that sexy mouth.

She placed her hands on my shoulders and rocked her hips forward, pulling me in deeper. "Mike," she whispered. "I'm close."

My phone rang again, and I cursed. I was not stopping right now. I slid my hands under her ass and moved her faster to the soundtrack of my ringtone and her moaning.

Her hands tightened and then her mouth fell open as a shudder worked its way through her body. I'd been so focused on getting her to come last night that I hadn't paid attention to the way she looked when she actually did.

She was so fucking perfect.

My phone beeped as a slew of text messages came through, but I had more important things on my mind. Like how to make Lauren's face do that all over again.

Her eyes fluttered open as she came back down to earth. "Do you need to answer that?"

I shook my head and clenched my teeth. I needed to focus. Just as her eyes closed and her mouth dropped open again, someone began beating on the front door.

"What the hell?" Lauren clutched her chest and froze.

I slid her off my lap and grabbed her clothes off the floor. "Go into the bedroom and lock the door. Okay?"

She nodded shakily, but obeyed. The person sounded like they were trying to break the goddamn door down.

I pulled my boxers on over my still painfully hard dick and grabbed my gun from the dining room table before going over to it. I looked through the peephole to find the last person in the world I wanted to see.

I threw it open with a snarled, "What the fuck do you want?"

My father laughed as he took me in. "Watch how you talk to me, Junior. Too busy boning Little Red Ridin' Hood to answer your phone? She's a piece."

I grabbed him by his shirt and growled, "Don't say a fucking thing about her."

He wrenched himself free and sarcastically responded, "We got a mess for you to clean up if you can spare some time out of your busy day."

I hadn't spoken to him in four years, and after thirty seconds, discovered I had missed nothing.

"Let me get dressed. Wait out here—you'll scare her."

He grinned like the Cheshire cat. "Oh, Junior. Afraid if she meets your daddy, she might wanna trade up? You fucked her. Now drop her and get back to work."

I resisted the urge to hit him. I didn't have any fear I couldn't take him, but knowing Grey would come down on me for it kept my hand at my side. Like a good little soldier.

Lauren waited until she heard the click of the lock on the front door before poking her head out of the bedroom. "What was that? Is everything okay?"

No. I'm indebted to an outlaw MC that expects me to drop everything every time they snap their fingers.

Instead, I gave her a reassuring smile. "Yeah, one of your neighbors came home drunk and ended up in the wrong apartment. I checked my messages, though. I've got to get down to the station to put out some fires. Can we finish this later?"

She looked over at the clock. "It's getting late and I've got to work tomorrow. Call me?"

I crossed the room in two strides and took her in my arms. "Absolutely. Get some sleep." After a quick kiss, I faced the firing squad waiting on her porch.

"Let's go."

My father was leaning against the railing on the stairs, leisurely smoking a cigarette. "No, fuck it. You've obviously got something more pressin' to deal with. What I wanna know is when you got desperate enough to fuck the same chick twice—that ain't your M.O."

He was right. It wasn't. And now I remembered why. The MC knew everything about me, including all the people in my life. They kept tabs on those people.

After vaguely admitting that her upbringing had been rough, would she really be okay with dating a guy who was in bed with a one-percenter motorcycle club?

He stubbed his cigarette out with his boot heel and then tossed it in front of Lauren's door.

I bent down and retrieved it. "Don't throw your shit down here. Show some respect."

He rolled his eyes. "Didn't realize I'd raised a fuckin' pussy and here I'd been proud of you for turnin' out just like your old man. You're on thin ice, dickhead. You know where to meet us."

My father left me standing on the stairs and fired up his Harley. I dutifully followed him, cursing the way my life had turned out with every step.

We drove down into the canyon and pulled up outside the old Wagon Wheel Motel. I killed my truck and stared wearily ahead at the various bikers and club whores roaming the property, feeling every bit of my thirty-one years.

At the tap on the driver's side window, I climbed out. "Hey, Goblin."

Goblin was this twenty-two-year-old kid who'd apparently had no higher aspirations for himself and thought an illegal club was a good career path. From what I'd heard, he was a gangbanger before, so maybe this was a step up.

"Mikey, hey. You know, since you're not a club member, you could call me Little Ricky. That's what my mama calls me. It's better, you know?"

I sighed. "Do I look like your fucking mother, kid?"

He shook his head and dejectedly made his way back into the club-house. I was in rare form tonight. At the rate I was going, I stood a real chance at pissing off every member before I left.

Grey walked out. "You're late for church."

I scratched at my beard. "Since when do I show up for church? I'm not patched in."

He opened the door and ushered me in. "Right now, I don't give a fuck if you've ever even ridden a bike. We've got problems."

The bikers all filed in and sat down, leaving me a spot near the back. Then Grey took my biggest fear and made it a reality. "We got word tonight that there's another MC moving into the area. They've contacted several of our guys, and I want it shut down before it turns into a fuckin' shit show."

I'd often wondered when they would pull me into a turf war. I could ensure there wasn't police presence when they were moving drugs and guns—paying off the right people when needed. Those were nothing compared to taking down another club.

If this new MC was looking to take over the area, they wouldn't play fairly. They'd take out bikers, families—even cops to get it done. Sweat ran down my back as I worked through every plausible scenario. "Who's your source?"

Grey looked back at me. "Excuse me?"

I stood and faced him. "Who's your source? These are some heavy accusations, Grey. I just want to know how reliable your source is."

His jaw tightened while the rest of his face remained blank. "You want sources? Alright, I've gotten the same story from both the Mexican Mafia and Lone Star Syndicate. The Sons of Death are tryin' to poach the local gangs. I didn't fuckin' take over this club to let it fall apart now.

"I want kuttes worn all the time. We fought and earned the rights to that lower rocker. We are the MC of Texas. I've reached out to our other chapters and they're sending in the troops. Mike, I want the entire force backing us. You see any of these guys, take them out. Broken taillights—driving a mile over the speed limit—I don't fucking care. Just send a message."

I nodded. *Sure, I'd just get the entire police force to back me in taking out a rival club.*

Absolutely.

Yeah, no way this was going to blow up in our fucking faces.

CHAPTER EIGHTEEN

Lauren: July 2014 (Age: 27)

"Please come over tonight," Elizabeth begged. "We could watch sappy chick flicks and cry because we'll never find a love like that."

I browsed the various pastas on aisle three like a visitor on a strange planet.

Angel Hair? Fettucine? Vermicelli?

My offer to cook for Mike came with one teensy-tiny drawback. I didn't actually know how to cook. It was on my list, along with all the other adult shit I was supposed to be doing, like owning matching bath towels and entertaining like Martha Stewart.

After an exhaustive day with Dr. Mulloy, the last thing I wanted to do was work for my dinner. Knowing takeout or a frozen dinner wouldn't cut it, I'd called Elizabeth for *'a meal so easy a toddler could make it.'*

Her answer had been immediate. "Spaghetti. It's so simple. And if you're feeling intimidated, just brown your ground beef and then use jarred pasta sauce."

She had also offered an in-person cooking lesson that would have conflicted with my date with Mike. Not that I could tell her that. No, thank you. I was not rubbing salt in that wound.

That, and I still wasn't entirely sure what he and I were.

"Hey, I would, but I made plans. I haven't seen these girls since college. But real quick, while I have you on the phone, should I get six or seven boxes of spaghetti?"

To be honest, I hadn't talked to the girls I went to college with since... well, college, actually.

Elizabeth laughed. "How many friends are you feeding? One box is plenty for four people."

I kept the one box of spaghetti and put the other five back.

"Look, I'm gonna let you go so that I can finish getting everything I need. I'll see you on Monday." I still needed ground beef and pasta sauce.

She sighed. "Okay, but if you change your mind, call me. I'll be here."

That was the problem with dating her soon to be ex-husband's best friend. There would never be a good time to tell her.

God, she'd probably see me as a traitor.

———

Mike: Leaving work soon. I'm swamped with this case at the moment, so just make yourself at home.

I read the text and eyes the large pot of bubbling water on the stovetop with a heavy sigh.

"The water needs to come to a vigorous boil," I mumbled, consulting the pasta box for advice. "But how do I know when that is?"

I already regretted my decision to try cooking. The sauce had at least been straightforward enough. Elizabeth had suggested browning the meat and draining it before adding the sauce, but I saved time by cooking them together.

After cranking the heat to high, I took a long swig from my wine glass. Drinking had taken away most of my cooking-related jitters.

My phone rang, and I answered with a slightly slurred, "Abuelita!"

"*Hola, mija.* How are you?" Hearing her voice made me feel like crying. I missed her fiercely and wished she lived closer so I could have her come over and walk me through the whole thing.

I tried to mask my emotions as I responded, "I'm doing great. I'm actually cooking!"

She made a noise that sounded a lot like laughter. "Oh? And what are you making?"

I frowned at the bubbling water. It still didn't look like it was boiling enough. "Um, spaghetti with meat sauce. I made a salad too. That was easy."

"*Mija*, did you use my trick and have the butcher grind up a roast for you? You get more meat for a much better price."

I had completely forgotten she did that.

"Yes, such a smart tip. Thanks, Abuelita. Um, how do you know if the water is boiling enough to add the pasta?"

She patiently replied, "Lauren, if it's bubbling a lot, it's ready. Just dump your pasta in."

I followed her suggestion before walking out front to sit on the porch swing. It was my first visit back since the night I lost my virginity and would be the first time I'd seen Mike since the night a drunk tried busting down my front door.

We were still in the awkward stage of getting to know each other, something our jobs made infinitely harder. Most nights, I fell into bed fully clothed. Alone.

He and I were stuck in a dance of two steps forward and three steps back. Texts were short and to the point. Phone calls hadn't lasted longer than five minutes.

I told myself it was because his week had been as hectic as mine. It was absolutely not because he'd changed his mind about me.

The thought left me with a pit in my stomach and a weight in my chest.

"*Mija?* Do you think that can be worked into your schedule?"

Shit. I'd zoned out.

"Abuelita," I began just as the smoke alarm began blaring from inside the house. "Um, I'm going to have to call you back. I have another call coming in."

"Lauren, is that the thing? *Como es que se llama esa mierda...* ah, smoke alarm! Did you—" I ended the call, following the smoke to the kitchen.

It was like something out of a nightmare. I turned off the burners and threw open the windows, trying to clear out the smoke. When the alarm continued its unholy screeching, I snagged a broom from the hall closet and waved it wildly beneath the detector.

I caught an empty jar of pasta sauce with the handle, sending it sailing off the counter and onto the floor, where it promptly shattered into a million pieces.

"Fuck me!" I roared, flipping the broom around to sweep the mess into a dustpan. In my infinite wisdom, I ran my palm over the wood floor, only to slice it open on a missed piece of glass. After wrapping my bleeding hand in paper towels, I did another pass with the broom, all while the alarm continued its death wail.

Once the smoke cleared, the source was impossible to miss. The spaghetti. I'd left the burner on high and all the water had evaporated. Maybe I hadn't added enough water from the start. Either way, blackened sticks that used to be pasta were all that remained.

I donned a pair of oven mitts and carried the pot out to the back porch step. At least I still had the sauce. I lifted the lid and stirred, shoulders sinking along with any hope of salvaging the meal. The sauce had scorched along the bottom of the pan, while the top still had bits of raw meat floating around in it.

My hand chose that moment to bleed through the towel and right into the pot of meat sauce. The tears I'd held at bay plummeted down my face. I wrapped my hand in another bundle of paper towels and grabbed the bottle of wine before heading for the porch swing.

If he'd been on the fence before, this pushed me into the nondatable category. Not knowing how to cook was one thing. Sucking entirely was another beast altogether. I tipped the bottle back and took a long, mournful drink.

Two bottles later and I felt just as shitty. My hand was still oozing blood. I kept bursting into tears. I couldn't cook ever again, the stress would kill me.

Mike's truck kicked up dust as it came down the driveway and I took another long swig to stifle the sob fighting to break free.

"Well, it's official. I'm about to be dumped."

He parked and got out with a huge grin on his face. One look at my bandaged hand and tear-stained face, and the grin faded.

"Lauren? What happened?" he asked, jogging up the steps.

I held up the bottle and gestured with it wildly. "I made you dinner. And, well... it turns out that I don't know how to cook. I should go."

My body swayed when I stood up, and Mike grabbed my shoulder to hold me steady. "Hey, calm down. I bet what you made is fine."

I snorted, "Well, the spaghetti is nothing but burnt sticks, and the pasta sauce has raw meat blended with scorched bits. Oh, and I bled in it on accident. It's a real gourmet experience."

After guiding me back to the swing, Mike disappeared into the house, only to reappear almost immediately with an unreadable expression on his face. "I get what's happened in there, but what happened to your hand?"

He reached out, and I let him remove the paper towels to inspect the cut on my palm.

"I set off the smoke alarm and then when I was trying to wave the smoke outside, I knocked over a jar of pasta sauce and it broke. I cut my hand trying to sweep that up," I blubbered, switching the wine bottle to the space between my legs so I could wipe the tears from my cheeks.

Mike pressed his lips into a flat line and looked away.

"Stop. Stop laughing. It's not funny."

His shoulders shook. "But, it kind of is. Jesus, darlin', you've had a day."

The sky turned red as the sun set, and I laid my head on his shoulder. "I'm sorry. I wanted to impress you."

He pulled the bottle from between my knees and took a drink before replying, "Oh, I'm impressed. Until now, I didn't think it was possible for someone to have so many things go wrong while trying to make spaghetti." I swatted him on the thigh and he grinned, "But you made up for it with dessert." Then he raised the bottle of wine in a toast.

I tapped my fingers against the bottle before replying sarcastically, "Yeah, I really saved the day."

"You know, I might have some Pop Tarts lying around somewhere."
Mike winked at me and took another swig.

I smiled. So, maybe I was no Susie Homemaker. I had remembered
the alcohol.

"You never had your dads teach you how to cook while growing
up?" Mike asked as he passed the bottle back to me.

Uh-oh.

I was two bottles past keeping my mouth shut. At this point in my
drinking, I'd hand over my social security card and bank information if
he asked for it.

I took the bottle from his hand and upended it for a little more
liquid courage. "Well, growing up, I lived with my bio mom. Mostly.
She was an addict and would go off on benders, leaving me to fend for
myself. She wasn't great at keeping the electricity and water on, so I
stuck to canned goods—soups and things that didn't require heat to be
eaten."

"And how did your dad come into the picture?" Mike asked gently.
His expression hadn't changed once during my little confession. Then
again, he was a detective, so keeping his face impassive was probably
part of the job.

"Josué was my guidance counselor at school. When he couldn't
reach Mon—my mother over some trouble I'd gotten into, he showed
up at the duplex I'd been staying in. If he hadn't shown up when he
did, I don't know what would have happened to me."

I paused with a shudder, remembering how close I'd come to death
that night and wanting to shut the memories down. "Josué isn't really
much of a cook, either. In college, I was more focused on proving to
the world I wasn't like her than I was on learning to scramble an egg
and never took the time. It sounds ridiculous, I know."

He took my uninjured hand in his. "Ridiculous? Red, statistically
speaking, you're an anomaly. Children of addicts are something like
eight times more likely to develop an addiction themselves—"

"Wait. Did you pull that number out of your ass, or is it something
they teach in cop school?" I asked, my words slurring together.

Mike looked away before answering, "Life taught me that one,
darlin'."

I squeezed his hand, bringing him back to the present.

"Crippling addiction to alcohol, notwithstanding, I'd say you turned out alright," he joked, bringing the bottle to my lips. "Who gives a fuck if you can cook or not? You got me for that."

We passed the wine back and forth, watching the fireworks light up the horizon. For the first time that night, I saw the situation from his perspective and could finally laugh about it.

CHAPTER NINETEEN

Mike: July 2014 (Age: 31)

I'd been avoiding David since his marriage imploded. Dating his soon-to-be ex-wife's friend wasn't likely to earn me any friendship points. He'd fallen into a bottle of whiskey when things went south and, given our earlier conversation, he hadn't found his way out yet.

David had some crackpot theory that Landon, Elizabeth's former lover, had broken into their house and was stalking her. As far as break-ins went, it ranked pretty low on my list of cases to solve. No prints and nothing taken other than a photograph.

To appease him, I'd looked into the guy and couldn't find so much as a parking ticket. Landon Scott was clean and had a solid alibi for the night of the break-in, meaning there was no chance of holding him indefinitely as David had so helpfully recommended.

Regardless, I owed him dinner and a sympathetic ear, even if I wanted to spend every free second with Lauren.

Between work and SPMC, free time was scarce. Keeping Grey happy involved arresting Sons of Death members for petty shit, which had gone about as well as I'd expected.

It wasn't a productive day unless I was getting death threats, right?

My phone buzzed with an incoming text.

Lauren: I promised Elizabeth I would help her pack. Looks like it's going to be a long night. I'll call you when I'm on my way home.

I stared sullenly at the message. I didn't know why I was getting bent out of shape over not seeing her. It wasn't like we hadn't been together almost every night for the past week.

One month in, and I'd officially fallen head over ass for Lauren. Anytime there was a lull in my schedule, my thoughts went to her. Maybe I'd never really been against monogamy—just anyone who wasn't her.

No one was more shocked than me.

Instead of twiddling my thumbs, waiting for David to show, I called her. Just because.

"Hey," she said in greeting.

I smiled, just like I did anytime I heard her voice. *You know, real manly shit.* "Hey yourself, Red. How's it going?"

There was a lot of background noise. "I've been recruited to pack up the guest bedroom and these boxes are," she huffed, "so fucking heavy. Why can't they just stay together so we don't have to play counselor?"

I laughed. "Darlin', I have no idea. Think you can break away early and meet me?"

"Mike Sullivan, are you trying to get into my panties?"

I damn sure was.

Sex with Lauren was like nothing I'd ever experienced. She was constantly checking in with me—making sure I was enjoying it as much as she was. It didn't seem to matter how many times I assured her I was having the best fucking time of my life. She was convinced she was lacking. Once, she'd even gone as far as insisting it couldn't be good for me because, and I quote, "I don't even know any tricks."

Knew enough to turn an ass hound into her man.

"I'm going to take your silence as a yes," she said when I didn't respond. "And, in that case, my answer is okay."

I beamed. "That's my girl. You text me the minute you're done—I'll fake a fucking heart attack if I have to."

"You got it, Tex," she chuckled.

"You started drinking without me? Fucker."

I quickly ended the call and took in the stranger seated across the from me. David's hair hung in greasy strands near his chin and remnants of food caked his beard.

He looked like he'd been living on the streets for the past month, not at the Holiday Inn down the road.

"Hey man," I said, trying not to stare. "Got here a little early and ordered a Guinness. I didn't know what you were drinking."

David eyed the drink menu like he was expecting it to throw a punch. "Who was on the phone? Fuck buddy of the week?"

I clenched my jaw and mentally repeated, *he just lost his marriage... he just lost his marriage...*

David didn't seem to notice and continued, "Damn. Maybe you had it right all along—if you just screw around, then you never have to worry about getting your heart broken. Cause I gotta tell ya, this fucking sucks."

The serve reappeared to take his order and David went back to staring absently at the wall behind my head. Any thoughts of telling him about Lauren were long gone. The guy was a train-wreck, gloating would have been in poor form.

"So," I tried. "She won't see you, but is she still seeing him?"

"I don't know—I guess I just assumed she was keeping us both at a distance while sorting everything out."

I nodded while scanning the menu. "I feel like I already asked, but did you ever suspect she was screwing someone else?"

David stared at the table before quietly admitting, "I saw nothing out of the ordinary. Looking back on it, though, the signs were there."

It was probably the first time in the entirety of our friendship I had nothing to say. An uncomfortable silence descended over the table. I looked over at the television in the bar, checking the score of the baseball game. A woman made eye contact with me before heading straight for our table.

"David Greene?" she asked with a forced smile.

He nodded, and I saw it coming before she ever even reached into her handbag.

Fuck.

She thrust a large manila envelope into his hands. "You've been served."

————

"Mmm... *McDonald's*. Dinner of champions," Lauren said from the foot of the stairs.

I looked up from the carton of French fries with a guilty grin before fishing the extra burger out of the bag. "You hungry? I cooked."

She smiled, but something was off. "I'm okay for now. Have you been waiting long?"

I gathered up the food while she unlocked the front door. "No, just a couple of minutes. Rough night?"

"You could say that," she responded, placing her purse and keys on the hook in the entryway before looking back at me. "Would it be alright if I just laid my head on your shoulder and pretended this day never happened?"

Food forgotten, I led her over to the couch. "Start at the beginning."

Lauren pulled her knees to her chest, making her appear even smaller than she already was, before laying against my arm. "Work was just... difficult. We had a patient that arrived a half-hour late for their first appointment and when I tried to explain why we would need to reschedule, he copped an attitude with me and blamed it on all the paperwork we emailed over for him to fill out. It was emailed three days ago and apparently, he's been working on it since then."

Lauren rubbed her temple as if reliving it made her head ache. I nestled her between my legs, with her back against my chest. As I massaged her neck and shoulders, I tried not to think too hard about what I'd become.

She leaned into my touch with a sigh before adding, "That's not the half of it. The prick told me if I refused to see his daughter, then I'd be sorry—something about waiting in the parking lot to work the 'uppity bitch' right out of me."

I didn't realize I was taking it out on her shoulders until she pulled away with a groan. I was livid. It was like David getting served times a thousand.

"Sorry, darlin'," I whispered, rubbing her back softly to make up for it.

She shrugged. "I think guys like that forget they're dealing with actual people. I had to dismiss them from the practice."

I was going to find this guy and work the douchebag out of him—I doubt there'd be anything left by the time I was done. I took a deep breath and calmly asked, "What was his name?"

She tilted her head back and looked up at me in amusement. "Why? You gonna arrest him?"

I shook my head, using every ounce of willpower to keep my voice calm. "Nah, you handled it fine—I just like to know these things in case he ever ends up getting booked down the road. We can make his stay... unpleasant."

I was absolutely going to go after him.

She gave me an upside-down smile and told me what I wanted to know, adding, "But that's only to be used if he ends up in the slammer."

I nodded dramatically. "Yes, Red. For official police use only."

I would give him to Grey. The thought made me smile.

She sat up and turned around to face me. "I thought the day couldn't get any worse and then I got to Elizabeth's. Mike, she's pregnant, and understandably freaking out."

My mouth fell open. "She's pregnant. Jess is pregnant. Wait—you're not pregnant, are you?" I playfully poked her in the ribs.

"Not even the slightest bit," Lauren said, dodging my finger. "Disappointed?"

I gave a mock sigh, still trying to cheer her up. "Guess we'll just have to keep practicing until we get it right, won't we?"

"That we will, Tex. Now, enough about my crappy day. Tell me about yours."

"Well," I cleared my throat, debating how much to reveal. "David was served, so that was fun."

Lauren sighed. "I knew Elizabeth was looking into her options. How does that even work? Did they just find him on a job site?"

"They found him at the restaurant—before we ate, I might add, which is why I had to make a pit stop at the Golden Arches. He looked like absolute dog shit, convinced Landon broke into their house. We're lucky management didn't call LE, because he was disturbing the peace, to put it mildly."

She leaned forward and placed a soft kiss against my chin. "It makes me feel so guilty. I'm the happiest I've ever been, but I can't share it with my best friend. I just wish there was some way for them to work this out."

Her emotions mirrored mine. There was a certain weariness I'd been carrying when I was around David. Like I didn't deserve to be happy if he wasn't.

I kissed her neck and blurted out, "Please tell me that won't be us."

Shit. Where the hell had that come from?

She regarded me with a serious expression that slowly turned into a smirk. "Seeing how you're the only man I've ever been with, I don't feel like it's fair to put these limitations on me. I just dipped my toe in the water. I haven't even experienced all the world can offer."

I pinched her arm, and she squeaked in surprise. "Stop. I'm serious."

Drop it, Mike.

I couldn't.

Not when there were words hung up in the back of my throat. I was nowhere ready to say them, but I was trying my best to communicate how much she meant to me.

She was the exception to my every rule, but it wasn't love. I couldn't recall ever caring about anything but myself.

It was just some long-term lust. I refused to accept anything else.

I couldn't recall if I'd ever truly loved anything in my life.

Early on, I'd learned nothing good lasted, and the experiences had left me jaded. I respected my mother, but her constant back and forth with my father made me hate her. I even admired Grey up to a certain point, but even that now tasted like bitterness.

There was nothing in my life I couldn't part with—except her.

And it concerned me.

She bit down on the corner of her lip and gave me a half smile. "Me too."

I frowned until she gave in. "Fine. I'm kidding. That won't be us—we have our shit together and we're not keeping secrets. Their relationship was failing long before they cheated—it happened when they stopped confiding in each other."

I blamed the weighted feeling in my chest on the fast food and not on the impact of her words. I couldn't confide in her—if she knew half the shit I'd done, she'd drop a restraining order on me before I'd even finished talking. My secrets would only put her in danger. Grey had been adamant that no one know about our deal.

Lauren hadn't had a peaceful life. It was on me to protect her now.

I pulled her into my arms and held on for dear life—wishing for the one millionth time since meeting her I was the man she imagined me to be.

Hell, I would've even settled for being Jack, a down-on-my-luck surfer.

His life seemed a hell of a lot simpler than mine.

CHAPTER TWENTY

Lauren: August 2014 (Age: 27)

W*here had it all gone wrong?*
Oh, I remembered. I'd opened my big mouth and ruined the entire evening.

After receiving a text from David asking me to check on Elizabeth, I'd agreed, thinking the two of them must have been working things out. Plus, a work emergency forced Mike to cancel our dinner plans, so it was that or sitting at home alone.

Over a carton of mint chocolate chip ice cream, she'd spilled the dirt on David. It was all terribly romantic. One second, they were arguing. Then he backed her against a wall and kissed the hell out of her.

The conversation took a hard right turn into a minefield when she mentioned Landon, and I slipped. "David thinks that he's the one who broke into your house."

I realized how it sounded the moment the words left my mouth and began backpedaling immediately. "Elizabeth, I shouldn't have said anything. Let's talk about something else. I know—how about those Oilers? I mean, they beat the Bears last night, but boy, has this season been rough. And they've got the Hurricanes in a couple of days. It doesn't look good right now."

Mike really liked baseball. He'd played in high school and was never one to miss an Arlington Oilers game. I knew enough, thanks to Josué's love of the game, to watch with him. Plus, it gave me a reprieve from the History channel.

Elizabeth did not give a damn about baseball. "You've been talking to David behind my back? Does he know I'm pregnant? Jesus, Lauren, I trusted you!"

"Wait! Elizabeth, please," I pleaded. "Just calm down!"

"Calm down? I need to calm down when yet another friend of mine has fallen under the spell that is David Greene?"

Oh, Jesus.

She thought I was like Jess? It felt as though my body was collapsing in on itself.

I held my hands up in surrender. "Stop—it's not what you think. I swear I haven't been talking to David. His text tonight was the first I've heard from him since everything happened."

I didn't know if the pregnancy hormones were making things worse, or if she was always this scary, but I took several steps back. Just in case.

"Then explain how you know what David suspects with the break-in. Because, from where I'm standing, it sure looks like you're talking to him behind my back."

So much for secrets…

"I'm sleeping with Mike!" I yelled over her. We stood in complete silence, each of us trying to regain our breath.

Her face fell. "What? Christ! I'm sorry—and congratulations? How long has this been going on? Why didn't you tell me?"

Because you and your husband had just split up?

"We've been sort of dating since the night we all went out together. And I was going to tell you, but I worried about what you'd think—worried we'd end up like this."

She reached toward me and I flinched until I realized she was pulling me into a hug. "I'm awful—I'm sorry. I'm not even going to blame this on pregnancy. I lost one friend already and couldn't bear it if I lost you, too."

"I know it's only been a couple of months, but I think I love him,"

I said, giving life to something that had been running around in my head for weeks.

It was crazy.

People didn't fall in love just like that. Certainly not after two months of dating. I wanted to believe it was just the sex, but that was only one piece of the puzzle. It was him—the way he was with me.

"He's a good guy," Elizabeth said, reaffirming my thoughts. "I don't know that he's ever dated anyone, really."

Which was exactly why I hadn't pushed to label our relationship.

I picked up Elizabeth's ultrasound pictures, trying to spot the baby in the sepia and black tones.

"So, Mike. Is he, um, big everywhere?"

"Elizabeth," I gasped, my face flaming with embarrassment. "You cannot ask people those things!"

She gnawed on her lower lip before admitting, "Seeing how David left me with a severe case of female blue balls, I'll take what I can get."

"I'm going to assume the hormones have taken over your body."

"Yes," she groaned. "If I'm not puking, I'm dreaming up ways to seduce David. So, because some of us are going through a bit of a dry spell, just tell me how the sex is."

"It's a good thing I like so you much, you pervert," I said with a laugh. "Phenomenal. Sex with Mike is absolutely phenomenal. Do you need to excuse yourself to deal with your *situation*? If so, I can play a couple of rounds of *Candy Crush* on my phone."

"You're killing me. That's all I get? Phenomenal?"

I instantly saw an image of Mike hovering above me, face fixed in concentration. It was enough to leave me breathless.

"Yep," I murmured distractedly. "If I say any more, I'm afraid you'll spontaneously combust in your chair."

Elizabeth buried her face in her hands. "How am I supposed to make it through the next thirty-one weeks of pregnancy in a constant state of arousal?"

"You'll be rubbing up against strangers on the street!" God knew I would if I had to give up sex. Now that I'd experienced it, I couldn't imagine living without it.

"You laugh now, Lauren. You won't be laughing when I move my chair over to yours at work, so I can hump your leg!"

"You wouldn't dare!"

She kicked off her shoes and stretched her feet out on the carpet with a sigh. Our spat was already a distant spot on the horizon, but I was still feeling conflicted.

"Elizabeth? Can I ask for some advice?"

She frowned. "If it's about relationships, I'm not so sure I'm the girl to ask."

I shook my head. "No, nothing like that. It's just—hypothetically speaking—if your mom was an addict who'd ignored you for most of your life, but had suddenly gotten sober in the last few months and wanted to see you, would you do it?" The words came out in a rush and I could see her head practically spinning as she took it all in.

It had been nagging at me since Monica had shown up in the parking lot, trying to pay me off. I didn't owe her a thing, but a small part of me felt like I needed to meet with her.

She mulled my words over. "Was she abusive to you?"

"No—she was neglectful, and well, she stole from me when she was using." Hearing the words out loud made it obvious my answer to meeting her should have been a resounding *Hell No*.

"I think maybe you hear her out. Just go in with an open mind and no expectations."

What the hell?

Given her frosty relationship with her own mother, I'd expected her to tell me that meeting with Monica was insanity. "Really?" I pushed. "Just meet with her?"

Elizabeth shrugged. "I mean, I wouldn't go into it with any expectations, but what's the harm?"

I nodded brightly, while a war waged in my mind.

The harm? Giving Monica any foothold into my life.

The last time had cost me my car. Knowing she was deep in a world of bikers had me concerned the stakes would be much higher this time around.

CHAPTER TWENTY-ONE

Lauren: August 2014 (Age: 27)

Two weeks later and I was feeling just as conflicted. I smoothed my skirt and picked at my manicure, jumping in my seat every time the bell jingled over the front door at *Perked Up*.

The lead ball in my gut had been with me since I woke up.

Monica had sobered up.

Big deal.

It didn't mean we had anything in common. Sure, we'd both hit rock bottom, but in my mind, I was the only one who had found a way out.

My head jerked up involuntarily when the bell jingled again. It wasn't her. Maybe she'd decided not to come, after all. I didn't know whether to feel relieved or disappointed.

The woman who walked in slung her Louis Vuitton over her shoulder and scanned the menu easily. I studied her, trying to place where I'd seen her before. She turned as if she felt my gaze and took her sunglasses off before asking, "You want something, Lauren?"

Monica?

My eyes went wide. "You? You don't look like you!"

Lauren, you can't just tell people they don't look like themselves.

The barista gave me a strange look while Monica shrugged it off and paid for her latte. After tucking her purse into one of the empty chairs much like a parent would a newborn, she settled into the seat across from mine.

"Didn't recognize me, did you?" she asked with a wide grin.

My breath caught as I took in the brilliantly white veneers. She hadn't had those when I saw her at the hospital. The transformation was so drastic, I could have passed her on the street and never known it.

Mouth still agape, I shook my head, fumbling to find the right words. "How? When? How?"

Monica took a tentative sip of her latte before answering, "Torch. I'd hit my absolute rock bottom when he stepped in. He helped me get clean and sober."

I wadded up a napkin just to give my hands something to do. Her response left me with more questions than answers.

How had a biker helped her get clean?

Weren't they all balls deep in that shit?

Balls deep?

Oh, Jesus. I was starting to think like Mike.

A part of me was happy for her. The other, bitter as hell. She sobered up for some biker, but not her own daughter.

She placed a hand on mine when I began picking at my nail polish again, stopping me. "Don't do that. Remember, a lady's nails—"

"Say a lot about who she is," I finished, surprised I still remembered. During the brief periods of lucidity, when Monica had sobered up long enough to remember she had a daughter, she would always insist on getting manicures. We could have been living on pork and beans for the week prior, but she always found a way for us to get our nails done.

Even though I was notorious for picking my polish off within a matter of days, I had subconsciously carried her mantra into adulthood.

That was when I looked at Monica—really looked at her. I didn't need a drug test to confirm what I already knew. She was telling the truth.

"So, you really did it. Congratulations."

What else was there to say?

Apparently, Torch had some magic touch I'd never possessed.

"I was horrible to you, Lauren." She paused, her eyes filling with tears. "Addiction brings out the worst in a person. My god—you had to practically raise yourself. I know there's nothing I can do to make up for that, and it's unfair of me to ask this of you, but I'd like to rebuild our relationship."

And there it was.

I had come prepared, knowing it was likely Monica wanted something. Her request still took me by surprise, though. I didn't know what to say—I'd spent most of my childhood hoping she would sober up and be the mother I needed her to be. Now that she wanted to try, it left me completely stumped.

Realizing it was doing nothing to calm my anxiety, I tossed the napkin aside and said, "Monica, I don't know that we can have the typical mother/daughter relationship. There's just been too much."

"I never expected it to be normal. Look at us. I grew up with addicts for parents and turned into one myself. You took the lemons that life gave you and made fucking lemonade."

Several heads turned in our direction, and she lowered her voice. "I don't deserve it, but I'd like another chance. I'm not gonna sit here and blame it on addiction, or tell you I did the best I could—it's obvious I didn't."

My eyes stung, and I was painfully aware of just how many people surrounded us. It was too public. I'd thought being here would be safer, but all it had done was expose more people to our drama. "This might not be the best place to have this conversation—"

She looked down at the table and I watched as tears fell in a steady stream. "I never told you this, but my parents lost custody of me pretty early on. The state shuffled me around in foster care. Some homes were good, and some were pretty fucking terrible." Her hands began shaking and without thinking, I reached across and placed them in mine.

Monica took a deep breath. "The last home I was in fostered five other teens. I went into it thinking the couple must have some very generous people with big hearts. It wasn't long before I realized they were only doing it for the state check. The—the husband was always touchy-feely, but I tried to convince myself he was just an affectionate —" Her words cut off in a sob and I realized where the conversation was headed. The sickness I'd felt in the pit of my stomach seemed to intensify as she forced herself to continue.

"He started coming into the bedroom I shared with another girl at night and forcing us to do things—said he'd throw us out if we told anyone. I got pregnant at sixteen and tried explaining myself to his wife, but she called me a whore and threw me out. I considered an abortion, but had no money."

"Excuse me," I said weakly, fleeing from the table and into the bathroom, where my body purged the coffee and muffin I'd consumed for breakfast.

The product of rape.

Monica was waiting outside the stall when I opened the door. Her eyes were overly bright with tears that had yet to be shed, while her face was streaked from the ones that had already escaped.

She ran a paper towel under the faucet and pressed it to my forehead. "Lauren, I'm so sorry. I wanted to be completely honest with you —no more sugarcoating my behavior to look better."

"Okay," I said, my voice little more than a whisper. "What did you do?"

"There was a home for unwed mothers and they took me in, no questions asked. I told myself I was going to do right by you." She shook her head. "I fucked that up. The first time they put you in foster care, I quit using. Cold turkey. I had this vision of what happened to me happening to you and knew I couldn't have lived with myself if it did. I also tried to make sure I never brought men around you. Probably means jack shit right now, but you deserve the truth."

I leaned over to clutch my thighs, my breaths labored. All those years spent in anger over being yanked out of foster homes had come from a deep-seated fear of me being raped. It was almost ironic, considering Josué had rescued me when I was seconds away from it.

Monica placed her hands on my back and rubbed. "It's okay. Deep breaths."

Once the panic subsided and my breaths evened out, she pulled me into a hug, apologizing over and over.

Knowing she had forced herself to get clean in order to keep custody—however short-lived it might have been—left me rethinking everything I'd believed about her for years.

"Take a walk with me?"

I clutched my rolling stomach, but gave a small nod, letting her lead me to a small park a couple of blocks from the coffee shop. We sat on a wrought-iron bench, watching the kids playing at the elementary school across the street.

"Is that why you turned to drugs?" I asked, shattering the silence. "Because of him?"

Monica exhaled softly and stared off into the distance. "Initially, yes. After you were born, I had this recurring nightmare about him breaking into the apartment. In it, he'd always start by abusing me until he'd hear you cry out from your bassinet and then he'd turn toward you with this awful grin on his face. The dreams had gotten so bad that I could barely function during the day. Every little sound made me jump."

I couldn't imagine. I still had nightmares about the men who broke into the duplex, but it had never been a daily thing.

"When I told my girlfriend, she put me in touch with a guy who dealt. Being high felt like floating. My brain didn't replay the abuse, and I didn't see his face. I was invincible. I wasn't a sleep-deprived new mother anymore, either. The first time I snorted coke, I stayed up all night cleaning the apartment. I scrubbed the baseboards until my hands were raw. You'd wake up every three hours, and I'd make you a bottle. Once you were asleep, I'd go right back to cleaning. I felt like I'd found a miracle drug. I could keep up with you and housework while not being forced to relive the abuse."

She stopped talking, and I looked away from the swings and over to her. Her lip quivered.

"It didn't stay like that, though, did it?"

She shook her head. "No, at first I'd use once a week, but then I noticed I didn't have as much energy, so I'd use a little more. When the cocaine failed, I switched to meth—was told it would give me a better high. From there it was like a wildfire—it started off small and manage-able and just turned into this monster, consuming everything within me."

Sounded like me and Mike.

The thought startled me. I'd told myself he was a player and planned to just dip my toe in the water. Instead, I'd run down the end of a long pier and jumped in headfirst. Now, he occupied most of my thoughts.

Was I being consumed by him?

I'd spent most of the morning feeling guilty. I hadn't exactly told him about my coffee date—he had enough going on at the moment. A lingerie model had come to Lubbock to meet with friends, only to disappear without a trace. Mike spent every waking moment at the station or out interviewing potential witnesses.

I convinced myself I didn't tell him because I was just trying to be a conscientious girl... friend. Friend who happened to be a girl. Were terms like 'boyfriend' and 'girlfriend' even used after high school?

How had we spent two months together without me knowing what we were?

I shook off thoughts of Mike and reached over to take Monica's hand in mine. "Okay."

She gave me a puzzled look, so I elaborated. "Okay. Let's do it. Let's give this whole relationship thing a try."

Her eyes welled up again, and she squeezed my fingers. "Thank you."

The bitterness and anger I'd held onto for too long gave way to something foreign.

Hope.

CHAPTER TWENTY-TWO

Mike: August 2014 (Age: 31)

I couldn't remember the last time I'd gotten eight hours of
uninterrupted sleep.

I rubbed my eyes wearily and took a sip of lukewarm coffee before
going back to staring at my computer screen. I was turning into the
stereotypical cop—eating most of my meals out of a bag and spending
the night at the station in front of my desk. If I wasn't parked in my
chair, I was revisiting the places the missing model was last seen.
There were more dead ends than leads. It was as if Ekaterina "Katya"
Egorichev simply walked out of her hotel room one day and fell off the
face of the earth.

Something wasn't adding up, but for the life of me, I couldn't put
my finger on what that something was.

To make matters worse, the department had rounded up ten Sons
of Death members, but they were like a hydra. It didn't matter how
many heads I cut off, three more grew back.

Lauren and I had only seen each other during the brief moments
our work schedules didn't overlap. Missing the hell out of her, I picked
up my desk phone and dialed her direct extension.

"Good Morning, *Mulloy Dental*, this is Lauren," she recited in her
best customer service voice.

Days and nights bled together inside these cinderblock walls, but hearing her voice made me light up like the fucking sun. "Hey, Red. Tell me something good."

"Hey yourself, Tex. Good news... good news—ooh, I got it. On this day in 1939, they televised a Major-League baseball game for the first time. I'm not sure it falls under 'good,' but it's definitely noteworthy considering how much you love the sport."

She was so damn cute.

"I'll take it," I said with a grin. "How's work?"

She lowered her voice. "Fine, I guess. How's it going with *The Thing?*"

Somewhere along the way, she'd gotten it in her head that we had to speak in code when referring to cases.

I sighed and massaged the back of my neck. Every part of my body hurt and longed for my bed. "Honestly, I'm exhausted. I just want an actual meal... and you."

"Don't tell me that while I'm at work," she groaned. "I'm going to have to go home at lunch and take care of this situation now. Any chance you can break away from the office for thirty minutes and give me a hand?"

Fuck.

I wanted to grab my keys and drive over to her office right now. I couldn't do it, though. The model's father was scheduled to come in for questioning. I couldn't discount anything at this point.

Landon Scott had been in a relationship with Ms. Egorichev and had been the one to report her missing when she failed to show for a dinner date. His involvement forced me to call David and Elizabeth in for questioning, where Elizabeth informed officers that Katia had ended her long-distance relationship with Landon after discovering his affair.

Perps who were guilty would almost always give themselves away. Slight changes to their original statement. Contradicting timelines. Displaying little to no emotion regarding the missing person. Eventually, they all slipped up.

Given his prior statements, which had led investigators to believe the two were still involved, Elizabeth's revelation felt like the break I'd been searching for.

It wasn't.

Not only did he stick to his original statement, Landon readily admitted to the infidelity and said the two had reconciled after going through counseling, a detail that checked out.

He'd even produced a ring and said he'd been planning to propose at the dinner she never showed up for. Security footage from the restaurant showed Landon sitting in a corner booth for over an hour, fidgeting with the ring box and checking his phone constantly. The restaurant's security cameras showed the two phone calls he claimed to have made to Katya's cell phone.

Just one more dead end.

"Did you fall asleep?" Lauren's soft voice brought me back to the present.

"No, just got a lot going on right now, darlin'. Listen, as much as I wish I could meet you for that lunch date, I'll be in the middle of interviews for most of the afternoon. I can call you on my way home. Fair warning, it might be pretty late."

The line was silent, and I worried that I'd upset her until she said, "Um, I might stay up a little later. Just text me. And, Mike? I get it. Go save the world."

I smiled. "And that's why I love you—" I froze the minute the words left my mouth.

What the fuck had I just said?

"I'vegottotakecareofsomestuffherebye." The words all ran together, and I hung up before she could respond. Then I laid my forehead against the cool wood of my desk in shame. I was so fucking sleep deprived I'd just told Lauren I loved her.

What if she started expecting things, like moving in together?

Or worse, marriage.

I pinched the bridge of my nose and inhaled deeply.

My desk phone beeped, before the intercom crackled with, "Detective Sullivan, Nikolay Egorichev is here to see you."

I sat back and rubbed my eyes. "Get him in a room."

Several minutes later, Noelle, an investigator, popped her head into my office. "He's in room one, Sullivan. We're ready when you are."

I nodded, still hung up on the fact I'd used the L word. What I wanted to do was skip the interview and get the fuck out of Dodge long enough to clear my head.

"You sticking around for a while?" I asked Noelle, letting my gaze drift down toward her tits.

She rolled her eyes. "Yeah, about that. I don't make the same mistake twice. So, and I mean this with all the respect in the world, fuck off, Sullivan."

The door slammed shut behind her, and I dropped my head to my hands, trying to remember.

Fuck me.

Christmas party. Three years ago.

What would I have said if she was receptive?

I needed to clear my head—scratch that. I needed sleep.

I got up and headed into the interrogation room. Thanks to my dickhead move, I was in for a world of fun.

CHAPTER TWENTY-THREE

Mike: August 2014 (Age: 31)

It was a little after twelve-thirty in the morning when I finally pulled into my driveway. I was no closer to solving my missing person's case than I'd been two weeks ago. But I needed a goddamned break and sleep in an actual bed.

Unfortunately, the dark blue Toyota parked in my driveway meant I was going to have to have a conversation I'd been running from since yesterday morning.

Shit.

I was going to be forced to tell Lauren I wasn't in love with her. Now. When I wanted nothing more than a long hot shower and my bed. It had the makings of an epic showdown—one I was absolutely going to lose, along with her.

The front door was unlocked, but the downstairs was dark. I peeked into the living room and kitchen, but both were empty. A swift check of the remaining rooms downstairs turned up nothing.

Something didn't feel right. It was quiet. Too quiet. I pulled my Glock from the back of my pants, wrestling with the worst-case scenarios in my mind.

What if the Sons of Death had shown up while I was gone?

My heart hammered in my chest as I crept up the stairs, pausing to check the bathroom and two spare bedrooms. The sinking feeling in the pit of my stomach became more pronounced as I moved toward the master bedroom.

Then, I saw her. Handcuffed to my headboard. In nothing but her bra. Her head hung at an awkward angle and I circled the bed, trying to figure out who'd done this to her. My cock didn't seem to give a fuck and was at midnight, ready to party.

I watched her chest rise and fall in a steady rhythm before releasing the breath I'd been holding.

"Red?" I whispered.

She blinked slowly before focusing on my face with a drowsy grin. "Hi, what time is it?"

I set my gun down on the nightstand and turned back to her. "Late. What are you—what do you have going on here?"

Lauren's teeth rested on her lower lip and she gave me a shy smile. "I told you I needed a hand. You couldn't come to me, so I came to you."

Oh, she was going to be coming for me.

I loosened my tie and tossed it on the floor. My shirt and slacks followed. She watched with a hungry look as I hooked my thumbs into the waistband of my boxer briefs, leisurely working them down my thighs.

"You planning on taking all night, Tex? I've still gotta drive home after this and somehow make myself look presentable enough for work at seven."

I kicked them off and climbed across the comforter to her. "Your pussy getting lonely, darlin'?" Her entire torso blazed red. "I'll take that as a yes. You need this?"

I pushed a finger into her wetness and she moaned softly, her eyes fluttering shut. "No, no, no. Keep those green eyes on me. You don't wanna miss anything. Now, what about this?" I added another finger and her eyes widened. "I can't hear you."

She nodded shakily and pushed against me. "Y-yes."

I fucked her lazily with my hand, as if we had all the time in the world. It wasn't what I wanted, but I hadn't been with her for what felt like an eternity. I wanted to make up for lost time by giving her more than five minutes of pleasure.

There it was again. I was putting her needs first.

Frustration gripped me and I thrust my fingers deeper, taking it out on her pussy. The cuffs rattled against the headboard and by the way she was clenching around me; I knew she was close. I leaned down to let my tongue flick against her and that was all she wrote.

Lauren's whole body shuddered against my hand as she began crying out words of nonsense. I pulled my hand free and sucked my fingers clean as she groaned. She tasted fucking delicious. I leaned across her and pulled a condom from the nightstand.

She watched me with a drunk expression on her face and I couldn't help myself. I leaned down and pressed a rough kiss to her neck before lightly taking her earlobe between my teeth.

She responded by lifting her hips up toward me, pussy glistening from my mouth and her orgasm. The only thing that would've made it better was if she'd taken her bra off. I wanted to remember her like this. Spread out before me, just begging to be fucked.

Good god almighty, what was she doing to me?

After ensuring I was good safety-wise, I pushed into her and her mouth fell open in that familiar silent scream. I had to fight the urge to lose control, pushing into her body until I couldn't go any further.

"God, you're so good at this," she whispered. Her half-lidded eyes looked up at me with reverence.

I'd gotten used to her hands digging into my back and shoulders, but the cuffs kept her at bay. It was by far the hottest sex we'd had yet. I angled her hips and began fucking her, knowing she'd come within seconds. She didn't disappoint. Her body began pushing back against mine at the same tempo, so I used my hips to speed up. She met me thrust for motherfucking thrust until her breathing stopped.

She ground against me and then released a small moan as her body flooded around me. "Oh, fuck."

I was ready to explode just from watching her, but I tried slowing it down. Her pussy disagreed with my plan and greedily gripped my cock like a fucking vice. I couldn't have pulled out even if I wanted to. I came loudly with a death grip on her hips, before collapsing onto her chest, sweat dripping off of me like water.

Fuck.

It just got better every time.

"Mike?" she whispered and moved away. It was time for the fighting portion of the evening. Luckily, I was still too high off of endorphins to care much.

I rolled onto my back and squeezed my eyes shut, ready to face the firing squad. The only thing missing was my last cigarette. "Yeah?"

She shifted around and I braced myself. "Um, could you get me out of these? I lost feeling in my arms an hour ago and I'm worried it might be permanent."

My eyes popped open, and I jumped up. "Jesus, Lauren. How long have you been like this?"

She stretched her neck. "Um, since eleven?"

Shit. It was a damn good thing I'd come home tonight. I found the key on the nightstand and quickly unfastened her, taking my time to get the blood flowing back into her arms.

"Thanks. I was afraid this was going to be one of those cautionary tales for adventurous young women everywhere." She smiled and my heart thudded in my chest.

It was just aftershocks from the amazing sex.

I laid back down beside her, still breathing hard. "Well, now it'll just be our little secret."

Just as I began to doze, Lauren got up. I cracked one eye open and watched as she bounced around the room, teeming with energy. "What are ya doing, Red?" I asked with a yawn, propping an arm behind my head.

She pulled her pink lacy boy-shorts up and over her shapely ass before bending over to grab the rest of her clothes. My eyes were wide open now and focused on her.

"I'm going home," she tossed over her shoulder nonchalantly as she dressed, flooding me with a sense of loss. I hadn't seen her for more than a quick fuck in weeks.

"Yeah? Tired of me already?" I was on thin ice.

She pulled a tank top over her head before responding, "Not at all.

You need to sleep, and I have to be at work in a few hours. Well, that, and I've gotta revive my arms."

I worked my jaw back and forth, struggling to get the words out. "Look, about what I said on the phone—"

"You didn't mean it. I know. It's not like we're serious—it's just sex."

The words were like a sucker punch to my gut, but I played it off. "Yeah... just sex."

She came over to where I was laying, sweeping her lips over mine. "Get some sleep."

I wanted to take it back—beg her to stay. Instead, I followed her to the front door and watched as she climbed into her car and drove away.

It wasn't just sex. It never had been.

CHAPTER TWENTY-FOUR

Lauren: September 2014 (Age: 27)

What was I doing with my life?

I stared at the search results on my office computer screen, wondering how I'd gotten embroiled in OPP—Other People's Problems. Not quite the level of drama Naughty By Nature rapped about in the nineties, but more than I wanted to be involved in.

I had enough of my own.

Like telling Mike it was just sex. Who did that? The words had just tumbled out of my mouth. A defense mechanism to protect myself from the inevitable—clinging to the illusion of control.

There was no control. And as for the inevitable, we were on a collision course headed straight for it. I felt it. The distance between us had become an ever-widening chasm filled with late nights, mountains of paperwork, and missing persons cases.

I gave him space, thinking I could gradually move in until he was eating out of the palm of my hand. But Mike wasn't a wild animal to be tamed.

Trying to pin down a self-proclaimed man whore—what the hell was wrong with me?

He was perfectly content to keep me at arm's length, and by saying it was just sex, I'd accepted his terms. Terms I never wanted in this weird state of limbo.

We weren't exclusive—we were nothing more than fuck buddies.

Nice job, Lauren. Way to respect yourself.

When Elizabeth invited me to tag along to an ultrasound appointment, I'd jumped at the opportunity to get away from the office and thoughts of Mike. My reprieve was short-lived as we'd run into David's Other Woman in the waiting room. I unleashed all my pent-up aggression from Mike on Jess in a way that made me cringe just thinking about it. It was later, while trying to collect my thoughts and lower my blood pressure out of the stroke range, that I overheard something I shouldn't have. Placing me smack dab in the middle of Other People's Problems.

I waited until I got back to the office before calling Mike to tell him what I'd overheard and my suspicions. Because he was a cop. Obviously. It wasn't like he'd become the person I wanted to call anytime something happened.

Our conversation had been brief and stilted, punctuated by the incessant clicking of his pen—something he seemed to do whenever he was deep in thought over something. Hours after we'd hung up, I realized we'd only discussed business. Like two complete strangers. He hadn't even had the courtesy to call me Red or throw in a darlin' at the end.

One week later and I couldn't focus on the mountain of tasks piling up on my desk. Elizabeth had cashed in her vacation hours and gone down to Galveston. With David. It seemed my friend's sleeping arrangements were just as convoluted as my own.

Instead of keeping busy covering Elizabeth's duty list, I was staring blankly at my computer screen, wondering why he hadn't called. The thought of him moving on to someone new left my stomach in knots.

"Good morning, Mulloy Dental. This is Lauren," I answered on autopilot.

"Lauren?" Elizabeth's teary voice came through the line.

Instantly on alert, I used my foot to shut the office door and sank down onto my chair. "What's wrong? Is the baby okay?"

Her sobs came harder, making it impossible to decipher what she was trying to say. "Sweetie, slow down. I can't understand you."

Several deep breaths later, Elizabeth choked out, "It's his. They faxed the paternity test results and Jess—they're having a son. I caught a cab to Houston. Just need you to help me find a flight back. Please."

After promising to see what I could do, she ended the call, and I went back to staring blankly at my computer. A tear fell to my keyboard, quickly followed by another. Soon, a downpour of emotions rained onto my desk. How was I supposed to help my friend? I could barely take care of myself.

There was a soft knock at my door and I fought to compose myself before weakly calling out, "Come in."

Proving it had a twisted sense of humor, the universe had delivered a swift kick to my lady-bits in the form of Mike Sullivan. I directed all of my attention to the surface of my desk and not the fact that he was standing in my tiny closet of an office. Close enough for me to smell the spice in his cologne.

He had never surprised me at work before. I didn't know what it meant, and the suspense was killing me.

"Red?" He slid coffee and a brown paper bag that smelled like cinnamon in front of me before kneeling beside my chair. "Hey, look at me."

I tried turning away, but he caught my chin, bringing my gaze to his. A tear spilled over onto my cheek as he searched my face, completely somber. As if whatever he was about to say caused him pain.

"I came to say I can't do it anymore," he admitted through a clenched jaw.

The words sent my heart plummeting through the floor. I'd known it wouldn't last, but hearing him say it still hurt like a bitch.

"Okay," I said, my voice sounding too calm even to me. I untangled myself from his grip, looking anywhere but at his face. If I did, I'd never be able to keep it together.

Everything ended eventually.

Mike was just another in a long line of heartbreaks I'd experienced in my twenty-seven years. Okay, so he was my first romantic relationship. Big deal. I would handle this setback the same way I'd handled all of life's disappointments—by pretending to be fine until I was alone and could silently sob into my hands or rage scream in the front seat of my car—depending on my mood.

Unfortunately, Mike didn't seem to catch the vibe and was still squatting next to my chair. Inexplicably. Maybe I was supposed to say or do something. Not like I had a lot of break-up experience.

He spun my chair around and rested his forearms on my thighs, holding me captive and making it impossible to avoid his beautiful but stupid face.

"Look at me," he commanded. I reluctantly faced him and the corner of his mouth tipped up in the smallest of grins.

Sadist.

"As I was saying, I can't do it. I can't do friends with benefits or fuck buddies—or whatever the hell the kids are calling it these days. Say something, Red. Anything."

My eyebrows were lost somewhere near my hairline. I was sure of it. "Wait—you mean, you're not here to tell me you never want to see me again?"

"You thought I was ending it and bringing you breakfast as—what —a consolation prize? God, I'm not that much of a dick, am I?"

I lifted my shoulder in a shrug, and he immediately began shaking his head.

"Don't answer that. I've made myself so goddamned crazy, thinking about you with someone else. I know I have an insane schedule right now, but I want more than a late-night fuck with you."

He shut up, clearly waiting for me to say something. Instead, I sat back, somehow holding on to my serious expression. "What are you saying?"

Mike rolled his eyes. "C'mon, Red. Don't make me spell it out for you. I want exclusivity and shit."

I pressed my lips together to keep from laughing. "And shit? How romantic. Where do I sign up?"

"Fuck. Just listen to me. I want you to be mine—my girlfriend. So, what do you say?" He rocked back on his heels and eyed me expectantly.

I nodded. "I say... okay."

He moved then, his mouth colliding roughly with mine. My heart beat out a frantic rhythm as I replayed his confession repeatedly in my head. *Girlfriend.* I swept my tongue over his lower lip, nipping his flesh between my teeth and accepting a truth I'd tried to deny for too long.

It had never been just sex. Our mouths moved together and even kissing seemed like the wrong word for what we were doing. This was possession.

I broke the connection almost reluctantly, pulling back to gather my wits and my thoughts. "Elizabeth," I panted.

Mike blinked in confusion. "What?"

"Airport paternity," I rushed to say, flubbing my words. "I mean, Elizabeth saw the paternity results and is on her way to the airport. I'm supposed to be finding her a flight home, but I keep coming back to what I told you I overheard at Elizabeth's appointment—"

"With Jess potentially bribing a nurse over a blood test," he finished for me, his thumb absently stroking the length of his jaw. I followed the movement, wondering why I couldn't have had an attack of conscience *after* our kiss. It wasn't like Elizabeth needed a flight immediately. She could have waited an extra five or ten minutes, allowing me to savor our first physical contact in a week, as well as my new title.

Girlfriend.

I sighed, and Mike's gaze instantly darkened. "Red, I'm gonna need you to keep it together and focus for a minute."

My smile faded. I wasn't a fan of Detective Mike and his condescending attitude. I much preferred Boyfriend Mike, who brought breakfast and kissed the hell out of me.

"Don't," he warned, tugging my hand from where it rested against my hip. "Please. You were right to end that kiss when you did, otherwise I might have been forced to take you on that little desk of yours. And let's be honest, darlin'. That hunk of wood isn't sturdy enough for all the kinky shit I've been dreaming up over the past week."

I released the breath I'd been holding, along with a low moan at the imagery his words incited. "O-okay. Strictly business."

"For now," he affirmed with a wink. "Now, why would Jess need to bribe a nurse, unless—"

"She's faking the pregnancy," I blurted out, gesturing to my computer screen. "I Googled it. You probably think it's crazy, but Jess doesn't look like someone who's twenty weeks pregnant—she doesn't even look like she's ten weeks pregnant!"

He laughed. "I was gonna go with what you said before, about the baby not being his, but this latest theory holds water, too. We just need proof."

"First, I have to find a flight for Elizabeth and then stall the divorce proceedings while I search for proof Jess is lying." I was rambling, trying to organize the chaos in my head.

"Lauren?"

"I don't understand why Elizabeth didn't tell David about the baby. Like, make him choose. But no, they're supposed to go before a judge next week and she's definitely not calling the divorce off now that she's seen the stupid paternity results."

"Red!"

I jumped and turned to where Mike was leaned against the door frame, clearly fighting the urge to laugh.

"This is serious, Mike."

He held his hands up in surrender. "Oh, I know, which is why I was going to suggest David file a motion for an emergency hearing—"

"How is speeding the divorce up going to help?" I interrupted to ask.

"We tell David that she's pregnant. In the emergency hearing, he'll ask for a pregnancy test. Bada-bing-bada-boom, more time to figure out what the hell Jess is up to." At my puzzled expression, he elaborated, "In the state of Texas, a judge won't grant a divorce when the woman is pregnant, except in domestic violence or other extreme situations, none of which applies to the Greene's."

Holy shit, maybe Detective Mike had his perks.

I took his face in my hands, plastering kisses along his jawline while murmuring, "Thank you. Thank you. Thank you."

His lips stretched into a wide grin. "If this is your way of saying thank you, remind me to do shit for you more often."

A sharp knock at the office door had us jumping apart guiltily. My lips and chin were still tingling from our kiss, meaning there was a fairly good chance I was suffering from a wicked case of beard burn. With no way of hiding it, I opened the door and hoped for the best.

"Mitzi's handpiece isn't working," Dr. Mulloy said, holding the offending between her thumb and index finger. "Can you call Henry Schein and find out if it's still under warranty?"

The color drained from Mike's face when he saw her, probably remembering how she'd behaved at David and Elizabeth's wedding. I mean, if I went to a wedding and got groped, I'd never forget the person's face.

"Absolutely. Dr. Mulloy, this is my boyfriend, Mike Sullivan."

He extended his hand, and she snatched it up. A little too quickly for my liking. "Oh, hello," she purred. "Pleasure to meet you."

He nodded and tried to retrieve his hand, clearly uncomfortable with the predatory look in her eyes. "Likewise."

She grinned again, letting her gaze linger on his crotch before moving back to me. "Lauren, just let me know what they say."

I agreed and closed the door behind her with a barely repressed growl. Mike stood in the same spot, completely pale.

"Are you okay?" I asked, running my hands over his chest. "I promise you this, she won't get handsy with you again. If she tries, I'll kick her ass."

He managed a weak smile and pulled me back into his arms. "I didn't know she was your boss."

I sighed, "Yeah, for seven years now. Lucky me."

He cupped my jaw in his calloused hand. "I've got to get back to the office. Why don't you call David while I make a few phone calls of my own—see if I can't get this nurse to crack. Oh, and Red? Be wearing this when I come over tonight. Got a real Boss Bitch vibe about it that I'd like to explore further."

CHAPTER TWENTY-FIVE

Lauren: September 2014 (Age: 27)

"I did it!"

Monica laughed on the other end of the line. "I think you missed your calling in life, Nancy Drew. You should've been a private investigator."

I leaned against the courthouse bricks and pulled my shirt away from my body, allowing the breeze to cool my overheated skin. When David told me he and Elizabeth were going to the courthouse this afternoon, I'd gone a little overboard.

Who knew it was poor form to burst into a courtroom, shouting, "I have information the court must hear!"

The court police hadn't welcomed my intrusion and were in the process of prying my hands from the courtroom door when David swept in, stealing my thunder.

I'd envisioned entering, guns blazing and documentation in hand. David and Elizabeth would have been in the middle of tearfully admitting they couldn't make their marriage work when I appeared, demanding they stop the proceedings. After brandishing the actual paternity test, I would have earned the respect of everyone present.

In reality, David and Elizabeth were in the middle of withdrawing their petition to divorce when I showed up. After soothing the cops' ruffled feathers, he'd led me to some random desk in the middle of a large room—nothing at all like I'd pictured in my fantasy.

My only moment of glory was when Nurse Rose broke the news. Jess had indeed faked her pregnancy and the paternity test results, using Elizabeth's blood. Seeing how happy David and Elizabeth were to discover they were having a son together somewhat made up for it, though.

"So, what's next, Detective? Got any other cases on your agenda?" Monica teased.

"You up for an early dinner? I could tell you all about my life as a PI on the mean streets of Lubbock."

"Oh yeah? I think I caught most of it," she said, her voice coming from behind me. I turned, shocked to see her standing on the courthouse steps. "Surprise."

I gasped, "I can't believe you came all the way down here!"

She watched my face hopefully. "You texted, and call me a sap, but I wanted to know how it turned out for them. You were very good."

I laughed and shook my head. "No, I was awful! Geez Louise, I had no idea what I was doing. Courtroom dramas need to step up their game. They are misleading the people."

"I thought you did great." When she reached out to squeeze my arm, I didn't pull away. Life was funny. Over the last month, we'd seen each other every week for coffee and things were going really well.

Not so well that I was ready to tell Mike about her, but maybe soon.

My phone began ringing, and I rifled through my purse for it. Seeing Mike's name on the screen never failed to send my pulse racing, but this time it was for an entirely different reason.

"Just give me a second," I mumbled to Monica, before hurrying down the sidewalk as if afraid to be spotted anywhere near my mother. "Hey there."

"Hey yourself," Mike drawled. "How'd it go?"

"Um," I squeaked, debating whether to tell him about the part where I threatened to call him down to deal with the court police.

"Really great. They decided not to go through with the divorce—hooray! How's it going with The Thing? Had any breaks in the case?"

"So when David said you burst into the courthouse like it was an episode of *Law & Order*, he was..."

"Exaggerating, obviously."

He chuckled. "I miss you."

I held my breath, afraid to ruin the moment. The man had me tied up in knots. If I opened my mouth, I love you might come pouring out.

After clearing my throat and any thoughts of proclaiming my undying love for the man on the other end of the line, I asked, "Are you working late tonight?"

He clicked his pen with a sigh. "Yep. I'm trying, Red. Believe me, I'd much rather be with you."

I nodded, trying to regain control of my emotions.

"You still there?"

I took a deep breath. "Yeah. I'm nodding."

I could hear the smile in his voice as he replied, "Right. I thought I sensed that. Listen, if I get out of here at a decent time, I'll swing by."

"Sounds good." My voice sounded falsely bright to my own ears, but he didn't seem to notice. I thought I knew what I was signing up for when I agreed to be his girlfriend a few days ago—thinking it'd be like the beginning of summer.

Instead, he was still investigating the case of the missing model, while juggling loads of other cases, too. I'd sacrificed dinner at seven for sex at three AM—or whatever ungodly hour he stepped away from his desk. Not that the sex wasn't amazing. I just wanted a deeper connection.

Call me old-fashioned, but I wanted intimate talks over long dinners. I wanted to argue over where to eat. I wanted to take a weekend trip out of the city.

I wanted a full eight hours of sleep.

I was making stupid mistakes at work due to sleep deprivation. It wouldn't be long before Dr. Mulloy noticed, either.

Maybe I wasn't cut out to be a cop's girlfriend.

"Everything okay?" Monica asked as I slipped the phone back into my purse.

I pushed the worry down and nodded. "All good. Let's grab that dinner."

CHAPTER TWENTY-SIX

Mike: October 2014 (Age: 31)

"We've got an issue."

It was the last thing I wanted to hear from Grey on a night that was supposed to be about Lauren.

Making her mine had come with its own set of problems. Like realizing the friend of hers I fucked in Galveston was actually her boss. Any chance of me seeing more of Lauren during daytime hours evaporated in an instant. Thanks to my shitty decision to fuck Solid Seven Sandra, I was stuck on nights for the foreseeable future. The few instances I'd managed to sneak away from work early, Grey was there to cock-block me with club shit.

It was taking a toll on me.

Just sex had been my M.O. for as long as I could remember. All the benefits of a relationship without the hassle of an actual relationship.

Until her.

The woman had slipped past my defenses since day one, consuming my thoughts and turning me into a possessive asshole almost overnight.

Just sex should have been right up my alley. Instead, I damn near drove myself mad, thinking about her with anyone who wasn't me. I knew she was about to come when she bit down on the left corner of her lower lip.

Me.

No one else.

God, I sounded like David. If I didn't watch it, I'd be the guy picking fights with strangers just for looking at her.

I met Grey outside the city.

"What do we have?"

He gestured up the road and clenched his jaw, the veins in his neck fighting to break through his skin as he forced out, "He was just a fuckin' kid."

I mentally prepared myself and headed toward the downed bike. The first thing I noticed was the prospect patch. The second was the fact that someone had gutted the kid like a goddamn fish. Overlapping stab wounds had an enormous gaping hole in his back.

His wide eyes met mine when I rolled him over with my boot.

Jesus.

He couldn't have been much older than eighteen. I thought I'd even seen him around once or twice back when he was still a hang around.

Grey broke the eerie stillness. "I'm takin' care of this tonight. Need your help."

I pinched the bridge of my nose, but nodded. "We thinking SOD?"

He shook his head. "I don't fuckin' know who else it would be, but seein' how they have a hard-on for knives, I'm bringing Comedian along. Need you to keep this under the radar, unless you're lookin' to earn your skull and crossbones."

Members who killed for the club earned a skull and crossbones patch. Something I had no desire to earn.

"Slight problem with that," I said. "I ain't a member of your club, old man. And I've got no plans to patch in."

He slapped my shoulder after we placed the prospect in the back of his truck. "Yet. Someday you'll come around to it. Be a helluva lot more fun than sitting behind a fuckin' desk all day."

He was right.

If I'd known all that being a detective entailed, I would have stayed on patrol. Before the tediousness of working a case start to finish, I was the guy on scene, collecting evidence and gathering information to pass along to the detectives.

The grass was always greener...

When I was on patrol, I wanted to be a detective. I wanted to work a case from start to finish. Like a puzzle. Now I was a detective doing just that and longed to be on patrol again.

I could mask a lot more of the club's activities than I would have if I'd remained on patrol. Somehow, that seemed more like a con than a pro, though.

"Monica says your girl is over the fuckin' moon for you," Grey noted casually, as if discussing our love lives was something we did every day. My thoughts came to a grinding halt as I wracked my brain for a Monica.

I turned to him, keeping my face blank. "Who?"

"Monica." Sensing I wasn't following, he elaborated. "Lauren's mother? Torch's Ol' Lady? Dark blue Toyota that was stolen? C'mon, Mikey, you know who I'm talkin' about."

My palms were slick with sweat. Fear was a strange reaction, considering I was standing mere feet from a dead body and hadn't thought twice about it.

Lauren was on speaking terms with the addict. I was new at the relationship stuff, but this felt like it at least deserved a mention.

Why hadn't she told me?

"The stolen car was Lauren's," I said to myself, putting the pieces in place. If I'd known, I would have—what? Outed myself as an associate of SPMC? Knowing she kept the relationship with her mother from me hurt, but it wasn't as if I wasn't keeping secrets of my own.

"Monica reached out to Lauren after getting clean—guess she wanted to make amends for the shit she did when she was fucked up." Grey shrugged and said, "Anyway, with you bein' a badge and all, makes sense Lauren wouldn't mention it."

The truth hit me like a sucker punch. It made perfect sense. But not for the same reason. The only conversations Lauren and I had as of late were in the bedroom, and this wasn't a topic for pillow talk.

"Haven't really seen much of her lately," I admitted with a sigh. I'd wanted to keep Lauren far away from the club and their shit. If her mother was in with a patch, it became virtually impossible. She could end up in the cross-hairs of this war as easily as any of us.

As if reading my thoughts, Grey added, "I'm keepin' an eye on her. With the Sons around, nobody's safe."

He waved a hand over the prospect's body. "You and I both know if they find out you're helpin' us, she'll be the target they go after next, Mikey."

Bile rose in my throat.

I couldn't keep her from the club, but I'd be damned if I didn't keep her safe.

CHAPTER TWENTY-SEVEN

Mike: October 2014 (Age: 31)

"Mmm... hello?"

Hearing the sleep in her voice, I glanced down at my watch and immediately winced. It was much later than I'd planned, but Grey had yet another mess for me to clean up.

"Hey, darlin'," I whispered. "Sorry to wake you."

"No, I was up—doing stuff," she said with a yawn.

Sure she was.

If I knew her, she'd been asleep since eight. "Have you seen the moon tonight?"

Lauren yawned again. Louder this time. "Hmm—the moon? Why? Is it doing tricks?"

I chuckled. "Something like that. Why don't you step outside and look?"

"Okay," she whispered softly. "Let me get my shoes."

The lock clicked on her front door, followed by the telltale squeak of it opening.

"You might have to go downstairs to get the full effect."

"Mike, is this really necessary? I'm pretty tired."

"Once in a lifetime sight, Red. Just go downstairs and head toward the street. Then you'll see what I'm talking about."

Lauren dragged herself downstairs, rubbing the sleep from her eyes, and I ducked out of sight behind some shrubbery. After taking a couple more steps, she stopped and stared up at the sky with a frown.

"Can you just tell me what I'm looking for?"

"How about the guy right in front of you?" I asked, standing up.

She stumbled back, bringing a hand up to her chest with a gasp. "Jesus Christ, Mike! You can't just go popping up out of bushes, scaring people."

I retrieved the cupcake with an unlit candle sticking out of it from the sidewalk, holding it out like a peace offering. "I wanted to be the first one to wish you a Happy Birthday, Red. Fucking candle wouldn't stay lit, though."

Lauren grinned as she took it from my hand. "You got me a birthday cake?"

"Technically, a birthday *cup*cake, but close enough."

Had Monica ever been sober long enough to celebrate her daughter's birthday? Given the tears, I assumed she hadn't.

She wrapped her free arm around my neck and whispered, "Could you be any sweeter?"

I considered the last week and a half. I wasn't sweet.

I was a fucking monster.

I'd been called in to help dispose of six Sons of Death members—well, what they'd left of them. Grey made sure they met the same end that Ian, the prospect, did. Kid hadn't even earned his road name yet.

SODMC wouldn't file a missing persons report. This was tit for tat. They now knew the score—take out one of Grey's and expect to lose six in retaliation.

I thought it was bad before, but this had morphed into a full-on war I had an active role in. Neither side would back down, and the bodies were going to keep stacking up.

Brushing the thought aside, I scooped her up and carried her over to my truck. "Got something I wanna show you, if can spare some time."

Lauren looked up at me with a smirk. "Oh, well, I had a date with my bed, but I guess I can spare some time for you."

The minute she buckled in, I handed her a bouquet of daisies. "Gift number two."

"Well, well, well. Look who's just full of surprises," she said with a lifted brow. "Where are we going?"

I made a right, already shaking my head. "Uh-uh, Darlin'. You're just gonna have to wait and see."

Grey had purchased some land about fifteen miles from town. With the sheer amount of blood on my hands, I figured he owed me one. I parked and got out, leaving Lauren dozing with her head against the window.

It took a minute to light the small bonfire and arrange the blankets in the truck's bed before I was ready to wake the birthday girl. She looked up at me with a sleepy smile as I opened the passenger door, keeping a hand on her shoulder to steady her.

"Is it time for my next present now?" she murmured.

Goddamn, I could wake up to that face for the rest of my life.

She cupped my cheek, suddenly alert. "Are you okay? You just got really pale."

I nodded. "Yeah. Low blood sugar or some shit. Come on." I led her around to the bed of the truck. "Happy Birthday!"

Lauren took it all in before laughing wildly. "Oh, my god! A bonfire?" She thrust her arms up in victory and fell back against the blankets with a contented sigh. "I've never been to a bonfire before."

I'd spent maybe ten dollars total on her gifts, but she was reacting as I'd dropped ten thousand. The problem was I hadn't known what she liked and had no fucking clue what to buy her. "You like it?"

She nodded with glowing eyes, cheeks flushed from the fire. "This is the best birthday ever."

I could've beaten my chest at that comment. I'd fucking done it.

After climbing up to join her, I reached for the wine I'd stashed among the blankets and filled a couple of Solo cups.

"A toast," I said, lifting mine. "To the birthday girl. Who is going to need a shitload of caffeine to survive the day."

We tapped the cups together and took a drink, savoring a silence that was anything but awkward. Lauren stared into the flames, one leg crossed over the other and a content smile playing on her lips. I stared at her, captivated by the strands of copper hair that had fallen over one eye.

When she reached up to tuck it behind her ear, I knew. I could search the entire fucking world and never find anyone who made me feel like she did.

I loved her.

Maybe it made me a pussy, but someday—someday, I'd tell her that in the middle of nowhere, next to a bonfire, I fell in love.

Sensing she was being watched, Lauren turned and lifted to pull her pajama pants down. It had become a habit for us. A way to pass the wee hours of the morning. My cock might have been ready to go, but it wasn't why I'd brought her here.

Balancing the cup between my legs, I pulled her back down. "Whoa there, darlin'. Slow down. That's not what tonight's about."

She cocked her head to the side and reached down to cup me through my jeans. "You sure about that, Tex? Seems a big part of you thinks that's exactly what tonight is about."

Jesus. I'd created a monster.

I swallowed the groan on my lips with a tight nod. "Just lay with me."

I lay back, and she nestled up against my side, one leg thrown over mine. Feeling the need to impress her, I began pointing out the various constellations Grey had taught me as a kid. "See the one that looks like a head on a winding tail? That's Aquarius, son of the king of Troy. Apparently, Zeus wanted to fuck him, so he turned him into an eagle and carried him off to serve as cupbearer to the gods—which is probably a euphemism."

"What about that one?" She pointed north of Aquarius.

"That would be Pegasus. See, Poseidon fucked Medusa, and she gave birth to Pegasus. Pretty sure I would've asked for a paternity test if I were Poseidon. The hero, Bellerophon, tamed him and rode him to defeat the chimera. But Zeus turned him into a fucking constellation —probably because Pegasus turned him down. Homeboy was a freak like that."

I was basing most of my material on stories Grey had told when I was a kid. The details had gotten a little fuzzy over the years.

She traced the tattoos on my arm. "I love you, Mike."

I went silent, trying to determine if it was the right time to confess I felt the same.

Sensing my hesitation, she added, "You don't have to say it back. I just wanted you to know that. No one's ever gone to this much trouble for my birthday and I—"

I rolled onto my side and faced her. It was right there, but no matter how artfully my brain arranged them, my mouth couldn't form the words.

Instead, I did what I knew best. I wrapped my right hand up in her hair and grazed my teeth against the point where her jawline and ear met. Her skin went from pink to red, back arching up off the blanket. Amid quiet moans, I inched my way down toward her mouth. She surprised me by tilting her face up, forcing my mouth to hers. And there it was—the jolt of attraction that sent my brain into a sexual frenzy.

Kissing her was the culmination of every wet dream I'd ever had.

Lauren must have felt the same way because her hands suddenly had a mind of their own. Her hips arched up, seeking mine, and I went into a pushup position as I moved over her. I took her hands in one of mine and pinned them over her head, our mouths coming together in a rough collision.

"Can we have sex now? Please?"

Her pleading tone brought a cocky grin to my face. "What's the matter, darlin'? All that Zeus talk got you hot and bothered?"

She tucked her bottom lip between her teeth and nodded. From there, instinct took over. I shoved my feelings to the back burner once again. Just like my old man had taught me.

CHAPTER TWENTY-EIGHT

Lauren: November 2014 (Age: 28)

"Apply the wax in a thin layer in the same direction as the hair growth," I read before taking a drink from the bottle of pinot noir sitting on the bathroom counter. I hadn't bothered with a glass because I was all class, all the time.

It was Mike's birthday and I should have been lying on my back with my legs spread like a frog's, but my esthetician, Annie, had canceled on me at the last minute.

Faced with the prospect of having to dig out the razor blade or tell him he was going to be taking a trip to the wilderness to find his birthday present, I decided to give at-home waxing a whirl.

He was supposed to be leaving work at seven, which left me with just under two hours to de-hair and slip into something revealing. Mike had gone to great lengths ensuring that my birthday was special. The least I could do was make sure that my lady-bits were in presentable party clothes for him.

Forty-five minutes and half a bottle of wine later, I was second-guessing the wisdom of my decision.

Using Mike's bathroom counter to prop my leg up, I took the popsicle stick of wax and applied it to my skin in a thin layer, just like the instructions said. "Thirty seconds to harden," I read aloud, skimming over the next section. "And then pull off in the opposite direction of hair growth."

Easy peasy.

I caught sight of myself in the mirror and immediately had to look away. No wonder they charged so much for these.

The view was... something else.

Feeling as though thirty seconds had come and gone, I tested the bottom edge of the wax before quickly yanking it up and off. I exhaled slowly and contorted my body to reveal my handiwork.

Okay. Not bad.

I didn't need an esthetician and eighty dollars. I was going to keep my dignity and do my own waxing from here on out.

I got through the next three sections without issue, making excellent time. My plan was to be in his bed with a bow wrapped around me in the next half-hour. There was Chinese takeout in the fridge downstairs and *Saving Private Ryan* waiting in the DVD player.

Everything was moving along swimmingly. While waiting for the next section to harden, I perused the instruction sheet, doing a double take on the large warning near the bottom.

WARNING! Never use on nipples, perianal, vaginal/genital areas, or on hairs inside nostrils, ears or on eyelids/eyelashes.

Jesus, who would be stupid enough to put it on their eyelashes?

A door slammed downstairs just as I lifted the edge of the wax.

Shit.

He wasn't supposed to be home for another hour. I rushed to yank the wax off and threw it into the trash can, wincing at the sting.

Was that red?

A soft knock sounded at the bathroom door.

"Uh, just give me a second," I mumbled, watching in horror as blood dripped steadily from the newly waxed area. This never happened at Annie's.

I was trying to work out how much blood loss was dangerous when the door burst open. In my rush to cover myself, I slipped on the puddle at my feet and fell back on my ass with a whimpered groan.

"Who the hell are you?" The stranger at the door shrieked, clutching the frame for support.

I'd never seen the woman before in my life and searched desperately for something to cover up with, as my hands weren't doing a stellar job.

"Uh," I said, fighting to keep the fear out of my voice. "Could you just give me a minute to, uh, cover everything?"

"Let me guess, he blew you off so you've broken in to get your revenge?" she asked, rolling her eyes. The snarky smirk on her face disappeared when she finally noticed the blood. "Jesus, what is this —*Fatal Attraction*? Did you cut your wrists? Got a bunny boiling on the stove?"

Well, she was just a barrel full of sunshine.

I reached up and snagged a washcloth from the vanity, holding it over my lady-bits to retain some sense of modesty.

"If you must know, I had a minor mishap with the wax. And there is no bunny or anything else on the stove, because I can't cook. Also, I'm Mike's girlfriend. Probably should have led with that one."

Noting my culinary skills before my relationship status was a clear sign I'd lost a lot of blood. Anything I said beyond this point couldn't be held against me.

The older woman's eyes widened. "Girlfriend? You've got to be joking. Michael doesn't have a girlfriend!"

Bleeding out and now thoroughly pissed off, I snapped, "And who the fuck are you to know so much about Mike's social life?"

Her hand shot up onto her hip. "I'm his mother, Betsy."

Oh, fuck.

I pasted a smile onto my face and extended my hand up to hers, immediately backpedaling. "Lauren. Pleasure to meet you."

She gave me a look of disgust as if I'd just offered her a live snake, refusing to take it. "What have you done to yourself?" She asked, gesturing toward the bloody washcloth. I didn't miss the way her nose turned up.

I slowly got back to my feet and immediately had to grip onto the counter as a wave of dizziness overtook me. "Ooh, watch out. The floor is wobbly right here."

Sensing she was about to witness me faint, Betsy sprang into action, grabbing my arm and leading me over to the edge of the tub. "Sit." I obeyed, and she knelt in front of me. "Let's see it."

Okay, having my boyfriend's mother all up in my lady-bits within five minutes of meeting was not how I pictured tonight going. It was a scenario I hadn't pictured playing out at any point in my life.

Reluctantly, I dropped the washcloth and spread my legs, fighting the flush creeping up my neck.

Betsy turned back to her purse and retrieved a small first aid kit. Before investigating the source of the blood, she calmly retrieved a pair of latex gloves and slipped them on.

I raised an eyebrow but kept my mouth shut and focused on the ceiling, praying the tub would swallow me whole.

"There's a small tear on the lip. You're not supposed to wax there— you know that, right? It's just for the bikini area." Her voice held a tone that only parents seemed to master.

I nodded. "I thought that was more of a guideline. How in the hell am I supposed to get all the hair off, then?"

She lifted her head with a frown. "Go to a professional." With a sigh, she added, "I've got some Steri-Strips that I'll put on it, but if that doesn't work, then you'll probably need to go in for stitches."

I shook my head. "Absolutely not. I would rather bleed to death on his bathroom floor."

She pulled a thin tube from the kit and handed it to me. "That's a bit dramatic, wouldn't you say? Apply this antibiotic cream three times a day and keep the area clean."

I marveled at her. "Are you a doctor?"

She stripped the gloves off and tossed them into the trashcan with a laugh. "No, just a mom. All moms know these things."

Apparently not all moms. Monica certainly never had a first aid kit in her purse. Knowing her, she probably didn't even know where the damn thing was located.

Once I was mostly put back together, I began the arduous task of cleaning up the floor. I was still naked from the waist down, but didn't see the point to covering up now that she'd seen everything.

"Can we agree to never speak of this to Mike?" I asked, after mopping up the last spot of blood.

I wasn't able to keep my modesty intact. The least she could do was help me keep this secret.

Betsy pursed her lips. "Well, that depends, Lana."

"It's Lauren," I corrected.

"I don't think it really matters, does it? Anyway, I just came into town for my son's birthday and I got us a reservation for two at his favorite steakhouse."

Suddenly feeling completely exposed, I grabbed a towel and wrapped it around my waist before sitting back down on the edge of the tub. "I'm going to go out on a limb here and assume you won't change that to three, right?"

"No. Now, you can leave and we'll pretend like this whole thing never happened. You stay, and he'll know about this within five minutes of hitting that door, along with my strong suspicion that you might have an STD. Are we clear, Lydia?" Betsy might have been beautiful, were it not for the pinched expression etched on her face.

It looked as if she'd been sucking lemons since birth.

I took in the half empty bottle of wine on the counter, the used wax strips in the trashcan, and me, perched half-naked on the tub.

It wasn't the most flattering representation.

I could have stood my ground and argued my way out of it, but my ego was bruised and my body was numb. I'd only ever been with her son, but Betsy had painted me as a slut. A diseased slut, at that.

I stalked past her without a word and began gathering my clothes from Mike's bedroom. She watched from the doorway with crossed arms, probably there to ensure I didn't steal anything.

"You know, I'm not what you think I am," I said over my shoulder. "I've been with your son since June—I love him. That might be hard for you to understand, but we make each other happy."

"And does he love you, too?"

My heart fell to my feet, but I kept my expression blank. "I think he does."

Her voice became impatient. "Has he told you?"

I shook my head and zipped up my jeans before reaching for my purse. "No. He hasn't told me."

It wasn't true. He had told me on the phone once, only to take it back later. He was close to telling me. I felt it. Something was still holding him back, though.

Her eyes went shiny for a brief second before the mask fell back into place. "Well, maybe he's just passing the time with you."

CHAPTER TWENTY-NINE

Lauren: November 2014 (Age: 28)

"She said he was just passing the time with me," I sighed, sticking another spoonful of rocky road ice cream in my mouth. It took three ibuprofen and two ice packs between my legs before I felt some relief.

The ice cream ha

'dn't hurt either.

Monica dropped her empty spoon back into the bowl. "That's bullshit. The man's in love with you. She knows it and just wants to intimidate you. What did you say?"

Knowing I couldn't call Mike and throw his mother under a bus, especially when I wasn't entirely sure he'd side with me, I called Monica. Not only had she dropped everything, but she'd shown up with my favorite ice cream—I was surprised she even remembered.

"I didn't say anything," I groaned, feeling like a wuss. "Just told Mike I had a migraine and called you."

He'd been clearly upset when I canceled, but what could I have said? *'Hey, your mom pieced my lady-bits back together and is now blackmailing me to get the evening alone with you?'*

Monica reached over and squeezed my leg. "She'll come around. How could she not? You're adorable."

I rolled my eyes. "You're just saying that because you're my mom."

Her smile grew. "Haven't been called Mom in twenty years. I'd forgotten how much I enjoyed hearing it until now."

She was right. I'd called her Monica for as long as I could remember.

"Well, you are my mother," I said, shrugging it off. "Enough about me. Tell me something about you. Something good to balance out this shit day."

"Okay." Monica grinned. "After seven hours of testing and one day of waiting impatiently, I passed my GED."

Ice cream forgotten, I threw my arms around her neck. "What? I didn't know you were going to take it. That's awesome!"

"I wanted to surprise you. I've been thinking about it since May and I thought, what the hell? It was time to make some lemonade with all the lemons life had given me. Like you did."

Her hopeful expression crushed the last line of my defenses. I leaned in for another hug, breathing in her familiar scent and feeling like a child again.

"I'm really proud of you, Monica," I managed after pulling away. "What's next?"

"Well, I'm going to college," she admitted, not making any attempt to hide her tears. "I've always wanted to be a nurse. I'm forty-four now —there's no time like the present, you know?"

I stirred the remaining ice cream around in the bowl before tentatively asking, "So, the bikers—they don't care about all of this? You getting your teeth fixed and going off to college?"

The smile faded. "I don't belong to them. I belong to Torch. He was an addict too, so it's like fate, you know? He said removing the reminders helped keep him clean, so he paid for my teeth and encouraged me to finish high school."

Without thinking, I blurted out, "Do you miss using?"

Immediately, I wanted to kick myself for it.

While Monica didn't seem bothered by the question, she was much quieter when she admitted, "Activities keep the mind occupied and not thinking about the next fix. Do I miss it? Yes. Every single day. But I keep a list in my pocket—all my reasons not to. There are some highs you can't get from drugs, like you calling me Mom just now. That's better than any fix."

I placed my ice cream down on the coffee table, staring blankly at the television.

Could I go back to having a mother?

Was past hurt so easily forgiven in the light of sobriety?

A soft knock on the door saved me from having to answer my own questions, and I eagerly hopped up to answer it.

Mike leaned against the brick exterior, mouth curved up in a sexy grin and a grocery bag dangling from his wrist.

"What are you doing here?"

"You said you had a migraine—thought I'd stop by and see if you needed a doctor."

My skin instantly prickled with lust, but Monica was less than six feet away. That, and my vagina was being held together with medical tape.

"I'm good, Tex. You should be out enjoying your birthday, not worrying about me. A few hours of sleep and I'll be good as new."

Why wasn't he out with his mother?

Mike peered over my shoulder, his grin fading. "Do you have company? I could have sworn I heard someone else when I got here."

Moment of truth.

I could lie and say it was the TV or get it over with and introduce him. I'd leave out the bikers. He didn't need those kinds of details. It'd be like Galveston, where we made it up. She would be Monica, recovering addict with a large inheritance and I would be the girlfriend who hadn't had her lady-bits in his mother's hands just hours before.

With a deep breath, I ushered him inside. "Mike, this is my mother, Monica McGuire. Monica, this is my boyfriend, Mike Sullivan."

He beamed and shook her hand while she shot me a grateful look.

Mom.

It was funny how such a small word could cause a shift in perception. As she and Mike talked, I realized it was the first time in my life that I felt like I was a normal person. My mom was meeting my boyfriend—no big deal.

If she could turn her entire life around, then maybe it wasn't crazy to think that Betsy could learn to like me. She'd come around once she saw how good he and I were together.

Right?

CHAPTER THIRTY

Mike: December 2014 (Age: 32)

"We had an agreement," Betsy hissed, reaching around Lauren to grab plates from the cabinet, narrowly missing her head with the door.

Lauren jumped out of the way and loudly whispered, "We had an agreement I wouldn't go out for his birthday. You never said anything about accepting his invitation to dinner so I could meet his mother."

I watched them continue bickering back and forth before stepping in. "Good to see that you two have met. I'm just gonna go upstairs and change clothes."

They both froze and then slowly turned around to face me.

"You're home early!" my mother exclaimed in an overly bright voice.

I'd envisioned them meeting and instantly becoming best friends—not trying to take each other's heads off with kitchen cabinets. Then again, my mother hung around my father voluntarily, so her idea of a good time and mine differed slightly.

Lauren kept her gaze on the counter, refusing to look at me. She was bright red, from the tips of her ears down to her collarbones. "Red, mind if I talk to you upstairs?"

I didn't miss the triumphant look my mother shot her as she left the kitchen. Meeting her mother had been a hell of a lot easier. Sure, she'd conspicuously left SPMC out of the introductions, but it was a step in the right direction.

So much so that I'd invited my mom out to meet her.

We reached my bedroom, and I turned to her. "So, you met my mother on my birthday?"

"Yes, I met your mother on your birthday. It didn't go well. End of story."

I loosened my tie. "Care to elaborate?"

"Am I being formally charged with something, Detective?" she asked, crossing her arms over her chest.

Damn. My mother had done a number on her.

I slipped out of my button-down and tossed it on the bed before approaching her. "Darlin', you know if I'm gonna question you, I'm using the cuffs to keep you compliant."

When that didn't earn me a grin, I began to worry. I pulled her into my arms, rubbing small circles along her back. "So, you and my mom don't get along. Big fucking deal. It doesn't change how I feel about you."

"I met your mom while I was performing a Brazilian wax on myself. She walked in right as I ripped the wax off, taking part of my labia majora—or was it minora—with me. She Steri-Stripped my lady-bits and then told me to stay away from you," she mumbled against my chest.

Steri-Stripped her lady-bits?

I brought my fist up to my mouth to keep from laughing.

Jesus, I would've paid good money to see a video of that.

My mother was the First-Aid Queen—had pieced me and my father back together more times than I could count. Lauren's confession also explained why I'd only gotten a blowjob on my birthday, despite my best efforts to return the favor.

She pushed off of my chest and glared angrily up at me. "Don't laugh at me. It could've happened to anyone. She also said she was going to tell you she thought I had an STD."

The laughter died in my throat. "She did what?"

I'd watched my mother self-destruct on multiple occasions after getting involved in my father's bullshit. I'd finally reached a point where it no longer affected me. She was a grown ass woman, and if she wanted to involve herself with a dumpster fire of a human, it was on her.

But breaking up my relationship with Lauren under some guise of caring crossed the line.

"Stay here," I commanded, before jogging back down the stairs.

My mother sat at the dining table with an expectant smile on her face. "How'd that go? Did you let her down gently?"

The urge to throttle her was so strong I had to lean down and grip the edge of the table with both hands. "Are you really trying to get rid of the one person who makes me happy?"

Her face paled. "You mean you two are serious?"

I rolled my eyes. "Cut the shit, Mom."

Lauren poked her head around the corner. "I'm just gonna go—give you two a chance to catch up."

"No, your ass is staying," I growled. "If anyone needs to leave, it's Betsy over here."

Lauren's phone rang, and she disappeared into the kitchen to answer it, leaving my mother and me to our stand-off.

"You need to apologize."

My mother finally managed a small nod. "Stay here. I'll go talk to her."

I was straightening the napkin next to my plate and debating on whether to move the silverware next when Lauren called my name.

"What's wrong? What did you do now?" I pointed at my mother, who began shaking her head, stabbing a finger in Lauren's direction.

"It's David," she said, covering the speaker. "He said Elizabeth received a text from me to go up to the office to print tomorrow's schedule in case we get snowed in tonight."

"Okay, and? What's the problem?"

Lauren frowned. "I didn't text her. He's up there now, and she's not answering her phone. I'm going to go let him in—"

"Truck. Now. I'll drive. Mom—"

She nodded and patted my arm. "I know the routine. I'll be here when you get back."

I had the dash lights flashing before my truck even hit the end of the dirt driveway.

"Lauren, did he say anything else?"

She shook her head. "No, just that she'd left after receiving the text and now he can't get a hold of her. Who would've texted her?"

I shook my head and ran my third red light. "I don't know. You're sure you didn't text her?"

She frowned. "I think I'd remember if I texted her. Maybe it was a glitch?"

We pulled into the parking lot of the dental office on two wheels. Lauren's hands shook violently as she worked to get the door unlocked and the lights on.

We were dealing with a crime scene.

Elizabeth's coat and purse were lying on the floor near some blood and what had to be vomit. I grabbed my cell phone and pulled up the tracking app on my phone, on the off-chance she had her phone. It pinged her location south of town and moving.

"Shit! Laur—call 911. Do not, under any circumstances, tell them I was here. David, truck!"

Lauren stared at a bloody handprint in horror, hand pressed to her mouth. "Mike, what's going on?"

"Somehow, she made it out of here with her phone." I held up the screen. "Whoever has her is just outside the city limits, heading south."

"Look at me," I commanded, taking Lauren by the shoulders and leading her away from the blood. She was clearly in shock, but I didn't have time to ease her fears or promise her everything would be okay.

"Need you to do what I say, alright? Tell the cops you came up here to meet Elizabeth and found this—don't touch anything. Okay?"

If I stuck around to go through the proper channels, Elizabeth would be another Katya—a case that grew colder every single day.

She bobbed her head in a shaky nod. "O-okay."

"That's my girl." I pressed my lips to her temple and jogged back to my truck, retrieving my Glock from the side pocket. David took the spare Smith & Wesson with a confused frown.

"We're gonna need these."

Meteorologists were calling this blizzard the storm of the century. Whoever took Elizabeth had to have known that and was counting on the snow to delay a proper search.

After double-checking her location, I fired off a quick text to Grey.

Me: 911—33°17'04.4"N 101°56'52.4"W.

He responded immediately.

10-4. North location.

"David, watch this," I ordered, passing my phone over the console. "Make sure her location doesn't move from that spot. Okay?"

He nodded, fear in his eyes. "She's twenty-eight weeks pregnant. Who would take her?"

I had an idea. And if I was right, we needed to get there sooner rather than later.

"We're going to find her," I vowed.

"Drive as fast as you fucking can, Mike."

I mashed the pedal to the floor. David gave me updates periodically, but otherwise, the cab of the truck was deathly quiet.

It was like Patrick all over again.

"I want to kill this guy myself," David said, yanking me back to the present.

"What?"

He continued talking, staring straight ahead. "You told me if there was ever a time that I needed it, you would cover for me. I wanna cash in that favor now."

I nodded immediately. "Consider it done."

CHAPTER THIRTY-ONE

Mike: December 2014 (Age: 32)

We tracked Elizabeth to an old farmhouse, hearing a scream the second we left the truck. The wind picked up, pelting us with sleet as we ran up the steps and inside.

There was nothing but silence as we quickly searched the house, coming up with nothing but empty rooms.

I pointed to a closed door and held a finger to my lips, mentally trying to convey the element of surprise was the only thing keeping us alive. "It's a basement. Go."

Instead of heeding my warning, David ran down the stairs, gun in hand. I made it all of three steps before realizing my suspicion was correct.

Landon Scott.

He had his arm around Elizabeth's throat, probably to keep her quiet. His grip was too tight, though, and he was now slowly choking her to death.

"David?" I questioned, prepared to honor my promise. Instead, my best friend stood with his gun trained on Landon and a look of complete helplessness on his face.

He couldn't do it—convinced he'd hit her instead.

A flash of movement caught of my eye and I trained my gun on it just in time to see the screwdriver sink into the space between Landon's shoulder blades. He dropped Elizabeth and turned on his attacker.

A woman.

His hand locked around her throat, squeezing as he backed her toward a wall. I brought the gun down and calmly fired a round through the back of his calf. The blast shattered his tibia and fibula, forcing them forward through the skin. Landon fell to the dirt floor with a groan, the woman trapped beneath him.

I pulled him off and recoiled at the sight of her. She looked like something from a Holocaust documentary. A walking skeleton, covered by nothing more than a thin layer of skin. I couldn't fathom where she'd gotten the energy to even stand, much less stab someone.

"I'm Detective Michael Sullivan," I said, kneeling in front of her, trying to match her face to any of the missing persons posters littering the desks and walls of the station. "Can you tell me your name, ma'am?"

"Ka-Katya," she whispered, refusing to meet my eyes.

There was no way. This woman looked nothing like the woman plastered across billboards and posters.

With wide eyes, I asked, "Egorichev?"

She nodded.

Holy fuck.

Shallow cuts and deep purple bruises marred her face, but when I tried inspecting them, she winced and jerked away.

"Mike, we're going to need an ambulance. She's in bad shape," David called from across the room. Elizabeth was panting heavily, fighting to sit up as blood spilled out from between her legs.

She bore down with a scream before losing consciousness. Left with no other options and praying that Grey was close, I called it in. Dispatch gave me the runaround before agreeing to send a chopper to meet us at a nearby highway junction.

Doing my best not to jar her broken body, I carried Katya out of the basement, carefully placing her in the backseat of my truck. The case that had plagued me for months was going to be closed, but it didn't leave me with a good feeling.

I should have known where she was all along. The motherfucker I'd interviewed repeatedly had her the entire time. Landon, the loving boyfriend who'd organized countless search parties and press conferences, had been stringing us along for months.

If I'd just kept a tail on him twenty-four hours a day, we would have found her much sooner.

Katya kept a death grip on my shirt, refusing to let me back out of the truck. Knowing Grey and his crew were going to be arriving any second, I passed my cell phone off to David in the front seat. If anyone ever got suspicious enough to check my location, it'd look like I was with him all night.

I gave him directions and managed to untangle Katya's hands from my shirt, promising her, "I'm going to take care of him. I will come to you, okay?"

Grey pulled up seconds after they left, worriedly asking, "You okay?"

I clenched my jaw. "Found my missing model and David's wife holed up in here. Fucker's wounded, but I need him alive. I promised David."

If Grey was surprised, he didn't show it. Instead, he cracked his neck and followed me inside. "The others should be here any second."

We dragged Landon up out of the basement while he cursed us both, bragging about his exploits. "You cops think you're so fucking smart, but you're not. You're all just a bunch of lackeys, standing around until your shift ends, hoping the next peon is the one who cracks the case for you. Laziness, Detective. Sheer laziness."

"Your death is going to be a slow one, asshole," I snarled, thinking of the countless hours spent trying to find Katya.

Shift work?

I'd sacrificed a proper relationship, jumping through hoops for the bastard.

"Yeah, rotting away in prison. Wonder how much free time I'll get to write letters. If I'm a model prisoner, I might even get early parole."

Grey smirked and swung his steel-toed boot out, catching Landon in his wounded leg and sending him face down in the dead grass with a shriek.

"Jesus, son. Oughta watch where you step."

Landon bit his tongue in the fall and spewed a mouthful of blood, screaming, "And who the fuck are you? The bad cop to Sullivan's good cop?"

Grey grinned. "I'm the motherfuckin' Pres of Silent Phoenix. I'd say that's about the farthest thing from a cop, wouldn't you?"

Grey slipped on a pair of gloves and forced a suddenly pale Landon into the driver's seat of his SUV, spilling blood on the seats and floorboard.

"It's a shame you tried to outrun the cops in this weather," I told him just as the cavalry arrived.

Comedian was the first one out. "Well, well. Looks like this one found himself in some trouble. Let's take a little trip." He dragged Landon over to his truck with a manic grin.

"You're a fucking cop, Sullivan! You can't just hand me over to a bunch of bikers. It goes against your fucking oath to serve and protect!"

I nodded. "You're right. More of a guideline than a rule, though. You know, I believe in following my own code—guess we're alike in that regard."

Landon struggled to get out of my father's truck. "I'll see you in Hell, Sullivan. You hear me?" My father caught him with an elbow and he immediately slumped over in the front seat.

"Looking forward to it," I muttered. I'd solved the case and kept my promise to David. As far as I was concerned, my hands were clean.

Grey directed another member to drop the truck as far away from the farmhouse as possible before turning to me. "We're heading out. He'll be up north when you're ready. You know the coordinates."

It was done.

Well, almost.

I pulled the burner phone from my back pocket. "Nikolay? It's Detective Sullivan. We got her. They've taken her to the hospital."

"Who was it?" he demanded.

I rubbed at the back of neck. "Landon Scott."

There was a long silence.

"My deal stands, Sullivan. Forty thousand if he never makes it to jail. I won't have Ekaterina subjected to him any further. Either you take the money or I'll find someone else, but that man's life will end soon."

It was a discussion he and I had multiple times throughout the investigation. Once I'd ruled him out as a suspect, he'd turned to plans of revenge, saying he knew people who could make her kidnapper disappear without a trace.

At the mention of cash, I was in. It didn't matter to me how his people dealt with it as long as I got the money. Elizabeth's involvement threw a wrench into things. My promise to David trumped the one I'd made Nikolay.

"My best friend's wife was found with your daughter. Believe me when I say it's being dealt with."

What the fuck was I doing—involving civilians in club business?

No way was Nikolay Egorichev just a civilian, though. I left most of my interviews, feeling as though I was the one being interrogated. My guess was CIA operative—maybe a spy. Either would explain the cash he had readily available to pay off lowly detectives like me.

"Call me when it's done and I'll get you the money. I expect proof, though."

This was no longer about being an accomplice to the club. I was in over my head. A dirty cop who accepted bribes to look the other way.

I'd lived with the man in the mirror for thirty-two years now. I just hoped after it was all said and done, I'd still be able to.

CHAPTER THIRTY-TWO

Lauren: December 2014 (Age: 28)

David murdered someone—had all but admitted it in a hospital room that felt as if it was shrinking by the second.

"I took care of my family," he said to Elizabeth, stroking her hair. "That's all you need to know, baby."

She nodded and squeezed his hand, the best she could do with her jaw wired shut. In addition to a broken jaw, Landon had fractured Elizabeth's finger and three ribs. But the baby had taken the brunt of the trauma. They delivered Kaden John Greene by emergency caesarean. He weighed just two pounds and eight ounces, and was currently fighting for his life in the NICU.

It was senseless.

Now, authorities were searching for a man they would never find. At least not alive, if David was to be believed.

I sat with the confession, struggling to understand how the guy who owned his own construction company had become a killer. Not that the bastard hadn't earned that very fate, but the technological advancements in DNA alone made it virtually impossible to get away with murder.

Yet David didn't seem concerned about a lifetime reservation behind bars. He was acting like a man who didn't believe the law would catch him, which was impossible. Unless he had help from the inside.

My god.

I'd spent the past forty-eight hours pacing the halls of the hospital, wondering where Mike had gone and why he wouldn't return my calls or texts. Everything he asked, I had done, answering countless questions for police as they searched the office and wrote up their reports. Yet I wracked my brain, wondering if I'd slipped up and said the wrong thing, something that warranted the radio silence he was subjecting me to.

"Excuse me," I choked out, bolting for the door.

"Lauren—Lauren, wait," David called after me, but I broke into a jog and lost him by a nurses' station.

I frantically mashed the call button for the elevator, each breath more labored than the last. David killed someone—would he kill me to keep it from getting out?

The doors finally slid open, and I rushed inside, scared in a way I never had been before. I leaned back against the cold metallic wall as the car descended, fighting with my morality.

It wasn't right, but that didn't mean it wasn't the right thing.

If it were me, would I have made the same decision?

Halfway across the parking lot and I realized why Mike had gone M.I.A. He'd crossed a line he knew he couldn't come back from. As I started my car and let the heat thaw my frozen limbs, I wondered if I could cross over to join him. I'd just come to accept the fact that my mother was cozied up with an outlaw biker. Now I was supposed to throw a crooked cop into the mix too?

If it came right down to it, was I even capable of walking away from him?

I told him I loved him.

Did that love have an expiration date? Or was it covered under a lifetime warranty? With transactions of the heart, what was the return policy?

———

The familiar dirt driveway greeted me just after midnight. It had taken all of an hour to reach a decision. After pacing my apartment, lost in hypotheticals and what-ifs, it hit me.

Mike had been the only man in my life for the last four and a half years. After one night in Galveston, I knew.

He was it for me.

Flaws and all.

The snow had melted and refroze to the point of becoming a skating rink and I began sliding the second my feet touched the ground. Thirty harrowing seconds later, I made it onto the porch and knocked softly at the door.

Two minutes after that, I realized I would be dead and frozen by the time he let me in. I tried the door handle, relieved when it opened.

"Mike?" I called softly, but the house remained dark and silent. I almost expected Betsy to jump out at me with Steri-Strips in her hands. The sight would likely send me to an early grave.

He was home. His truck was outside. After checking the living and dining rooms, I moved into the kitchen where I found him hunched over the table, a bottle of tequila clenched in his fist.

"Mike?"

His head shot up, and he instinctively reached for his gun.

"It's me!" I shouted. Mike lowered the weapon, but refused to meet my gaze.

"I know why you're here," he whispered, the resignation in his voice damn near breaking me. He looked wretched, like he hadn't slept in days.

"Are you drunk?" I asked, gesturing toward the bottle, but he shook his head.

"No, and not for lack of trying, either. David told me you knew."

I slipped my jacket off before pulling a chair out to join him at the table. "I do, and I won't lie to you. It threw me." His eyes dropped back down to the tequila bottle. "But I would've made the same call."

Mike looked up in surprise. "You would have? Well, darlin', that shocks the shit out of me."

I took a deep breath and blurted out, "My mom's in a biker gang and not the type you see doing charity drives at Christmas. I didn't know how to tell you before—" I trailed off, suddenly unable to finish the sentence.

Before you killed someone.

He laughed. "Yeah, that's a deal breaker for me."

"Are you serious?" I asked, feeling my heart plummet.

He kicked his chair back and knelt next to me, taking my hands in his. I didn't miss the way they shook, much like mine had for the past forty-eight hours.

"No," he whispered. "I've been sitting here for days, trying to find the right words. When David said you knew, I thought that was it. It's supposed to be black and white—right and wrong. Yet, I keep finding myself in gray areas."

There it was.

He had just put into words what I'd struggled with since allowing Monica back into my life. I hadn't had the first clue how to reconcile my recovering addict of a mother with the image of a biker's Ol' Lady.

"I do too. Maybe loving someone means spending time in the in-between areas."

"I went and saw Katya earlier—the woman found with Elizabeth."

I nodded, encouraging him to continue.

"Wanted to see how she was. I guess she'd seen the same news blurb Elizabeth had because she was in pretty bad shape by the time I got there."

I couldn't imagine what she was going through.

"Her father showed up and wanted to know if it was done." Mike cleared his throat, looking a bit like a deer in the headlights. "Nikolay offered me forty grand to ensure Landon never made it to jail. I took it, Lauren. I took the money."

I mashed my lips together to keep from gasping, settling for a small nod instead.

Murder. Bribery. It made me sick.

If it had been me, what would my family have done?

Without a doubt, I knew Josué, Isaac—even Monica—would stop at nothing to get me back. Forty grand was a small price to pay for the peace of mind in knowing your daughter was safe.

"Katya said it was blood money. And she's right. I'm a hired killer.

Even if I didn't put the final bullet in him, I'm still responsible and deep down, I just can't shake the feeling this is all gonna go south." Mike went quiet for a beat before asking, "Are you willing to be labeled an accessory after the fact if I go down for first degree murder?"

My pulse raced at the thought of going to prison. I swallowed the saliva that had pooled in my mouth before replying, "I love you. The rest is just details."

He rocked back on his heels and studied my face before his face split into a grin. "Jesus Christ, Red. You must have a screw loose to want to stay, but I'm not letting you back out now."

I smiled, even as my stomach twisted itself into knots.

He cupped my chin, bringing his forehead to rest against mine. "I love you. It feels like I've loved you since we met in Galveston, and I'm sick of fighting it."

Three words I'd been waiting for since the day I met him. When I wasn't the daughter of an addict and he wasn't a dirty cop.

We were just Jack and Charlotte.

Maybe it wasn't the fairy tale I'd longed for as a child, but loving him in the gray areas was a hell of a lot better than the lukewarm emotions I'd experienced with anyone else.

"While we're discussing honesty," I said carefully, Mike's eyes already narrowing in suspicion. "I hate historical documentaries."

The corner of his mouth curved up. "So, when you told me you loved them..."

I winced. "Lies."

"Alright, I guess it's only fair that I admit you are, without a doubt, the worst cook I've ever met."

"Rude." I tried to cuff him upside the head, but he caught my hand, his lips brushing across the inside of my wrist. I shuddered with pleasure at the contact, suddenly a fan of the honesty game.

"What shows do you like, darlin'?" he whispered, tracing my jawline with his mouth.

"M-mainly, true crime and sci-fi stuff," I stuttered, biting back a moan as he trailed kisses down the column of my throat.

Mike's eyes darkened. "Murder and zombies, huh? Ever thought about adding some cooking shows to that mix?"

"You know what, you c—" The retort died on my tongue when he tugged the wide neckline of my sweater down, letting his tongue explore the valley of my breasts.

"Don't misunderstand," he whispered, hovering over the swell of cleavage spilling out over the cups of my bra. "I fucking love your kinks, darlin'."

"Don't tease me," I pleaded, shifting forward. I wanted more. Everything. Him. "Please."

Mike lifted me off the chair with a growl, his hands moving to my hips. I locked my arms around his neck, hissing at the feel of his hard length pressed up against my body. He suckled my nipples through the lace of my bra. Rough pulls that left them puckered into tight points.

We made it as far as the living room.

"Any other confessions?" He asked, lowering me onto the couch. His hands made quick work of my sweater and bra, before he resumed his tour of my breasts. "C'mon, my ego can handle it."

The ache between my thighs had temporarily knocked my speech setting offline, rendering me incapable of responding with anything more than moans and whimpers.

His mouth closed over my nipple, and the breath left my body. I arched up toward him, silently begging him to take it. Take it all. He sucked harder, lashing me with his tongue—catching my flesh between his teeth and holding me hostage at the border of pleasure and pain.

I palmed him through the front of his jeans, blindly searching for the zipper while he continued his assault.

He released my breast with a loud pop, panting, "C'mon, Red. Don't keep me in suspense."

I stayed silent and ran the heel of my palm over his erection, completely focused on my task of freeing him from the confines of his jeans.

My lips parted in an exhale. Holy shit, he'd gone commando. I gripped his shaft, stroking him from root to tip. Again. And Again.

Mike migrated over to my other breast with a growl, devouring me in a way I would never come down from.

"Don't stop. Please," I croaked, having strung enough words into a plea for more.

His hands moved lower, pausing once he unzipped my jeans.

Waiting.

The man was trying to kill me.

"Please," I murmured again, letting my legs fall open in invitation. When he didn't move, I gave him a confession guaranteed to stroke his ego. "You want my honesty?"

He pulled back, one brow already cocked high on his forehead as he nodded. Convinced I had his full, undivided attention, I slipped out from under him and stood in front of the couch, thumbs hooked in the waistband of my jeans.

"See, I have this fantasy," I began, tugging the denim down my hips. "You're in it, and you—" I paused to step out of my pants, kicking them aside.

His throat bobbed in a swallow. "What—what do I do?"

I tugged lightly on a strand of my hair and took a hesitant step toward him, whispering, "You're in charge, controlling how fast or slow we go. You could make love to me gently, or force me to take you deep. Hard. Using my body to feel good."

An involuntary shiver worked its way through my body, tightening my abused and aching nipples. Just when I thought I was going to combust, Mike pulled me onto his lap, dragged my panties to the side, and drove a finger into me with a force that bordered on savage.

"Mike," I groaned when he stopped just as suddenly. Feeling the heat of his stare, I reluctantly opened my eyes.

"I could fucking watch you like this all night long, baby. But right now, I need to taste you."

My face heated, but I kept my eyes on his as he lay me back, dropping to his knees between my thighs. He discarded my drenched panties on the coffee table before moving in to sweep his tongue over my clit.

I gasped and gripped the back of his head, preventing another escape attempt. "Patience, darlin'," he chuckled. "I'll get you there."

I was soaked by the time Mike slid two fingers into me. My skin heated, like a can of gasoline that had just had a match thrown into it. His tongue and hand worked in a rhythm that didn't seem physically possible. My back arched up off the couch and my hands sought his hair, needing something to ground me.

I didn't have to tell him what to do. His tongue knew just where to stroke, and he lapped at my sensitive nub until I was riding a wave of pleasure unlike any I'd experienced before with him.

Higher and higher.

"Come for me."

My inner muscles fluttered around his flexing fingers and I kept a death grip on his hair, refusing to come back down to earth.

"Darlin'?" Mike groaned.

My chest rose and fell steadily, but otherwise, I didn't move.

He tried again. "Darlin', you're gonna have to let go of me. Your legs are like a goddamned vice."

I picked my head up and smiled at the sight of his blond head caught between my thighs. I released him and he sat up, exaggeratedly coughing, before running the back of his hand across his mouth.

"Better?" I asked.

"Oh, I'd say I'm better than okay, Red. What do you think?" He winked and stepped out of his jeans.

He was hard as a rock, and I wanted nothing more than to feel my body stretching around him. I was aching for it. Every. Single. Inch.

"Shit," he cursed, searching the pockets of his pants. "I need to run upstairs for a condom—"

The arousal flowing through my veins and clouding my judgment had other thoughts. "Don't. Just take me bare," I begged.

Mike's gaze darkened and stalked back over to the couch. I took the hem of his t-shirt in my hands and lifted, admiring the sheen of sweat clinging to his muscles—the colorful ink that covered almost every inch of skin.

He let me remove the shirt before forcing me over the back of the couch. My breasts brushed against the cool leather, sending goose-bumps over my skin. I instinctively pushed back against him when his teeth sank into the curve of my ass.

"More."

"That's my girl," he praised, nudging my thighs wider and aligning his shaft at my entrance. "Hands on the couch, baby."

Mike took his sweet time feeding me his cock, inch by glorious inch. I dug my toes into the junction behind his knees, fighting to keep him from pulling out. He chuckled at my greediness and thrust his hips forward, forcing my body to accommodate him.

All of him.

Once he was fully seated, he pulled me back against his chest. His hands roamed my skin—skimming my lower belly and then up to cup my breasts, anchoring me to him.

If I thought I was hot before, I was a raging inferno now. Each slow, deliberate thrust pushed me closer to the edge of a cliff. I gripped the back of the couch and tightened my inner muscles around his shaft, feeling another orgasm building.

"Look at me," Mike commanded through clenched teeth.

I tipped my head back. He looked like a warrior in the middle of battle, hovering over me, his features tight as he fought to stay in control. I was high on dopamine, feeling like a goddess beneath this gorgeous man.

"You and me," he panted against my lips. "You and me."

I gave a jerky nod, every nerve ending in my body lighting up like a runway. Sensing I was close, he picked up the pace, ramming into me almost frantically. At the last second, his hands locked around my breasts, squeezing my nipples between his thumb and forefinger.

My vision began blurred and the world around me went white. His teeth connected in the space where my shoulder and neck met and I screamed his name, plummeting over the edge.

"I love you," Mike rasped, cupping my throat in his hand. I was still coming when I felt him swell inside me, his thrusts turning shallow. I rocked my hips, urging him deeper and prolonging my own orgasm.

"I—I love you too," I whispered when I finally came down. My back arched against his chest and he dropped his other hand down to the apex of my thighs, regaining speed. We could've been hurtling toward a brick wall and I wouldn't have stopped him.

It felt so much bigger than just our bodies connecting. It was as if our souls had fused together. Each thrust cast out our sins—each sigh, another exhalation of doubt.

"Please," I begged.

I didn't know if my body was capable of another orgasm, but I was willing to try. His thrusts became desperate, and he gripped my shoulders hard, using my body to find his own release.

"Yes," I moaned, keeping pace with each thrust. My pleasure increased to where it bordered on pain as he reached a fever pitch. I fell apart with a silent cry, all sound lost within my chest.

"Lauren," Mike growled, holding me in a death grip as he flooded my body. Despite the slight chill in the room, our skin glistened with sweat. He collapsed onto me, forcing me back over the couch with a breathless pant.

We lay together, with him still buried deep inside me. I wasn't the daughter of a biker chick and he wasn't a man who had helped commit a murder.

We were just Jack and Charlotte back on a beach in Galveston.

Two people without a care in the world.

CHAPTER THIRTY-THREE

Mike: January 2015 (Age: 32)

"Someone's in a good mood," David noted from the doorway into my office.

The grin on my face had become a permanent fixture on my face since the night Lauren discovered the truth and stayed anyway.

So, maybe I hadn't been entirely honest.

There was no way in hell she would have stayed if I'd told her everything. But just as soon as Grey's fucking war was over and I was convinced there were no targets on her back, I'd come clean about Silent Phoenix.

Ease her into it.

Only, this war seemed far from over. The Sons of Death played by their own rules. They didn't give a fuck about club bitches or hang arounds. It hadn't mattered whether someone was just associated with Silent Phoenix or a patched-in member. The Sons viewed everyone as an enemy to be destroyed.

Until then, there was absolutely no fucking reason for me to involve her.

"What the hell brings you to my neck of the woods?" I asked, pushing my thoughts aside for the time being.

David clapped me on the back before sinking down into a chair in front of my desk. It was strange—he was clearly exhausted, but upbeat about it.

"Beth kicked me out of the hospital for a bit. She's still working on nursing Kaden and said I made her frustrated with all my hovering. Work's being handled by Tony right now, so I thought I'd check in with you," he said, drumming his fingers on the armrests.

"We haven't really talked much recently, and I wanna know how the investigation is going."

I knew what he was really asking—*did Lauren leave because of the Landon thing? And if so, should we be worried?*

"Life is good," I said with a reassuring smile, clicking a pen in my hand. "Working this Landon Scott case has been trying, but we're gonna find him. While I've got you here, mind if I ask you something?"

His shoulders, which had just relaxed, immediately arched back up in defense. "What?"

I reached into my suit jacket and pulled out a ring box, tossing it over to him. "You think it's too soon?"

David popped it open with a grin before pitching his voice higher. "Do you know how many years I've waited for this Michael Sullivan? I knew if I was patient enough, I'd make an honest man out of you one day."

I flipped him off. "Cut the shit, dickhead. It's for Lauren."

"What did I tell you on my wedding day? I said this was going to happen. I recall you telling me I was full of shit."

"Never mind," I sighed. "You were obviously the wrong fucking person to ask about this. I should have—"

"It's perfect. But you're asking the man who proposed to Beth after just a couple of months of dating her, though."

I nodded. "This is true. Just figure I'm gonna be thirty-three this year and—I don't know—I like the idea of settling down."

"When you know, you know," David agreed with a distant look in his eyes. "So, how are you planning on asking her?"

I pinched the bridge of my nose and looked down at my desk calendar. "Jesus, I don't know. I thought about doing some big weekend getaway in February, but everyone fucking proposes in

February. And I still haven't met her dads—need to ask for their blessing."

The smirk reappeared on David's face. "I love this—it's so fucking strange to see you like this. Like seeing a dog walk around in a three-piece suit. Absolutely bizarre."

I chucked my pen at his head. The prepaid I kept on me for club business alerted me to an incoming text. Jarvis had installed a burner app, so it displayed a different number every time I placed a call or text.

Restricted: Hold until further instruction. Sons involved. Not safe to release. Possible overnight. Be ready. -G

What?

It didn't make any sense.

Usually Grey gave me a phone call if there were any members coming through the station. If I had enough of a warning, I could usually smuggle them right back out before they even made it to booking.

This was different.

He had never once asked me to hold a club member. His big thing was getting them out and back on the street. I read the text again, trying to decide if it warranted a phone call or not.

If Grey thought the police station was a safe house, it meant the Sons were plotting something big.

"Everything alright?" David asked.

"Yeah. Just had something come up." I gave the text one last look before shoving my phone back into my pocket. "You should go home and get some sleep. You look like ass."

David nodded sleepily. "Yeah, I just might do that. If Beth calls, tell her I'm with you and have been the whole time. If she finds out I'm getting sleep, she might castrate me."

I grinned. "Sounds like marital bliss, man. Keep me posted on Kaden. I'd like to meet him once he gets out."

David slid the ring box back across the desk. "Yeah, he's still being fed mainly by a feeding tube. So, he's gonna have to get strong enough to nurse or take a bottle before they decide to release him. He's a fighter, though. Let me know how it goes with Lauren."

His eyes shone as he talked about his son. I wondered if my own father had ever once looked like that when talking about me. Had he even held me as a baby? I couldn't remember, and as far as I knew, there was no photographic evidence to support it.

"Speak of the devil," David said, blocking the doorway with his body.

"Hey, David," Lauren replied, but her voice sounded different.

I stuffed the box back inside my suit jacket and tried to look relaxed as David turned to let her into the office. She walked in almost robotically. He frowned at me over her head before shutting the door, leaving us alone.

"Hey, Red. Didn't expect to see you until tonight." My heart was still beating unsteadily as I sank down into my chair.

"I'm sorry to bother you at work, but I'm in trouble," she admitted, finally meeting my eyes.

My mind immediately jumped to the Sons of Death when I saw she'd been crying. Somehow, they'd figured out I was helping the club and gone after her.

"Look, Lauren—"

"The police arrested my mother for possession and driving under the influence." Her voice cracked. She paused to regain her composure before adding, "She didn't do it, Mike. She's clean."

Trying to comfort family members who wanted to believe the person they loved wasn't using again had always been one of the harder parts of my job.

"I know it's hard to believe that she could betray your trust like this, but sometimes, the addiction is stronger than reason," I said, reciting the same spiel I'd spouted off hundreds of times before. "We can't ever know what goes through a user's head when they relapse—"

Lauren shoved her chair back and came over the desk. "Don't you dare spout off the same shit you tell everyone else! I'm your girlfriend, goddammit! And I'm telling you something about this is wrong!"

"I get—" I tried, before she was pacing the length of my office, talking over me.

"My mother called me, and she sounded fine! Scared, but sober. Said she'd overheard something she shouldn't have. That's why she's sitting in jail."

I grabbed a pen and began clicking it at random. "What did she overhear? Where was she when she overheard it?"

She shook her head. "I don't know. She said it wasn't safe to talk about it over the phone. She thought they might be listening."

Oh, fuck.

Lauren had been played.

"Lauren, this is the same woman who stole your car," I said, struggling to keep the judgment out of my voice. "Who's to say she isn't taking you for a ride right now?"

Her mouth fell into a flat line and she asked, "How the hell did you know about that?"

Shit.

Grey told me. You know, after I helped him return the car to you. But, it's fine because we weren't together then.

I kept my posture relaxed. "I'm a cop, darlin'. Surely you knew I'd run a background check on you."

I regretted saying it almost immediately, but didn't exactly have an alternative option loaded and ready to go.

Lauren's eyes darkened and her jaw muscles clenched as she stalked toward my desk. "You ran a fucking background check on me without my consent? Who does that?"

I waved my hand. "Look, just let me explain. I researched you—I wanted to get to know you better."

Yeah, that was worse.

"Then fucking ask me, asshole!" she shouted, the veins in her neck bulging. "That's how people get to know each other. Not by running background checks on the other person without them knowing! Now, are you going to help me or continue to waste my time?"

I tried to move my chair out of the line of fire without her noticing.

I got it. She was clinging to this hope her mother had stayed sober, despite a shitload of evidence to the contrary. Willing to cover all my bases, I pulled the prepaid from my back pocket and replied to the last text received.

Me: Female?

Within seconds, it was buzzing with an incoming message.

Restricted: Affirmative. Hold overnight.

Great.

Her mother was being targeted by the Sons and Grey wanted her held until he could neutralize the threat.

And there was absolutely no way for me to tell her any of it.

"Lauren, I'm not sure it's such a good idea to take any action until we get all the facts."

A flush worked its way up her throat and into her face, and I wasn't afraid to admit that the woman fucking terrified me.

Lauren stabbed a shaking finger at me, hissing, "Oh, so you'll bend over backward for David, but not me? I'm not even asking you to cover up a murder—all I need is for my mother to be taken to a secure location so that I can find out what's going on."

She retrieved her coat off the back of the chair and slipped it on before adding, "Guess that's too much for a crooked cop like you to handle, though."

"Just hear me out," I said, meeting her by the door. "I can't bend the rules on this one. I need you to trust me on this. It's all going to be fine."

The words were right there in my throat. She looked absolutely devastated. I wanted to fix it—wanted to tell her that her mother was much safer in here than she was on the streets.

But, I couldn't.

I couldn't let Lauren get mixed up in Grey's shit.

She wrenched back when I reached out to grip her shoulder, growling, "Don't touch me. I can't even look at you right now, Mike."

I didn't run after her when she stormed out, even though I wanted to. If I told her about the club, I'd have to admit how I got mixed up with them in the first place.

What could I say—*Hey Lauren, I'm in deep with an outlaw MC and they're keeping your mom safe by locking her up, okay? How'd I end up in bed with criminals? Well, darlin', I'm the son of a psychopathic biker. Oh, and by the way, I committed my first murder at eighteen and they covered it up. So, I guess I owe them. Oh, and by the way, do you wanna marry me?*

Yeah, there was no way that conversation was going to go any better than the one we'd just had.

She left me alone in my office with a diamond ring and shitload of guilt.

CHAPTER THIRTY-FOUR

Lauren: January 2015 (Age: 28)

I'd planned to lie on the couch, binge-watching *Dateline* before meeting Mike for dinner.

Until my phone rang.

"This call will be recorded and monitored. You have a collect call from—*Monica*—an inmate in the Lubbock County Detention Facility. Your telephone service provider does not allow collect calls. If you would like to accept this and future calls, you must establish a pre-pay account. We accept Visa and Mastercard. If you would like to set up an account and accept this call, please press four."

After grabbing my purse and handing over my emergency credit card information, it dawned on me. My mother was in jail. Again.

"Lauren?"

"Mom?" I asked, eyes stinging with tears. "What happened?"

"I got arrested—DUI and possession of heroin," she whispered, choking on the words. "I'm still clean, though, I swear."

Initially, I was livid, thinking she'd blown months of sobriety for a heroin fix. But meth and coke had always been her go-to. I wasn't naïve enough to think she could stay sober around bikers, but it still didn't make sense.

"Lauren, listen to my voice," she'd demanded. "You've been around me when I'm using. Do I sound fucked up to you? I think—I think I'm being targeted."

"What happened?" I sobbed. "Help me understand."

"I can't say much, but I overheard something I shouldn't have, and I think this is retaliation for that. I know they're monitoring this call."

She went silent for a beat. "Lauren, I need you to get me out of here."

It was the stuff of crime thrillers, but I knew she was telling the truth. I couldn't imagine what she'd overheard that warranted a trip to jail, but I had no way of getting her out.

"What about Torch?"

"I—I can't call him," my mother sighed. "Go to Mike—tell him what's happened. He'll know what to do."

The thought of involving Mike in my family drama was almost worse than finding out she was using again. Until I considered what he'd done for David. If anyone could help me get her out, it was him.

"Lauren, baby, I swear to you on my life I am sober right now. Tell him—hell, he can come do a blood test on me now. He is the only one who will know what to do."

He hadn't.

Helping his friend hide a body was all well and good, but god forbid he bail his girlfriend's mother out of jail.

Damn you, Mike Sullivan.

Did he know how hard it had been for me to even approach him, much less admit to needing help?

Would he have cared?

I checked my cell phone again—praying for a text, a phone call—anything that would help me get my mother out of jail.

Nothing.

"Motherfucker!" I screamed, punching the mattress. I had gnawed my fingernails down to the quick, replaying the last thing my mother said to me before her time was up.

"I love you... okay?"

Why hadn't I said it back? The question had plagued my thoughts most of the night, to the point I thinking about calling Mike to apologize for my outburst. I wasn't sorry, but I didn't want my mother spending another night in a cell.

Just as I reached for my phone, there was a knock at my front door. It was just a little after four AM, and there was only one person I knew who would show up this early, which meant he'd finally come to his senses.

I ran down the hallway and threw open the front door. "I knew you'd—" The words died on my tongue as I took in the two uniformed police officers on my porch.

The one with short and spiky blonde hair displayed her badge and asked, "Are you Lauren McGuire?"

I nodded dumbly. "Why are you here?"

Had Mike sent them in his place? The lack of sleep and shitload of stress had left me thoroughly confused.

"I'm Officer Sorensen and this is Officer Richards," she said, gesturing toward her partner, a man with silver hair and a thick mustache that probably doubled as a food catchall. "May we come in?"

I nodded again and let Officer Sorensen lead me over to my couch.

"Why don't you have a seat, Lauren?"

Wasn't I supposed to be the one to offer that?

She sat down next to me. "We're sorry to wake you, but we found Monica McGuire dead early this morning."

I stared blankly at her, waiting for the camera crew and Mike to come through the front door and tell me it was all a joke. A bubble of hysterical laughter broke free from my tight chest. "Nice one. Did Mike put you up to this? My mother's sitting in jail and has been since yesterday afternoon."

"We understand it may be difficult to process," Officer Sorensen said, patting my leg. "But the identification recovered matched her information."

I shook my head and scooted further away from her. "No, she's in jail. Trust me, I would know if she'd gotten out. I guess there has to be a bail hearing and apparently that can take a couple of days."

Officer Richards, who hadn't bothered to say a goddamned word at any point since they arrived, suddenly got chatty. "The decedent was in possession of your contact information, among other... items. Her effects are being held for you at the coroner's office."

I was on my feet in an instant, chest heaving. "Decedent? What are you, Sherlock Holmes? You're not listening to me. Monica is sitting in jail. They charged her with possession and a DUI—they don't let you out for those things when no one has posted bail!"

Officer Sorensen stood up. "Would you like for us to take you down to the coroner's office to make an identification?"

I bit my lip, but nodded. "But I'm telling you, you've got the wrong person."

We drove across town in silence. My finger hovered over the screen of my phone. I wanted to call Mike, but didn't know what to say. Maybe we'd said everything back in his office.

He hadn't been willing to help me free Monica, which didn't exactly leave us with a lot of options for our relationship. I wanted to uncover the truth and find the person responsible for setting her up. He made it clear he didn't want to get his hands dirty.

After pulling up in front of a nondescript building downtown, the officers led me to a small room with a table, some chairs, and an upholstered love seat. Monotonous elevator music played softly in the background. I brushed my wild hair off of my forehead and sat down at the table, feeling more tired than I could ever remember being in my life.

A woman walked in with a clipboard in her hand, taking the seat across from mine. "Hello, Lauren. My name is Brynn Kelly. I'm a crisis counselor here. I'm going to be with you as long as you need me to be."

I shook my head. "This isn't going to take up much of your time. My mother is sitting in jail—there's been a mix-up."

"Okay," Brynn said with an encouraging nod before pointing to the clipboard. "The identification will be done by photograph right here in this room. The photograph will be upside down. When you turn it over, you'll see a face surrounded by a blue sheet. She looks like she's sleeping. I can stay here as long as needed until you feel comfortable enough to look."

She placed the clipboard in front of me and I stared at the back of the picture for a brief second before flipping it over. I wanted to get this over with and prove them—

My mother's face stared up at me, her ivory skin now tinged a grayish-blue.

"No," I moaned, feeling as if someone had sucked the air from the room. The blood drained from my face and I barely got my hand up over my mouth before I began dry heaving.

Brynn grabbed a trash can and held it out for me.

"I don't understand," I sobbed, running the back of my hand across my mouth. "My mother—she was supposed to be in jail."

She went into counselor mode, going over resources and handing me pamphlets on grief. I stared at them blankly before ripping them in half and tossing the scraps to the ground. The trash can was next. I launched it against the beige wall with a growl.

My legs buckled, and I fell into a heap on the carpet, feeling as though I was being devoured by grief and rage. It didn't matter how deeply I inhaled, I couldn't get enough air into my lungs and felt as if I was hovering a few feet above my body.

I screamed until my throat was raw, while Brynn sat silently at the table. I wanted to punch her—to hit her until she felt this pain as keenly as I did.

"Who would do this to her? Who would hurt her like this?" I forced out through clenched teeth.

"She was found with a needle in her arm. The coroner is running a screen on her, but it looks like an overdose at this point."

No. I wasn't accepting that.

My mother had gotten sober—she wouldn't have gone back to that. She swore to me and I believed her.

Over the years, I'd built up a wall, knowing there would be a day when Monica went too far and OD'ed. But that was then. I had seen how good she could be sober. I'd seen how hard she worked getting her GED, and she was going to be starting school in just a few weeks.

"I need to talk to my mom," I said firmly, wiping the snot from my nose. "She hasn't bought her books yet. She needs to order them or they won't be here in time for class."

I was rambling, but everything had become surreal. She wasn't gone. Not when we were just starting to figure things out.

Brynn began talking softly again, but the ringing in my ears drowned out most of her words.

"We're supposed to have dinner, and she wanted me to help her find a nice dress to impress Mike. Do you think *Dillards* would have something?"

She knelt on the floor and took my hand in hers, her eyes shiny. "Lauren, we're going to get you some help. Okay?"

I tried inhaling again, but could only manage a shallow breath. "You need to help her. Just tell her I'm waiting in here. Go get her!"

My sobs turned violent again, and I curled up in the fetal position until paramedics arrived.

I never got to tell her I loved her, too.

CHAPTER THIRTY-FIVE

Lauren: January 2015 (Age: 28)

Four hours and several sedatives later, I lay on my couch, staring at the cardboard box on the coffee table.

It was a heartbreaking sight, seeing someone's entire life condensed into one box.

Monica had been much more than four walls of cardboard. She'd been a rape survivor. A mother. A GED recipient. A woman who had figured out her purpose in life, only to have it snuffed out at forty-four.

I ignored the knocking at the front door and wrapped my arms around myself, freezing despite the amount of blankets on my body. The hospital had gotten in touch with Josué, and he and Isaac's flight was scheduled to land in an hour.

The knocking stopped. I went back to staring at the box until I heard the unmistakable sound of a key sliding into the lock. Someone was trying to get inside.

I jerked upright with a startled cry when the lock clicked, clutching my cell phone to my chest as the front door burst open. Mike rushed toward me, his eyes wild as they searched my face.

"I just heard," he exclaimed breathlessly.

Just a few short hours ago, I prayed he would show up. Now that he was here, I wanted him to leave. He was the reason she was lying on a cold metal slab.

"Y-you did this!" I screamed when he tried reaching for me. "You told me to trust you and now she's dead!"

His face fell, and he fumbled with his words. "Lauren, I swear to god, if I'd known this would be the outcome—I would have stayed on shift. I would have made sure she stayed locked up."

"You motherfucker!" I barreled into him, raking my bloody fingernails down his face. He tried to latch onto my upper arms and I drove the heel of my hand into his nose, breaking the contact.

"You killed her! You said to trust you, but you lied!"

Blood ran down his face from his wounds, but he kept advancing on me. "Baby, please don't do this. I can fix it."

"Fix it?" I shrieked. "How in the fuck can you fix this? You killed my mother, you bastard. You took her away—just when things were good, you destroyed it."

Mike used his shirt to wipe the blood from his face before coming toward me again. As if in defiance, tears and blood continued to freely flow down his cheeks. "Please, baby, let me hold you. Just let me make it right."

I didn't tell her how much I loved her.

"Stay the fuck away from me!" A guttural roar broke free from my chest and I shoved him, stumbling back against the couch. Fight gone, I sank down onto a cushion in defeat, panting from the exertion.

I wanted to tell her that Mike and I were fighting—wanted her to come over with a pint of rocky road and make it all better.

But I couldn't.

I could never call her again.

She would never see me get married.

Never get a chance to become a grandmother.

The realization reopened the gaping wound in my chest. Mike had taken her from me.

"She didn't overdose," I said hoarsely, fighting the tremors in my body.

"Baby, they found her with a needle in her arm."

"She was murdered!" I snapped. "And her blood is all over your hands!"

He sighed, "Lauren, if you'd just let me—"

I jumped back onto my feet and grabbed a fistful of his shirt with one hand, while pummeling him as hard as I could with the other.

"You." I slapped him across the face.

"Mother." The fist that had been holding his shirt connected with his abdomen.

"Fucker." My knee came up into his groin. "I wish it had been you."

He stood stoically, taking the abuse, before admitting, "I wish it had been me, too."

We stared at each other in silence. My body quaked with grief over the loss of not only my mom, but him as well. He was physically standing in front of me, but what we'd shared together was long gone.

Regardless of what he wanted to believe, Mike had signed her death warrant by refusing to help me. And that was something I could never forgive.

"Get out," I croaked.

He shook his head. "If you'd just let me stay—"

"Get. Out." I enunciated each word before pointing toward the door.

This time, he listened.

I collapsed onto the couch with a strangled sob, hearing my mother's voice singing softly in my head. It almost sounded like a lullaby, something hauntingly familiar. Maybe she'd sung it to me as a baby.

But she was no longer around to tell me.

My mother hadn't killed herself—someone had wanted her silent.

I stared listlessly through the balcony doors. A bird landed on the railing and watched me curiously for a moment before flying away. I could hear the traffic down on the street. It all felt wrong.

Life was carrying on normally outside—as if her life had meant nothing. As if she hadn't mattered.

My mother had been more than just a statistic or a number.

"Mom?" I asked, my voice raspy with tears. "I don't know if you're somewhere you can still hear me, but I love you too."

Sobs overtook me again, and I wrapped my arms around myself, trying to shield my soul from the tragedy of it all—aching for my mommy to hold me, promising I would be okay.

But I wouldn't be okay. Not while her killer still roamed the streets and cops like Mike accepted bribes at every turn. No one was going to put much legwork into finding out what really happened to a former junkie.

She would not become a cold case. And a morally bankrupt detective and gang of outlaw bikers couldn't stop me from uncovering the people responsible.

I was going to find her killer.

And then I was going to make them pay.

CHAPTER THIRTY-SIX

Mike: February 2015 (Age: 32)

"It's just a regular night out with the woman you love," I muttered to myself, sinking into the lumpy mattress.

No matter how many times I said it, it still didn't seem real. I watched her as she moved around the hotel bathroom effortlessly, brushing through her long red hair and dabbing perfume on her wrists.

I made the mistake of looking up, catching sight of myself in the large mirror above the desk. I winced. Jesus Christ, I looked like shit.

Worse than shit, if that was even possible.

My hair desperately needed a cut and my beard—seemed I was trying to compete with Homeless Joe, who hung around outside Inked on Broadway. There was something white caught in it, too.

I walked the four steps over to the mirror, stiffening when I realized it was remnants from the blow I'd snorted an hour ago.

Fuck me.

She had already warned me I was on thin ice when I showed up forty-five minutes late. The last thing I needed was for her to realize I was sampling illicit drugs in my free time. I brushed the white powder from my upper lip and reached for my tie.

My father had been right—a little blow really helped clear the old conscience, putting perspective back where it needed to be.

"C'mon, Mikey. Get your shit together," I hissed at my swaying reflection.

She began humming from the bathroom and the vibrations went straight to my cock. I caught sight of her backside as she did beauty shit to her face.

I should have been focused on straightening my tie, but my eyes wandered off task with every glimpse of her in the mirror. She caught me watching from the bathroom doorway and winked, a blush creeping up into her cheeks. She couldn't hide her emotions. The pale skin would always give it away.

But Christ, was she was beautiful.

I should think so, as she was my wife.

"Good to go, Slick?" she asked, stepping into her heels.

"Ready if you are, Cam."

What the fuck was I doing?

I had asked myself that very question about a hundred times since stepping off the elevator. It was one I'd avoided answering for over a month now. Not that anything good would have come from it, anyway.

What was done was done. I had to learn to live with the consequences of my actions, which I was doing. I drowned myself in a bottle of tequila and when that didn't do the trick, snorted a few lines until the slate was clean again.

Fuck, I was a goddamn success story here.

"You nervous?" Cam turned to me on the elevator ride down, fidgeting with her black dress.

I paused for a moment to fully take her in. Goddamn, she was a looker. Her tits weren't anything to write home about and she acted more like one of the guys, but she was mine.

Unlike Lauren.

Screw you, brain. Nobody invited you to this party.

Cam cocked her head to the side, waiting for an answer to her question.

What was it?

Oh, right. "Course not, babe. It's dinner with you—what's there to be nervous about?"

She opened her mouth and then closed it, giving me an odd look.

Convinced I'd missed a spot, I ran a finger under my nose. When my hand came away clean, I shrugged and asked, "Why? You feeling nervous?"

"A bit," she admitted.

I guided her back against the wall of the elevator with a grin, bringing my mouth down to hers. "Relax, sweetheart. It's just dinner— me and you."

Cam cleared her throat and stuttered, "Well, and the prostitute."

"You got me a hooker? Best wife ever!" I felt like clapping my hands in glee, but settled for crushing her to my chest. Maybe this was a late birthday gift—or was it an anniversary of something? How long had we been together?

Her brow furrowed. "I... guess. Are you okay?"

My hands slipped down to cup her ass through the thin material of her dress, and she let out a soft moan. She felt nice in my hands. Different, but nice. "You ever been fucked in an elevator?"

We pulled apart reluctantly when the doors opened onto the ground floor. I gave her a wink and sauntered off in search of my *gift*.

Cam caught up and looped her arm through mine, leading me down a long corridor and into a dimly lit bar.

My, my. Weren't we fancy?

This hotel seemed a little too highbrow for what we were about to do, but fuck, I was pumped.

"Who are we looking for, sweetheart?" I asked as I swiped my index finger absently across my gums, praying there was just enough residue left on my hands to give me a little bump. I was feeling fantastic now—no sense in coming down right as we met our girl.

I hadn't screwed two chicks at once in a long time. And I had a feeling this was going to be one for the record books.

Cam chose a deserted corner of the bar. It was a good choice. We didn't need an audience. I pulled a chair out, temporarily distracted by the glint of my wedding band. The sight made my pulse race, leaving me with a sudden urge to bolt from the hotel.

If we were going to convince this girl to come back to our room, I had to keep my head on straight. "Gonna grab a drink. You need one?"

She stopped scanning the bar and nodded absently. "Club soda, please."

Club soda for the lady and a fuck ton of liquor for the gentleman.

I approached the bar and waited impatiently for the bartender to quit eye-fucking every woman that walked in.

"Hey man," I called, raising my finger. "Can I get a club soda and a *Campo Azul Añejo* on the rocks? Oh, and I want it in a snifter. Thanks." I turned back toward Cam without waiting for a response.

"Uh, guy?" The bartender started. "We carry *Dulce Vida Añejo*—it's a Texas tequila. Will that work?"

Would that work? Let me see. Would no tip work?

Instead of spouting off and causing a scene, I ground my teeth and nodded. "Sure. Sounds great."

A man in a black suit had joined Cam at the table. He looked like he was going to a funeral. If he laid a hand on my wife, he'd soon be attending his own.

I needed to hit someone—was itching for a fight. It had been too long.

But first, hookers.

"Thank you, but I'm not sure I could do that," Cam said to the man as I walked up with the drinks.

He ran his hand down her arm. "You're overthinking it. Do you know how much money people would pay for a redhead?"

I set the club soda down so hard it splashed over the sides. "I'd like to know."

The man's eyes widened. "I don't mean to insult you, but surely you can see how beautiful your woman is. It's not unreasonable to think there's a market for her."

Cam patted my arm. "Babe, it's fine. It's just something to consider." She turned back to the man. "Gavin, we're really just interested in having another woman join us for now."

"You know my terms," Gavin said with a thoughtful nod.

I took a sip of the tequila, praying the liquor would bring me back down enough to calm the rage that had been building since we'd made it downstairs. "I'd like to go over the terms again and see what my wife picked out. I'm not fucking anything less than a ten tonight."

He pulled out his phone and sent a text. "That can be arranged. Now, as for the money—"

Gesturing with my glass, I asked, "Yo, Gav—what's the going rate for more than just vanilla sex?"

"Babe," Cam warned, discreetly pinching my thigh under the table.

I dropped the hand that was on her shoulder down into the V of her dress while maintaining eye contact with Gavin. "You ever just wanna spice things up, man?" My fingers dipped under the fabric and he nodded dumbly.

"Absolutely. Which is why I'm bringing in my best girl. Luciana is well-versed in many areas." He paused and gestured toward a woman walking into the bar. My cock was hard the minute she came into view.

Seemed my new friend Gavin had gone and gotten me a goddamn twelve.

Luciana slid into the vacant seat across from us. "Hello."

"Hi," Cam mumbled, dipping her head to hide the pink in her cheeks.

I thrust my hand out. "Hello, beautiful. You DTF?"

Luciana blinked slowly as she took my hand. "DTF?"

I ran my thumb along her knuckles. "Down to fuck, doll."

Gavin leaned back against the booth seat. "You need to pay first. It's five hundred for an hour of straight... *vanilla* sex."

I clicked my tongue against my teeth. "Gavin, my man. You know that won't do—I've got needs. How much for anal?"

Cam choked on her club soda and I reluctantly let go of Luciana's hand to pound her on the back.

Gavin grinned. "Anal's gonna cost you another three."

I pursed my lips and nodded. "Alright, how about fisting? I'm talking about me fisting her... her fisting my girl... them fisting each other while I watch. Where are we at now with cost?"

"Let's say eleven hundred for an hour—whatever the hell you want, as long as it doesn't leave a mark. Think you can handle that?"

He regarded me carefully while I studied Luciana. She'd taken something, judging by the glassy, vacant stare in her eyes. They were half-open, as if she'd just woken up from a deep sleep. We'd been discussing her for the last two minutes, but she was too far gone to even notice. She wasn't much older than eighteen—couldn't have been. Her very real tits still defied gravity.

My hard-on disappeared. This wasn't turning out to be nearly as much fun as I'd hoped. Before I could voice those concerns, Cam was already handing over a wad of cash from her purse.

"We've got a room upstairs, if that works."

Gavin nodded and pushed Luciana from the booth. "Go. I'll meet you outside when you're done."

"But what about my cut?"

He slapped her ass. "You'll get it when the nice couple here is satisfied. Now go."

With barely open eyes, she did as she was told. Shit, I needed to rally—Cam had just spent a nice chunk of change to get me what I wanted.

As soon as the elevator doors closed, Luciana pressed her lips to the side of Cam's head. "Want me to go down on you?" she asked in a bored tone.

Yes, I'd be up for that.

Cam shook her head and moved closer to me. "Let's just wait until we get into the room. I don't want us to be interrupted."

Fucking Cam... killjoy.

We got off on our floor and Cam fished the room key from her purse before opening the door into... *a lot of fucking people in police gear.*

"Hands on your head!" someone yelled.

Oh, fuck.

I instinctively raised my arms, knowing I was utterly screwed. I was going to get hit with solicitation, at the very least. If they ran a tox screen, I'd be looking at possession and influence charges on top of the others.

Goddammit.

My entire career was about to go down the shitter, and it was all Lauren's fault. Maybe she hadn't led my dick to hire a hooker, but she had broken my goddamn heart. Surely, she had to take some responsibility for the aftermath.

While several officers patted me and Cam down, two others led a dazed Luciana out of the room in handcuffs.

"Nice work, Detectives," Masterson said with a grin. "We busted her pimp outside, and thanks to Mike's seemingly pointless questions, we might even have enough to get the other girls off the street as well."

This was a fucking sting operation?

Had I known that all along?

Was I even really married to Cam?

"Fuck, Sullivan," Cam said, pulling a wire from the inside of her dress. "Thought you were gonna blow our cover when you stuck your hand down my dress. Way to make her pimp feel comfortable, though."

I bobbed my head up and down in a slow nod. I had a sneaking suspicion I wasn't actually married. And I was really starting to suspect they had moved me from CAP to Vice.

Fuck me.

Cam gave me a breathless grin as the officers moved around the room. "We did it, Slick. You are good—even had me going there for a bit. I swear, that's why you're the best for undercover."

My dick gave a painful lurch, reminding me I'd gotten nothing in this little exchange. "What are you doing after this?"

Her smile faltered. "You mean after the paperwork? I don't know— I've been living this case for the past few months. I don't know what to do with myself now."

"Have a drink with me. Let's celebrate."

She agreed, her eyes lighting up at the suggestion. I wondered how many drinks it would take before she and Lauren were indistinguishable. My chest tightened at the thought of her, and I briefly considered the possibility that I was dying.

It wouldn't have been the worst thing.

———

"Thought about this for so long," I slurred against Cam's ear. The department had rented the hotel room for the night—it would have been a damn shame to let it go to waste.

"You have? I thought you were seeing someone." Her cheeks were pink, despite her words.

"Didn't work out—couldn't get you out of my head."

Lie.

I had never once seen her as anything other than a co-worker. Yet the tequila flowing through my veins wanted me to believe she was Lauren. Or maybe a one-night substitute.

Ignoring the large warning signs flashing in my head, I cupped her face in my hands and kissed her. She didn't feel right. Her taste was unfamiliar. Foreign. Lauren's mouth had always fit mine perfectly and the taste of her lips—a man could get drunk off of it.

I really needed my brain to shut that shit down.

I broke away from her and pulled a bottle of whiskey from the mini-bar in our suite—needing to silence my brain's not so helpful reminders of what I'd lost. I sucked it down, dimly aware of the burn.

My dick had gone as limp as a sock puppet the minute things got hot and heavy. It was shit that didn't happen to Michael Sullivan Jr.

Cam snuck up from behind and wrapped her arms around me, letting her hands roam across my stomach.

"You okay?" she whispered, her breath hot against my skin.

I nodded.

C'mon, dick. You can do this.

Nothing.

She pressed kisses to my spine, her hand sliding down to cup my balls.

"Whiskey dick?" she questioned, the disappointment heavy in her voice.

I broke away and turned to face her. No way I was going to rally. Lauren had permanently taken up residence inside my head—throwing open the front door every so often to scream, "You killed her!"

I had, hadn't I?

According to the department, a glitch in the system showed the charges had been dropped, so they released her and ruined the only fucking thing that had ever gone right for me.

Unofficially, Monica died because I went home to sleep. Would she have overdosed had I stayed? Maybe. Maybe not.

Cam, having given up on an answer, dropped to her knees and took me in her mouth. She could suck until her goddamn lips went numb. There was no way I was getting hard now.

The hair fell across her eyes, almost completely shielding her face from view.

Hold up. With her head like that, she almost looked like Lauren. It was enough to send the blood rushing back down to my cock.

She looked up at me with a grin, and it was gone. Again. Not willing to play another round of up or down, I hauled Cam to her feet and threw her face down onto the mattress.

Gentlemen, put your rally caps on—we're in the bottom of the ninth, with the bases loaded and a full count.

She wiggled her hips, and I focused only on her ass as I slipped the condom on and guided my cock inside of her.

"I dreamt about this—knew you'd feel amazing," I groaned, but I was picturing Lauren's face. Cam was here because she happened to resemble a woman who would never be mine again.

It was time to hit one out of the park and permanently erase her from memory.

CHAPTER THIRTY-SEVEN

Lauren: February 2015 (Age: 28)

F our weeks.

Days. Hours. Minutes. Seconds. All spent without her.

Even though Josué and Isaac tried convincing me it was a bad idea, I returned to work immediately. No one knew about Monica. Bringing her up now would have only raised questions I couldn't answer.

I alternated between grief and rage the first week. A part of me wanted to accept the police theory of an overdose, just because it was easier for my heart to take. Once an addict, always an addict.

It was only when I asked to see her body that I got the truth. Whoever killed her had been powerful enough to silence not only the entire police department, but the coroner's office as well.

The crisis counselor had been right about one thing. She had looked like she was sleeping. Were it not for the sudden urge to hold her hand one last time, I would have left, thinking she'd relapsed.

When Monica told me she'd been arrested, I'd wanted nothing more than to drive down to the station and sit with her hand in mine until they sorted the whole mess out.

I'd pulled her hand from beneath the paper thin sheet, trying to ignore the gray pallor clinging to her skin. That was when I knew, without a doubt, that my mother was murdered. Her fingernails were broken, leaving behind a mess of bloody nail beds. I'd immediately snatched the other hand, only to find similar damage.

When I brought it to the coroner's attention, he'd insisted addict's hands always looked bad.

Not Monica's.

Never Monica's.

Within hours of being released, they had found her five blocks from the police station with clear defensive wounds on her hands, yet no one was looking into it.

No one seemed to think that her death seemed suspicious.

No one but me.

Dara leaned into my office. "Lauren, I'm still waiting for that order from last week. Dr. Mulloy wants you to call them and see what the problem is."

Shit.

I'd written it on a sticky note. I began shuffling enormous stacks of paper from one side of the desk to the other, praying I'd buried the order somewhere in there.

Had I thrown it away?

She gave me a strange look. "Are you okay?"

I nodded absently, still tearing apart my desk. "Uh-huh. Tell Doc it's being taken care of."

Before she could say anything else, I pushed the office door closed with my foot and dropped my head on my desk, sending several stacks of papers onto the floor.

I was losing my ever-loving mind.

As a giant middle finger, my brain conjured up his face.

Mike.

My stomach gave a lurch, and I slowly inhaled and exhaled until the nausea passed. There was a light knock on the door before Elizabeth poked her head in. "Hey," she said softly. "Is everything okay?"

She had just come back from maternity leave, having taken a couple of extra weeks to be at the hospital with Kaden. He was still in the NICU, so she was still spending her every free moment there until they could release him.

I mashed my lips into a thin line to stop them from trembling before shaking my head.

She slipped in and closed the door behind her. "What happened? Is it Mike?"

Was it?

I'd been so immersed in my grief I didn't even know the specifics of it anymore.

The words were on the tip of my tongue. I wanted to blurt them out—to unburden my soul, if only temporarily. Could I do that to a woman who'd gone through her own hell, though? If I told her about my mother and what I suspected, would she become a target?

Without knowing who Monica had upset, it was hard to say. So, I settled for a version of the truth. "Mike and I broke up," I admitted with a strangled sob.

Elizabeth pulled me into her arms. "Oh, Lauren, no. Was it because of—"

I cut her off with a quick shake of my head. The last thing I wanted was for her to think the abduction or Landon's murder had anything to do with what happened. "No. It just wasn't meant to be."

She pursed her lips. "Did he cheat on you?"

I almost wished it were as easy as infidelity. Maybe then we would have had a chance of working through it. It was strange, when we became serious, cheating had been my biggest fear. Never in a million years would I have guessed he would have had a hand in ending my mother's life.

My own hand tightened into a fist as I replied, "No—look, I can't cry anymore today. I'm at my max. Can we talk about something else? How are you?"

Elizabeth leaned back against the door with a small sigh. "I'm... I'm here. Kaden's getting stronger every day, but I ache to have him home. I don't like leaving him there at night with the nurses. He needs his mom." She swiped a finger under each eye, brushing away the tears.

"But, how are you? You know, since everything?" I pressed.

"Physically, I'm back to normal. I stay busy during the day and it's like being given a reprieve." She paused. "Night is different. At night, I can't escape the nightmares."

I took her hand in mine. "What if we kept each other busy? God knows I'm barely keeping my head above water here."

Elizabeth took in my dishevelment, along with the monstrosity formerly known as my desk. "I can see that. Man, did he do a number on you. I'm half tempted to drive down to the station and give him a piece of my mind. But I won't... unless that's something you want me to do."

I smiled weakly. "If you really want to help me, you can find a pink Post-It note with an order written on it and get it overnighted so I don't lose my job."

She squeezed my hand. "Done. Maybe you could come up to the hospital with me during lunch. David's stuck on a job site and won't be able to break away until later. It'd be nice to have some company."

"Done."

Releasing my hand, Elizabeth began sorting through the papers on my desk. "Mike's an idiot. You know that, right? Letting you go—it makes no sense. He was crazy about you."

I kept my head down and made a non-committal sound as I searched for the elusive order. Feelings had nothing to do with it. His actions had spoken louder than any words. When shit went south for him, I put aside my personal feelings and supported him, yet he hadn't been willing to do the same for me.

Hadn't that said it all?

My brain had come to terms with it, but my heart?

The jury was still out on that one.

CHAPTER THIRTY-EIGHT

Lauren: February 2015 (Age: 28)

"Have a good night," I called to Dara as I walked out. We'd stayed late on the phone with our dental supply company, ensuring they would deliver her order first thing in the morning.

I pulled the keys from my purse, only to freeze when I looked up.

There he was. Again.

He'd been waiting outside for the last month—standing near his motorcycle in the corner of the parking lot.

Just watching.

At first, his presence frightened me, but he had never followed me out of the parking lot. I assumed he was one of Torch's brothers, or whatever the hell it was they called each other. Every time I considered approaching the man to ask just what the hell he thought he was doing, my courage fled, and I bolted for the safety of my car.

He continued to stare me down as I tossed my purse into the passenger seat, arms crossed over his chest. Maybe it was because my entire day had been a nightmare, but instead of running, I slammed the driver's side door and marched over.

He never changed his stance, but a grin slowly spread across his face as I got within a couple of feet.

"Who the fuck do you think you are?" I spat out before my brain could consider the consequences.

He clicked his tongue across his teeth. "Aren't you feisty? Reminds me of someone else. Oh, that's right... your mama."

I sucked in a quick breath as the grief washed over me. I'd meant for my voice to come out strong, but only managed to whisper, "Why are you here?"

He grinned again. "Maybe I just wanted to see how you were—see what you know."

I heard the threat beneath the smile. He was testing me to see if I knew the real reason Monica was no longer alive. If I gave him any sign I knew the truth, I imagined I'd end up just like she had.

I tucked my right hand into my pocket and wrapped my other around my bicep, willing myself to stop shaking. "Did Torch send you? If he did, tell him to man up and face me himself. I wanna know how Monica got those drugs—did he give them to her?"

It was a lie, but I needed him to think I was clueless. His gaze darkened as he studied my face for any signs I was deceiving him.

I tilted my chin up defiantly and looked him straight in the eyes. "What—you covering for him now?"

He latched onto my upper arm, his grip causing me to cry out in pain. I tried to move out of his grasp, but he only tightened his hold. "You want Torch, bitch? Go find him yourself. I ain't his mother."

I jerked my arm free, hissing through clenched teeth, "You think I haven't tried? If I knew where he was, I'd be there. Instead, I'm standing here with you—getting nowhere. Oh, and call me bitch one more time and I'll remove your balls."

My stomach wasn't on board with my sudden bravery streak and was eagerly trying to talk me out of it in favor of vomiting. Being with Mike had left me feeling invincible. It was only after my mouth began picking fights that my body couldn't win I remembered he was gone. Unless I wanted to end up dead, I was going to have to keep my wits about me.

Something strange happened when the biker came toward me. Instead of cowering, I stood my ground, feeling a strange sense of calm wash over me. Death was no longer something to fear, but something closer to a friend. I readied my body for the blow, undoubtedly headed my way, but he stopped at the last second with a warning.

"Watch your back. Bitch."

I exhaled a shaky breath and ran for my car, completely spent. I'd just challenged a biker and somehow lived to tell the tale. If there had been even the smallest doubts someone had killed Monica, my encounter with the biker had laid all of them to rest.

I made it to my apartment and up the stairs on wobbly legs. The box mocked me from the coffee table. I knew I needed to open it and go through her things, but doing so added a sense of finality. If I left it alone, then it wasn't real.

Despite the urn resting on the mantle of my fireplace, my mind was still clinging to this hope it was all a nightmare. I placed my palm on the gunmetal container and took several deep breaths, trying to ground. The funeral home had talked with me about caskets, but it wasn't right. Monica had lived her entire life in darkness. I couldn't bring myself to put her down in the earth to live in it for eternity.

I blinked away the tears that seemed to form at the drop of a hat these days and returned my attention to the box. A few weeks ago, I'd mustered up the strength to touch it, but couldn't bring myself to pull off the lid.

But if I had any hope of solving her murder, I was going to have to do the hard things. I took a step forward and then another until it was right in front of me. I could do this. Like ripping off a Band-Aid. With another deep breath, I lifted the lid and tossed it to the floor.

Her purse was lying on its side with the wallet peeking out from the top. I grabbed the strap with numb fingers and set it on my lap. That was all there was. No letter naming her killer or a clue to lead me down the right path.

Just her purse and wallet. I checked the interior and found her cell phone was missing. I wondered if the police station still had it, before remembering they weren't treating her death as a homicide. There was no reason for them to hold on to any of her possessions.

I could ask Mike to track it...

The thought hit me, sending a fresh round of tears streaming down my face. *Why?* Why did I do this to myself? What part of me was sadistic enough to continue digging at the open wound instead of letting it heal?

I ran the back of my hand and forearm across my eyes before opening up the wallet. Everything seemed to be there. There was cash in one pocket and her driver's license in another. Another cursory search of her purse turned up nothing other than a business card.

I'd avoided opening the damn thing for a month and it held nothing. All those nights spent lying in bed, wondering what she'd left behind.

She left nothing.

In frustration, I flipped the purse upside down and held it open, shaking vigorously.

Before I could work up the nerve to launch it across the room, the fabric separated beneath my fingers. I turned it right side up and ran my fingers along the bottom until I felt the seam.

I reached in and pulled a bundle of papers free with a soft exhale. She'd known they would go through her things. A hidden pocket inside a purse wasn't something a man would typically look for.

A folded piece of notebook paper caught my eye, and I slid it from the stack. In her loopy handwriting, she'd written:

1) Lauren

2) Torch

3) Future Grandchildren

I stared at it in confusion until it clicked. I had asked her before if she missed using and she'd said, *"Yes, every day, but I keep a list in my pocket of all the reasons not to."*

I let out a small sob and clutched the tattered paper to my chest, rocking back and forth on the couch. This was the list—with the three things that had kept her sober. It was simple, yet my heart felt as though someone had forced it through a meat grinder seeing it in writing.

The papers fell from my hands as I leaned over and clutched my knees—the air ripped from my lungs. They blended into one large blur as my eyes filled again. My grief was a bottomless pit that pulled me down a little more each time I inhaled.

Maybe it would have been easier to have kept my walls up with her.

But if I had, I never would've understood the woman behind the addict.

My phone buzzed with an incoming call. Josué. I declined it and went back to hugging my knees. I had dodged every single one of his calls this week, knowing he meant well, but packing up my entire life and moving to Austin would not fix me. It would probably only make things worse. Being waited on hand and foot with nothing to distract my mind was a recipe for disaster.

One person who hadn't reached out was Mike. No phone calls. No texts. I guess he figured we'd said all there was to say the morning my mother died.

I still didn't understand his reluctance to help. He could have moved her to a temporary safe-house and it would've been enough to keep her alive. Instead, he'd chosen to go home. And while he was sleeping peacefully, she was dying on a dirty street.

Josué left yet another voicemail, probably begging me to change my mind. But I wasn't leaving Lubbock behind. Not until I knew who killed Monica.

I ran my hands through my hair and stared blankly at the beige carpet beneath my feet. A paper coaster peeked out from beneath the couch. Seeing my mother's handwriting on the back, I picked it up.

SOD.

Roll over?

Chon.

Unable to decipher the random words, I flipped it to the front side.

Leather & Lace.

Now that I'd heard of. A seedy little bar just north of the city limits, nestled in between a boarded-up strip club and an adult video store.

I grabbed my purse and headed for the door. My stalker biker had said if I wanted Torch to go find him myself, so that was exactly what I was going to do. Even if he wasn't at the bar, someone there would know where I could find him.

Armed with nothing but my rage, I punched the accelerator to the floor. It was late, and I had no solid plan of attack, but I wasn't about to let it stop me from confronting Torch. The biker hadn't shown his face once since she passed—as if she'd meant nothing to him.

Gravel kicked up under my car with loud thuds as I pulled into the crowded parking lot just after eleven. Each pop had me white knuckling the steering wheel while searching for a place to park.

"This is fine," I told myself, finding a small space near the dumpsters in the back. I hadn't bothered to change out of my work clothes and my heels sank almost immediately. I trudged through weeds that had sprouted up from beneath the gravel and made my way to the front door, suddenly wishing I'd taken a shot of something beforehand.

Deciding I had nothing left to lose, I stepped inside and was immediately assaulted by the heavy fog of cigarette smoke. It took a second to make out the men gathered near the bar. Men who looked like they could kill with a single look.

Okay. No big deal.

I would just grab a table near the back and wait for Torch to show his face. A pair of arms stopped me before I'd even made it all the way inside and my entire plan went out the window.

"Where the fuck do you think you're going, bitch?"

I was done with being called a bitch. Enough that I spun around and grabbed a fistful of the biker's shirt, hissing, "I'm here to see Torch. Bitch."

His blue-green eyes narrowed, and I realized the words were a mistake. Because this man—he was something other than human. He looked like someone who unalived people for sport. His thick wiry beard hung down to his chest. The sides of his head were shaved with long charcoal-colored hair descending the back of his neck like a mane.

He was obviously half-Viking, half-Norse god.

And one hundred percent pissed off.

He raised an arm that was bigger than my entire body and locked his hand around my throat like a vise, sending me back. My head made a dull thud as it connected with the brick wall.

"What did you just call me?" he asked, grinning as if I amused him. Or maybe he was just considering how he could make my death slow and gruesome.

The barrel of his gun dug into my forehead. The sound of it

cocking further reinforced the idea I should have kept my damn mouth shut and stayed at home. My pulse thrummed wildly against his palm, the hairs on the backs of my arms standing at full attention.

Just when I thought I was immune to feeling anything other than soul-crushing grief, the numbness that had blanketed me over the last month evaporated.

"I-I-I," I stuttered, all strength gone from my voice. I suddenly had a strong aversion to dying.

Another biker felt me up. "She's clean," he noted casually to the biker holding the gun.

"The Sons must be the dumbest assholes alive, sending you to our bar without a weapon." His hand tightened around my throat. "Won't be a mistake they make twice, though."

My brain went haywire, searching for something to say—anything to make him reconsider killing me. "M-Monica," I forced through lips that no longer felt like mine. All the blood in my body had taken up residence in my stomach.

He jabbed the barrel of the gun deeper against my skull until it felt like it was going to go right through the bone and into my brain. "Monica? Who the fuck is Monica?"

"Torch's Ol' Lady," I croaked, seeing black spots in the corners of my vision. "Need to talk to him."

A quiet voice from across the room cut through the silence. "Back off, Carnage. It's Lauren."

Carnage immediately released my throat and lowered me back to my feet before holstering his gun. "Fuck," he whispered with wide eyes. "I'd appreciate you not mentioning this to Sullivan."

Sullivan?

Wait... the bikers were afraid of Mike?

Carnage rubbed the area where he'd just held a gun and led me over to a table on the other side of the bar. When Torch looked up from his empty pint glass, my heart stuttered.

I'd assumed he'd already moved on and forgotten my mother, but it was clear he was just as bad, if not worse off, than I was. His long mahogany brown hair hung in unwashed clumps, the dark blue bags under his eyes a stark contrast against the paleness of his face. The man was hanging on by a thread.

He waved Carnage off, and I sat down across from him, my hands still shaking badly from my near-death experience.

"I'm sorry about that. Didn't know it was you." He lowered his head, staring listlessly at the tabletop, as if waiting for his next cue.

"Um, Torch?" I chewed the corner of my lip, trying to figure out how to say what needed to be said when another biker approached, sliding two beers in front of us. Somewhere between him walking back to the bar and a long drink to steady my nerves, I decided honesty was the best policy. "Monica didn't overdose."

His head shot up. "Lauren, trust me, I don't want to believe it anymore than you. But facts are facts. I don't know how she got the H, but I'll never forgive myself for it."

I glanced around the room to make sure no one was listening in. "She was arrested for possession and being under the influence the day before—did you know that?"

He shook his head, his hand coming up to rest against the side of his face. "No, she texted to say she was spendin' the day with you. Said she'd be back Sunday."

I blew out a frustrated breath. "Then someone had her phone. She was in jail the entire day. I know how Monica gets—" I corrected myself. "How she got when she was high. But that wasn't it. She said she pissed off the wrong people, overheard something she shouldn't have. Do you know anything about this?"

He slid the full pint of beer off to the side and leaned in. "What did she overhear? Was it somethin' with the club?"

I shook my head. "I don't know. She didn't tell me before... before..." My eyes welled up and I looked down at my lap.

"Sorry about your ma, kid," a biker with a long graying beard said, patting me on the head. I was still staring at him in surprise when three more perfect strangers walked up and offered their condolences as well.

"I got the next round," offered one, and I nodded before looking back down at the floor. It was what I'd needed without even knowing it.

Acknowledgment.

She hadn't been perfect in life—far from it, actually. Until now, I hadn't known how to honor the woman who gave me life. Sharing beers with the men she'd considered family seemed fitting somehow.

Torch waited until the bikers drifted back to their tables before asking, "Lauren, how do you know she wasn't lyin'? I wanna believe you, doll. I do. But Monica and me—we had demons. Hell, I fuckin' relapsed when I heard she was—" His voice cut off and I looked up to see him shaking with silent sobs.

I slipped my hand into his. "Hey, I know how it looks, but she didn't relapse—"

He stopped me. "But how do you know?" His eyes pleaded for me to lie. To say I'd made a mistake.

I couldn't lie, even if it was easier to swallow. "I saw her—after, I mean. Her—" There she was, surrounded by blue sheets and cold as ice. My throat tightened. "Her fingernails were broken off..."

It wasn't firm evidence, and I wasn't expecting it to be enough to convince him of what I knew. Torch's grip on my hand grew tighter, squeezing to the point of pain.

The noise made me jump. I thought he broke my hand until I saw the pool of beer spreading across the table. He'd shattered the pint glass in his other hand. Some shards were still embedded in his palm, and I freed myself from his grip to frantically search for a napkin.

"FUCKING HELL!" he roared, and I cowered. The bar went silent again, curious bikers looking in our direction.

"Torch?" the gray bearded one questioned.

"Not now, Wolverine," he snapped, storming away from the table and out of the bar, leaving a trail of blood in his wake.

"Torch!" I called out, running after him. "Wait!"

He took long strides across the gravel, refusing to slow down as I stumbled in my heels after him.

Carnage came flying out of the front doors with his gun drawn. "Torch, what the fuck?"

He turned, the fury barely contained on his face. "They killed my girl!" Then he calmly walked over to the side of the bar and drove his fists into the bricks with an anguished wail. Repeatedly. Until his hands were raw and bloody.

But he didn't stop.

I covered my mouth, trying to stifle the sobs that had risen at witnessing his grief. Carnage looked at me questioningly.

"Call Grey. Tell him the Sons got Monica," Torch called out, stepping away from the building with a breathless pant.

The Sons?

Carnage growled, "If the Sons are responsible for what happened to your girl, I'll help you kill 'em myself, brother."

"Who are the Sons?"

The men ignored my question and formulated their game plan in hushed tones.

Torch finally looked up and made eye contact with me, shaking the blood off his right hand. A hand that was obviously broken in several places. "Lauren's gonna need club protection."

I shook my head. "No, what I need is for you to tell me who the Sons are. I have a right to know."

He went to reach for me before realizing both hands were still dripping blood. "Let's get you home, kid. I'll come to you once I know somethin'."

"I'm not a kid," I snapped. "You already know something—why won't you let me help you?"

Carnage laughed deeply. "You help us? That's fuckin' hilarious!"

"Fine, I'll do it myself," I spat, turning to stomp-walk back to my car. I was tits deep in this investigation—it was mine. The only reason I'd come was to feel Torch out, see where his head was at. Instead, I'd been given an impromptu memorial service for my mother before he and the rest of the club swiped the whole thing out from under me.

I wasn't waiting around for them to solve this case.

The night sky caught my attention on the angry drive back to my apartment. It was hard to see the stars with the light pollution, but I knew they were there.

Just like Mike.

He hadn't been in the picture for over a month, yet I still felt his presence. The sky was another reminder of him, and I couldn't look up without seeing his face.

The same stars we'd gazed up at just a few short months ago had been there to witness the implosion of our relationship.

Celebrations. Tragedy.

Was there any higher power in the galaxy that had fought for us? Love should come with an off switch—a way for the broken-hearted to heal in peace. I didn't need the universe providing constant reminders of the man who'd destroyed my world. It was ironic, considering cops were sworn to serve and protect.

I wrapped my jacket tighter around my body as I stepped out of my car, feeling a chill that had nothing to do with the weather.

When would the hurting stop? At what point would Mike be nothing more than a distant memory?

Could I reclaim songs and events for myself, or would thoughts of him haunt me forever? Was our love like the stars in the sky—something that would remain for all eternity?

I came to a sudden stop at the top of the stairs. Someone had kicked my front door in and spray-painted bold red letters across it.

STAY AWAY.

CHAPTER THIRTY-NINE

Mike: February 2015 (Age: 32)

"Hold still."

The blonde giggled and stuck her ass in the air. Again. It was becoming quite the game for her.

I placed my hand on the small of her back and forced her to the floor. "Lay there. Just like that."

This time, she listened. Maybe she heard the frustration in my voice. I didn't know, and to be honest, I didn't care as long as she stayed still.

I laid out two lines of coke along her spine, taking my time to make sure they were neat and even before grabbing my straw and water glass from the nightstand. I snorted a little water into each nostril, wincing at the burn.

It was going to be worth it—a little pain for a shitload of pleasure.

"Can I move?" she whined, slightly squirming on the carpet.

I shook my head even though I was aware she couldn't see me. "Move and you'll be paying me tonight. Not the other way around."

She sighed, "You sure this is how you want to spend your time? I could do other stuff for you—or you could share. Then we could both have fun."

There was no way I was wasting good blow on a hooker. And after my one-night stand with Cam, sex was out of the fucking question. It didn't matter how many times I'd pictured Lauren's face since then. My dick had gone on strike.

I snorted the first line and lay back, letting my head rest against the edge of the mattress, feeling nothing. I'd probably need another seven before I felt anything remotely close to euphoric.

It was at that moment that Hooker Number Two strolled into the bedroom, squealing in delight at the line of snow on Hooker Number One's back. She'd passed out on the couch for hours and I'd actually been looking forward to only having to pay one bimbo tonight.

"Now, it's a party!" She clapped her hands and jumped up and down, fake tits frozen in place. I stared down at my boxers, but my cock refused to come out to play.

"I get you fake tits and you still can't rise to the occasion? You might as well call yourself a pussy," I muttered, before snorting the second line.

Hooker Number Two began pouting when she realized I wasn't sharing.

I rolled my eyes, still waiting on The Best High of my life. My old man was so full of shit sometimes. "Two, what fucking bills do you pay around here that entitle you to my blow?"

Her nose wrinkled up. "Two? I told you my name is *Tru*. And excuse the fuck outta me, but you promised a party. I don't see no fucking party around here. Just a sad man in his underwear who can't even get it up."

Hooker Number One began giggling into the carpet as I jumped to my feet.

Screw that.

I got up and went to the kitchen. I knew what the problem was—I was still sober. An issue I planned on remedying right the fuck now. I unscrewed the top from the bottle of *Patrón Añejo* and tipped it back.

Within seconds, my eyes were streaming, but I continued chugging. Now it was a race to see which was going to fuck me up first—the blow or the tequila.

Hooker Number Two began a slow clap as soon as she rounded the corner. "Now, this? This is a party." She reached for the bottle, but I took a step back.

"No, s'mine. I'm the one who had his heart shattered into a million fucking pieces. I need a drink more than anybody."

Two frowned again. "You wanna talk about it?"

In a move that surprised even me, I nodded. "Yeah... I do. But first, I need another bump."

She followed me back into the bedroom where One was still lying face down on the floor.

"I haven't moved a muscle, I swear," she said, her voice muffled against the carpet.

I fought back a laugh. "You realize I snorted the blow off of you, right?"

She rolled over onto her back with a giggle and spread her legs wide, pointing to her bare pussy. "Now that you're feelin' good, you wanna?"

I froze just as Two chimed in, "Girl, he can't. He's got a broken heart."

Yep. Gather around hookers—it's story time.

One immediately sat up, tucking her knees into her chest. "What happened to you?"

I laid out another couple of lines on the nightstand and inhaled. I needed the coke to rewire my brain—anything to give me a fighting chance at leading a normal life.

Well, semi-normal.

The girls sat naked before me, waiting not for sex, but for me to tell them about the redhead who'd broken my heart.

Oh, how the mighty had fallen.

I took a deep breath and began, the coke finally giving me the slightest hint at euphoria. I had to pause several times throughout the story to snort a few more lines, washing each one down with a shot of tequila.

My tale of woe enraptured one and Two. They didn't move from their spots on the carpet as I recounted how Lauren had gotten it all wrong while pacing the bedroom.

Mr. Owl, how many lines of blow does it take to get my ex out of my mind?

Let's find out.

One. Two. Three—Nine.

Goddamn. I was floating. It had taken nine lines of blow and a fifth of tequila to get me there, but I'd finally done it. I was no longer blaming myself for Monica's death.

It felt good up here. I didn't want to come back down. Ever.

Nothing hurt.

I thought of her and it wasn't like my guts were being ripped from my stomach. I'd finally found the perfect mix—I just hadn't been doing enough blow.

My father was right—it was some damn fine stuff.

CHAPTER FORTY

Mike: February 2015 (Age: 32)

The porch swing creaked beneath me. I opened my eyes reluctantly. I was still high and more than a little drunk, but I felt good. Invincible. Didn't mean I didn't want to catch a little shut-eye, though.

"Mind if I sit here?"

I sat up quickly, careening into the chain holding the swing up. "Lauren?"

She let the screen door close softly behind her. "I'm sorry to wake you."

I rubbed my eyes. "You're really here."

One and Two better have shown themselves out, or I was going to have some explaining to do.

Lauren smiled and settled in next to me, her head on my chest. "I missed you," she whispered, and I was sure my heart was going to break through my ribs at a moment's notice.

I wrapped my arms around her and squeezed. "Shouldn't have left that morning. I should've stayed and fought for us. If I could go back, I would've stayed at the station all night."

Her hand came up and covered my mouth. "Shhhh... I believe you.

She overdosed. If it hadn't happened that night, it would've been another."

I nodded, more than a little surprised at how well she seemed to be taking it.

"I need you, Mikey," she moaned, climbing across my lap to straddle me. Without waiting for a response, she leaned down, covering my mouth with hers. She tasted different, like cigarettes. Seemed I wasn't the only one who'd turned to bad habits after the break-up.

I tried reaching for her, but my arms felt heavy. Weighted. Her teeth caught on my tongue and I winced. "Getting a little kinky there, Red?"

"Maybe," she admitted with an innocent smirk. "Is this good?" She asked, roughly running the backs of her knuckles up and down my sternum.

I groaned. "Not really."

She definitely knew about the hookers.

Lauren's hands fisted in my hair and she bit down on my tongue again until the copper tang of blood flooded my mouth. Her hitting me, I got. This? Not so much.

"Darlin', stop. I can explain."

She bit down on her lower lip and popped me in the chest with her fist before I could say another word. "Yeah? What is there to explain? I'm in love with you, Mike."

"You have a funny way of showing it," I wheezed.

"Look at me," she commanded, slapping at my cheeks. Her lips went back to mine, sending my brain pretty conflicting signals.

This was worse than the morning after her mom died. I wanted to get her off my lap before she went after the family jewels, but my whole body hurt.

"Mikey? Fuck." A voice cursed, and I jerked my head left and right, only to find myself alone again.

"Lauren?" I was beyond fucked up, but surely I would have remembered seeing her leave. The porch faded away, leaving me in complete darkness.

That settled it. I was never using again.

Leave it to Comedian to lace the coke with something dangerous, ruining any chance of a good time. I fought to remain wherever I was, as surreal as it was. But my body was being physically moved by something beyond my control.

"Mikey, open your eyes! Goddammit!" The voice was vaguely familiar, but it sure as shit didn't belong to Lauren.

A blast of cold hit my body, sending me plummeting back to earth. I fought to hold on, but the high faded almost instantly.

"N-n-n-no," I groaned.

"There we go," he panted, shifting my body. "There we go. You're alright."

I opened my eyes and immediately turned my head, trying to avoid the cold water from the showerhead.

"G-Grey?" I questioned, when the out-of-focus face came into view.

He peered into my eyes. "Christ, kid. Damn near gave me a heart attack. You fuckin' OD'ed. Jesus." He sat back on his heels, the water pelting both of us in its icy spray, and I saw something I'd never seen in his eyes before.

Terror.

"Mmm f-f-fine," I grumbled. My limbs were heavy.

Grey shook his head. "No, you fuckin' aren't. Found you face down in your own puke, Mikey. You started seizing on the goddamn floor. Eli's on his way over. Tell me where you got the drugs."

I tried to shrug, but couldn't move my shoulder more than an inch.

He brushed the hair back off of my forehead and checked my eyes. "Let me guess, Comedian? You can't pull this shit anymore—you're better than he is."

I shook my head. "S-same."

Grey grabbed me by the shoulders and shook hard enough to rattle the few remaining brain cells around.

"You're not him, Mikey!" he growled, pinching the bridge of his nose and squeezing his eyes shut. "Christ, if I hadn't shown up, you'd be dead. Was that your plan?"

"I killed Monica! W-why'd you make me k-keep her there?" I forced out through chattering teeth.

He looked at me in shock. "How did you kill Monica? Did you give her the drugs?"

I shook my head slowly. "You sent me a t-text—said to hold her in jail. I did what you said, and she died."

His eyed widened, and he moved out of the shower to kneel on the tile. "You got a text to keep her in jail? What was she arrested for?"

I closed my eyes again, wanting to give in to the oblivion, but it was just out of arm's reach. "T-told me it was safer there. Then she went and overdosed."

Talking required every ounce of my focus. My tongue was completely numb, as was the back of throat.

Grey studied my face, as if he were working a puzzle. "Do you still have those messages? Maybe we could have Jarvis trace the number."

If I had the strength, I would have been scratching my head in confusion. "Trace the number? Why? It doesn't change the fact that she got the drugs and ended herself, does it?"

He rubbed at the scruff on his jawline with the back of his thumb. The man fidgeted more than I did when working through something in his head. "Lauren showed up at *Leather & Lace* tonight."

I was suddenly fighting for soberness. "What the hell was she doing at the bar?"

"Way I heard it, she showed up, demanding to speak to Torch. Even managed to get Carnage riled up to the point he pulled his gun on her," Grey said with a grim smile.

My chest constricted painfully. "Is she—did he?" I knew what those men were, and women who came in alone were usually never seen again. If she got hurt, Grey was going to have some dead bikers on his hands.

"Hey." He placed his hand on my arm. "Lauren's alright. She's lookin' into her ma's death and shit ain't addin' up. Let's get you out of here and we'll talk." Grey reached up and shut the water off before handing me a towel.

"I've been over this a thousand times," I protested as he pulled me to my feet and guided me back to my bed. One and Two had taken off at some point, probably with all of my valuables.

Grey reached for my wet boxers and I jerked back. "Whoa, old man! I got this. Just toss me a pair from the top drawer, will ya?"

Jesus. I'd do damn near anything for the club, but I wasn't letting their Pres come anywhere near my dick

He had the decency to turn around while I pulled on a dry pair of underwear, before giving me the look. An expression that all but guaranteed I wouldn't be getting a lot of sleep anytime soon.

"I think Lauren's right about Monica being murdered. Look, I didn't text you that night—hell, I didn't even know about the arrest until you told me. There were clear defensive wounds on her hands. Torch thinks the Sons are responsible and I'm inclined to agree, especially after talking to you."

I lay back against the pillows and closed my eyes. Instead of the guilt lessening, I felt even more responsible. I'd turned my girlfriend's mother over to a bunch of monsters. "Grey, if the Sons are responsible, then they've got someone in the department on their payroll. The official story is that a computer glitch led to Monica being released that night. You're the only one who knows how to reach me on that phone. So, if you didn't text me, who the fuck did?"

He clicked his tongue against his teeth. "Thought we had the upper hand with these assholes, but I just don't know anymore. Need you to see what you can do on your end. If they're in with a badge, I wanna know who. The Sons ain't known for coverin' up a death and Lauren's convinced Monica overheard something she shouldn't have. If they think she knows something, she might become their next target."

I was almost completely sober again and feeling incredibly sick, knowing I'd brought this down on her. I'd followed orders like a good soldier, never once questioning where those orders were actually coming from. "Need to go talk to her," I mumbled as I tried to sit up.

Grey placed a hand on my chest. "Eli's on his way. You need to detox—get all that shit out of your system. Addiction runs in your family. You can't use and keep her safe."

"Is that so?" I asked with a sarcastic laugh. "Comedian get drunk enough to share the family secrets?"

The bed shifted as he stood up and stretched. "Somethin' like that. Just promise me you'll keep it in check."

"It hurts," I admitted with a slow exhale. "It hurts so fucking bad, Grey."

The only relief I'd felt in over a month had come as an overdose. It didn't leave me with much hope for the future.

He rubbed absently at the back of his head. "Love's a bitch, kid. I was a lot like you back in the day. Fucked around a lot—never had anything serious. Until Celia. Once she came into the picture, that was it for me."

"How nice for you, old man, but I got my girl's mom killed. You tell me how in the fuck that works out happily for anyone."

Sure, he straddled that line between outlaw and husband just fine, but he had no goddamn idea when it came to the things I'd done.

Grey chewed at his lip before nodding to himself. "That's why she left—she blames you for Monica?" I nodded, and he continued. "I thought maybe you'd gotten cold feet. So, what? Seems to me like you've got even more motivation to find out who's behind this now. Trust me, it ain't love unless it rips your fucking guts out."

He wasn't wrong. Loving Lauren had eviscerated me. And I hadn't even known how badly I needed her until she'd shown up to David and Elizabeth's anniversary party.

Need.

The emotion had never benefited me in the past. Need had led to me being indebted to the club. It didn't matter. Lauren held the same power over me and I would never move on.

She was it.

I pressed my fingers to my eyelids. Now was a fine time to realize my heart was going to be hers until I took my last breath.

Grey hovered in the background when Eli showed up. God forbid his number one detective croak on him. As the club doctor checked my vitals, the full impact of Grey's suspicions hit me.

If the Sons of Death took out Monica because she knew something, they had to be watching Lauren closely right about now. And they wouldn't hesitate to kill her.

I nodded at Grey. "I'm in, but I want club protection on her at all times."

"Already taken care of."

There wasn't any way to fix what I'd done, but I would still do everything in my power to keep her safe. That had to be enough for now.

CHAPTER FORTY-ONE

Lauren: March 2015 (Age: 28)

"*Hola*, Lauren. How's it hanging today?"

I looked up from my bag to see the range officer grinning at me. He couldn't have been much older than twenty-two, but was extremely knowledgeable about all things gun-related.

"I'm doing good, LR. Just can't stay away." He gave me a knowing smile and walked down to the next lane.

As much as I wanted to leave work and go home to bed, I needed more practice. That, and I didn't exactly feel safe there anymore. Not only had they tagged my front door, but my entire apartment had been ransacked.

I refused to become another one of their victims and had taken to studying Monica's notes every chance I got. Not that I was making much headway. I had seven scraps of paper with various names and dates scrawled on them, a coaster from a biker bar, and a business card that featured a smiley face with a gun pointed at its head.

Not the makings of a substantial case.

All I wanted was to wallow in self-pity. I also wanted to call up Mike because my heart was clearly on a self-destructive kick. Instead, I bought myself a handgun and took a basics class.

If another biker had the audacity to pull a gun on me again, I wanted to be ready to put a bullet between his eyes without hesitation. I couldn't rely on the police to save me—they were just as corrupt as the bikers.

I laid out my Glock 19 and a box of ammo before digging through my bag to find my eyes and ears. I was the girl who'd shown up completely clueless on my first day. At check-in, the front staff asked if I had my eyes and ears. I'd responded with an exasperated, *"Obviously."*

Once everyone had stopped laughing, I learned they were referring to protective gear. My cheeks had burned the rest of my visit, but I made sure I knew the lingo after that.

I released the magazine and began loading just as LR walked up. I was starting to think he never took a day off. At first I thought it was because he loved helping people, but he paid little attention to anyone else on the range. Just me.

"Got any plans after this?" he casually asked.

I hid a small smile. "Just going home. What about you?"

What was the harm in flirting with the RO?

He was pretty cute with his black hair spiked messily on top of his head. There was an intensity to his brown eyes, and I found it hard to stare into them for longer than a few seconds. He might not have had Mike's build, but there was some definition in his arms. He just needed a little more time with the free weights.

"I—uh, I was gonna grab a bite to eat," LR said, inspecting my gun before meeting my eyes again. "You interested?"

I took the gun from his hand, keeping it pointed downrange. Was I in any shape to date someone? Absolutely not. But sharing a meal with someone other than myself was too appealing to pass up.

"Sure. Sounds good."

He left with another grin and I focused on my target, envisioning Parking Lot Biker's face with every pull of the trigger.

Torch had peppered me with questions when I told him about my stalker—*Was he wearing a leather vest? What patches were on display?*

I hadn't paid attention to what was on his vest, but promised I would look the next time he showed up. But he hadn't, and I could only speculate where he'd gone.

The only biker waiting for me when I left work now was Torch. He sat on his motorcycle with a lit cigarette dangling from his lips, glaring.

A search of the names on Monica's list hadn't turned up anything either. According to the internet, these men didn't exist. Torch continued for any information I could give, but I wasn't handing anything over until I knew what it meant.

I was back to square one, tirelessly searching for anything that would lead me to her killer. Torch believed it was another group of bikers, but it could have just as easily been someone she knew.

What had she overheard?

Finding the answer had become an obsession. I couldn't sleep. Thanks to a chronic upset stomach, I wasn't eating much, either. Between my mother and Mike, I was one crisis away from a nervous breakdown.

———

"So, what got you interested in guns?" LR asked in between bites of his sandwich at a little cafe just blocks from the range.

I swallowed my soup. "As a single woman, I felt it was time to learn. Not like the world's getting any safer, you know?"

He took another bite and chewed before asking, "You don't want a man to take care of you?"

Right to the point.

"Nope. I enjoy being alone."

It was a lie, but what could I say?

I fell in love with a crooked cop and broke up with him when he wouldn't bend the rules for me. This led to my mother dying and me holding him person-ally responsible. Would you like to go on a second date sometime?

"Maybe you just haven't been with the right guy yet," he said with a wink, his eyes full of mischief.

My cheeks flamed, and I dropped my eyes back down to my soup bowl. "Maybe?"

He wasn't Mike.

Not even close.

I still wasn't sure whether that was a good or bad thing. We sat quietly, each of us picking at our food and searching for something to talk about. I suddenly wished we'd gone to a bar instead—at least we would have had alcohol to break the tension.

"What does LR stand for?" I ventured, hoping it was enough of a conversation starter to at least get us through dinner.

His entire face lit up. "It stands for Little Ricky. My ma was a big fan of I Love Lucy and named me after Lucy's kid. Sometimes, I tell myself, 'Little Ricky, you are a grown ass man, time to get a grown ass name.' Man, I don't know, though. It's hard to give it up."

I couldn't help it and grinned along with him. "I think Little Ricky has a lot more character than LR."

He bit into his sandwich and, with a full mouth, responded, "Well then, call me Little Ricky. It'll be our thing."

Our thing—as if we were already together. What would dating a younger guy be like? Sure, he was fine as hell, but would I just compare him to Mike?

When he reached for my hand, I didn't pull away, even as everything inside of me screamed to let go.

What was wrong with me?

Somehow mistaking my hesitation for encouragement, he leaned in and pressed his lips to mine. I felt nothing—not even the smallest hint of a spark. It was disappointing.

Little Ricky's face was baby smooth, where Mike's had been scruffy. His lips were fuller and softer, but I missed the roughness. His kiss was lacking the things I loved most—the things that had been unique to Mike.

His tongue slipped between my lips, and I tried to conjure up something—anything to blur the memories.

"You're beautiful, *mi sirenita*," he praised against my lips, his hand still tangled up in my hair. The soft smile disappeared as suddenly as it appeared. "Son of a bitch," he muttered under his breath.

I turned and immediately dropped into a crouch when I saw what he was looking at. Or rather, *who* he was looking at.

"Did he see me?" I hissed from my hiding spot under the table.

"Oh I saw you, darlin'. Saw him. Saw you. Saw it all."

Shit.

I sat up and reluctantly faced the man who refused to vacate my brain, no matter how many eviction notices I sent. "Mike, hello. I didn't see you there."

He looked amazing, and I hated him a little more. It would have been easier had he looked like he'd just crawled out of a dumpster. But no, here he was, standing in front of me, looking just as he had when we were together. It was throwing the old lady-bits into quite the tailspin.

Traitorous bitches.

"Hello," he parroted back, lip twitching against a smile. "Mind if I join you?"

"I—I think—"

He slid into the booth next to me while I was still trying to stammer out a response and thrust a hand toward Little Ricky. "Sup, man? I'm Mike. I'm sure Lauren's mentioned me."

Little Ricky didn't take the bait, keeping his hand on the table. "Hasn't said a damn word to me. And you and I have already met, *cabrón.*"

This time, I was the one frowning. "You have? When?"

They had a silent conversation with their eyes before Little Ricky explained. "This guy comes down to the range now and then. Acts like a complete prick too—drives my boss fucking loco."

"Really?" I asked.

Mike's glare turned murderous and he bit out, "Yep. Be nice if they'd hire a RO who actually knows what the fuck he's talking about. Maybe then I'd be nicer to deal with." He grabbed the extra silverware and stole a spoonful of my soup. "It's good. You sure you don't want it, baby?"

I ground my teeth together. "I did until you started eating it. And don't call me that."

Mike shrugged and took another bite before reaching across the table for the uneaten half of Little Ricky's sandwich. He took a bite and immediately grimaced. "Pastrami? C'mon, man."

I pretended to be looking for something inside my purse to avoid having to make eye contact with either of them, knowing, without a doubt, my cheeks were flaming red.

"You ready, Lauren?" Little Ricky asked, giving Mike the side eye.

What?

I'd driven myself and met him here, and he knew it.

"Actually, I'll take her home," Mike interjected with a smirk.

"Over my dead body, ass—"

Mike was out of the booth and on him, snarling, "You fucker—you know what she means to me!"

He threw a punch but missed, giving Little Ricky enough time to slide free from the booth. He swiped Mike's legs out from under him, sending him down to the linoleum floor with a loud squeak.

"*Me cago en tu puta madre,*" Little Ricky hissed before launching himself on top of Mike.

"Oh, is that Spanish for *I have a small dick*? It's alright, little buddy," Mike growled back at him, slapping at his face.

The two looked like they were locked in a passionate embrace as they flopped across the floor. Neither one seemed capable of landing a solid hit—it was like watching toddlers fight.

Any minute now Mike was going to cry out, "Little Ricky pinched me!"

I slid out of the booth, only to be elbowed out of the way by a manager and several onlookers. I fought my way forward, standing on tiptoe to see over the other patrons' shoulders.

Like boxers in the tenth round, they were panting heavily with their arms wrapped around each other, each placing weak blows into the other's back. The manager tried separating them and barely dodged a blow off the side of his head before shouting, "That's it—I'm calling the cops!"

"I'm a cop!" Mike exclaimed, shoving Little Ricky aside to get to his feet again. He displayed his badge, and like magic, everyone immediately backed down.

Typical. Completely and utterly typical.

I rolled my eyes and retrieved my purse, heading for the front of the restaurant.

"Lauren?" Both men called after me, but I kept walking, right through the front door.

I was feet from my car when my breath hitched. My eyes stung, but I blinked, refusing to give him the privilege of seeing me cry.

"Red—c'mon, darlin'. Wait. Let me talk to you." Mike caught the sleeve of my jacket just as I reached my car door, pulling me back.

"There you go again," I snapped, wrenching my arm free. "Whipping out your badge to get out of a bind. God forbid you do the same for someone else. Must be nice to not have the rules apply to you."

His face fell. "Lauren, I did what I had to do. The guy was going to call the police—"

"Let's get out of here, *mi sirenita*," Little Ricky interrupted.

I pointed at my car. "I drove myself—remember?"

He nodded and stuck his hands into his jacket pockets, rocking back and forth on his heels against the frigid wind. "Well... we could grab coffee or something."

His split lip was swelling.

"I think I've had enough excitement for one night. I'll just plan on seeing you tomorrow night at the range."

"Over my dead body," Mike muttered, and I gave him a chilly look. He had fared about as well as Little Ricky and was going to have a hell of a time driving home with one eye as the other was almost swollen shut.

"I'll deal with you in a minute."

Little Ricky nodded. "It's cool. I'll see you tomorrow night." He leaned in and gave me a kiss on the cheek while Mike grumbled obscenities in the background.

Once he was gone, I turned back to Detective Douchebag. "I'm leaving and I'd appreciate it if you didn't follow me again. You've done enough."

He stepped into my path, blocking me. The smell of him enveloped me like a warm hug and every feeling bubbled up to the surface. Emotions I'd fought so hard to invoke with Little Ricky easily came back with Mike in front of me.

"Darlin', I think about you every day. I can't let you leave upset. I still love you." His face was the picture of innocence as he stood in front of me, arms crossed over his body.

I wanted to rake my nails down his cheeks again until he remembered why I wouldn't take him back. He'd gotten my mother killed. And, just like that, him showing up was no longer amusing or cute. It was a dick move.

"Typical Mike Sullivan, thinking that because you want something, it's automatically yours for the taking. Well, flash your badge all you want, asshole. I'm not interested."

I tried to sidestep him, but he caught my arm at the last second, pulling me up against his warm body. It took everything in me not to throw my arms around him and hold on for dear life, but I managed. Just barely.

"Lauren, I love you. Can't that be enough?" His eyes pleaded for acceptance, his hands shaking against my back.

As much as I wanted to say yes, I wouldn't dishonor my mother like that.

"No," I said, before my eyes clouded and my throat tightened. "I told you I would stay with you even if it meant going to prison, but you—"

My voice cracked as the first tear fell and I had to fight to get my thoughts out. "But you wouldn't do the same for me. I loved you in those gray areas, while you only saw black and white with me. And I deserved better—she deserved better."

"Lauren—I—" His words tapered off. He stepped back, letting me go.

The remaining tears hit my cheeks as I pulled out of the parking lot, blindly cranking the stereo volume up.

"You get five minutes to cry," I told myself, amid the flood. "And then you are going to suck it up and stop being a little bitch."

I sucked in a ragged breath as the first bars of 'Come a Little Closer' by Dierks Bentley began to play before hurriedly changing the station.

I needed something angry, not another reminder of the handsome blond surfer who'd asked me to dance on a beach. I punched the next button, exhaling a soft sigh of relief as the familiar guitar riff of 'Seven Nation Army' filled the car.

Five minutes to fall apart.

And then, I was going to banish Michael Sullivan Jr. from my thoughts forever.

I hoped.

CHAPTER FORTY-TWO

Mike: April 2015 (Age: 32)

I blindly felt for my phone, pulled from a dead sleep and dreams of Lauren.

It was all I did lately.

Tonight, she'd married Little Ricky and started a family with the prick. The two then had a daughter they lovingly referred to as Little Lauren, and their son—Littlest Little Ricky. Lauren had never looked happier.

It was a goddamned nightmare.

Little Ricky was supposed to keep a discreet watch over Lauren—not ram his goddamned tongue down her throat in front of me. I clenched my jaw, remembering how it had taken three of Grey's men to hold me back when I'd shown up to confront the prick later.

"Hello?" I answered groggily, trying to clear my mind. The ensuing silence had me on high alert. "Lauren, baby, are you okay?"

"Detective, this is Katya Egorichev. I'm sorry to wake you."

"What's going on now?" I asked, stifling a yawn. I might have been more interested had she not called on and off over the last three months, convinced someone was stalking her. Every conversation led back to Landon Scott. Despite giving her his college ring, she had somehow convinced herself the man was still alive.

If the woman hadn't been through the fucking ringer already, I would have recommended a psych eval because she had definitely lost touch with reality.

She sniffled into the phone before clearing her throat. "Um, there was a note on the door to my condo when I got home tonight."

I hastily rubbed the sleep from my eyes and sat up. "What did it say? Did you see anyone?"

"It said, *These days when I see you, you make it look like I'm see-through.* I swear, I didn't see a soul, though. How did he get into my building, Detective?"

I reached over to turn on the bedside lamp and grabbed my notebook. After recording the latest message, I asked, "Has there been anything else? Any specific people you keep seeing around?"

There was the unmistakable clink of glass on glass.

"What are you doing right now, Katya?"

"Drinking, Detective," she responded in a flat tone. "It's the only way to get through the nights. To answer your question, no. There's just been this and the *Victoria's Secret* catalog with, *What do you know about the disappearance of Katya Egorichev?* written on it.

"You said not to worry, but—" Her voice broke. "I'm starting to worry."

Fuck, I wanted a drink.

I wanted to ask her what was in the glass—wanted to hear the liquid sloshing up against the sides of the bottle. But first, I needed to calm her the fuck down before she did something stupid, like admit Landon was dead over an unsecured line.

"Okay, I've got the catalog incident noted," I reassured her. I didn't, but that was only because I'd been certain it didn't exist. She swore she came home to her condo and found a catalog, published after she went missing, hidden under the comforter on her bed. The problem was local police officers couldn't find any record of its existence.

"Remember what we talked about. I am pouring every resource into finding Landon. You need to stay safe until we get him, though."

We both knew the guy was dead, but I felt bound to mention we were looking for him every time we spoke—needing to cover my ass should anyone be listening in.

"I'm being careful, Detective. I promise you that."

I wanted to believe her—I did—but I broke out in a cold sweat every time I saw her name on my caller ID. Katya was a wild card, always one bad day away from revealing everything.

After promising to look into the latest note, we hung up. If there was a copycat masquerading as Landon, what was the motive? Were they trying to scare her or convince her to come clean because they had somehow figured out Landon Scott was dead?

My thoughts made going back to sleep impossible. What was my promise to David going to cost me? If the dominos fell, they'd lock me up and throw away the key. I doubted even Grey's club connections would be enough to bust me out.

And if I was behind bars, who would keep Lauren safe?

I went back over the details, convinced Grey was on to something. It was looking like someone had killed Monica to keep her quiet.

I wasn't the only double-agent hiding behind a badge, which made looking into her death that much harder. If the Sons of Death got wind of me looking into an open and shut case, they wouldn't hesitate to go after Lauren.

Grey was right—she was my weak spot and the first person they would take out to get to me.

Knowing I needed to get evidence without arousing suspicion, I turned to Jeremy—or Jarvis, as he was known within the club. Not only a kick-ass realtor who'd helped me find my place, but he was a master hacker, too. Guy could probably tap into the DoD website without breaking a sweat.

As if he'd hacked my brain and read my thoughts, my phone lit up with a text from the man himself.

Jarvis: I'm not liking this autopsy report.

Me: No shit. I don't fucking like it either. If it didn't exist, I'd still have Lauren.

She may have left me standing in a parking lot alone after I crashed her little date, but there was still something there. A spark. If she was still willing to go toe to toe with me, maybe she felt it, too.

Jarvis: Someone tampered with it. I haven't been able to get into the original yet. Just wanted to give you a head's up. You and Goblin sort shit out yet?

I rolled my eyes.

Me: What are you—my fucking therapist? Wake me up when you actually have something.

Goblin. It was a fitting club name for Little Ricky—sneaky little shit. I cracked my knuckles and leaned back against the headboard with a sigh.

Well, it was official.

I had surpassed David as the surliest bastard alive.

Thanks to Katya, I wanted a fucking bottle of tequila to go with my memories of Lauren.

CHAPTER FORTY-THREE

Mike: April 2015 (Age: 32)

"*Chingate*! She wants a real man—not some *chocha*!"

My fist caught him in the abdomen and he immediately doubled over with a loud groan. Sensing I wouldn't get another opportunity, I began pummeling him with all I had. "Mine. She's mine!"

"Holy fuckin' shit!" Grey roared, stepping into the large living area of the clubhouse. "Fuckin' warned you two about this!"

Little Ricky landed one on my jaw and I stumbled back into the wall, vision blurring. Before I could collect my bearings, he let out a small roar and charged toward me.

Grey grabbed me and hauled me over to the opposite side of the room. "Fuck, Mikey—what'd I tell you?"

I shrugged and wiped the blood from my nose like a defiant teen. "I don't know, old man. You say a lot of shit."

Little Ricky fought against my father and Carnage in his attempts to get to me. "You don't deserve her, *cabrón*."

I pointed an unsteady finger at Grey. "Thought you were shutting him down. He fucking took her out again!"

Little Ricky grinned widely from across the room and gestured toward his chest. "You forgot to mention those amazing tits—I took those out too! *Mi sirenita* is a ten."

"Motherfucker!" I roared.

Grey halted me with one arm. "Let him talk—I'll fuckin' deal with him later. Look at me," he insisted, gripping my chin. "You been drinkin' again?"

"No," I lied, trying to look anywhere but his eyes.

He sighed and dropped his hand. "I can smell the tequila on your breath, kid. Said you were quittin'."

I leaned back against the wood-paneled wall for support. "No, you told me that alcoholism ran in my family and assumed I was quitting. I never agreed to it."

His blue eyes narrowed in frustration. "Called you down here to help with club business. You even capable of that anymore? Seems to me if you're not chasin' after your ex, you're buried in the fuckin' bottle. Gotta be honest here—I ain't got an ounce of confidence in you anymore."

I flinched at his words. If I wasn't indispensable to the club anymore, then I was as good as dead in their minds.

Hadn't they made that abundantly clear over the years?

Unfortunately, I was still a Sullivan, and we didn't know how to back down without a fight.

"So, I can go home then?" I asked sarcastically.

Grey smiled through clenched teeth and then, without saying a word, drove his fist into my stomach. I dropped to my knees with a loud grunt, reeling from the blow and struggling to keep the tequila in.

"Might wanna watch your mouth, Junior. Pres ain't in a jokin' mood tonight," Comedian cheerily called from across the room.

I responded with my middle finger and fought through another round of nausea as I rocked on all fours. It was a losing battle. I turned my head and vomited onto the cement floor near Grey's boots.

"Tried to take it easy on ya, kid. But, enough is enough. Man the fuck up and help me out here. You're my eyes and ears on the inside and right now—someone in your department is passing along information to the Sons."

I wracked my brain, but no one came to mind. I had been treated the same way by all of my colleagues and superiors. If someone had it out for SPMC, then I'd completely missed it.

In all honesty, since giving up sobriety, I had missed a lot of things.

"I haven't seen anything, but I'm on it," I assured Grey, but he continued to stare daggers at me.

"You're on it? Well, maybe you can explain what happened over at *Inked on Broadway* today. C'mon, Mikey, don't get shy now. Tell the entire club how you're fuckin' handling this situation." He crossed his arms over his chest.

Shit.

Inked on Broadway had been a part of the club from the very beginning. While they did well enough on their own, the tattoo parlor was still loaded with dirty money from all of Grey's exploits.

Gun money. Drug money. You name it. It all flowed through my old man's body shop, *Inked*, the bars, six car washes, and several other mom and pop businesses. Grey always kept his deposits at roughly the same amount and never enough to draw suspicion from the banks.

"Keep it under ten grand and we're golden," he'd once boasted.

I cleared my throat; the tequila having seared off what remained of my tonsils. "Uh, something happened at Inked? It didn't come through the station."

Maybe it had.

At the moment, I couldn't recall if I'd even come through the station.

Carnage winced and turned away, while my father grinned from ear to ear. "Junior, you got to get a handle on your drinkin'."

If he was telling me to lay off the drinking, then I was worse off than I'd initially thought. I gave him a weak thumbs up before turning back to face Grey.

He didn't look amused. In fact, I got the distinct impression he was seconds away from snapping me in half. "*Inked* has been taken over by every fuckin' agency in the country. Criminal Investigation Unit from the IRS, FinCEN and OIA from the Office of Terrorism and Financial Intelligence, as well as the goddamn FBI and DEA," He snapped, ticking each agency off on his fingers with a poorly controlled rage.

"The feds froze our assets while they investigate accusations of money laundering. So please, Detective, tell me what the fuck you're doin' to help us."

The room spun around me and, for the first time in a while, it had nothing to do with the tequila. This wasn't me going down for murder anymore—it was all of us going down for such a vast array of shit I couldn't even fathom prison sentences and fines.

We were fucked, and Grey was right yet again. I had to sober up for good and find the snitch before the federal government came crashing down on all of our fucking heads.

I looked around the room at all the men who'd become like family over the years. All wore matching somber expressions—shit, even Little Ricky looked scared. Crossbones looked like he wanted to punch someone—probably me. He'd never forgiven me for arresting him back in 2009 and, given the way things were going, I couldn't say I blamed him.

I had to put my bullshit personal feelings aside and take care of this.

If I got a handle on this, then it might help me with the Monica situation. That would help me with Lauren. This wasn't over.

Not by a long shot.

I looked at Grey. "May I?"

He nodded, and I ran through the speech in my head.

Okay, Mike. Sober up. Any time now is good.

With a deep breath, I began. "Alright, motherfuckers, listen up. The Sons are trying to take over. Right now, it looks pretty fucking awful for us."

Grey cocked his head to the side. Seemed my motivational speech was severely lacking in motivation.

I cleared my throat and tried again. "What I mean is we've been here before with other clubs. It's war, plain and simple. From here on out, no displaying colors in public—you might as well stick a fucking target on your back. No going off on your own. Find a buddy. That goes for family members too. The Sons won't hesitate to take out your Ol' Lady. Gentlemen, you fucking own this area. It's time to act like it."

Carnage piped up from the back of the room. "How the fuck are we acting like we own the town if we're shedding our kuttes? They're going to see us as a bunch of pussies."

I smiled patiently. Now we were in my territory. I'd read *The Art of War* cover to cover—shit, I'd lived my entire life in a war-zone. I was at home there.

"Well, Carnage, as my good buddy Sun Tzu would say, *'Appear weak when you are strong, and strong when you are weak.'* Who gives a fuck what they call the club? *'All war is deception'*—my bro said that one too. I'll take care of the legal side of things, but it's time to rally the fucking troops. Grey, call in the other chapters. We need to convince the Sons we're backing down when, in reality, we're building a motherfucking army!"

Comedian beamed at me and began clapping. "There ya go, Junior!" He yelled, and the others followed his lead.

Grey nodded to himself, never taking his eyes off of me. "You heard the man." He raised his voice above the others. "Make it happen!"

Fuck, I should have been a speechwriter.

CHAPTER FORTY-FOUR

Lauren: April 2015 (Age: 28)

The banging on the roof got louder, but I tried my best to block it out and complete payroll. Luckily, it was a half day. I didn't think my nerves could handle a full eight hours of this.

A piece of equipment fell with a large thud that seemed to shake the entire building and sent my pen falling to the floor. I was bending to retrieve it when my office door burst open.

I scrambled back with a strangled gasp as Dr. Mulloy marched in, hissing, "What the hell, Lauren? Why is there a six-man crew up on the roof when I have a full clinic?"

I stared stupidly at her. "But... but, it's Friday. Why are you here?"

She blinked incredulously. "It's fucking Monday! Good lord, are you hungover? Still drunk?"

I pursed my lips before softly replying, "Something like that." It wasn't alcohol that had me behaving erratically, but sleep deprivation—the most dangerous drug around.

Now I was losing touch with reality.

I was sure I'd scheduled the roofers to come Friday and pointed to the appointment on my desk calendar. "They're supposed to come on the thirteenth."

She lifted several stacks of paper from my desktop. "Look at the month, Lauren. This is your calendar for March. We're in April now."

I dropped my head into my hands and groaned. "Sandra, I'm so sorry. I've just got a lot on my plate right now."

"It's Dr. Mulloy, Lauren," she said with a sniff. "Can you explain to me why you're drunk on a Monday morning? You and the boyfriend have a long weekend?"

She always made a point to ask about him and while I usually remained non-committal on it, I was exhausted. "Actually, we broke up."

"Did something happen? Was it another woman?" she asked, tucking a strand of hair behind her ear.

I closed my eyes against the sudden tension headache and fought back tears. "No... it just didn't work out. Listen, I really need to go talk to the roofers to see if I can reschedule. I'll get this taken care of for you. It won't happen again, I promise."

She remained in the doorway, staring as if I'd grown three heads. "Are you sure you're okay to be here? Do you need to take the after-noon off?"

I quickly shook my head and went back to the computer screen. I didn't trust her sudden kindness. Sandra wasn't known for doing anything out of the goodness of her heart. There was a catch. Until I knew what it was, I was better off working through my broken heart up here.

Elizabeth caught up to me as I headed toward the roof access room.

"Hey... wait up."

I slowed my stride and turned. "What's wrong?"

The corner of her mouth lifted in a small smile. "I could ask you the same thing. Did Doc go crazy? I tried to warn you, but was too late."

I pressed the palm of my hand gently against my forehead, desperate for relief. "It was fine. Just having an off day. How are you? Have they said if Kaden will get to come home soon?"

Elizabeth bit down on her lower lip. "Well, that's kind of why I wanted to talk to you. He's almost up to eighty percent bottle feedings and they've said he'll be released as soon as he does. Lauren, I just don't think that I can manage all of his care and work full time. I'm sorry."

I shook my head and pulled her into a hug, my mind swirling with a massive to-do list.

Get the roofers off the building.

Find a new patient coordinator.

Work on remembering what day it is.

Call the police department and ask for a copy of Monica's autopsy report.

Stop thinking about a certain detective.

Get back to the gym.

Avenge my mother's death.

"It's fine. Honestly, I expected it. You take care of that sweet boy."

It wasn't fine. It was just one more chink in my armor. I was unraveling more and more every day, descending into a madness I wasn't certain I could recover from.

My apartment resembled a TV detective's office, with post-it notes and push-pins littering the walls. I stayed up all night scrawling down anything that seemed vital. In the harsh light of day, though, the notes looked like nothing more than the ramblings of a crazy person.

It wasn't too far from the truth.

Grief was strange.

Some days, I wasn't sure I could get out of bed and cover up the fact that I'd been crying most of the night. Then there were days when I woke up and felt nothing. I'd stare at my reflection in the bathroom, wondering why the thought of Monica wasn't reducing me to tears. Those days were the worst—it was as if I was already forgetting her.

CHAPTER FORTY-FIVE

Lauren: April 2015 (Age: 28)

"I'm sorry, Ms. Santiago-McGuire. To access that information, you'll need to come down to the station and fill out a form. Once that's processed, it could take up to six weeks."

It was ridiculous. One call to Mike and I would have had the report in my hands the same day. But I still had my pride, along with the remnants of the broken heart he'd left me with before.

I pushed the metal pin in between the plates near the bottom of the leg extension machine and lifted the weight up with a huff. My quads burned, but I powered through four sets on nothing but fury. I doubted I'd be able to walk tomorrow.

I finished my last rep and headed for the bench press machine. I hadn't been to the gym in months and, for the life of me, couldn't fathom why I was jumping from machine to machine with no clear workout plan in mind.

Kind of like my life.

At work, I was still struggling to stay on top of things—something that had not gone unnoticed by Dr. Mulloy.

"If you can't manage this office during your little break-up, I'm going to need to find someone who can. How do we have a past due balance with two of our

*suppliers? If I've got a hold on my accounts, I can't order. If I can't order, I can't
see patients. If I can't see patients, then we're all fucked. Do you understand?"*

A meathead grinned appreciatively at me from where he lingered
nearby, clearly waiting to chat.

"Not even if my life depended on it," I paused long enough to
mutter while loading more plates onto the bar. He muttered a curse
under his breath before stalking off to find his next target, and I went
back to kicking my ass—both physically and mentally.

The last thing my upended life needed in it was another man.
Something I'd realized the night Mike and Little Ricky turned a quiet
cafe into an MMA ring. I wasn't ready to date—not now, maybe never.

Unfortunately, Little Ricky hadn't taken the hint. No matter how
many times I changed my shooting schedule to dodge him, he
somehow showed up at the range every single time I was there.

We had shared one kiss. One lackluster, firework-free kiss.
According to him, though, we were about to embark on a magical
journey.

No, seriously.

Those were his exact words. If I gave him one night in my bed,
then I would never again want for another man.

Again, exact words.

Once I'd stopped laughing long enough to respond, I'd politely
asked if we could just be friends and then promptly found a new place
to practice. If the text he'd sent me earlier this afternoon was any indicator, he wouldn't give up.

LR: Mi sirenita, let me stay over.

"You almost done with this machine?"

I tilted my head back on the bench until my eyes connected with a
giant of a man. "Um, I just started. I still have two more sets."

He nodded. "I'll wait. You need a spotter?"

I frowned. "No, I'm good. See?" The bar slipped from my grasp
and I was bracing myself for the crushed collar bone that was
undoubtedly coming my way when the giant swooped in and
caught it.

"Yeah, you look like you've got this all under control here," he noted, fighting a smile. "I'm Jimmy."

He returned the bar and helped me into a sitting position.

"Lauren," I responded breathlessly, the blood rushing out of my head.

I took a second to collect my bearings and admire the way his gray hoodie and black joggers clung to his massive frame. His chestnut brown hair was close cropped on the sides, but longer on top with the part cut into it. Obviously, it took time and good hair gel for it to look as perfect as it did.

His eyes were a deep shade of blue. Where Mike's were more of an electric blue, Jimmy's were darker, like a wolf's. My eyes roamed over the stubble on his chiseled jawbone and the full lips most women would kill to have.

Lips that were now turned up in an amused smirk.

"Right," I murmured, feeling my face heat. There was no hiding the way I'd been shamelessly drinking him in. "Great to meet you. I'm going to go die now."

He let out a deep chuckle. The vibrations of it were probably being felt throughout the entire gym. "No need for that. Look, I need a spotter and my buddy flaked out on me. Why don't you stay? I could put you through my work-out."

I nodded. "Okay, but I'm kind of on a mission to inflict as much pain as possible on my muscles."

Jimmy pointed to several machines. "I think this place has every-thing we need to make that happen. You're doing what? Chest and biceps? Chest and triceps?"

I shrugged. "I was sort of doing a mix of everything—legs, arms, chest..."

He let out something that sounded suspiciously like laughter before composing his face back into a serious expression. "Okay then, let's pick maybe two of those, yeah?"

"Fine. Let's see what you got, Jimmy."

He moved through the chest and bicep workout with ease while I worked valiantly to remain standing. The man was a well-oiled machine, while I was somewhere near old toaster. I huffed right alongside him, refusing to admit defeat by throwing myself down on the mats.

An eternity later, he took a swig from his water bottle and grinned. "Well, what'd you think?"

What'd I think?

That my arms were made of spaghetti.

I sat down on an empty bench and rested my forearms on my thighs. "Um," I huffed. "That was a good beginner work-out. Thanks."

He prodded my shoe with the tip of his. "Beginner workout? I thought you were going to flatline on me several times."

I shook my head, looking like a wet dog as the sweat flew in different directions. "Did not. I was great."

Jimmy held out his hand to me and I slipped mine into it without a second thought. "Oh. I was going to give you a high-five," he explained.

I immediately dropped it.

"Sorry, thought you were helping me up off of this bench. I guess I can spend the night down here. Maybe the morning crew will find me." It was a lie, but better than confessing I thought he was trying to hold my hand.

His eyes darkened as he reached for me again. "Jesus, sorry. Here." He easily lifted me and my chest collided with his stomach. Like something out of a movie, our eyes locked, and we instinctively moved closer together.

Unlike with Little Ricky, I was expecting this kiss.

Jimmy froze at the last second and straightened. "I've—I've gotta hit the shower. It's pretty late. If you've got time to wait around, I can walk you out."

I nodded, and all but ran for the women's locker room. I stopped in front of a full-length mirror and checked myself over. My nose was clear and my makeup was still relatively in place. I sniffed my armpits and checked my breath before deciding I smelled fine.

It was the first time since January someone had distracted me from the crushing disappointment that had become my life. Without his presence, my mind fell back into the familiar abyss.

I stripped out of my sweaty tank and retrieved the waistband holster from my gym bag. It was nothing more than military grade black elastic, but with the hot pink ribbon corseted up the back, I actually felt sexy wearing it. I slid the mag back into my Glock before holstering it with shaky hands. The workout had done a number on my arm muscles. I slipped a baggy green t-shirt over my head and gave myself a final glance in the mirror, fighting to purge thoughts of Mike from my brain.

Jimmy waited just outside the locker room, casually leaning against a wall like a magazine model. His hair was damp, but still perfectly in place, and I wondered if the water just beaded off.

"You ready?" he asked.

I nodded. "Sure. Thanks for the escort."

He opened his mouth as if to say something before turning toward the exit. I followed behind, the scent of his cologne creating a trail of sorts.

"I've got a bike," he said, retrieving a cherry red helmet from the front desk.

Of course he did.

"You're a biker."

He gave me a confused smile. "Was that a question or a statement?"

"I've just run into a lot of bikers lately," I admitted with a sigh. "It's like I can't walk outside without finding one."

"You got something against motorcycles?"

I slung my bag across my back. "No—just the gangs you all belong to."

Jimmy chuckled as if I'd said something incredibly witty. "*Gang?* Lauren, I just ride a motorcycle. It's nothing more than a mode of transportation."

I was turning into one of those crazy people on the street, convinced the government was hiding listening devices inside supermarket produce.

"I'm sorry," I said, massaging the back of my neck and wishing I could disappear into the concrete beneath my feet. "I'm just exhausted and—"

"Can I have your number?"

"What?" I snorted. "Didn't get enough insults tonight?"

Jimmy cocked his head to the side and studied my face. "Something like that. So, is that a yes?"

What are you doing, Red?

His voice was so clear I could have sworn he was standing right behind me. I'd officially gone off the deep end if the voice in my head.

Jimmy saw me hesitate. "Hey, if you're not comfortable giving it to me, no big deal. I just thought in case I don't see you again, I'd better ask."

Was I really going to live out the rest of my life, afraid to take a chance on falling in love again because of what Mike did?

"Tell you what. Why don't we not see each other again on Friday at eight? I can put you through my workout this time."

I was going to get over Mike Sullivan. I just needed to distract my heart long enough for it to piece itself back together.

He grinned. "It's not a date."

We said our goodbyes, and I sank into the driver's seat with a happy sigh. So, it wasn't like it was with Mike. That was probably a good thing. I had to wait for a break in traffic before pulling out of the parking lot, one downside to living in a college town.

As I merged into the far-right lane and approached my exit, I noticed a motorcycle in my rearview mirror.

Jimmy.

When he made the same turn, I shook my head with a laugh and cranked up my music. If he was trying to catch up with me, I was going to pretend like I didn't notice. While Will.i.am and Britney were encouraging me to scream and shout, I kept my eyes on the rearview mirror, silently encouraging him to keep up.

Unfortunately, Jimmy was content to remain three cars behind me. I merged into the left lane to get on the Loop and he followed, only speeding up once we were on the freeway.

It was then I noticed that the rider on the motorcycle was wearing a black helmet with a tinted visor.

It wasn't Jimmy.

There were probably other cars that had followed mine from the gym, all going to different destinations. I tried convincing myself it was just a weird coincidence, even as my pulse raced.

When I changed lanes, the motorcyclist moved with me immediately. Okay, he was definitely following me. My exit was coming up on the right, but I didn't want to lead him to my doorstep. Instead, I passed it and then picked up speed before moving back into the middle lane.

The motorcycle did the same, weaving in and out of cars to keep pace with me. He could have easily taken me, but continued to stay three cars back, as if he thought I was oblivious to him.

My brain frantically ran through emergency protocol, urging me to call the police. I resisted. They had all but ignored my mother's death. Why would they suddenly lift a finger to help me now?

The exit sign for University Ave loomed ahead. I would not get another shot. I moved into the left lane and waited for him to follow before crossing back over three lanes of traffic to make the exit amid multiple horns honking. The motorcyclist tried and failed to do the same, getting swept back up into traffic.

I wound my way back toward my apartment, changing up streets every few blocks. My heart was pounding fiercely in my chest, but a glance in the rearview mirror confirmed I'd lost him for good.

As I entered my apartment complex parking lot, I cut the headlights and coasted into my parking spot. The deep rumble of a bike cut through the sounds of crickets, causing my heart to stumble in my chest.

Fuck.

I slid down in the driver's seat, praying he hadn't memorized my car and would drive on once he saw a bunch of empty vehicles.

I wasn't that lucky, and he wasn't that stupid.

The muffler growled as he came to a stop right behind my car, boxing me in. I could see everything from the side mirror, including the moment he noticed me.

He killed the bike and removed the helmet before reaching behind his back—probably searching for a good murder weapon.

I fought through the paralyzing fear and threw the door open, running like hell for my apartment. He tackled me from behind in a bear hug just as I reached the stairs; the momentum sending my body tumbling forward.

My chin slammed against the concrete steps, forcing my teeth together. The man slapped a hand over my mouth when I cried out, pressing the sharp point of a blade to my throat in warning. I remembered the gun in my waistband, but with his weight on top of me and a knife to my neck, I was helpless.

"Shhhh... you open that pretty mouth again and I'll cut your fucking tongue out," he crooned in a thick Spanish accent. It was a threat that was unmistakable in any language.

I nodded my assent before he decided to slit my throat and be done with it, cursing myself for my stupidity.

What was the point of carrying a gun if I wasn't going to use it?

After roughly yanking me up, he marched up the stairs to the door of my apartment. He knew where I lived—had probably been watching me all along. An icy chill ran the length of my spine.

"Unlock the door, bitch," he hissed with alcohol-laced breath. "And remember, if you scream, I will gut you like a pig before your neighbors can even get their lights on."

I nodded again and shakily inserted the key into the lock. It took me several tries to get it open, but I finally succeeded. The man shoved me forward, and I fell onto the carpet with a soft groan.

He turned the lock behind him with a cruel smirk. "You keep digging into things. Let's see if I can help you remember to mind your own business. My name is Chon Ramos—you'll be screaming it when you beg me for your life later."

A click sounded from somewhere behind his head in the dark living room. "Chonny, Chonny, Chonny," a voice tsked. "You broke biker rule number one, my man. Always check your surroundings before starting a torture session. C'mon, this ain't amateur hour. Now drop the fucking knife and step away from the redhead."

I sat up, wincing from the pain radiating throughout my body. "Little Ricky? What the hell are you doing here?"

CHAPTER FORTY-SIX

Mike: April 2015 (Age: 32)

"We got a problem, Mikey."

The statement sent me racing toward Lauren's, the worst thoughts imaginable running on a loop in my head. He wouldn't say if she was hurt—in fact, he said nothing else other than, "Get here. Now."

The motorcycle sitting behind her car and the trail of blood leading up the stairs to her apartment didn't do jack shit in alleviating my fears. It just made them even more tangible.

Little Ricky ushered me in to where a short and stocky Latino sat bound to one of Lauren's dining room chairs, his fat lip twisted into a scowl. His kutte identified him as a Son and I resisted the urge to crush his facial bones beneath my fist.

I needed answers. But first, I needed to make sure she was okay. "Where's Lauren?"

Little Ricky pointed, and I sprinted down the hall, not giving a fuck if I woke every downstairs neighbor in the building. "Lauren?"

She sat on the bathroom floor with torn leggings, bandaging a wound on her knee. When she saw me, she immediately jumped to her feet. "What the hell? Who let you in?"

I ignored the anger, distracted by the wound on her chin. "He did this to you?"

She nodded, and I stalked back down the hallway. "You laid hands on my girl?" I roared into the man's face.

He grinned. "*La puta* didn't get half of what she deserves."

I swung my fist into his chin. His nose. His eyes. Completely blinded by rage. Little Ricky finally stepped in to pull me off.

"C'mon, Mikey. Keep it together," he warned. "We need to know why he's here. Thought we could take him for a drive, loosen up his tongue a bit, you know?" He patted me gently on the back with one hand while keeping a gun trained on the biker with the other. Once my breathing regulated, he moved away.

"I want you to leave."

I spun around to face Lauren. "You're shitting me, right? You want me to leave you with the man who wanted to kill you?"

She propped a hand on her hip and narrowed her eyes at me. Before, I would have thought it was cute as hell. Right now, though? I wanted to wring her slender neck.

"Better him than you. At least he's upfront about what he is. I can't say the same for you," she snapped, tilting her bruised and bloody chin up at me defiantly.

I caught the sides of her face in my hands, growling, "Goddamn it! Why won't you let me help you?"

"Let it go, Mike."

"I can't! Darlin', worrying about you is like a second full-time job I never signed up for," I forced through clenched teeth, squeezing the sides of her face harder as the anger devoured what little resolve I had left.

"Well, you can quit your second job because I'm good," she bit out, jaw tightening beneath my hands. "I wouldn't want you to pull a muscle stressing over my life."

Little Ricky cleared his throat to get our attention. "Uh, should I just keep the gun on this prick until you're done fighting, or can we get this fucking show on the road?"

I turned around and threw my hands up. "Fuck, Rick. Give me a minute here."

Lauren moved faster than I would have thought possible. One second she had her hands on her hips and the next she'd pulled a gun from underneath her shirt.

"No one is leaving until I get some answers! I deserve to know why Chon here followed me home and how Little Ricky got inside my apartment. No, scratch that! I wanna know why he called you, of all people. You two hate each other!"

Her hand shook, and I watched her trigger finger warily. I had to calm her down before she put bullet holes in all of us.

"Jesus, Red. You had a gun the entire time? Why didn't you pull that? Could've saved me a trip down here."

She aimed the gun at my head with a glare. "Go to hell, Mike."

I held my hands up. "Please, just hear me out. I want to keep you safe, but you're messing with some dangerous people."

I couldn't fathom what she'd done to provoke their club, but there wasn't a snowball's chance in hell I'd be able to keep her safe if she continued down this path.

Keeping the gun trained on me, Lauren sighed. "I don't know if you're even capable of it anymore, but I deserve to know the truth."

"Little Ricky works with me," I began. I wasn't sure where to go from there.

No way was I telling her he was a biker. That would only lead to me having to admit he was watching her for the club—a club I was in deep with. No, thank you. I was in enough hot water as it was.

Her eyes widened. "You're a cop?"

Little Ricky nodded, while giving me a death stare. "Yep. Serving and protecting—all that shit."

Her nose crinkled. "But, you look like you're in a gang—"

"Undercover, *mi sirenita*," he said as he hauled the biker outside, giving us a minute alone.

Lauren mouthed the word *undercover* to herself, but didn't lower her weapon.

"Do it," I said, leaning in until the barrel of the gun butted against my forehead. "Pull the fucking trigger if it'll make you feel better. I had nothing to do with what happened to your mom, though. I swear."

Her lower lip quivered, but she kept her index finger alongside the frame of the gun and away from the trigger, giving me hope she didn't really want to end my life.

I continued talking, keeping my voice low and calm. "It's okay, Red. I get it, but I need you to know I'm doing everything in my power to find out who did this."

The gun dug into my skin, but I kept my eyes on hers. An eternity later, she lowered the gun, sliding it back into the holster on her waist. "I need you to go," she whispered.

I caught her arm and tugged her closer. "Why can't you just trust me and leave it alone?"

Her lips parted slightly and her eyes dilated before she shook it off. "Because she was my mom—because I loved her and she died alone." Her voice cracked. "She died because I trusted you and left it alone."

What could I say? She was absolutely right.

I stroked her shoulder with my thumb. "I failed you. That's a mistake I have to live with the rest of my life, but one I won't make again with you."

"Was Little Ricky hanging around because it was his job to watch me?" she asked, leaning into my touch.

"At first, yeah," I admitted with a nod. "Cops—uh, they look out for each other. Him taking you out was never part of the deal, though."

Lauren's lips turned up in a soft smile. "Explains why you lost your mind when you saw us together. Look, I know you want me to stay out of it, but I won't. And I know that you're going to be just as stubborn as I am, so I've got a proposition."

"I enjoy being propositioned, darlin'."

This was it.

I was going to get a second chance to make things right.

Instead, she finished with, "I'd like for us to be friends. If we're going to have to work together on this, let's at least make it amicable."

I frowned. I didn't want to be her fucking friend.

Lauren regarded me silently before settling her head against my chest. I cautiously wrapped my arms around both shoulders, pulling her up against my body, still wary of the gun between us.

"I can't offer you anything else right now, but I also don't have the strength to fight with you anymore. I'm exhausted, Mike."

I nodded. "Okay. We'll be friends. For now." I lifted her face up to mine. "Are you sure you're okay? Do you want me to take you to get checked out?"

She shook her head. "He tackled me and I fell. That's it. Little Ricky stopped him before—before anything else could happen."

I led her into the kitchen and found some ibuprofen buried in a cabinet. I shook three out into her hand and grabbed her a bottled water from the fridge.

"Take these and call me in the morning. Let me know how you are. Friends do that, right?"

She nodded. "Sure."

CHAPTER FORTY-SEVEN

Mike: May 2015 (Age: 32)

S he never called.

April moved into May, but my phone remained silent. We'd hauled the biker down to the canyon, but the only thing he copped to was the fact that Lauren had requested Monica's autopsy report. After forty-eight hours of sleep deprivation, he'd still refused to give up the officers involved. Anytime his eyes had closed, Grey blasted AC/DC. Still, the son of a bitch wouldn't break.

We took our time breaking down his body, but he'd remained silent until Comedian pumped a couple of rounds into his stomach. From there, I'd gotten nothing but his groans of agony as he bled to death.

"Ladies and gentlemen, on behalf of the flight crew, welcome to Denver."

People began unbuckling and reaching into overhead bins to get their belongings while I sat, staring blankly out over the tarmac, wondering what my next step was.

While I hadn't heard from Lauren, my phone had been blowing up daily with calls from Katya. Another note appeared on her door, leaving me with no choice but to go to Colorado and investigate.

Unofficially, of course.

Recent erratic behavior had landed her in the tabloids after a paparazzo spotted her with a football player known more for his off-field antics than anything else. The press was salivating for a story. I didn't trust she wouldn't give them one. Her father admitted she'd been experiencing blackouts—losing hours, sometimes even days.

The woman was a fucking thorn in my side. I couldn't get my own shit taken care of because I was constantly being pulled back to babysit her gorgeous ass—and not in a fun way that involved both of us naked.

If I'd left Landon to rot in prison, my hands would have been clean. I wouldn't have given a damn if Katya ran down 16th Street buck naked, while singing the fucking Star-Spangled Banner at the top of her lungs. Okay, I'd probably want a front-row seat to that show.

Without a time machine, the best I could do was try to talk some fucking sense into her.

Katya's father buzzed me into the building, warning me she was in the middle of another 'episode.' I looked past him to where she sat on a low ottoman, staring blankly through the wall of windows overlooking the city.

She'd lost more weight, leaving her with sunken cheeks and a haggard appearance. I froze about halfway across the room as images from the night of the rescue flooded my memory. The medical report was as clear as day—the photographs documenting the extensive abuse she'd suffered at the hands of a person she once loved.

I knelt in front of her, my earlier anger draining away. She blinked slowly, as if just realizing I was there. "I thought you weren't coming until next week."

Her father was right. The blackouts were messing with her mind. I sighed. "We've been over this, remember? I told you I'd be here this week."

Her eyes widened with surprise, and she shook her head. I had to look away—she was like a small child. Fragile.

Her father reappeared with a mug of hot tea, giving me an almost stern look. "Detective, she is not sleeping well."

"Nikolay, you and I both know she's trying to avoid sleeping all together."

Katya placed the mug on a nearby table and wandered into the kitchen.

He handed me the letters. "She's falling apart. I told myself she was getting better, but I was wrong. I kept her schedule full so she would not dwell in the past. These notes and messages have made things difficult. Her mind—it has become her prison."

I studied them, trying to make sense of the contents. The guy had a thing for song lyrics.

My darling, you looked wonderful tonight, the latest one read. Attached was a photo of Katya as she left her condo earlier the same evening.

No wonder she was paranoid. In the fractured parts of her brain, she was convinced Landon had discovered a way to get back at her. Even in death.

She cried out suddenly and Nikolay and I raced into the kitchen to find her hunched over the counter. She sucked in a ragged breath, clutching her cell phone in her trembling hands.

I pried it loose from her grip.

Landon Scott: I desire the things that will destroy me in the end...

Nikolay read the message over my shoulder and weakly muttered, "Jesus Christ."

We were in big trouble.

Whoever was behind the messages knew exactly what had happened to Landon. I massaged my temples. "Katya, you're sure you haven't talked to anyone? You didn't mention it to a shrink or one of your girlfriends?"

I sounded like I was on the verge of joining in her panic attack.

"Detective, my daughter has already told you she didn't talk to anyone."

She glanced longingly at her water bottle and I snapped, "Yeah Nikolay, she also wants us to believe that it's only water in that bottle of hers, too. You'll forgive me if I don't trust her judgment right now."

"Yeah?" Katya snapped, slapping a hand against the granite countertop. "And you're nothing but a dirty cop whose judgment is more questionable than mine. Yet, here we are."

Her phone began chiming. We reached for it at the same time.

Landon Scott tagged you in a post.

Landon Scott tagged you in a post.
Landon Scott tagged you in a post.

She clicked on the notification, and her missing person flyer popped up. Someone had posted repeatedly it on Landon's social media page. The caption was the same on every single one.

What do you know about the disappearance of Katya Egorichev?

Who the fuck was this guy?

A SODMC member? An ex of hers with a vendetta? Just some random crazy? Who had the knowledge to hack a dead man's social media accounts?

"You said he was dead!" she screamed at me.

"He is! I swear to you!" I reached for her arm, but she recoiled instantly and slapped my hand away. She didn't like to be touched.

"Then who the fuck is on his account?"

"Detective, where is Landon Scott?" Nikolay asked, pulling a sobbing Katya into his arms. "I paid you to do a job. It appears the job was not done."

Oh, hell no.

Katya gutted me with another one of her wide-eyed looks. "Mike— I've been to every psychologist in the area, but nothing helps! Do you know what that's like? I'm scared to fall asleep... I'm scared to stay awake—I used to love the city and now I'm scared to even leave my building! You're saying there's a chance he's still out there?"

Nikolay fought to keep her steady as she descended into hysteria.

It was the last thing I wanted to do. But, it was this or be labeled a liar.

"You want proof he's gone? Look!"

I scrolled through my club phone until I found the picture of Landon's corpse. She managed one look before her knees buckled.

Katya had lived since December, convinced Landon was lurking somewhere around Denver, just waiting to strike again. This was the only way she was going to move forward. She buried her face in her father's jacket and sobbed.

I lowered my voice. "It's not him. I told you I took care of it. Now, what I'm trying to do is figure out who's behind this. I need your help, Katya."

She continued sobbing and shook her head. "I've told you everything I know. I haven't spoken to anyone about it. I can barely talk about what happened to me, much less what happened to him."

I looked back at her father. "Nikolay, you've got to get her out of here. Until we can trace these messages, I don't think it's safe for her."

I'd arranged something similar with Lauren. From what I heard, she was incredibly pissed off, but safe.

"Detective, believe me when I say I know a thing or two about hiding. I will keep my daughter safe."

There it was again. Vague references to a life before his daughter. I was leaning more toward spy than CIA operative, only because he would have had an arsenal at his disposal with the latter and wouldn't have relied on a local detective.

A CIA black site would have been helpful when dealing with Chon last month. Maybe someone there could have gotten him to talk. While Nikolay worked to convince his daughter to leave, I checked my messages, finding a recent one from Grey.

Grey: When are you coming back?

I sighed.

Me: If I can get her to leave Denver tonight, I can be on the first flight home tomorrow morning. Is Lauren okay?

I would leave for the airport immediately if she wasn't okay. Minutes later, he responded.

Grey: Feds are gone. Investigation closed. Lauren's seeing someone.

A man of few words, but every single one of them packed a punch. The Feds didn't just call off investigations, and Lauren didn't see anyone but me. I wanted to punch something until my hands bled—to grab the bottle of vodka Katya was trying to pass off as water and suck it down.

Fuck sobriety.

Fuck her.

Fuck this.

Instead, I interrupted a moment between Katya and Nikolay and snapped, "I say we get her out of Denver tonight. I've got my guys working on tracing everything. Without knowing who or what we're dealing with, it's for the best."

So, I hadn't exactly alerted the authorities just yet, but I was going to take care of that, just as soon as my blood pressure dropped back down into a normal range.

For good measure, I used my other phone to email the Arapahoe County Sheriff's office with all the information on Katya's case. This could be a good thing; having the authorities convinced Landon was still out there. I was going to fix this.

I stabbed out a quick reply to Grey.

Me: I'm getting out of here tonight. Why'd the Feds call it off? That strike you as strange?

Katya approached. "I'll do it. If you think it'll keep me safe, I'll leave. I don't know what to tell my agent—they're expecting me to fly out to California on Monday."

Grey: Someone's toying with us—get back and we'll talk.

No shit. That someone was pretty powerful if they were yanking the Feds around.

Nikolay offered his cabin in the mountains—some place called Cedar Ridge. It sounded like the perfect place to relax. As I was using my vacation time to work, it was obvious I didn't know jack shit about the concept.

One fire out. Eight million to go.

As if on cue, my phone began ringing.

CHAPTER FORTY-EIGHT

Lauren: May 2015 (Age: 28)

"No, wait. I can do it. Stop making me laugh!" I leaned forward with another giggle before grabbing the bar. I'd always done bicep curls while sitting down, but Jimmy had me standing up to work my core at the same time.

I met him for that first gym date, despite everything working against me. The morning after the attack, I woke up feeling as though a bus had hit me. At the sound of male voices coming from my living room, I'd hastily rubbed the sleep from my eyes and grabbed my gun. Torch, Isaac, and Josué had thrown the half-full cardboard boxes to the floor when I burst into the living room like some cop in a cheesy TV drama, shouting, "Freeze!"

The three had stood sheepishly, each looking to the other to offer an explanation. After some hesitation, the truth had eventually come out. I was being moved to Torch's house, because apparently, the safest place to hide from one biker was in another's home.

I'd refused, but it soon became apparent everyone there was under strict orders to get me out of the apartment, with or without my consent.

I wasn't sure what surprised me more—Mike staying in touch with my fathers after our break-up or not being able to leave well enough alone where I was concerned.

Friends didn't behave like that.

Just another painful reminder it was Mike's world, and we were all just lucky enough to live in it. I hadn't faulted him for the decision, but the execution was awful. It was as if he didn't know how to have a normal relationship—everything had to be shrouded in lies and mystery. And the realization that he would never change pushed me back into a state of numbness. I would not allow myself to feel anything for him ever again.

A pop on my ass brought me back to the present.

I looked over my shoulder with a grin. "What was that for?"

Jimmy winked. "You got lazy with those last two reps... and my hand got lonely."

The man was, in a word, amazing.

Where Mike was closed off, Jimmy was an open book.

Working out together had led to coffee dates. Coffee dates had led to dinner and movie dates. And I had a sneaking suspicion dinner and movie dates were going to lead to sleepovers.

Soon.

We'd held hands. Sex was obviously the next step. After our first coffee date, Jimmy had leaned in to kiss me. I'd suddenly realized my shoelace had come untied and dropped to my knee, avoiding it entirely.

I'd rushed things before, with Mike. This time around, I wanted to play it smart.

"Want to come back to my place?" Jimmy asked as we walked out together, hand in hand, after finishing the last set. I stumbled, and he caught my arm before I face-planted on the sidewalk. "Easy."

I righted myself and faced him. "Um, it's late, and I've got to work tomorrow."

"I thought you could meet Puck," he said, unable to mask his disappointment. "Maybe another night."

Puck was Jimmy's adorable chocolate lab—he'd shown me pictures the first time we had coffee. I was all for meeting his dog, but wasn't ready to take things further just yet. I had to think fast, or he was going to think I was friend-zoning him and there was no coming back from that.

I grabbed the front of his shirt and pulled him down, whispering, "Kiss me," against his throat. His massive hands cupped my face and his mouth dipped down over mine.

There was a small spark. I almost breathed a sigh of relief. I wasn't broken. I could still kiss a man who wasn't Mike and feel something. Any second now, the spark would ignite into a bonfire of lust, breaking the spell I'd been under since January.

The scruff on his face chafed against my skin and his tongue fought to gain entrance to my mouth as I caught his lower lip with my teeth, nipping lightly.

Yep. Any minute now.

Bonfire.

Fireworks.

I was going to be overwhelmed with emotion and would beg to be taken back to his house. Puck would not get a proper introduction because Jimmy and I were going to be shedding clothes like we were in the middle of a Texas heat wave.

Bones would be jumped.

Jimmy broke the kiss with a sigh. "Text me when you get home, okay?"

No.

So, my lady-bits were just feeling a little grumpy. I'd been close, though. I just knew it. Five more seconds and I would have been in that sweet spot.

I tried to hide my frustration and promised to text him the moment I got home before grabbing my keys. After scanning the parking lot for any suspicious vehicles near mine, I pressed the fob to unlock the doors, only to jump back when a dark figure stood up.

"Who is he?"

I reflexively reached for my gun before snapping, "Jesus Christ, Mike! What did I tell you about jumping out at people?"

He gave me a lazy grin. "You're getting quicker on the draw, darlin'. Now tell me, who the fuck was that guy?"

I shrugged. "We work out together."

"Yeah, he was working something out. Have you fucked him?" At my answering glare, he immediately began backpedaling. "I just—shit. I don't know how to be friends with you."

"Obviously," I deadpanned. "You forced me out of my apartment without talking to me first."

He at least had the audacity to look ashamed. "I'm doing the best I can. I was stuck interrogating that Ramos guy and didn't break away long enough to talk to you face to face. For that, I'm sorry. I just thought if one biker was after you, it wouldn't be long before others were too."

I'd known that, hadn't I?

"Did he make bail? Should I be looking over my shoulder?"

His eyes flashed with something, but it was gone in an instant. "They came after you because you requested Monica's autopsy report."

I swallowed, my mouth suddenly dry. "But that means—someone tipped them off at the police department, doesn't it?"

Mike ran a hand roughly across his face. "Yeah, that's exactly what it fucking means. Someone on the inside is in their pocket."

"How do we figure out who it is?"

He smirked. "We, Red?"

I stabbed my index finger into his chest. "Yeah, Tex. *We.* You've got a mole, and they may be the reason my mother got killed. You need my help."

"Does that mean you don't blame me anymore?" Mike asked, his smile fading.

My voice came out softer than I intended. "I know it wasn't you, but it was never about that. I came to you for help and suddenly you were freaking Barney Fife."

He leaned against the side of my car with a resigned sigh. "So, what's your plan?"

I hesitated. *What was my plan?* "What if I go in and ask them to reopen her case? I doubt I'll get very far, but it would send a message to the biker gang that I'm not backing—"

Mike slammed his fist down on top of my car. "Absofuckinglutely not, Red. I'm not putting your life in danger to catch a cop!"

I moved until we were toe to toe. "You don't get to make that call! I said I was helping you. End of story."

One minute we were glaring at each other and the next, his hand was on my jaw, pulling me up against his chest. Even before our mouths collided, I was a raging inferno of desire.

Lady-bits, you disloyal bitches.

His mouth was unforgiving, as if he was pouring his anger into me. Instead of pushing away, I pulled him closer, melting into his touch. His tongue slipped easily between my lips, feeling like home and reminding me I would never feel with anyone else what I felt with him.

My hands frantically climbed his arms, stopping once I reached his muscular biceps. How many nights had I gripped him just like this as he moved in and out of me?

I moaned at the memory and his hands moved to my ass, lifting me easily up against the side of my car. I squeezed my thighs tightly around his waist, afraid he might disappear at any second.

My mind was running rampant. I needed to remember why things hadn't worked before. I needed to stay because his arms were the only place that felt safe anymore.

It wasn't just a kiss. It was an apology. An atonement. The heat from his mouth scorched away all of our sins against each other. He nipped at my lips while his hands freed the elastic from my hair. He threaded his hands through my scalp and gently pulled each tendril down around my face. I tilted my head to the side, allowing him better access, never once breaking contact with his mouth.

Little Ricky was too young.

Jimmy was too soft.

Mike was just right.

My life had become a damn nursery rhyme somewhere in the last two minutes. His lips reluctantly left my mouth and traveled down to my neck and all coherent thought stuttered to a stop as my body broke out in goosebumps. I wanted him inside of me.

Damn the consequences.

My hands clawed futilely at his shirt until he pulled away and set me back down on solid ground.

"Why'd you stop?" I whispered breathlessly.

Mike glanced around, refusing to make eye contact with me. "I'm not fucking you in a parking lot. We just got caught up in the moment. That's it."

His chest heaved with each breath, and I knew he was full of shit. I took his shirt in my hands. "Really? Just caught up in a moment? It's that easy for you?"

He pulled my hands free and gripped them tightly in his. "You think this is easy for me, Lauren? I want to hate fuck you until you feel me in your veins. Then I want to slow it down and make love to you until you can't find a reason for us not to be together. You want to place yourself in the path of an oncoming train and force me to sit back and watch."

I shook my head, trying to clear away images of him hate fucking me. It turned me on more than it should have. I was certain my lady-bits were turning blue. "Don't be dramatic, Mike. I'm not trying to kill myself—I want to help. I could be your partner—"

He cut me off. "Partner? I wanted to make you my wife!"

I stood there, dumbfounded. "Wife?"

He squeezed his eyes shut and roared, "Fuck!"

"Mike, answer me. You were going to propose?" My voice was unsteady, but it couldn't be helped in light of his revelation.

He'd admitted he loved me after rescuing Elizabeth. I knew he was committed, but never imagined he was gearing up to propose marriage. It left me with mixed emotions—disappointment and bitterness ranking near the top.

If he hadn't been a cop, would we have been planning our wedding right now? If he'd offered to help me that night with the same outcome, would I have made a different decision?

He got his breathing back under control before answering, "I—I don't know, Lauren. Does it matter now?"

I tried to sound casual. "Hey, you brought it up, Tex." My chest tightened, and I felt like weeping over everything we'd lost that night.

"I've got to go. I'll call you once I figure out who the mole is." Without waiting for a response, he stormed back across the parking lot to his truck.

My face grew warm and tears pricked the back of my eyelids, but I refused to fall apart right now. I was going to have to reach out to the police department again. With or without his help.

I watched him drive away, feeling a small sense of relief when my phone alerted me to an incoming text.

It wasn't from Mike, though.

Jimmy: Are you okay? Did you make it home?

A lone tear broke free and slid down my cheek. I felt dirty. Cheap. I'd thrown myself at Mike mere minutes after kissing Jimmy. It was disgusting.

I tapped out a quick reply.

Me: Got hung up. Almost home now. Same time tomorrow?

Mike was determined to never let my heart forget what we'd had, however brief it had been. Every time we touched, he left an imprint on my body, further ruining me for any other man.

If I stayed away, how long would it take to forget what his touch had felt like? The way his lips parted slightly when he leaned in for a kiss? How long would it be before I could fully inhale without feeling the stabbing pain of losing him all over again?

CHAPTER FORTY-NINE

Mike: May 2015 (Age: 32)

"Hey, you got a minute?" I called after Grey as he stepped outside the clubhouse.

Before, he'd done an excellent job of keeping me out of his shit. Now, I was making weekly trips to the canyon for club business. That was the problem with being a great speechwriter—suddenly everyone else became lazy as fuck.

I'd dodged a kutte for years and had no plans of patching in now just to fill the role of club cheerleader.

Fuck that.

Grey slowed his steps to look back at me. "What's on your mind, kid?"

"It's Lauren. She thinks she might have a way to smoke out the mole." I'd outright refused to let her put herself in danger again and was hoping Grey might have a better alternative.

He took a couple of puffs from the lit cigar in his hand before asking, "What's she got?"

I shook my head. "Not out here in the open—officers only."

Grey blew a perfect ring of smoke in my direction. "Mikey, you know my guys take an oath when they patch in—even have them fill out a fuckin' application. If I trust 'em with my life, you can too."

I wanted to believe him. I did. But Feds had infiltrated clubs before and with his recent shit, I wasn't taking any chances. "Officers or nothing, old man. That's the best I can do."

He nodded. "You got it. Head back in and I'll round 'em up."

I knew the oath all Silent Phoenix members took. Shit, I'd taken an oath of my own and look at how well I'd held up my end of that.

1. *As a member of Silent Phoenix MC, I will never use my patch for personal gain.*
2. *As a member of Silent Phoenix MC, I will never mess with a brother's Ol' Lady.*
3. *As a member of Silent Phoenix MC, I will never cause one of my brothers to end up on the wrong side of the law in any way, shape, or form.*
4. *As a member of Silent Phoenix MC, I will never steal from one of my brothers.*
5. *As a member of Silent Phoenix MC, I will never lie to my Pres or my brothers.*

I had the damn thing memorized before I was eight. My old man beat it into me. I was to be a shining example to my brothers long before I was old enough to pledge. Trouble was, even as a kid, I kind of thought the whole thing was bullshit.

People broke promises every day. Comedian had vowed to love my mother, yet fucked around on her any chance he got. He'd promised to come to my little league baseball games, yet I'd look up from the outfield every game to see my mother sitting alone. Grey would watch me from the fence, but it wasn't the same.

Human nature dictated a need to let other humans down. I'd come to terms with that shit a long time ago. Grey, for whatever reason, held out this hope that people would be who they pledged to be.

The bikers filed in, one by one, scowls on all of their faces. Grey had interrupted their fucking or using, and nobody enjoyed being pulled away from that. Wolverine followed in last, and I gave Grey a look.

"What? He's a Lifer. I ain't throwin' him out."

Sensing I was about to lose what little control I had over the room, I began. "Gentlemen, I will just take a moment of your time and you can get back to being balls deep in pussy and whatever illicit drugs strike your fancy. This is about my girl."

Carnage rolled his eyes and mimed jacking himself off.

"Carnage, pumpkin, you can go back to fucking yourself as soon as this meeting is over. Just give me a goddamned second of your time for now, okay?"

He slammed his hands down on the table, but immediately sat back when Grey shook his head.

"As I was saying, my girl has a plan for getting our mole in the department. She wants to waltz in and press for them to reopen her mother's case in light of recent evidence. I think it's a fucking stupid—"

"What evidence does she have?" Jarvis asked, at the same time as Bear.

I shrugged. "How the fuck am I supposed to know?"

Little Ricky piped up, his pen poised over a notebook. Apparently, he thought this counted as a meeting and was in secretary mode. "I searched her apartment up and down that night. If she had evidence, I never saw it. The wall she made was information we already had. Whoever took out Monica was good and didn't leave behind a trace."

I knew about the wall and had noted it the night we saved her from Chon Ramos. Little Ricky was supposed to have been in and out of her apartment before she got home from the gym. Her storyboard of a wall was the reason she was still with us. He'd gotten hung up taking pictures of it. Any problems I had with him disappeared the minute he saved her life. I owed him one.

Grey released another couple of smoke rings. "I say we do it. If the mole thinks she has evidence against the Sons, they're gonna be fallin' all over themselves to get to her. She's still alive because they don't believe she knows enough to become a threat."

Without thinking, I growled, "Then what the fuck was Chon Ramos planning? To cook her dinner?"

The table went silent, waiting for Grey to lash out at me. Admittedly, I deserved it. Instead of losing his shit, he sat back with an unreadable expression on his face. "I think he was going to rough her up to send a message to us. Wouldn't be the first time the tactic's been used."

I thought back to the afternoon at Inked, from Celia's knowledge of a biker's tattooed dick to the circular scar on her hip. Grey's cryptic response suddenly took on a new meaning.

Jesus.

Had his enemies gone after her? If so, I doubted there were any left to tell the tale.

"You think it's a good plan?" He, of all people, was supposed to think it was a terrible idea and come up with something better. Safer.

"When's this takin' place?" My father asked, a bored expression on his face. He'd definitely been in the middle of a bimbo bender—blow too, judging by his eyes.

I shrugged again, frustrated the club was sanctioning this asinine idea. "We haven't decided."

Grey stood up, signaling that the meeting was over. "Get a date and we'll catch us a fuckin' mole."

CHAPTER FIFTY

Lauren: May 2015 (Age: 28)

"Are you sure he won't break?" I lifted Kaden's legs up as if they were made of glass, trying to slide a clean diaper under his tiny bum.

Elizabeth watched amusedly over my shoulder. "Lauren, babies are pretty resilient. I think he'll make it through a diaper change."

"But, this sock thing on his foot with the wire," I protested as I unsnapped the minuscule buttons on his onesie. "What if I pull it off?"

She laughed. "Look at him. He's fine. If it comes off, we'll put it right back on."

Kaden stared up at me with wide eyes, as if even he knew I wasn't qualified. "Hey there," I cooed, but his expression remained serious. "I won't hurt you... I mean, I probably won't hurt you. It's not my intention to hurt you—"

"Lauren?"

"Hmm?" I muttered distractedly before looking at Elizabeth.

"Just change the damn diaper."

Got it.

It took me ten minutes, an extra three diapers, and one change of clothes before I had Kaden settled peacefully in my arms.

"That was easier than I thought," I exclaimed.

Elizabeth's eyebrows drew down, and she pursed her lips. "I wouldn't quit your day job just yet. You've got to be quick with little boys. They fire at will."

Kaden's mouth fell open as he inhaled and exhaled loudly, his little chest working hard with each breath. "Is this okay? Does he need some oxygen?"

Elizabeth leaned across the chair and checked his monitor. "He's good, just a noisy sleeper. Relax, Lauren. You're doing great."

I tried to take my mind off the stress of holding a preemie, wondering how Elizabeth got even a second of sleep. I would have been a sleep-deprived monster. Yet here she was, looking like a supermodel.

She beamed at me. "I've been meaning to ask—how are things going since what's his face?"

Since discovering the break-up, Elizabeth had taken to calling Mike anything but his actual name. My favorite was *Detective Dickhead*.

I covered Kaden's exposed ear. "It's going about as *shitastic* as you can imagine."

Elizabeth's smile faded. "I'm sorry—why won't you tell me what happened between you two? Maybe I could help. I mean, I've kind of seen it all at this point."

The clock ticked on the wall, punctuating the silence while I wrestled with what to do. I wanted to explain it to her, if for nothing else other than to see if she thought I made the wrong call.

Then I considered the note spray-painted across my apartment door and being attacked by a biker. There was no way I could put that on her.

"There's really nothing to tell. The bad-boy and the virgin only work out in the movies and romance novels—never in real life."

She pursed her lips, unable to mask her hurt. "Fine. We'll leave it at that."

"Look, I'm here under false pretenses. I said I was just here to hold the baby, but I'm actually here to hold him and get some advice. When you and David separated, did you forget things about him? Like maybe you forgot the way he looks when he first wakes up... or something kind of like that?"

Elizabeth nodded to herself, idly spinning her wedding ring around her finger. "Some details were fuzzy, but with David there was always this clarity. I was almost hyperaware of him once he was gone. Little things reminded me of him—why are you asking? Is it because you're having a tough time forgetting Mike—shit—*Deputy Dipshit?*"

If I admitted I was struggling to move on and Elizabeth shared the tidbit with David, it would get back to Mike before the night was over.

"Not exactly," I hedged. "I—um—I met someone."

Elizabeth clapped her hands together softly. "I knew it! You have that look—it's the same one you had with—well, that obviously doesn't matter, does it? Shut up, Elizabeth. Okay."

I laughed even though her observation had struck a nerve.She was right.

I was in love.

It was just with the wrong man.

What I felt for Jimmy was like a candle, flickering and fleeting. But Mike—those feelings were like a floodlight, blinding me to anything else in the room.

"I really like him and he makes me laugh—"

"So, what's the problem?" Elizabeth interjected.

I exhaled slowly. "Before Mike, there was no one. So, I had nothing to compare him to. With Jimmy I feel like I'm critiquing him—looking for some sign he's not right for me."

Kaden grumbled in his sleep and began sucking on his bottom lip. I stroked his cheek before returning my attention to Elizabeth.

She looked almost sheepish. "Have you and this Jimmy—you know?"

I shook my head.

"I shouldn't even tell you this. Okay, fine, I will tell you. But if you ever tell a soul, I'll deny everything. Maybe you should, uh, sleep with this guy and see how you feel after. If you still have doubts, then he's not the right fit."

I frowned. "Why does any of that have to be a secret?"

"Because Mike has been my friend for a long time. And I don't want to be known as a backstabber or traitor to my friends. I just think you deserve a chance at happiness and should take the opportunity and see what happens."

"Okay." I nodded. "I'll think about it, and I promise to never tell a soul about what we discussed here today. Kaden, you better not rat us out either." I tickled his chest and his eyes opened briefly before he was out again.

I could have a meaningful relationship with someone other than Mike. I just had to put myself out there more with Jimmy.

Taking down a mole in the police department, while sleeping with someone new at the same time?

I was turning into a real femme fatale over here and could only hope I didn't lure Jimmy right into the middle of my problems.

CHAPTER FIFTY-ONE

Mike: May 2015 (Age: 32)

"Come to Denver. It's gorgeous," I muttered angrily to myself as I disembarked the plane, earning myself a condescending stare from a blue-haired old woman wearing a paisley neck pillow as if she was making a fashion statement.

"The fuck are you looking at?" I sneered before storming off the jet-bridge. It wasn't Blue-Hair's fault, but Lauren's. She refused to back down on her plan, even threatening to cut me out of it if I argued with her one more time.

I was living in my own private Hell.

The person leaving messages for Katya wasn't some run-of-the-mill crazy living in his parent's basement but someone who knew their way around the system.

Blue Hair caught up to me, swatting me upside the head with her paisley neck pillow. "You kiss your mother with that mouth, mister? You need to learn some respect. Kids these days…"

She continued muttering to herself and headed toward the train. I held back, figuring waiting for the next one was the best way to guarantee I remained concussion free.

I was fucking cursed.

By the time I reached Katya's cabin in Cedar Ridge, it was

completely dark and she was nowhere to be found. I tried her cell phone several times, but it kept going straight to voicemail. I was mentally debating the pros and cons of performing a B&E when she finally answered.

"Hey Mike," she answered cheerfully. "Calling to tell me I can come home and give up my dreams of becoming a mountain-woman?"

"Where are you, Katya?" I asked, trying to keep my tone casual. Turned out casual had left the fucking building hours ago.

Her voice was quiet as she admitted, "I got a job. I needed to get out of the house."

I rubbed at my forehead wearily. "I'm at the cabin. We need to talk." I hung up and got comfortable on her porch swing—steadying my breathing and working out a way to tell her she couldn't go back to the city yet.

A half-hour later, Katya appeared, unsteadily pushing a bicycle up the steep driveway. There was a truck right on her heels, the headlights damn near blinding me as they hit the front of the house.

I reached for my gun, belatedly remembering I locked it away in my luggage. "Who's this?" I asked as she drew closer to the house.

She shrugged and dropped her bike onto the gravel, as if this sort of thing happened to her all the time. "Some guy I pissed off."

The man parked and got out. "Is she okay? I just wanted to make sure she made it home safely."

I walked toward him, unarmed, but hopefully sending a message. "She said she upset you. Did you hurt her?"

Katya fell over and immediately began crying and muttering to herself. She gathered up her things before crawling across the gravel path. Her knees were going to be a bloody mess.

I grabbed her arm and hauled her back onto her feet. "What in the hell are you rambling about over here?"

A dog joined the man as they made their way into the house next door. "Hey, I'm not finished talking to you," I called out.

Katya shook her head and patted my chest. "Don't—he's fine. It's me."

Once inside, I glared at her. "Couldn't just wait and see what I had to say, could you? You had to get blitzed beforehand."

She took a long swig from the vodka bottle in her hand and slurred, "What do you need, Detective?"

I watched her throat bob in a swallow, my mouth watering. I didn't give a fuck that it wasn't tequila—it was liquor and I had deprived my body for too long.

"Thought you stopped drinking," I said, dropping onto the couch in the living room with a groan, my body desperate for sleep. "Your dad said you were sober when we last spoke."

Katya shrugged halfheartedly. "So, I started again tonight. It's just a minor setback."

Christ, she sounded just like me.

I massaged my temple, trying to ward off the headache forming behind my eyes. "You can't keep doing this to yourself. Eventually, you're going to have to work through what he did to you."

I may as well have been talking to myself. I could get high or wasted, but at some point, I was going to have to come to terms with the fact that my actions led to Monica's death. If only I'd followed up on that mysterious text with a phone call to Grey, it would have changed everything. As it was, I had to live with my secrets or risk losing Lauren forever. The half-ass thing we had going was better than nothing. If she knew about the text, she'd never forgive me.

Katya ignored me and took another drink. "I'm doing the best I can. Is that why you drove all this way? To make sure I wasn't drinking again? Because that seems like a wasted trip. You could've texted, 'Katya, are you still drinking your life away?' and I would've said, 'Yep. Fucking everything up like normal.' And you wouldn't have had to drive up here. Mission accomplished."

"Look, I don't have good news," I hesitantly admitted. "We've looked into those Facebook messages and posts. The messages are coming from multiple IP addresses, pinging all over the goddamn place. Probably hiding behind a proxy server to mask their location."

I retrieved the Victoria's Secret catalog from the inside pocket of my jacket. She'd sworn someone had left a copy in her bedroom, but the police hadn't believed her. Hell, I hadn't believed her and had stopped by her condo to do a little digging of my own. It was resting on her pillow, waiting for her to come back home.

I held it up, and the color drained from her already pale face. "This was on your bed."

Her expression confirmed my fears. The stalker had been inside her condo since she'd been in Cedar Ridge.

"I'm not giving up—but you can't go home until we find them," I added, plucking the vodka from her hands and taking a long swig myself. Just enough to take the edge off. The flight had been turbulent. I was running on fumes.

"Do you think it's the same person who was leaving things on my door? Was there anything else?" Her hands shook as she reached for the bottle again.

I handed it over reluctantly and stared down at the hardwood floor. "Yeah. I had people watching your front door, but I guess the perp spotted them. I found the note on your Jeep down in the parking garage. Security cameras came up blank, though. How they got into your condo is beyond me."

"What did it say?" she asked softly.

"*You deserve the moon and the stars laid at your feet. Give me one more chance.* They want you to think it's Landon, obviously."

She didn't respond, just calmly tipped the bottle back to finish it. The glass slipped through her fingers and fell to the coffee table with a dull bang.

"I can't stay here forever, Mike. You promised me you'd end this. And you still don't know who this person is?" She stood up, swaying violently.

This was why I dreaded coming up here. After everything Katya had been through, she deserved to go home. Just like Lauren deserved to go back to her apartment. Without knowing who the real enemy was, though, it wasn't safe for either of them.

"I said I'd fix it, just—"

"This is your fault! You could have arrested Landon. People would've seen him for the monster he was, but you took justice into your own hands. You swore to uphold the law, and you broke your vow then. Why should now be any different?"

Despite being obviously drunk, Katya spun on her heel to walk away. I grabbed her arm and yanked her back toward me. Same fucking topic every time. She may as well have been Lauren.

I snarled, "I'm getting real fucking sick of trying to explain why I did what I did. You wanna accuse me of being corrupt? Fine. Just remember who saved your ass that night."

She slapped me and I reared back, stunned. "I never once asked you to do that!"

Fuck this.

I shoved her into a wall. "Don't hit me. You hear that? Can you process what I'm saying with all the alcohol in your system?"

She let out a low growl and began striking my head and chest with her fists. I snatched both of her arms, pinning them above her head. It felt too familiar. When Lauren took her anger out on me, it felt warranted. With Katya, it just pissed me off. We were fighting to regain our breath when I made the mistake of looking down at her.

I dropped my head down next to her face and inhaled. She smelled nothing like Lauren. It didn't matter. Once she turned her head and brushed her lips against mine, my remaining thread of control snapped.

The same hands hellbent on hurting me moments before now caressed my cheeks gently as she deepened the kiss. I moved my mouth roughly over hers, growing harder by the second.

I lifted Katya, letting her guide me to the bedroom. Just getting it out of my system. I'd work my frustration out on her body, proving my dick wasn't broken. My heart, maybe. But, I could only fix one thing at a time.

If I ever stepped foot in a therapist's office, they were going to cancel the rest of their appointments for the day and spend it trying to diagnose why I was so fucked up.

I laid her back on the bed and stripped her pants off before staring down in horror. I was so fucking sleep deprived I could have sworn I she still bore the injuries from the night I saved her. When I blinked, they were gone, and I silently chastised myself for not grabbing a coffee before leaving the city.

Her t-shirt came off next, followed shortly after by her bra. I just needed to get her naked and beneath me. Nothing else mattered. I ran my tongue across her skin, resisting the urge to sink my teeth into her flesh until she cried out. Rage flowed through my veins. I had the urge to hurt her—to inflict pain on her because she wasn't Lauren.

What the fuck was wrong with me?

Her eyes fluttered shut, and I saw the police report as clear as day in my mind. Katya had been violently raped and beaten, and I was a fucking monster to even think about laying a hand on her.

I poured all of my effort into licking and sucking my way down her body, trying to give her pleasure.

"Like this?" I asked, checking in. "Is it okay?"

Katya stiffened when I slipped beneath the waistband of her panties, and I yanked my hand back. She'd seen my thoughts—knew I was no better than Landon Scott.

I was forcing her to relive what he did.

Katya looked up at me. "Why'd you stop?"

I laughed bitterly, feeling as if I was breathing through a straw. "Really? You're lying there as if I'm about to hurt—Jesus, Katya. Have you been with anyone since it happened?"

The realization left me with the urge to take a cold shower and scrub my skin until every disgusting thought I'd had was gone.

"No, but you could fix that," she said, trying to reach for me.

I shook my head and backed up. "Absolutely not. We're not doing this."

"What? Why not?"

My dick, still painfully confined in my jeans, helpfully reminded me I hadn't had sex since February. I moved back to the bed and was about to make my move when I heard my father's voice.

She's fine with it. Fuck, she's practically begging for it. That pussy is aching for a real man to remind her of what she's good for.

"I can't!" I snapped. "It wouldn't be right."

She pulled her clothes back on, muttering, "Since when did you care about what's right?"

When a gorgeous redhead asked me to dance on a beach.

When I saw her walk down the hallway at David and Elizabeth's house, and thought for a brief second that maybe life did hand out fairy tales.

That was when I started caring about what was right. When I held her in my arms, I wanted to be on the right side of things—more than anything I'd ever wanted before in my life.

I shook my head. "Stop. Enough with the blaming. There's another woman—"

Katya covered her face in mortification. "You're married? Oh—"

"I'm not married. Just fucking listen, for once in your life. When shit went down, I was involved with someone, and I lost her because of it. I have to live with those regrets for the rest of my life."

She lowered her hands and gave me a pointed look. "You're not married? Then why can't we—"

"Stop, Katya! You think I don't want to? Jesus, your body is perfect. Most guys in my situation wouldn't hesitate to fuck a supermodel, but I'm not the type of guy who's gonna stick around for breakfast, though."

I would not sink to Comedian's level. I refused to push Katya into sex just because I needed to get off. She was liable to end up in a psych ward.

"I don't expect you to stick around," she said, giving me her best *fuck me* stare. "You can leave right once we're done."

I wasn't biting. "I can't. Katya, I saw you that night. I saw what he did to you—I've read the medical report a thousand times, for Christ's sake. I look at you and I see the photos that were taken in the hospital. Every cut, every bruise, every abrasion documented in writing and full-color photos. I know he raped you, but I can't put you back together. I can't have a one-night stand with you—not with knowing all I do."

Realization hit me like a slap in the face. I was worse than a monster. I'd turned into my father. Years spent fighting it for nothing. I ran the back of my hand angrily across my eyes as tears fell. I thought I'd wanted to hurt Katya, but really, I wanted to hurt myself.

I'd wasted years trying to be better—trying to be someone I could tolerate seeing in the mirror every morning. But the apple hadn't fallen far from the tree. I'd been so hellbent on getting Lauren back, I never once stopped to consider if I even deserved her.

And deep down, I knew I didn't.

She needed a warrior, not some depraved man-child. A child who hadn't questioned the text on Monica. I wanted to believe I was just following orders, but in reality, I was nothing more than a puppet on a string.

"I don't need your pity, Detective," Katya bitterly replied.

I looked up at her in surprise. "You think I pity you? No, I honestly can't even fathom how you survived four months with him. I get it—you drink until you don't see his face when you close your eyes. I drink because every time I close my eyes, I see—" I pinched the bridge of my nose to stop the flow of tears.

My father hunting a woman like an animal. Patrick convulsing on the ground. Lauren's face the morning her mother was murdered. But I couldn't say it—couldn't throw my burdens on her shoulders. The woman had carried enough.

I wasn't my father. Michael Sullivan, Sr. would have taken what he wanted, regardless. Didn't leave me feeling any better about myself, though.

Katya wrapped herself around me, whispering, "I'm sorry, Mike. I'm so sorry. It's like I'm beyond saving—irreparably damaged."

Just two lost souls waiting in Purgatory. Like some fucked up version of a Pink Floyd song.

"You're not," I reassured her. "You've been through hell, but I truly believe you can find your way back. Might have to fight to get there, but if anyone can do it, it's you. Come here." I tucked her into bed and snagged an extra pillow before moving to the floor.

She went still, only to jerk herself awake seconds later.

"Sleep, Katya," I whispered up to her. "I'm here. I'll wake you if it gets bad."

"Would you have killed him without the money?" she quietly asked.

It was a question I'd often considered since December. After the shit I put him through with Patrick, I owed David. But fulfilling one promise had set off a chain of events that led to me losing Lauren.

I finally answered. "I didn't think the baby—Kaden—was going to make it. Hell, if I'm being honest, I didn't think any of you were. David is my best friend. I thought if he was going to lose everything, he had a right to look his family's killer in the eye—to serve his own brand of justice.

"What your father offered—the forty grand—it's a lot of money. I thought I could set it aside—maybe buy a ring. You know, happily ever after shit. I never considered my actions with Landon would ensure I didn't have a future with her. To answer your question, I would've done it without the money. Even knowing what it was going to cost me."

She grew quiet again, and I thought she'd finally fallen asleep until her soft voice startled me. "I wouldn't have let you. I would have let him kill me first."

Her breathing evened out not long after, but I knew she wasn't sleeping peacefully. People like us never got peace. Not even in the quiet moments.

The words resonated, though. There were days I wished I would have let Grey kill me. It would've been an honorable death.

Maybe the only honorable thing I'd ever done.

CHAPTER FIFTY-TWO

Lauren: June 2015 (Age: 28)

Operation Sleep with Jimmy was a go.

O The slow tempo pop song blasted through my headphones and left me fighting the urge to drop it like it was hot by the free weights.

After finishing his last set of pull-downs, Jimmy indicated it was my turn. I raised my arms seductively overhead, bringing the bar down in time with the music.

I just needed to free my mind of all the doubt and not be a stranger anymore.

Tonight was about setting my spirit free.

It was the only way to be.

What we were going to achieve was going to make up for all the empty words between us—I just knew it.

Jimmy needed to wear a condom. Mike had forgotten, but I was wiser now. Besides getting me in the mood, the song was giving some really sound advice.

I finished my last rep and stood up, unable to resist a sexy little hip thrust to the beat of music only I could hear.

Yeah, Jimmy, that's right. Tonight, you're getting all of this.

He gave me a puzzled look, slipping my headphones off my head and onto his. I tried to snatch them back, but only reached his shoulders.

"Spice Girls, huh?" The confused expression gave way to an amused smirk. "You're throwing it back to the nineties tonight, aren't you?"

I crossed my arms over my chest. "I want my headphones back."

Before placing them back on my head, he leaned down to whisper, "Get it on. Get it on."

My cheeks grew warm, and I looked away. He didn't understand. Losing my virginity had been a relatively simple decision once I found the right guy.

But sex with someone else?

Simply put, if you'd done something once, it was damn near impossible to do again.

My brow furrowed. That didn't sound right.

If you did something a lot, it got... harder with time?

I slowly lifted my gaze to find Jimmy still staring down at me. "Hello," I managed weakly, earning me another grin from him.

"Hello. So, was that a hint? Because I can think of another way to burn calories." He chewed on the corner of his lip, impatiently awaiting my response.

Not trusting my voice, I nodded slowly.

Jimmy bent down and grabbed his gym bag before wrapping a massive arm behind my knees, throwing me over his shoulder. "We'll take my truck."

"You have a truck and a bike?" I asked breathlessly.

He laughed, his chest vibrating against my pelvis. "Oh, yeah. I'm the full package."

Package.

The word immediately made me think of dirty things. My pulse raced and my body flooded with heat. I knew it. After that kiss, I just knew the spark would ignite into this.

I was going to do the sex—*shit*—have sex. Right.

Jimmy stroked my thigh while navigating traffic lights and crowded city streets, as if my leg had become his own personal stick shift. When we reached his house, he didn't even take the time to pull all the way into the garage before grabbing my hand and tugging me across the seats toward him.

Puck greeted us at the door, jumping up and down at the prospect of meeting someone new. My thighs stung from where his tail caught me through the thin material of my leggings.

I watched as Jimmy tried to wrestle the pup down, unable to tear my eyes away from the bulge in his sweatpants.

If Puck was excited, then Jimmy was damn near ecstatic.

I pushed my lips together to keep the nervous giggle at bay as he dragged me through the house, not stopping until we reached his bedroom. He toed off his shoes, and I followed suit, heart pounding.

"I can't wait. I'm sorry," he murmured against my hair, his hands slipping beneath the waistband of my leggings to pull me closer. Thanks to the height difference, his erection was now firmly pressed up against my sports bra, reminding me of just how long I'd kept him waiting over the past month.

He rolled his hips forward, further pressing his hard length against my chest. I couldn't help the moan that escaped my lips.

"Don't be sorry," I whispered against his stomach, suddenly feeling very unsure about my plan.

He was so much bigger than me—what if it didn't fit?

Jimmy ground his hips against my body with a low growl, shamelessly using his grip on my ass for leverage. His fingers dug into my flesh and I wrapped my legs around him, trying to ignore the way his touch conjured up memories of Mike.

I would think about Mike tomorrow when I went to the station. Tonight was about Jimmy and forgetting. He sucked my bottom lip in between his teeth and all thoughts of Mike fled to the dark recesses of my mind.

"I didn't think you'd ever come meet Puck," he panted as he broke the kiss.

I glanced around the empty bedroom and toward the closed door. "Is he even in here?"

"Oh," he sighed. "He's probably still out in the living room. Want me to grab him?"

I cupped his face in my hand, guiding his eyes back to mine. "God no. Don't stop now."

He carried me over to a bed as big as he was, spreading me across it like a feast. I watched as he stripped out of his tank top, devouring his washboard abs and well-defined pecs. No need to trick my body into sleeping with him. It seemed to get there just fine on its own.

Sex with him was going to be the cherry on top of the sundae.

He pulled his sweatpants off, and I sucked in a breath. I was going to have to retract my statement. There was no way that was going near my lady-bits.

"Um, Jimmy," I protested. "I don't... I don't—"

He shook his head and crawled onto the bed with purpose—like a lion going after a gazelle. Or, in my case, an elephant going after a field mouse.

"No way, babe. I've dreamt about having you in my bed since the night you tried to kill yourself on the bench press. I'll make it fit."

I'll make it fit.

The words flooded my senses with lust. With four words, he'd made me forget what I was supposed to be fighting against.

"Show me that body, Lauren. Let me see you," he huskily whispered, running his tongue along my jawline and sending another tingle of pleasure through my body.

Damn. He was good.

I pulled my t-shirt over my head with a dry mouth, followed by my sports bra and leggings. I tossed all three over the side of the bed and held my arms up above my head with a giggle. "Here I am."

Jimmy stroked himself with a grin. "Come here."

He pulled me across his chest until I was straddling him. This was it. My one-way ticket out of *Sullivanville*.

"You forgot your protection," he said with a smile.

I froze. "You don't have condoms?"

He shook his head. "No—I mean, yes, I have condoms. You don't have your gun, though."

I still had my holster on, but my gun was still in the locker room at the gym. It didn't matter. I'd get it tomorrow. "I don't need it for this, do I?"

"Nope," he ground out, brushing up against my core. His thumb made soft circles around my clit and I hissed through my teeth, rocking into his hand. He slid a finger inside me and my head fell back, leaving me feeling as if I might spontaneously combust without warning.

You like that, Red?

"Yes. Yes. Yes. Don't stop, Mike!" The words came out in little puffs as my breaths grew shorter.

"No—don't stop!" I whimpered when his hand stilled beneath me.

"Who's Mike?" Jimmy asked, his eyebrows drawing together in a tight line.

"Who?" I repeated dumbly. Sensing there was no way of digging myself out of the massive hole my mouth had created, I stroked his chest with a fingernail and whispered, "Jimmy, I'm so close. Please let me come for you."

His jaw tightened as he fought over whether to say something. In the end, hormones won and his hand began moving inside of me again.

I closed my eyes, seeing not Jimmy but Mike beneath me, blue eyes sparkling mischievously. He'd always taken getting me off as a challenge.

One was never enough.

Sparks flashed behind my eyes. I cried out, clenching Jimmy's hand between my thighs. The urge to yell Mike's name was even stronger, leaving me with a sick feeling in the pit of my stomach.

What was wrong with me?

"Hey," Jimmy said softly, bringing me back to reality. "You're so beautiful when you come apart."

My lower lip quivered, and I jerked my chin in an abrupt nod, knowing my words would be drowned out by my tears.

I didn't deserve this man.

What I deserved was a friendly punch to the face. Or maybe the lady-bits—give them a nice reboot until they played nicely. *Didn't they know Mike was no good for us?*

"My turn?" Jimmy asked with a hopeful grin, grasping my hips in his hands. I let him slide me back toward his waiting dick, struck with a sudden sense of performance anxiety.

Moment of truth. Would sleeping with him be the antidote to the poison Mike had left in my veins?

Only one way to find out.

Keeping one hand locked on my waist, he rifled through his night-stand for a condom, flashing me another panty-melting grin as he tore the package with his teeth. "You ready, baby?"

I meant to nod and say something seductive. Instead, a strangled sob worked its way out and I vigorously began shaking my head. My breaths came in labored pants and where there should have been fire-works, I saw black spots.

Jimmy dropped the condom onto the comforter and pulled me to his chest. "Shhhh... I've got you."

"I can't breathe! I can't—breathe," I gasped, desperately trying to free myself from his grasp.

His hold loosened, and I crawled to the side of the bed, wrapping my arms around my torso. Something was wrong. The air I was sucking in wasn't reaching my lungs. I didn't know where it was going, but felt like a fish out of water with every desperate gasp.

Jimmy grabbed onto my arms, placing my left hand against my chest and my right against my belly. "Breathe in through your nose, nice and slow. Feel your chest rise with your left hand and sink in with your right. That a girl. Just like that."

Tears spilled down my cheeks, dripping onto my chest and his arms. I couldn't speak, so I continued breathing, just like he'd shown me. Until I felt in control again.

"You're having a panic attack," he calmly noted. "Is this something you've experienced before?"

I nodded weakly in response, wishing I could teleport to Torch's house, avoiding what was sure to be the most awkward conversation of my life.

Since my mother's murder, my body had been through the full gamut of grief—from denial to feeling as if I'd gone up against a heavy-weight boxing champ. And lost.

But this was the first attack I'd had over the loss of Mike.

Jimmy rocked back on his heels, giving me space and a complete view of the impressive hard-on he was still sporting.

I was a friggin' disaster.

"I'm sorry, Jimmy," I said, upon finding my voice again. I'd call a cab, and we could pretend the whole thing never happened. If I shifted my workouts around, we wouldn't even have to deal with any uncomfortable run-ins.

He tucked several strands of hair behind my ear. "You haven't been with anyone since—" His voice trailed off and he looked at me helplessly.

"Since?"

His eyes went dark, and he looked away. "Since Mike."

I struggled to corral my thoughts into something resembling a question. "You know Mike?"

Jimmy rubbed at his temple and squeezed his eyes shut before forcing out, "You said his name, Lauren. It's obvious you haven't been with anyone since him. It's why you brushed me off at first."

"That's not true," I argued. "How would you even know that?"

I looked at him—really looked at him—and finally saw what I'd missed. It was in his eyes.

Pain.

Loss.

He swallowed hard. "I've been in your shoes before—"

"I hope not," I deadpanned. "They'd never fit you."

Jimmy's expression remained somber. "I lost my fiancée a couple of years ago. The first time I tried to *get back in the saddle*, I cried like a fucking baby and we ended up watching movies instead. Come on."

He tossed me a t-shirt that fell to my knees like a dress and slipped on a pair of athletic shorts. I let him lead me to the living room, still feeling out of sorts.

Puck woke from his spot on the couch. Instead of jumping up to greet me, he grumbled and turned away.

Sorry, buddy.

Jimmy channel surfed like a professional, not spending more than half a second on each channel.

"Here we go," he said. "This is good. *Band of Brothers*—have you seen it?"

I stared at the screen, feeling my throat tighten. "No. I—I haven't seen—" The tears began falling again and lowered my gaze to my lap.

Forget teleportation.

I wanted the floor to swallow me whole right about now.

It had to be a historical documentary.

My heart was in a vice tonight, with every event putting just a little more pressure on it. I didn't know how much more I could take before the chambers caved in.

I began bawling like a lunatic again, and he hurriedly switched off the television. "Okay—we could play a card game. Or read a book."

"I'm sorry, Jimmy," I wailed. "We can watch the movie. See, I'm fine now."

I sniffled and tried to ignore the river of tears cascading down my cheeks.

"Let's try this," he suggested, landing on an infomercial.

I agreed, and the house descended into silence again, minus the random sounds Puck made as he dreamed from the end of the couch. I lay with my head on Jimmy's shoulder, ashamed of my reaction and plagued with the fear that Mike Sullivan had broken me permanently.

"Jimmy?" I asked quietly.

He muted the television and leaned down. "Yeah?"

I swallowed nervously. "You said you'd been here before—um, did you ever talk to your fiancée—or ex-fiancée—about things? Like to work it out? Or maybe just gain closure?"

Jimmy's nostrils flared and his jaw went tight, but this time it had nothing to do with desire. "Well..." His mouth twisted up, as if the words in his mouth pained him. "She died, Lauren."

I didn't know what to say—I was up to my eyeballs in my grief and the one thing I never wanted to hear was an apology. So, I kept my mouth shut and gripped his arm a little tighter, feeling like the world's biggest asshole.

"Does it get better?" I whispered, even though my heart had already given me the answer.

He clenched his jaw again. "I'm still waiting..."

That was when I knew Mike was going to be in my blood forever. I'd given him my heart and until he gave it back, I was enslaved to him.

CHAPTER FIFTY-THREE

Lauren: June 2015 (Age: 28)

"*Good morning, and we're back with a product you're all going to love. Tired of caked-on food?*"

I blinked slowly until the television screen came into focus. Then I blinked again at the unfamiliar surroundings before remembering where I was.

I lay sprawled across Jimmy with my head tucked under his chin, his arm resting on my thigh. Puck snored heavily from the other end of the couch. One bleary-eyed glance at my watch and I was up and racing to find my clothes.

Puck was on my heels in an instant, quickly followed by Jimmy. "What—what's wrong? What happened?"

I tugged my leggings on and began searching for my socks. "I have an appointment this morning at eight, and I still have to get my car and bag from the gym," I growled in frustration.

I was supposed to be at the station to formally request they open Monica's case in an hour. At the rate I was moving, I was going to be doing a walk of shame in last night's gym clothes.

Jimmy watched in amusement as I scurried back and forth, trying to make sure I had everything I needed. "I'll give you a ride back to the gym."

I nodded distractedly and laced up my shoes, suddenly feeling a little nervous at the prospect of going down to the station with no ideas who the mole might be.

We drove back to the gym in silence. This time around, Jimmy kept his hand on the steering wheel.

As he pulled into an empty spot close to the front doors, I turned to ask, "Will we—I mean, can we still work out together? Or is that weird now?"

He stared ahead through the windshield. "I think as long as we've decided to just be friends, it's fine. If we're going to go back and forth on it, it'd probably be best if we ended it now."

"That's fair. I wish it could be you, you know? You're a good guy."

He unbuckled and opened the door. "And Mike's not a good guy?"

I followed him inside the gym. "There are just a lot of gray areas with him." I puffed my cheeks out and exhaled roughly. "That about sums it up."

Unless I wanted to find myself in an even more uncomfortable position, I couldn't say more.

"Are you going to help me get ready, too?" I asked when Jimmy followed me to the locker room door.

He glanced around the gym, as if he too had just noticed it. "I guess I don't have anywhere to be right now. I'll just make sure you get your stuff and get out of here. Okay?"

"Thanks." I quickly retrieved my gym bag, tucking my gun back into its holster. Jimmy was still waiting in the hallway and we walked toward the exit in silence.

Why couldn't I want the nice guy? The man was incredibly sexy, had a great personality, nice house, and the most adorable dog ever. And I felt the same way about him as I did about the guy who delivered mail to the office.

Nothing.

The spark had only lasted for a second before flickering out completely. I couldn't have a bad boy complex if I'd only ever been with one guy, right?

I wondered if Jimmy's mind was going in the same direction as mine when he shifted closer, but before I could ask, his arm shot out, knocking me to the pavement just outside the front doors.

In an instant, his body came down over mine. I opened my mouth to protest when a loud pop and the sound of glass breaking shattered the silence. I struggled to move—to make sense of what was happening—but the arm on my chest kept me pinned against the concrete.

A deafening bang left my ears ringing and my head swimming in confusion. I took in the weapon clutched in Jimmy's hand, watching in horrified fascination as he fired on a black suburban with a gun I didn't know he had on him.

Someone in the suburban leaned out the window and I let out a sharp cry as they shot out the windows on my car before tossing a flaming bottle into the backseat.

Jimmy fired off another round, striking the man in the head, before the vehicle tore out of the parking lot, tires squealing. From start to finish, the entire thing had lasted maybe sixty seconds.

But it felt longer.

Gym employees raced outside, staring at the fireball that had once been my car. Someone nearby yelled they were calling 911, while another checked in with Jimmy to see if we needed an ambulance.

I kept a death grip on his shirt, too scared to move. What if they came back?

"You okay?" he asked gruffly, his hand tightening around my shoulder.

I nodded shakily, tears already leaking from the corners of my eyes. "Are you?"

"I'm fine." He calmly holstered his gun inside the waistband of his jeans and asked, "Is there someone who wants you dead? Because that was an attempted hit. Either they had the wrong target or you're a wanted woman. I took out one, but there'll be more."

I took a deep breath, fighting the sob lodged in my throat. "I—I was supposed to meet with the police department this morning. My mother—someone killed her, but they ruled it a drug overdose. I was going to get the case reopened with new evidence. Obviously, they don't like that plan."

Jimmy looked out toward the street again before running a hand roughly across his face. "No, they damn sure don't. Is there anyone you can call? Someone who could get you to a safe-house?"

Who was this guy?

What happened to the funny giant with no secrets?

Normal people didn't react like Jason Bourne in a crisis, did they?

I retrieved my phone from the small pocket of my leggings, wincing at the pain in my left elbow. Just another reminder I wouldn't make it out of this unscathed. He answered before it even rang.

"Lauren? Are you okay?"

My voice cracked as I whispered, "No. Someone just tried to kill me."

Mike cursed before asking, "Where are you, baby? Are they still there? Can you get somewhere safe?"

I shook my head and tried to speak before Jimmy plucked the phone from my hand.

"4th and Milwaukee. Asset is safe, but the rabbit has fled."

I stared at him incredulously. My head must have hit the pavement harder than I thought. Gym employees tried to help us up, but Jimmy kept a tight hold on my shoulder.

"Jimmy?" I asked, shifting into a sitting position.

"Hmm?" he responded absently, checking my body for injuries.

"What the hell was that? Rabbits and assets?"

His brow furrowed, and he frowned back at me. "What? What are you talking about? You're not making any sense. Let's get you inside."

I attempted to argue, but he handed me off to a female employee before stepping back outside to wait for the cops. Maybe he wasn't the open book I'd pegged him for.

CHAPTER FIFTY-FOUR

Mike: June 2015 (Age: 32)

The fire department was trying to put out the remains of a burning car when I arrived on scene.

Lauren's burning car.

I jumped out of my truck and ran for the crowd, hoping like hell she was nowhere near the damn thing when it happened.

Her skyscraper of a gym partner met me on the sidewalk. "Where is she?" I demanded. "Were you the one I talked to on the phone?"

He jerked a thumb toward the building and nodded. "Yeah, she's okay—they're keeping her calm inside."

I ran my hands roughly across my face and began pacing. "What I need to know is why she was here. She doesn't work out in the mornings—it goes against her entire routine."

The giraffe squeezed the back of his neck and grimaced. "She stayed with me last night, man. We were just here to get her car."

I kept my face passive, but inside, my blood was boiling. *How was that for a nice kick in the balls first thing in the morning?* I couldn't convince her to have dinner with me, but Chuckles over here was getting her overnight? *Fuck.*

He'd been inside of her—*nope*—couldn't go there right now. I needed to concentrate and keep a clear head.

"Who would have known she'd be here?" I asked pointedly.

Obviously not me.

He shrugged. "Look, nothing happened between us. Well, we did fool around a bit, but—"

I held my hand up. "Please stop. I don't need the details of your love life. This is a case—nothing more. If I'm going to help her, then I need to know who knew her schedule, besides you."

"I don't really know her schedule," Stretch reiterated. "We work out together and last night she came over. That's it. As far as knowing her schedule, she mentioned some Mike guy?"

Well, well, well.

"Oh, yeah?" I asked, unable to mask my grin. "What'd she say about Mike?"

"That he has a gigantic head and an even bigger mouth," said a voice from behind.

Lauren gave me a tired smile, her elbow cradled in her palm. I ached to hold her, but not in front of the Eiffel Tower. I knew my limits and while I could handle a black eye, this guy would obliterate me.

"Sounds about right for him," I answered, trying to keep the mood light before Lurch pounded me into the pavement.

Lauren bit down on her lip and looked between the two of us as if deciding something. Then she shocked the hell out of me by stepping forward to wrap her arms around my waist.

I winced and looked over at Treetop, but his face was a mask of indifference. I tentatively brought my arms around her, letting her cry into my chest.

"How did they know I was here?"

I brought my hand up and cupped the back of her head. "I don't know, baby, but I'm gonna find out. No one else knew you were going downtown today, did they?"

She shook her head, hiccuping, "I only told you—Mike, if Jimmy hadn't been here, they would've... I wouldn't—"

I tightened my hold on her, silencing her before she could finish the thought. For the first time since January, I felt like I was glimpsing the sunlight. This wasn't me kissing her in a parking lot in between bouts of fighting. She had come to me willingly this time. I wasn't about to let my mind wander back into the dark, thinking of her near death.

I looked up at Jimmy. "Thank you."

He nodded as another detective walked up and handed him a leather wallet. "That was some quick thinking, firing back on them like that."

I watched them both while Lauren moved to get closer, like she was trying to crawl inside of me. The guy had to be another badge—his jargon on the phone wasn't something a civilian would typically use. If he was a cop, I would've recognized him.

Maybe ex-military?

"Hey, Red?" I asked, so only she could hear me. "What happened exactly?"

Lauren looked up at me with her tear-streaked face and my heart damn near stopped in my chest. A million years could pass and I would still want only her. I glanced toward Jimmy and Detective Rangel, but they were deep in their own conversation. Lauren followed my gaze and nodded.

This was why she was so goddamned perfect for me. We didn't even need words, because she almost always knew where my head was at.

With a low voice, she replied, "We were walking out and, I'll admit, I wasn't paying much attention to anything else. Jimmy shoved me down, covered my body with his, and somehow had his gun drawn before they'd even gotten within range of us. He hit one guy and then they took off. It was like Rambo or something." Lauren laughed, but then immediately began crying again.

I tucked her head up against my chest and rocked her. "I've got you, baby. It's alright. I've got you."

It wasn't alright, though.

Someone had tried to kill her. And the only people who knew her plans for this morning were me, her, and Silent Phoenix.

Somebody owed me an explanation before I went on a fucking rampage.

CHAPTER FIFTY-FIVE

Mike: July 2015 (Age: 32)

I stared at my laptop screen and then back down at the notebook lying open on my kitchen table.

My conversation with Grey had gone nowhere. He was adamant it couldn't have been any of his guys because he could account for every single club officer during the time in question. I'd made a list of my own and had spent the last five hours cross-referencing names with locations.

To make matters worse, another model had gone missing in the Denver area. Katya's friend, Christine Stevens. It was no coincidence she disappeared on the six-month anniversary of Katya's rescue, either.

I switched screens, poring over anything that looked like a connection between the two cases. Katya and Christine were both models and had mutual female friends, but that's where the similarities ended. Outside of work events, the two rarely spent time together.

I tapped my pen against the pad of paper, trying to recreate the timeline of events leading up to Katya's disappearance. The Arapahoe County Sheriff's Department focused their efforts on tracking down Landon Scott. As I knew where that trail led, I looked for anything to tie the two cases together.

When I reached a dead end, I flipped back over to Lauren's case. If the club officers were accounted for, then maybe one of them opened their mouth to a club whore or Ol' Lady.

The whole fucking thing was fishy. If the Sons were that concerned with Lauren, why hadn't they attempted something before now?

At the guttural roar of a motorcycle outside, I grabbed my fun and headed to the front door.

"Come and get me, motherfuckers," I growled, checking my mag before sliding it back in. The noise from the straight pipes was thunderous, rattling the windowpanes like heavy bass from a speaker.

I threw open the front door and sauntered out, fury fueling each step. The rider threw off his helmet while his passenger sat stock-still.

"Mike, it's me! It's Torch!" He waved his hands.

I lowered my weapon, calling out, "Who'd you bring with you?"

The passenger pulled their helmet off to reveal long red hair. "Me, Tex. Thanks for the ride," Lauren said, patting Torch's arm.

He nodded and took off down the dirt road, his brake lights casting her in a red glow. She tucked the helmet under her arm and tentatively approached me. "You gonna put the gun away?"

I holstered it and gestured toward the porch swing. She had on a leather jacket, looking every bit the part of a biker's Ol' Lady. It made me feel sick. When she met me, she'd been a virgin with her life semi-together. I felt responsible for the shift.

"Nice jacket," I offered as she sat down.

"Thanks—it was my mom's." She shrugged out of it and kicked off her cowboy boots, setting the swing in motion.

I leaned against the front railing, watching her curiously. "Are we gonna talk about why you're here at—" I checked my watch. "Eleven-thirty at night?"

Lauren lifted her feet until just her toes were resting against the wood before dropping her heels back down. "I need you." She lowered her eyes to the porch. "I tried to move on with Jimmy. Elizabeth said I should have sex with someone else, but I couldn't do it. Shit, I wasn't supposed to tell you that last part."

I let out a bitter laugh. "You tried to take advice from someone who nearly died from her own affair?"

Elizabeth was going to get an earful the next time I saw her.

Lauren scowled at the patio. "Be nice. I just—I—I still love you, okay?" She looked up at me sadly. "Loving you hurt me, but I don't know how to stop. And I hate myself for it."

Just twist that knife a little deeper in my chest, darlin'.

With a deep breath, I cleared my thoughts. No more cases involving missing models. No more shady MCs firebombing cars like the goddamned Taliban.

Just Lauren.

It had always been just Lauren.

"I need you," she whispered again, her voice catching. "I just need to feel safe and I've only ever had that with you."

If I were to die right now, with her words ringing in my ears, then I'd go out a fortunate man.

I crossed the porch and scooped her into my arms. She didn't argue, just held on tightly as I carried her inside and upstairs. A tear slipped free from the corner of her eye as I laid her back on the bed and I pressed my lips to it.

I wanted to put her back together.

The only way I knew how.

Her pulse thrummed in her neck as she looked up at me with eyes that were even greener than usual against her purple tank top.

I grasped the hem and pulled it up and over her head, another tear spilling down her cheek. My tongue lapped it up, and I moved to her denim shorts, hands shaking as I unfastened them, knowing she was watching me with those wide eyes. Eyes that somehow saw past the facade and down into the blackness of my soul.

The night was warm, but her skin raised up as I slid the shorts off. I paused and stared down at her spread across my bed and realized I'd been starving—dying for what we had since she ended things in January.

I'd been fucking drowning in drugs and booze, but she was my lifeline. We had wasted so much time hating each other when we were the only ones who could save the other.

I brought my mouth down and pressed a light kiss against her belly. Her breath quivered, so I moved a little lower. Each stuttered exhale led me down until my nose brushed against the lips of her pussy.

I pressed my mouth to her through the panties and her hips rolled forward as she let out a soft sigh. Her hands found my hair, and she ran her fingers through it. Unlike our first time, I didn't want to rush this.

I pulled the lacy scrap of fabric to the side and ran my tongue over her clit, earning myself another full body shudder. Her nipples were straining against the mesh of her bra. With one hand, I remedied the situation and freed them.

So fucking perfect.

Her lips parted on a soft exhale when I took them in my hands, making me think maybe she needed me just as badly as I needed her. I pressed my tongue against her teeth until she let me in, my body instinctively driving into hers. The denim brushed up against her core and she whimpered, letting her hips rock back to meet me.

I did it again, and two more tears made the trek down her cheeks. When I tried to pull back, she shook her head. "Please don't stop."

Using my arms to brace myself on either side of her, I rolled my hips forward again and again until her mouth fell open and her hands dug into the sheets.

Lauren's body was something I wanted to worship for the rest of my life. Being forced to live without her for months only reiterated the fact that I never wanted to be apart from her again. I wanted her in my bed every night—her body pressed up against mine. Wanted to watch it change as she carried my children.

A tear trickled down my cheek, but I dropped to my knees before she could see. I took my time stripping her panties off before parting her thighs with my hands.

I thrust two fingers inside her tight channel and her back arched, forcing her perfect pussy onto my face. My tears mixed with saliva as I licked and sucked her flesh like it was my goddamn job. Lauren panted and clawed at the sheets above me, urging me on.

I wanted her back.

Charlotte and Jack.

Everything my father had always claimed was nothing more than bullshit. My ring on her finger. Mine for all eternity.

Christ, I wasn't David. I was a fucking biker.

I peeled my mouth off with a growl and stripped out of my clothes before lining the head of my cock up with her body. It slipped in easily, but Lauren immediately moved back.

"Condom," she panted.

I ground my teeth in frustration, but nodded. "Yep. I'll wrap it up."

Trying to knock her up in order to keep her with me was admittedly a dick move, but my brain wasn't rational. Not with her.

I took a deep breath and retrieved a condom from the back pocket of my jeans. This time, she didn't resist as I slowly sank into her and wrapped a hand around my neck, pulling my mouth back down over hers.

"I like tasting me on your lips," she murmured, and I fought the urge to come.

We easily found our rhythm, even after months apart, as if we'd never left. I plunged in and her body bore down on me—pushing me out, drawing me back in. Just like it used to be, before everything fell apart.

"I fucking hate you," Lauren whispered as she clenched around me, mouth falling open in a silent scream.

The words were like a blow to the head, but I gritted my teeth and thrust harder, hissing, "I fucking hate you too." Her pussy tightened around me at the confession.

This was the hate fucking we'd needed to work through all the shit I'd put her through.

She sucked in a ragged breath and a tear fell, soon followed by another. They fell so quickly I couldn't even tell where one began and the other ended.

"I'm so sorry, baby," I whispered against her throat. "So fucking sorry."

Lauren tried to inhale as a sob broke free, her raw pain the soundtrack to our fucking. She thrust a hand into my chest and pushed until I was lying on my back. Her hips held me in place as she sank back down on me.

The tears ran in rivets down her chest, pooling on my stomach, as she rocked on top of me.

"It hurts," she gasped. "I hurt so much."

"I know," I croaked, feeling it too.

Her hands came down to rest on my chest. "I want to forget, Mike. I just want to forget for a while."

I took my cue and gripped her hips tightly in my hands, forcing her sweat-slicked body back and my cock even deeper. Her cries went silent again and I couldn't hold back. I let myself come with her, somehow convinced I'd fixed us.

I loved her so damn much that her pain tore me apart.

When I woke up the next morning to an empty bed, I knew I'd only been fooling myself. There was no making up for what I'd done to her. I just wish I'd known before permanently handing over my heart.

To be continued...

––––––

Need more Mike and Lauren? Missing Celia and Grey? Keep reading for a sneak peek of *The Traitor*, book four of the SPMC series. Order today by tapping **HERE**!

––––––

Confused about the recommended reading order? Look no further!

Deserter (Book 1 in the Silent Phoenix MC Series)
Protector (Book 2 in the Silent Phoenix MC Series)
Renegade (Book 3 in the Silent Phoenix MC Series)
Traitor (Book 4 in the Silent Phoenix MC Series)
Savior (Book 5 in the Silent Phoenix MC Series)

* Operation Fit-ish (Book 1 in the Operation Duet)
* Operation Annulment (Book 2 in the Operation Duet)

*Optional, but will enhance your reading experience.

––––––

Worried that you'll miss my next release? Click here to receive an email notification the minute it goes live!

Want to be the first to know when my books go on sale? Follow me on BookBub!

For new release alerts, follow me on Amazon!

PREVIEW OF THE TRAITOR

ABOUT THE BOOK

Every war has its casualties...

We were just naive enough to believe it wouldn't hit so close to home.

The Sons are toying with us—moving people around like chess pieces.

Surrounded by enemies, it's impossible to know who's on my side.

Keeping my family and club out of the line of fire is my number one priority.

I almost lost her once before.

The breath will leave my body before I let it happen again.

The Traitor is available for purchase now. Simply tap on the title, or read on for a sneak peek at what's to come.

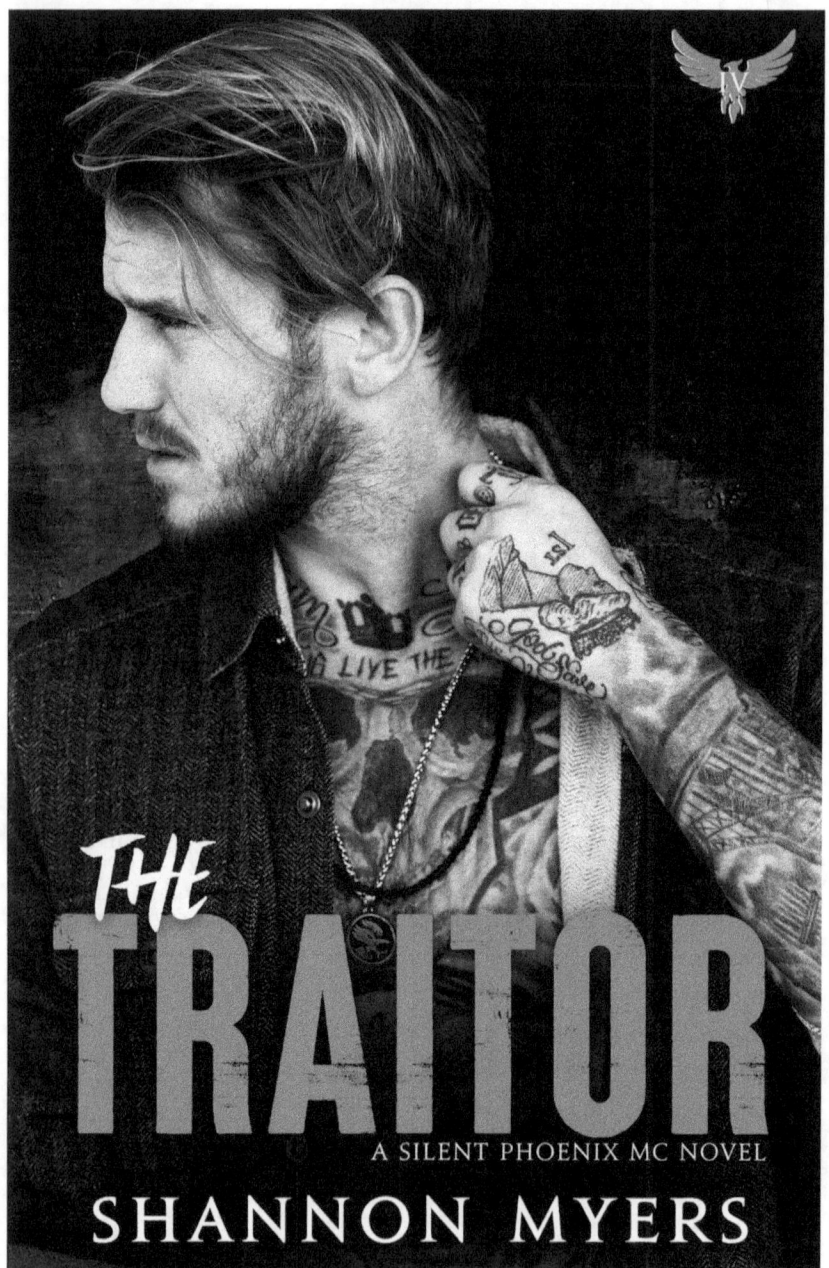

THE TRAITOR

Lauren: July 2015

I was going to get fired. It was really just a matter of when. I'd lost an invoice, and another vender hadn't been paid on time. It might have been manageable had Dr. Mulloy not called an order in herself today. When they explained there was a hold on our account because of nonpayment, she'd stormed into my office, guns blazing.

"What the hell is wrong with you?" she'd hissed. "Do you realize how this makes me look? Like I'm not seeing enough patients to cover the bills. Lauren, this is unacceptable. I don't care how late you have to stay, but you will stay and make sure every single account is up to date."

It was now almost nine, and I was just pulling into the driveway. Torch's bike was missing, but at least I could visit with *Abuelita* for a few minutes before collapsing from exhaustion. She'd been with us for two weeks, but hadn't mentioned any specifics for going back to Denver. Torch and I weren't complaining. The house was clean and there was always something to eat. With the third bedroom, I doubted either of us would have cared if she moved in permanently.

I let myself in, tossing my keys and purse on the small hall table. A table that hadn't come from Torch. There were hints of my mother all over the house. I found her presence comforting.

"*Abuelita?*" I called out, walking through the dark house.

When I flipped on the light to find a man sitting on the couch, I screamed.

"She's not here right now," said the large blond biker.

I took one look at the leather vest and reached for my Glock.

He placed his hand on the gun in his lap. "Wouldn't do that, Lauren. I'm a lot faster than I look and I didn't come here to put a bullet in your head. If I had, I would've dropped you in the hall as you put your keys down."

I let my shirt fall back over the holster, hands shaking violently. "W-why are you here? Where's my grandmother?"

He took his hand off the gun. "Torch took her to the movies. Needed a chance to talk to you. Alone."

I tried to imagine my grandmother on the back of a motorcycle, but failed. The man was menacing, yet strangely familiar.

"What could we possibly have to talk about?" I asked, crossing my arms over my chest to hide the shaking.

He grinned. "I like you—most people would be cowerin' right now. I wanna talk about why the fuck your car burned to the ground in a gym parkin' lot. Who knew you were tryin' to get your mother's case reopened?"

I fell into a nearby chair, shocked. It shouldn't have come as a surprise the bikers were watching my every move. But it did. "I—I told Mike, my ex. He's a cop, but—"

"I know who Mike is," he interjected. "No one else knew?"

I shook my head. The man continued staring, as if waiting for me to crack and admit I'd given the story to *CNN* as well.

"I swear to you. No one else knows."

"That means I've got a fuckin' rat in my clubhouse then. No wonder he didn't trust them." He stroked his beard, staring right through me.

I realized who he was when I looked into his eyes.

"You brought my car back, didn't you? You're Jared—no—Josh. Don't tell me, it's Jeremiah."

Why couldn't I remember?

The biker watched patiently before offering, "Do you want to keep guessin', or should I just tell you?"

I sighed and gestured for him to go on. "Just tell me. I'm too tired to think."

He laughed deeply. "It's Jamie. And, yes. I brought your car that night."

"So close," I lamented.

"You didn't tell anyone other than Mikey," Jamie reiterated as he paced the room. "And I know he's not a rat, so that leaves one of the club members."

I watched him walk from one side of the room to the other, wondering if Mikey and Mike were the same person.

"How am I supposed to help you with this?"

He stopped. "Did Monica leave you anything the night she died? I know she told you she'd overheard some shit. Might mean nothing to you, but it could to me."

"Back here." Without another thought, I grabbed his arm and led him down the hall to my bedroom. He didn't resist when I walked into the closet and slid a section of hangers back.

Jamie's brow raised as he took in my wall of clues and he let out a low whistle. "Wow. You're quite the detective. Walk me through this." He pulled a small notebook from his back pocket along with a pen, waiting for me to give him something.

I took a deep breath. "Okay, I found these bits of paper, but I haven't been able to make sense of them." I pulled one scrap free and held it up for him to see. "Like this—Brianne. October 2. I searched the archives for any public record relating to a Brianne and the date October 2. Nothing came up, though."

He nodded, and I moved down to the coaster. I removed the tack and handed it to him, pointing out the name at the bottom. "This meant nothing to me until Chon Ramos tried to kill me. I'm assuming they're the same person."

Jamie turned it over in his hands. "Leather & Lace."

I nodded. "Yeah. That's what led me to Torch. I don't know what *SOD* and *roll over* mean—do you?"

He clicked the pen on and off in frustration, his jaw tightening. "SOD is the Sons of Death MC. Roll over means someone turned on the club. Fuck!"

He roared the words, and I shrank back, instantly realizing I'd just trapped myself inside a small closet with a biker who probably killed girls like me for breakfast—*wait, that wasn't how the saying went.*

Ate girls like me for breakfast?

It wasn't much better, although Jamie was pretty handsome for an older man. I doubt I would complain much if he wanted to eat me.

When he paused to pinch the bridge of his nose, I gasped.

He gave me an odd look. "Are you okay?"

I nodded shakily. "I—I thought I saw a mouse."

He laughed lightly and went back to studying the wall, while I focused on his profile, the pieces falling into place.

The pen clicking.

The blue eyes.

Fuck, even his profile was a dead ringer.

The resemblance was uncanny. Jamie knew Mike wasn't the rat because a father would never suspect his son.

And Mike was most definitely Jamie's son.

It was why Carnage had apologized profusely when Torch told him I belonged to Mike. I knew next to nothing about bikers and their gangs or clubs, but I was pretty sure you couldn't mess with the head honcho's family.

Oh god.

Mike was in deep with outlaw bikers, but if he was the son of the leader, wouldn't that mean he would have done everything in his power to keep Monica safe?

What if I'd made a horrible mistake?

———

The Traitor is available for purchase now. Order it by tapping here.

ACKNOWLEDGMENTS

As always, this book would not have been possible without some amazing people.

Rebecca Pau- Thank you for stepping in to help me in a pinch with sequel covers and teasers. I really would be lost without you.

Bloggers- Thank you for your willingness to read and promote my work. I would be nothing without you guys!

Readers- You push me to release a book that tops the last. While I'd hoped to release Mike's story as one book, thank you for your patience and understanding when it morphed into two.

J. Law- Thank you for being my person. You are the Lauren to my Beth and the Reese's to my Pieces. Your willingness to discuss the inane facts of my stories and work them into something that makes sense keeps me sane. Bitches for life!

Wendi- You're the best PA ever. Seriously, your willingness to drop everything and help me out has made my life so much easier. Thank you for keeping me organized and prepared during this crazy journey and for becoming my friend in the process.

Ashley- Thank you for all of your information on Indie publishing this year and for being the one who broke the news that Renegade was going to be two books. I appreciate all the motivation you send my way and am lucky to call you my friend.

Family & Friends- Thank you for supporting my crazy little dream and for your willingness to promote my smut to your friends. I love you guys to the moon and back.

Zach- There are never enough words for me to communicate how much you mean to me. It doesn't matter how busy you are, you always have time to hear my troublesome plot points and help me gain a better understanding of the male psyche. Never leave me, because I'll find you!

ABOUT THE AUTHOR

Shannon is a born and raised Texan. She grew up inventing clever stories, usually to get herself out of trouble. Her mother was not amused. In junior high, she began writing fractured fairy tales from the villain's point of view and that was the moment she knew that she was going to use her powers for evil instead of good.

After an unplanned surgery in 2014 and a long pity party, she decided to pen a novel about the worst thing that could happen to a person in order to cheer herself up. She's twisted like that. Thus, *From This Day Forward* was born and the rest, as they say, is history.

She resides in the Texas desert with a posse of men (nothing like she'd imagined in fantasies) and plethora of fur babies.

Find her online at: http://shannonshaemyers.com
Or in her reader group: https://www.facebook.com/
groups/630229377127363/

ALSO BY SHANNON MYERS

From This Day Forward Duet

(David & Elizabeth's Story)

From This Day Forward

Forsaking All Others

Standalone Novels

(*Travis & Katya's Story*)

You Save Me

Operation Series

(*Dakota & Zane's Story*)

Operation Fit-ish

(*Kate and Nate's Story*)

Operation Annulment

Silent Phoenix MC Series

(*Grey & Celia's Story*)

The Deserter (Book One)

The Protector (Book Two)

The Renegade (Book Three)

The Traitor (Book Four)

The Savior (Book Five)

The Mercenary (Book Six) *Coming 2022*

Fairest Series

(*Charm & Neve's Story*)

Through The Woods

(Killian & Ariana's Story)

Wait For It

<u>Fictioned Series</u>

(Hayden & Jake's Story)

Protagonized

www.ingramcontent.com/pod-product-compliance
Lightning Source LLC
Chambersburg PA
CBHW050919030726
47503CB00007BB/2370